Praise for Ocean Echoes

"Through beautifully descriptive writing, the reader is transported from the Atlantic Ocean to the Pacific via the Panama Canal. I could feel the rolling of the waves, hear the metal locks of the Panama Canal, see the colorful sea life, and smell and taste the salty water. I learned so much about the ocean and its mysteries, all while getting engrossed in Ellen's life and rooting for her to find the peace she so desperately seeks. A terrific debut novel that will appeal to a wide variety of fiction fans."   - Carrie Rubin, author of *Eating Bull* and *The Seneca Scourge*

"Magnificent and fragile, this is a love story about our ocean told through the eyes of a talented author. Sheila's debut novel has an important message, and she pulls it off with an effortless style that's both entertaining and educational." - Britt Skrabanek, author of *Beneath the Satin Gloves* and *Nola Fran Evie*

"Ocean Echoes is a well-written story with layered characters who are struggling to understand not only the ocean, but themselves as well. There were plot twists that kept me turning the pages late at night to finish and discover the truth." - Charissa Stastny, author of *Between Hope and the Highway*

"Hurst's story is suspenseful, fascinating, and well-plotted. I particularly enjoyed the dives Ellen and her assistant, Ryan, take while on the research cruise, and loved the historical aspects of the tale. Ocean Echoes is a first-rate environmental thriller, and it's most highly recommended." - Jack Magnus, *Readers' Favorite 5-Star Review*

"The author has taken me on a discovery as much as she did her protagonist. I don't know what it is about the way the prose is written, but my mind is still filled with these images of the vast blue, divers traversing the ocean below. Ocean conservationists will want to get this book into as many readers' hands as possible." - Benjamin Ookami, *Readers' Favorite 5-Star Review*

"The author adorns this tale of discovery with droplets of magic and science fiction. Readers are taken under the water whenever the protagonist makes one of her dives and they will never want to come up for air. If there's a reader out there that wishes to be near the ocean but finds it difficult wherever they are, I would absolutely want that reader to read this book." - Cee-Jay Aurinko, *Hub Pages*

Ocean Echoes

Thank you for all your encouragement. It means so much to me.

Love!
Sandra

Ocean Echoes

~

A Novel

Sheila Hurst

Library of Congress Cataloging-in-Publication Data
Hurst, Sheila.
Ocean echoes / Sheila Hurst

ISBN 9780998077819

ISBN: 099807781X

1. Ocean – Fiction. 2. Science & Environment – Fiction. 3. Contemporary Fiction. 4. Adventure – Fiction. 5. Massachusetts – Fiction.

This is a work of fiction. Names, characters, places, and incidents either are the product of the author's imagination or are used fictitiously, and any resemblance to actual persons, living or dead, businesses, companies, events or locales is entirely coincidental. Cover design by Mario Lampic.

Table of Contents

To the dreamers

Prologue

I N THE BLUE-GREEN water near a forgotten island, at the point where it becomes impossible to tell what is truly blue and what is truly green, creatures breed. They do not breed like most animals. They do not invade one another, grope or grasp, coax or clutch, moan or scream. They simply eject some part of themselves out into the world and wait.

Made of 95 percent water, they are much more a part of their environment than most. To be sure, they still need their protective skin, though it is largely transparent and blends into the surroundings, barely separating the water they are made of from the water they live in. They need the protective skin, yet they have no need for a heart or brain. Instead, it is as if they become these organs themselves, pulsing through the ocean just as a heart pulses and echoes through the body. They drift, they propel through the clear blue green, they eat, and they breed.

CHAPTER 1

D AVID KATU THOUGHT of the ocean as a deranged relative. He had no choice but to grow up with it. It had always been there, surrounding his life with whispers and secrets. The ocean gave him presents: rocks and shells, ancient sea creatures, bits of other lands he would never visit, and once a message in a bottle all the way from Australia.

As he grew, he discovered the ocean could be as unpredictable as family. It could turn on a person for no reason at all. It could cradle him, buoy him up, then send him crashing down onto the sand, sputtering and spent, the shell of a man. Still, the ocean was family.

Luckily, Kalani wasn't quite as unpredictable, though she did have her moments. David studied her shadow as she slept. His fingers brushed along her arm to feel the warmth of her skin, then he moved them up to touch her hair as it spilled everywhere in waves. He stayed a moment longer to listen to her breathe. When he could delay no longer, he slid out of bed so as not to wake her.

He crept around in the dark while preparing to leave. His feet found the shorts he always wore and he bent down to pull them on along with a clean shirt. He felt his way out. His children slept on, little bundles rising and falling with promise, their breathing as rhythmic as the ocean.

Outside, he took a deep breath of the tropical air to feel it seep into his body. The day pretended to be light and cool, but he felt the electricity of certain change coming through the dark. The air had been stirred up, still a long way off. It must be a thunderstorm but it wouldn't come until late afternoon.

David brushed by the leaves and vines that reached out along the path, causing cool water droplets to tickle his arms. The path felt alive under his feet. He could be walking on damp skin instead of hardened dirt. Roots came through like twisted spines. He tried not to put too much weight into each step. Soon his feet felt the grit of sand and the leaves opened to a moonlit beach. His rowboat sat off to the side, waiting.

He stroked its rough hull while tracing the grooves and scratches. Years ago, he'd painted a fish there, hoping the silver glimmer would attract real ones. The paint had started to flake away, making it look scaly and more alive. He touched the fish once more for good luck and gave his boat a final hollow pat before turning it over. His oars and gear sat in the sand. He placed them inside with a clatter and pushed off from shore.

"Wait, Papa, wait!" A child's voice trickled through the darkness. David looked back and could barely make out the shape of Roberto, his youngest, running toward him.

"Roberto, you know I can't take you with me. I'll be going too far out today."

"Why not? I'm old enough now. Besides, you go out too far every day."

David chuckled and climbed out of the boat so he could hug his son.

"Well, that's true. Maybe someday I will not have to go out so far."

"But by then I'll be all grown up."

He ruffled his eight-year-old's shiny black hair. Roberto looked so much like him that he could be looking back through time. Even his grin looked the same. David recognized the mischief in it.

"You've still got more growing to do. I'll take you out soon enough. Now run home before your mama misses you."

"They're all still sleeping," Roberto yelled back over his shoulder as he bounced away through the sand. His son looked so small and skinny. He wanted to fill him up with all the goodness of the world.

His family grew from ancient Polynesian, Spanish, and English blood. They were seafarers and adventurers, fishermen and pirates, and the best of them all still beat through his children's hearts. His ancestors traveled thousands of miles through the open ocean while navigating by the stars and flight patterns of birds. He felt his ancestors with him whenever he journeyed with the ocean.

David eased into his boat and pushed off to feel the release of land. He pulled the oars as the winds picked up. The waves splashed and drenched his clean shirt. He rowed on.

Dawn used to be an early enough start for a fisherman. Now he made sure to be out long before the faintest light. He had to catch more fish. His family depended on him for that. Still, he caught less every day and kept rowing farther away.

He turned back only once to see the Man in the Rock. The rock rose out of the waves with the chiseled face of a man screaming. Hazy clouds and bursts of moonlight gave life to the face. The man had always been there, held captive by the rock. People said he had been trapped long ago. David didn't like to think of him as a prisoner. Instead, he thought of him as a watchdog or protector warning evil away from his island.

The wind blew the clouds away and the moon lit the water to make it shine like liquid fire. With the way it shimmered like that, the light could be coming from below the surface. The ocean's soul twinkled there for his eyes only. He spent many mornings like this, gazing into the water, thinking of all that hid in the ocean's depths. Dark waters hold fluid light mysteries. The phrase came to him from out of the air. An uneasiness rose with the words to prickle his skin.

David felt around in his boat for the yaqona. The clay bottle always felt like ice, making it easy to find when everything else felt warm and sticky. Once he opened the bottle, the spicy scent of earth mingled with the sea air. He poured the yaqona into the ocean as his offering to the shark god Minawaka. The stream sparkled as it seeped into the water. Minawaka would be pleased.

A flicker of light or movement caught his eye. A patch of water off to the side appeared darker and flatter than the rest. It looked like something pressed down on the waves, though nothing was there.

He grabbed his flashlight and swept the beam across the water's surface. It glowed dark red. He searched with his light to see if a body might be floating in the water. Nothing. Then the water pulsed. It happened so fast, he wasn't sure it happened at all. He closed his eyes, figuring they must be playing tricks. He needed more sleep. But with his eyes closed even for a moment, his feelings took over and screamed that something was wrong.

He opened his eyes in time to see a red wave rise toward him out of the flat water, a wave that moved against the current and clutched his boat, causing it to capsize into the dark ocean.

C H A P T E R   2

ELLEN SCANNED THE jellyfish swarm that had been reported off the Cape Cod coast. It could reach shore soon. The jellyfish might also head out to sea or disappear in the ocean depths. For now, they drifted. Something she could understand.

Her tiny research boat bucked in the wind. She gripped the railing to steady herself just as the ocean lurched up to spray her face. If she fell overboard, she'd end up right in the middle of the swarm. Ellen pulled her Detroit Tigers baseball cap down over her eyes. The late afternoon sun cast long, spindly shadows. Her lump of a ponytail dangled like a question mark as she held onto the rocking boat to survey the area. The ocean smelled like life. She took a deep breath and filled herself up with it.

Sand jellies. They were rare in the North Atlantic. Marcus, the senior scientist in her lab, had heard about the swarm and emailed an excited message asking her to get out there right away to collect samples. Somehow, she managed to find the jellyfish before they drifted too far or dispersed. Hundreds of sand jellies. They looked like blisters resting below the surface. Waves sent ripples through their gelatinous bodies, making them shudder.

Ellen fastened a sampling jar to a ten-foot pole and slid on heavy-duty gloves. She dipped the jar into the black water, hunted around a bit, then pulled the contraption up with a sand jelly tucked inside.

While hoping the pole wouldn't break, she swung her catch up and over to the deck. She dropped the pole and clamped the lid on as the boat continued to sway. Now the sand jelly could be examined. Its translucence made that easy. She could look right inside even as it remained impossible to know and understand.

There would always be more to know. Any discovery only led to more questions. Scientists couldn't be sure exactly how many jellyfish were out there; they only knew the population seemed to be increasing. Normally, any increase in ocean life would be good news but jellyfish thrive in acidic waters.

So if jellyfish populations kept on increasing, it could be a warning sign: an omen of a catastrophic future. But then the truth could turn on itself so easily and in a few more years, the opposite might be true. Meanwhile, she had to collect and interpret all the clues to predict the future, the real truth, before it arrived.

Tentacles serpentined inside the jar while looking longer than normal. Ellen gazed into the sand jelly. This type intrigued her because its body could inflate, though no one knew exactly why. It had been crammed into the sampling jar so if it did inflate, it might break through the glass. She tightened the lid.

Swarms didn't usually appear in the North Atlantic in late September, especially not from a species rarely found in the area.

Lately, jellyfish appearances felt more like invasions. Swarms congregated. They stretched out for miles. Now the jellyfish within those swarms were growing larger. Ellen shivered despite the sun while staring into the swarm as it blistered below the surface.

~

Rows of samples waited on the counter back in the lab. Ellen glanced at the glass bottles, each with a sand jelly hovering inside, before hurrying back out to the boat to grab the rest of the gear.

She stumbled on the dock and looked back to see what she tripped over, but nothing was there. At times it felt as if the outside world conspired against her while she kept tripping over it or falling against it. Her dad used to call her the fastest moving cast in the Midwest because of her tendency to fall out of trees, not as graceful as a leaf, but more like a nut hurtling to the ground. As she grew older, her clumsiness only worsened. Science took the place of daydreams. While wondering so much about the world, she'd forget where she was in it. Then she'd walk right into a fence or fall down a few stairs before getting back up again. Something always seemed to be in the way.

It didn't help that her hair kept falling in her eyes to obstruct her view. But then she liked to use her hair as a shield, especially while reading. With dark eyes to match her dark hair, she had always felt too plain in a world that valued vibrant color. Even now, in her mid-thirties, she still felt like that awkward girl who spent her days reading, learning, searching.

Ellen took the last box of gear from the boat and closed it up. She'd collected a dozen samples after spending hours out on the water. Marcus would have to be impressed.

The samples glistened while sitting on the counter, making her think of wrapped up gifts. She couldn't wait to peek inside their lives. They could reveal so many secrets, including where they came from and the purpose behind inflating their bodies. Her lab might even be able to determine why such a rare species would suddenly appear in a North Atlantic swarm. A discovery like that could bring in more funding.

Before heading off to a meeting in DC, Marcus warned everyone that if the program manager cut their funding again, there would have to be another layoff. It would be between Ellen and one other scientist.

The swarm had appeared just in time.

Ellen rushed back into the lab while thinking of all the discoveries yet to be made. If only she could empty her hands and get back to work. Then she stepped on an unraveled shoelace. As she fell, her box of gear flew and collided with the jellyfish samples. Ellen leapt up from the floor in time to see the jars wobble, then crash into the sink. Breaking glass crunched into shattered dreams.

She looked into the sink as the last jellyfish slid down the drain. She had to salvage everything. She had to seize that second and reverse it all somehow. Without thinking, she reached into the drain and grabbed a tentacle. The tentacle broke off in her hand, leaving nothing but a burning sting. An angry red welt rose up right away, a reminder of everything she had lost.

CHAPTER 3

THERE IS A reason love is red. Love burns into a person. Other colors surround us, waving gray or blue without leaving much of an impression. Red will always be noticed. Love leaves that kind of a mark. Love changes us forever.

Ellen still thought of that day. The day she gave up on love. Her mind returned there whenever she wasn't concentrating on work. She thought of it every night before finally sleeping. She should have stopped thinking of it by now, but it had become a constant ache that she couldn't help but touch, as if to test it to see if it was still there. And it always was.

She had loved Paul too much. It was a dangerous love, the kind a person could get lost in. At first she floundered around in it, then she sank into the depths and finally, she completely gave herself up to it.

They met back in graduate school. She remembered his wire-framed glasses, his short brown hair, his gentleness and grace. He walked right over in the lab while navigating a few empty stools, then nodded with a smile and sat next to her. He seemed to take it for granted that they would be lab partners, then later, life partners. Ellen never knew what to do. She felt so awkward and nervous around him. She wondered why he chose her, why he sat next to her, of all the empty seats he could have chosen.

A few classes later, his safety glasses fogged up during an experiment. He looked so ridiculous that she couldn't help but laugh. Her laughter made everyone stare at them, but that didn't faze him at all. He took his glasses off, wiped them down, then glanced over with a smile in his eyes. After that, his eyes always smiled at her. She liked to think they shared a private joke, even if she had no idea what the joke was.

She had never been in love before. In high school, she decided she'd rather spend time with her dog than with boys. In college, the boys seemed even worse than in high school. She stayed away and didn't get to know many of them. She heard stories from friends and that was enough. By graduate school, she was so immersed in her studies that she didn't have time to think of anything else; until Paul sat next to her in lab class.

As soon as he sat there, she felt attracted to the smell of him more than anything else. He smelled of warmth and light, sheets drying in the sun, and the books she loved so much. She kept breathing him in, then she breathed him in too much. She let herself get carried away.

Paul studied the swimming behavior of marine animals for robotic applications. Not exactly the sort of thing she studied, but he always acted interested in her ideas. His questions drew the passion out of her and excited her about her own research. She told him everything. She gave him everything. Then one day everything changed.

Ocean Echoes

That day started off normally enough. The autumn morning was full of crunch and crackle as they walked to the bakery for blueberry scones and coffee. Shadows and light played, creating colors too brilliant to look at for long. A falling leaf flashed bright yellow, a shard of stained glass, as if made of the sun itself. A sun flake. It sparked something inside. Everything could have been made of glass on the verge of breaking.

Of course, there had been doubts. Little background noises barely audible. But they were perfect for each other. They pushed each other further, made each other better. They were supposed to get married after graduate school and then the life they'd been preparing for all along could finally begin.

They settled in at the kitchen table with their scones and coffee. Paul put his glasses on, turned to read the paper, and suddenly everything felt too domestic. She imagined every Sunday morning for years and decades to come, and just as suddenly she didn't want it. She realized she never wanted it.

When the phone rang, Paul jumped up to answer it. He talked in a low voice while glancing at her, then brought the phone into another room and closed the door. Still, she could hear his whoop of joy as soon as he hung up. He rushed out to tell her the news.

"They're offering me a job in San Francisco. Can you believe it? It's all based on one of my research papers. It's a great offer, everything we've ever wanted. Aren't you excited?"

"What paper is that?"

"Oh, just one of the latest ones I've been working on. It wasn't even all that great. I don't know why it would have gotten their attention, but it did. They want me to head a new robotics division out there and the job starts as soon as we graduate. I won't even have to look for funding. They already have the grants; they just need more people to do the work. They said I was exactly the kind of person they've been looking for."

"And all this is based on a mystery paper I've never even seen? Can I read it?"

"You wouldn't want to read it. It's all boring robotics stuff."

"But we always help each other with our research. I've read all your other papers. Why can't I read this one?"

Paul's face turned pale. He searched her eyes for something before saying, "Okay, I'll go get it."

Once she started reading his paper, she saw why he didn't want to show it to her. It detailed her theories on the movement of jellyfish and he put them all out there as if they were his own. As she read each sentence, each paragraph, she felt a chill creep through her. A pinprick of rage bloomed inside and she nurtured it as she fed it more words from the research paper with his name on it. His name, only his, even though the words contained her theories. Ideas and theories she'd been working on for years.

"You could have at least mentioned me in the acknowledgements," she said when she finished reading it. They were still sitting at the kitchen table, the scones half eaten and crumbling, the coffee cold. She wanted to throw the research paper at him, rip it into shreds, yell and scream. But the cold chill covered the burning rage. It disconnected her from everything, from her life, her ideas, from Paul, from love. She felt it creep in and take over and grow.

"But no one knows who you are, so there didn't seem to be a point in mentioning you."

She laughed an icy laugh. "And you just made sure that no one will ever know my name, since you took all my ideas and called them your own."

"It's not like that. This is a paper on robotics, that's not your field."

She couldn't get any more words out by then. They were all frozen inside.

Paul reached over and touched her hand. "You'll still come to San Francisco with me, won't you? It's a great place to live and raise a family."

Ellen pulled away, ran her fingers through her straight black hair, then left them clenched there while leaning against the table. She looked down at the scone crumbs and examined the fabric of her jeans. Tiny intersections.

"Is that why you did it? Because you figured we'd get married and have a family anyway, so then my research wouldn't matter as much as yours?"

"I don't get it. We're a team, remember? I honestly didn't think you'd care."

"If we were a team, you would have given me a little credit. You know how hard I've been working on all this. All I ever wanted was to make a difference, and you just took that chance away. Now you're going off to do that instead. With my ideas and my research."

"That's not the way it is. Come with me. We'll make a difference together."

"I'd have to give up everything. My research is here. Everything is here. I'll have to come up with some new ideas now, but this is where I need to be."

As soon as she pulled the ring off, she felt lighter. She looked at the never-ending circle and the red mark it left on her finger, then gave the ring back to Paul while still loving his touch.

"Are you sure?"

She nodded, though she wasn't sure.

"You know I'll always love you, right?"

Tears stung at the thought. She closed her eyes and tried to wipe it all away.

If something had to be given up, it wasn't going to be her research. That thought was worse than giving up on love. She rubbed the red mark on her finger and wondered if she would ever be able to truly love again.

CHAPTER 4

H ER HOME MOVED and swayed. She loved the motion, the gentle soothing of the rocking: up and then down, just like life, just like breathing. It was one of the few things that relaxed her. All the scattered choices, all the decisions she still regretted, brought her to this place and to this life of perpetual movement.

Ellen leaned into the plastic seat of *Soliton*, her falling-apart houseboat, and watched the dark waves as if they held all the answers. The waves reflected nothing back while sloshing in all directions. Maybe she should have married Paul all those years ago, even if he did steal her research. She could have kept giving him all her ideas. Then those ideas might have had a chance of getting out there. She tried to picture that kind of a life. She wondered if she would have been happier.

The red welt on her hand still lingered. Since the jellyfish sting changed the look of her palm, it might change her destiny. Another line added: another adventure or detour. She touched the new line while thinking how funny it would be if we were all born with directions on our palms even as we continued to flounder around, always wondering what to do.

Fog streamed through the morning air to engulf and obscure everything. With a flutter of wings, a seagull appeared out of the gloom and perched on the edge of the boat. He kept an eye on her while watching out for fish. When she least expected it, he spread his wings and swooped down to the water, skimming the surface and plucking out his prize. Ellen toasted him with her coffee, feeling a lingering kinship. These days, he was probably the closest she'd ever come to having a pet.

Deep Harbor still looked to be sleeping. Its clapboard buildings stood silhouetted against the brightening sky. Scattered on a stretch of land between the ocean and Snake Pond, the village contained a marina with a handful of boat slips, a post office, coffee shops, and tourist traps where anything from sweatshirts to sharks' teeth to pirate treasure could be found. Deep Harbor Marine Institute sat in the middle of it all. Usually, Ellen thought it helped to live in the shadow of her workplace, but every once in a while it took a certain amount of willpower to cross the street and walk into that formidable brick building.

She swept her hair back to get it out of her face long enough to check her email messages. A tentacle of hair immediately slipped free to fall across her eyes. She tucked it behind her ear and opened her laptop. Most of the 153 messages that had come through between midnight and 6 AM had to do with the Atoll Islands research cruise. Adrenaline rushed through her as she read the subject lines. There was still so much to do.

No scientists had ever been where they were going. Most of the atolls that formed the Pacific island chain were uninhabited. On a map, they looked like a mass of tiny dots practically lost out in an expanse of blue. The area had just been designated a marine sanctuary and their mission would be to survey the island reefs and waters. But the ocean had a way of hiding its secrets. With most of the ocean still unexplored and unseen by human eyes, it remained one of the greatest mysteries of all time. For as long as she could remember, Ellen wanted to solve it.

If it hadn't been for the upcoming research cruise, Marcus probably would have laid her off right after the jellyfish catastrophe, but she was the only lab member scheduled to go and it was too late to change the paperwork. Now this expedition could either help generate funding or put an end to her research career. It would be her last chance, but failing or succeeding would be out of her control. A successful cruise would mean being able to find and document a variety of jellyfish while finding any at all would be left up to pure luck.

She kept seeing those jellyfish samples disappear down the drain. She couldn't let everything slide down there with them. It had taken most of the day to collect the samples and once they were gone, it was too late to collect more. Right after the catastrophe, she went back out to find them but they had vanished with the daylight. Marcus still wouldn't talk to her. The lab members all treated her differently now, as if she might already be gone. Whenever they talked about their research, Ellen thought she saw a flicker in their eyes that said they were laughing at her. She'd have to turn everything around with this cruise.

Ellen closed her laptop with a click and stretched her small frame into something that might resemble stature. She grabbed a towel and left *Soliton* to dance on the waves without her.

CHAPTER 5

A QUIET EERINESS pervaded as she walked across the street to work. No cars or tourists to maneuver around, no noise or movement at all except for a shiver of wind in the trees lining the red brick building. Far ahead on the street, a dog trotted along and stopped as if trying to sniff out signs of life.

Ellen jerked the heavy door open. The hallway formed a dark tunnel of potential insanity. She groped along the wall for the light switch and squinted at the resulting bright emptiness. No one was crazy enough to show up at work this early.

Since her houseboat's shower was really more of a hose, she showered in the scuba divers' locker room before dressing in faded jeans and a cotton shirt. The only socks she could find consisted of a long pink polka-dotted one and a short fuzzy purple one. Life was too hectic for matching socks. Luckily, her sneakers and jeans covered up most of the fashion disaster.

After drying her hair and sweeping it back into the usual ponytail, she felt ready for anything. Or almost anything. She walked out of the locker room and right into something very solid. The solid mass took the form of Ryan Turner, her research assistant. She felt her face flush, then willed it to stop, feeling ridiculous.

"Sorry, didn't see you there," Ryan said. His slow smile only made Ellen's face feel hotter.

"No problem," she managed to say while turning to escape down the hall before he noticed that her face was probably completely red. She felt it with her hand, trying to cool it down somehow. After taking a few steps away, she bumped into a stack of empty plastic buckets that stood against the wall. The resulting clatter was too much to bear. While making sure not to look back, she reached down and propped the buckets up as if nothing had happened. Hopefully Ryan wasn't still there watching the whole scene. She couldn't bring herself to look.

Why did she hire such a good-looking research assistant? She chastised herself as she continued to slink down the hall and up the stairs to her office. He was just a kid, really. In his late twenties at the most and that already felt like a lifetime ago. Most days when they were working together it didn't matter at all that he looked like he'd been out surfing, all tanned with light brown hair kept a little long, falling in his eyes enough to make anyone want to reach out and pet him.

She was probably still frazzled from the whole jellyfish catastrophe and then Ryan caught her off guard. That was all. Ellen tried to calm herself down before stumbling off into another disaster. She hadn't felt anyone's body against hers like that in such a long time. Maybe that was the problem.

In her office, she turned on her computer with a sigh of relief. Time to once again enter into a different world: the world of jellyfish. She still hadn't fully figured out the jellyfish world or the human world, but at least jellyfish didn't expect much from her. She just observed, learned along the way, and continued to investigate.

Ellen loved jellyfish for many reasons. They were so graceful, the way they moved with the currents, suspended as if in mid-air while propelling onward. She thought they looked like souls might look, hiding nothing, always seemingly at peace, their clear or pink bodies naturally becoming part of the water surrounding them. But like humans, jellyfish are filled with contradictions. While looking so peaceful, they hide the fact that they are predators. Their tentacles will reach out, sting, and can kill small ocean animals. Depending on the type of jellyfish, they can even kill humans.

Her first jellyfish encounter happened to be with a Portuguese Man-o-War. She was twelve years old at the time and had been visiting her grandmother in Florida. Ellen remembered the excitement of swimming in the ocean instead of the usual lake and kept diving under the waves to feel the water pound and rush off her back. Then she heard a powerful rumbling and turned to see a wall of water curl over her. Without thinking, she dove right in.

When her head popped back up, pain stabbed her neck and shoulder. She glanced down to see something clinging there. It looked like she'd grown another head. The light-blue air sac of a jellyfish stuck out from her shoulder and nodded in the breeze. Instinctively, she swiped it off and sent the second head flying back into the waves. But the tentacles stayed on her neck and kept stinging. More waves rushed at her, causing her to stumble. She forced herself to stand against them and ran back to shore.

Her grandmother tried to get the clinging tentacles off, but whenever she pulled at one it would break in a desperate attempt to stay on Ellen's skin. After a few minutes, Ellen's neck started to swell. She couldn't catch her breath. An ambulance had to be called to bring her to the hospital. Strangers hovered as she gasped for air. At the hospital, the doctor told her if the jellyfish had stung her neck an inch or so higher it could have killed her. So a jellyfish almost got the best of her that time. But then, she had only been twelve years old.

For Christmas that year, her grandmother sent a book about jellyfish complete with pictures of all different types, colors, and sizes. They floated through the pages like clouds billowing through an ocean sky. Yellow jellyfish suns brightened the sky with rays of trailing tentacles.

She learned that a Portuguese Man-o-War isn't just one jellyfish. It's actually a colony of four different individuals, living together and dependent on each other for survival. The jellyfish that looked like a second head was called the gas-filled float. She remembered seeing it bounce away on the waves after brushing it off, a hazy blue bubble looking lonely, and she was sorry that she had caused the destruction of the colony.

While flipping through the pages, Ellen couldn't believe how many kinds of jellyfish there were, how beautiful they all were, and how lethal they could be. From then on, she wanted to know all about them.

She continued to search through her emails. Most had to do with the upcoming research cruise but a few changes from co-authors popped up. She tried to incorporate all the changes into their journal article while hoping to send it off so that she could focus on the cruise. She'd have to talk with Ryan later about some of the supplies that needed to be ordered. But for now, the last thing she wanted to do was see him again. She'd probably make an even bigger fool out of herself than she had earlier.

At times like this, she felt like a cartoon drawn with shaky lines. She rubbed the indentation that appeared between her eyebrows. She knew it contributed to a permanent look of concentration, something she didn't always want to carry around. Touching it had become a habit, an attempt to rub away time.

Ellen checked the time on her computer: 10:25 already. The staff meeting was at 10:30. It didn't look like she'd be able to finish the article before then, so she closed out and headed off to the meeting.

CHAPTER 6

———— ∿ ————

H EAVY CEILING-TO-FLOOR DRAPERY lined one wall of the conference room, covering windows no one ever saw. While the drapes might have been orange or gold back in the 70s when they were still the newest thing, they had matured to a mottled brown design. No one noticed the decor or the general grayness of the room and people. They were all used to such things by now.

A few researchers sat at a rectangular table while sipping coffee or stood in line to get coffee and cookies. There were about thirty scientists in the department but only a handful regularly attended these meetings. Some were out on research cruises or at conferences; others were just missing in action. Although the building mostly consisted of one straight hallway, a surprising number of nooks and crannies existed where employees could hide whenever it came time for a meeting.

Ellen's chair screeched when she pulled it away from the conference table. Those already sitting at the table brushed their eyes over her. She plunked herself down and suddenly became interested in the mottled brown curtains.

When she dropped her gaze to the table, she noticed a newspaper with the headline, "Indonesian Earthquake and Tsunami Could Herald Larger Quake." Another story read, "We Couldn't Outrun Killer Wave: Death Toll Reaches Four Hundred."

She stared at the pictures of destroyed homes. Another disaster. So far, 2010 had been filled with them. The year started off with the earthquake in Haiti that killed two hundred and thirty thousand people. Then the Deepwater Horizon explosion. Now this. The research cruise would be heading toward the tsunami area. Too bad she didn't study earthquakes or tsunamis.

Jerry, an older scientist who looked suspiciously like a walrus, harrumphed and coughed and began the meeting with, "Okay, we all know government funding isn't what it used to be. It's been steadily declining for years now. So the point of this meeting is to come up with alternative agencies or companies to submit proposals to for funding. Anybody have any ideas?"

They all looked at each other. Ellen felt an urge to get up and leave. The only reason she'd come to this meeting was for the chance to hear of alternative funding. Now she was faced with a room drained of ideas and light. At least the cookies weren't too stale. She stayed seated, chewed, and looked from face to face, hoping for a little illumination.

Jerry watched Ellen as she chewed. A hint of saliva seemed to form around the corners of his mouth at the sight of her cookies. His drooping mustache promptly mopped the area so she couldn't be sure.

Assuming she wouldn't be laid off right after the cruise, her research funds were due to run out in a year. More projects should have been funded for subsequent years by now, but like Jerry said, government funding wasn't what it used to be. Each day, each week, each month brought her closer to the end of her project. Without more funding, she couldn't do her research and if she couldn't do that, then all her sacrifices, all her studying, all her years of work would be for nothing.

After the meeting, Ellen sent an email off to Ryan listing all the things that needed to be done before the cruise. She did this more for her own state of mind than anything else; figuring if she listed everything out, it wouldn't feel so ominous. She sent the email off and went back to her paper while hoping to finish it in the next hour or two. Then a message came back from Ryan with questions on some of the things she wanted done. She forced herself to get up and walk two doors down to his office.

Ryan slouched in a chair with his feet propped up on his desk and a laptop cradled in his lap. When he saw her, he put his feet back on the floor but still looked a little too relaxed and gave her that slow smile again. Prepared for it this time, Ellen was determined to act more like a real supervisor.

"Just thought I'd check in. Is everything going okay?"

"Yeah, no problem."

"There's still a lot to do. Are you sure you're not feeling bombarded by it all?"

He shrugged. "No problem for me."

"Okay, you'll have to go through our diving equipment. It's all packed away in boxes in the basement. See if there's anything that looks damaged and if there's a wet suit that will fit you. If you can't find a wet suit that fits, you'll have to buy a new one and anything else that needs to be replaced. We'll definitely need to rent more oxygen tanks so those should be ordered today. What else?"

Ryan's eyes widened. "I don't know. What else?"

"You'll need a high-quality underwater camera. I have one so I'll have to remember to pack that. It's better if we both have one in case one of us gets a chance at taking a good picture. And gloves, we always need lots of gloves, preferably very heavy duty so that we won't get stung through them. And some extra containers to store any specimens in and another laptop."

Ryan looked at her lips and grinned, then looked away and started jotting down notes.

"Okay, what kind of a camera and what kind of laptop do you want?"

"I guess the same as the ones we already have unless there's something better out there by now."

"Sounds good. I'll take care of it. Don't worry about anything."

"Great. Thank you."

Ellen turned to leave, glad that she had acted more professional than this morning. No one would ever guess she'd actually been thinking about his arms while she talked on like that, and how the light hairs looked soft against his tanned skin. The problem mainly seemed to be whenever he caught her off guard. She'd have to make sure not to get caught off guard again, to at least act like a real supervisor, even if she didn't feel like one.

She turned into the bathroom, washed her hands, and looked up to see chocolate smudges all over her mouth from the cookies.

So much for acting like a real supervisor. No wonder Ryan had been grinning at her like that. She envied Jerry's mustache. At least it covered everything up.

CHAPTER 7

D ARKNESS CAME WITH the rain and still no David. Kalani waited for him to throw the door open, wind whipping behind, letting in the cold damp air. Then everything would be all right again. He would be excited by the storm. Even if he hadn't caught any fish, he would be happy. These storms always energized him. They used to joke that the lightning bolts woke him up like a Frankenstein.

Kalani opened the door a crack to see palm trees bending and swaying in the wind like rubber toys. The sky puffed up with dark gray. Neighborhood children ran laughing by, splashing in puddles: plink, plink, plink. Maya perked up when she heard their laughter. Kalani gave her a look to let her know there was no way she'd be going out to play. It was bad enough that David and the other children were out there.

Maya bent her head over her book again, letting the dark curtain of her hair fall between them. Kalani tended the fire, stirring it with a stick. David would need a good fire to come home to. She knew he would be soaking wet and would want the energy of fire and lightning.

Roberto, her youngest, came home first while riding a gust of cold air. Still no David. She peeled Roberto's clothes off and hung them by the fire to dry. He danced around the crackling flames, quivering while refusing to admit he could be cold. She gave him dry clothes and a blanket.

"Make sure to keep this on and keep your sister company. I'm going out to look for Papa."

"But he's not there. I didn't see Papa or his boat anywhere."

"He's out there somewhere. We just need to find him." Kalani closed the door and stepped into the breath of a howling monster. She held a blanket over her head, using it as a shield before running toward the beach with wet leaves slapping, trying to hold her back.

The waves grumbled and roared. They reached for her and tried to take her away too.

"Isn't my husband enough?" She shouted to the beast. "You can't have both of us, but if you bring him back you can have me. Okay? Take me and bring him back. Please, please bring him back."

The waves reached and exploded in response. She searched each wave, expecting to see David stuck in one of them. She waited for the ocean to give him up, to bring him back. But there was nothing. Nothing but steel gray waves. She collapsed on the drenched sand. The sky cried along with her as the rain continued to fall.

CHAPTER 8

━━━━━ ⌒ ━━━━━

A S THE DEPARTURE date for the cruise drew closer, Ellen internally became more frantic. She remained calm on the outside while volcanoes or hydrothermal vents bubbled beneath the surface.

Hydrothermal vents had become famous at the institute ever since scientists discovered life in the deepest ocean. Before that, everyone assumed the sun was necessary for life. But with no access to the sun, these life forms used chemicals from seafloor vents to create their own energy. They found a way to survive.

Figuring her stomach felt like some strange life form, Ellen hoped it would also be able to create its own energy. While pondering all this, she realized she'd been exposed to too much workplace propaganda if her stomach made her think of hydrothermal vents.

She stood with her hands on her hips and examined the lab. Ryan had been a big help. Most of their gear had been dragged out of hiding and cleaned, with replacement gear due for delivery any day now. Some equipment had been packed and labeled, waiting only for the ship to arrive. The ship wasn't due in port until two days before the cruise so those last days would be spent hauling everything out to the dock and loading it onto the ship.

Ellen scoffed at the word "cruise," which called up images of never-ending buffets decorated with ice sculptures and pools shaped like spouting whales. The ship they'd be using along with other scientists and researchers from all over the world, the *Eagle*, was a huge black metal, clanging, echoing basin. Ellen had been on the ship for other experiments so she knew what to expect. Beds came in the form of bunked steel frames with army-issue scratchy blankets. Laboratories stayed crowded and sweaty at all hours of the day and night. But they wouldn't be there for luxury. They would be there to discover the unknown.

Most of the scientists on the cruise would be international coral and plankton researchers. Coral and plankton had ties to climate change and the politics of the day consequently funded the science. Jellyfish weren't considered as important but they were up there for the same reason.

Ellen sometimes had the feeling that other scientists regarded jellyfish as frivolous and so they thought it fitting that a woman studied them. But she would always smile at the thought, since anyone who believed such things must not know jellyfish at all. She would then imagine the jellyfish stinging the scientists, and the smile would grow.

She heard a scuffling noise and turned with the smile still spread across her face. Ryan stood there with his arms folded and smiled back.

"This looks great," Ellen said while waving her arm around the lab. "Thank you for organizing all this."

"No problem. Want to go celebrate with a beer? It's Thirsty Thursday, all kinds of drink and appetizer specials across the street."

Ellen looked at her watch: 4:30. It was tempting since it wouldn't be too crowded at The Pirate yet. She rationalized that if she did sit with Ryan over a beer, it could help break the ice before the cruise. Then maybe she wouldn't feel so awkward around him and would be able to concentrate on her work. Possibly. As long as she only had one beer. After two or more she just might end up in his lap.

"Okay, but I've got a couple more things to do around here so why don't you go ahead and I'll meet you there?"

"Great, see you there."

She wasn't sure what she could possibly finish doing in the next ten minutes or so, but she also wasn't sure about walking into The Pirate with Ryan. People could talk, after all, and they did have wild imaginations. It would be better to supposedly run into him there.

The Pirate, located on Snake Pond and across the street from work, exuded the scent and feel of a cave or hideout. It had been built from the remnants of a shipwreck and everything in the place creaked with ancient wood. When walking in off the street, at first only darkness can be seen. A long room with a polished bar hugging one wall gradually comes into view. Eyes adjust and shadows of people leaning against the bar begin to form.

While Ellen faced the long dark room, she noticed the smell of beer-soaked wood more than anything else: sticky wood from years of beer swilling and spilling. She detected the smell of the sea mixed in there too, perhaps still part of the wood ever since the shipwreck, but then realized that smell most likely came from the ocean outside.

A pirate complete with an eye patch and striped baggy pants materialized from the darkness. Before she had the chance to say anything to the pirate waiter, one of the bar shadows moved toward her. The shadow turned out to be Ryan.

"Want to get a table instead of sitting at the bar? I thought some of the engineers were going to be here but it looks like they've decided not to come over."

"Sure," Ellen said without thinking. Except that sitting at a table might look more intimate than sitting at the bar. People could get the wrong idea. She glanced around. At least she didn't see anyone from work yet.

Lethal-looking anchors stuck out from wooden walls. A gigantic whalebone, scarred with apparent life and death struggles, hung suspended from the ceiling. Ryan ducked under the whalebone as they walked to the table. They continued to the end of the long dark room, past a stone fireplace with the burnt-in smell of centuries of fires, and turned down a cavernous hallway. The hallway led out to a deck with scattered tables and rippling water all around. It seemed like a good place to hide.

The pirate waiter brought over a basket of bread and menus stamped with a skull and crossbones insignia. Ellen noticed a tattoo on his arm with the same skull and crossbones design. She wondered if it could be a fake tattoo worn only as part of his work uniform or if he was really that into being a supposed pirate.

"We're just going to have drinks," she said when the pirate tried to hand them the menus.

"Ah, very well then, might as well keep the bread fer yerselves. What can I get fer ya?"

Ellen decided the tattoo must be real and they both ordered beers. The pirate looked pleased and sauntered away, leaving them alone out on the deck. The late afternoon took on a soft glow. Ellen noticed that Ryan's eyes held an inner light like honey and questioned whether this was such a good idea after all.

CHAPTER 9

R YAN REACHED OVER, took some bread from the basket, and tore a piece off. "Good thing he left the bread. I like feeding the ducks out here."

As if on cue, ducks started to glide toward him from all corners of the pond. Ryan threw a chunk of bread into the water and the ducks darted so quickly toward it that it was impossible to tell what happened between the ripples and flapping wings until one finally grabbed the prize and gulped it down.

Ellen laughed at the commotion. "I always feel bad for the ones that don't get any bread."

"Yeah, me too." Ryan threw another piece out to a smaller duck on the fringe of the group. The duck managed to catch it in his mouth before the bread hit the water or anyone could fight over it.

Ryan had never said anything about the jellyfish catastrophe. Ellen figured he must know about it. He must have heard something. Hopefully he hadn't been laughing about it along with everyone else.

"So do you like working here?" She asked to push the image of jellyfish sliding down the drain out of her mind.

"Yeah, I love it. Don't you?"

"Sure, I love the research anyway, not so much the bureaucracy."

"You probably run into that more than me. All I have to do is take orders from you."

"And you like taking orders from me?"

"Yeah. It's great working with you."

The pirate brought their beers over and Ellen took a sip as soon as hers touched the table.

After taking a gulp of his, Ryan asked, "What are these cruises like anyway? I mean, I know it all depends on what the research is and how long the whole thing lasts. But what's it like for you when you go out on a cruise?"

"It's a lot of work. I'll make sure to order you around as much as possible."

"That's good. Just wanted to make sure."

"It'll depend on the ship's schedule, but once we get there we'll have to try to get as many dives in as possible and in lots of different locations. At least it's much easier diving in the clear blue water than around here, where sometimes you can't even see your hand in front of your face."

"Yeah, I've been on dives like that, especially after it's rained and the bottom's all stirred up. Then you can't see anything."

"You'd think there would be more plankton in the warmer tropical waters, but the tropical water is so clear because it's basically a desert for that kind of life."

"That's weird." Ryan threw more bread into the water. This time a bass jumped up to the surface and snatched the prize away from the ducks.

"Plankton typically prefer a colder environment so the ocean around here is full of plankton, and that's why we can hardly see anything when we're diving."

"That's funny, I thought it was because of pollution or something, at least when the bottom's not all churned up by the rain."

Ellen took another sip of her beer. "No, well, not all of it anyway."

"That's good to know. Makes me feel a little better about diving out there."

"Plankton can be microscopic too. Think of that. We're out there swimming through all kinds of life that we can't even see. Ocean life like that produces about half of the oxygen in the atmosphere."

"Wow, you always hear about trees doing that but never plankton."

"That's true. Plankton should probably get more credit." Ellen stopped, realizing she shouldn't be talking so much about plankton. But talking about science was usually easier than talking about anything else.

Fish now swarmed beneath the group of ducks. The fish swam so close to the surface that their faces could be seen peering up through the murky water. One pouted and stared right at them, waiting for more food to fly.

"Those fish have the same expression on their faces as the dog I had when I was little," Ellen said. "He'd get that look whenever he wanted a treat."

Silver, her golden retriever, had been her best friend through elementary school into high school. He'd been her shadow, her protector, her guardian angel. She missed him still.

Ellen took a gulp of her beer and wondered why Ryan kept looking like a teddy bear. He didn't seem to be that furry. She had to be sure not to order another beer.

"So where are you from?" She asked. "I know you live nearby now, but where did you grow up?"

"Not too far from here. I haven't really traveled around all that much."

"After this cruise you won't be able to say that anymore. The Atoll Islands are halfway around the world."

"You make it sound pretty exciting, like we'll be modern day explorers or something." Ryan threw more bread into the water and the fish and ducks started fighting.

"Those fish are vicious," Ellen said. "Imagine something like that underneath you, slithering around and biting."

She immediately wished she hadn't said that and felt her face flush again. Then the pirate appeared with two fresh beers.

"You wanted another one, didn't you?" Ryan asked. "I signaled to him to get us these."

"You signaled to him? I didn't even see him around anywhere."

"He was watching from inside."

Ellen felt a little giddy and started laughing. "What is he, a pirate or a spy?"

"Just a crazy person if you ask me, but the beers are good and cold at least."

"Yes, they are. But this will have to be my last one unless we want to start giving the ducks and fish some of the beer too."

"Sounds like a cool experiment," Ryan said. "I wonder if they'd get all happy and stop fighting then, maybe get to know each other a little better."

"Maybe. But we're not going to find out because I'm not going to pour my beer out at them."

"Yeah, me neither." Ryan took a sip and looked at her over his glass.

Ellen felt the deck shake with the thumping steps of other people. She turned her head toward the invaders and saw that they were work people. Great. A group of three guys around Ryan's age walked over to their table.

"Hey, mind if we join you?" They asked as they brought their chairs over.

"No, we were just wondering where you were," Ryan said.

"Got held up by some psycho scientist," one of them said as he settled in and rolled his eyes. Then he turned to Ellen. "No offense of course, you're not technically one of the psychos."

"Thanks." Ellen took a swig of her beer.

"Hey, don't you have a houseboat out there?" Another one asked. "Which one is yours?"

"You can't see it from here. It's farther out."

The truth was she could see it but she wasn't about to tell them which one was hers. They might try to get her to invite them all aboard or something. She could almost hear the rumors now: Ellen taking on four young studs on her boat after getting drunk at The Pirate.

"Too bad," he said. "I love boats," which only confirmed her suspicions.

Ellen emptied her beer. "Well, I've got to get going. Still lots to do before the cruise."

She gave Ryan some money for the beers and turned to go, hoping she wouldn't sway too much as she walked away.

"See you tomorrow," Ryan called out.

As she stepped off the deck and into the restaurant to leave, Ellen heard laughter behind her. She could only hope the laughter wasn't directed toward her. With nothing better to do, she walked across the street and went back to work.

She could still hear the laughter even as she sat at the computer in her office. Hearing it as she walked away reminded her of junior high when everyone suddenly decided to call her "Uppity Ellen." At the time, she knew it all started because her last name happened to be Upton. Still, she couldn't help but be offended. She never thought of herself as "uppity" in any way. But when they kept calling her that while laughing about it all through junior high, she began to wonder. It made her realize there can be a gap, sometimes a large one, between the person we know we are and the person others see. Even to this day, she recalled the taunting with a cringe.

CHAPTER 10

—◦—

S EA FOAM CLOUDS rippled into morning sky. Ellen performed her daily ritual of sitting out on *Soliton* with her coffee but didn't see her seagull pet. This time, the water drew her attention more than anything else. The surface looked so still and flat. She glanced over the edge of the boat and saw an abstract painting there with clouds and sky swirling together, constantly changing along with the movement of the water.

The fish she had seen last night were under there somewhere. She wondered if they noticed the abstract painting shimmering above. But then, we usually have one hanging over us too, she thought as she stretched and looked up at the sky.

She decided to concentrate on work for the entire day. Her work would be her haven, as it had been so many times in the past. And like usual, there was no time for anything else. She had to somehow finish everything and get ready to be away for four weeks.

On the way to the office, she ran into Oscar, a scientist in his late sixties. His graying hair stuck out at complicated angles and usually made her think of a Muppet. She figured he must grab constant fistfuls while researching, resulting in an electrified look. But pervading his personality more than anything else was the fact that he acted so distracted all the time. It was as if equations were constantly running and multiplying through his head. Ellen could practically see them flashing there in his eyes while he made a slight attempt to look past them and focus on her.

"Oh, uh, Ellen, I've been meaning to ask you, will you be going to the conference on carbon cycling?"

"I'll be leaving soon for a cruise to the Atoll Islands, so no conferences for me for a while."

"Yes, yes, of course. Well, good luck with that," Oscar said while already looking beyond her and back into his land of equations.

A spark of amusement might have ignited his eyes when he said good luck, but it was probably just her imagination. They couldn't still be laughing at her for losing those jellyfish samples. There should be a time limit on mockery.

Ellen walked into her office and gratefully shut the door behind her. Yes, everything was truly connected if even jellyfish had something to do with the ocean taking in carbon and offsetting climate change. And perhaps because everything was so connected, it felt good to shut her door for now.

She spent the day sending off emails while making sure all the supplies needed for the cruise had been delivered. She talked with Ryan only through email, perhaps the best way to communicate after all.

Ellen knew she kept pushing men away, whether consciously or subconsciously, but she couldn't help it. The one person she let herself love ended up taking too much. She couldn't let that happen again. Besides, they all acted like they wanted something from her. And whatever that happened to be, she knew it was something she couldn't fully give.

Just a generation or two ago, women scientists weren't allowed on research ships. That seemed unbelievable to her now. She once heard a woman give a speech describing what it was like to be a female scientist in the 1950s. The speaker, tall and thin with white hair slicked back into a bun, told the audience that her colleagues still thought of it as bad luck for a woman to be on a ship, especially a research cruise that would be out at sea for weeks at a time with only men aboard. They told her she should stay home where she belonged and that she wouldn't be allowed to go on the cruise.

"I felt I had as much of a right to go and conduct my research as anyone else, no matter what they said," she told the dark auditorium. "So I did what any reasonable person would do under the circumstances: I stowed away."

The scattered audience chuckled and coughed in response.

"We were out at sea by the time I was discovered. The men on the ship were so enraged that I would think to do such a thing, that they turned the ship around and traveled all the way back to the dock. Then they escorted me off the ship as if I could be some kind of a criminal. They brought me down to the dock and pushed me away in front of the entire crew. All because I wanted to do my research."

Ellen didn't believe it at first. How could anything like that ever happen? And it hadn't been that long ago. She thought of that story often. It did show how far women had come, but it also served as a warning. While looking around at some of the much older men she worked with, she thought she could see this sort of mentality in their eyes, that perhaps they saw her more as a woman than as a scientist or colleague. But that would only make her want to work harder and she would once again disappear into the world of jellyfish.

An email blinked in from her program manager with a subject line that announced "future results." Ellen opened it with a growing feeling of dread. As she read the message, dread turned to agitation. It said if she couldn't come up with quantifiable results in three months, her funding would be reassigned.

She suspected something like that might happen after the jellyfish catastrophe but now it stared at her in black and white. At least she could still make an earth-shattering discovery within the next few weeks so that her entire future wouldn't be taken away. She knew she was dreaming, but sometimes denial and dreams were the best options.

After seeing that, she needed some air and perhaps pizza. She tried not to worry about her disappearing future while drifting in a daze down to the nearest pizza place. The kids behind the counter sang along to The Rolling Stones with a passion that made the songs sound new as they shoveled pizzas into and out of brick ovens. She ordered her small pizza, then noticed an empty stool by the wall and collapsed onto it.

Splashes of rainbow colors brightened the cement floor, giving it the appearance of a gigantic tie-dye shirt. Whenever the oven opened, warm smells of oregano and baked bread taunted her.

Teenagers and families filled the place. A couple of teenagers kept their hands in each other's back pockets while whispering together. The girl glanced over and stared in mid-whisper. Ellen looked back down at the tie-dyed floor.

The kid behind the counter cut her pizza with clunky precision before slipping it into a cardboard box. Ellen stood up to pay, hoping to get back to *Soliton* as quickly as possible.

Once aboard, she opened the box right away and took a huge bite. While still chewing, she climbed down below to grab a beer. She had forgotten how well pizza and beer go together. She brought the beer back up and sat outside.

Both the sunlight and the warm weather faded a little too fast. Everything took on a gray edge as the light dissipated. Ellen took a gulp of the sea air while wolfing down the pizza, mixing the salty ocean taste in with her food. From her boat, only a tiny corner of the deck could be seen where she and Ryan had sat out the night before. She couldn't see any people but they must be out there somewhere. Churning waves carried distant voices. She concentrated on the sound of the waves rather than the voices. The ducks glided over and she threw some pizza crust to them.

CHAPTER 11

⸻ ∽ ⸻

E LLEN JUMPED WHEN her office phone rang. No one ever
called her office. She usually communicated with everyone
through email. The ring sounded foreign, too high pitched, a si-
ren warning of impending danger. It could be her program manager. She didn't want to answer, but grabbed the phone to stop
it from ringing.

"Dr. Upton, I presume?"

"Yes?"

"Don't you recognize the voice of an ex-fiancée?"

"Paul?"

"That's right. Good guess. Hey, I'm on my way down for a
visit."

"You're what? Why?"

"Because I want to see you, that's why. And I was in Boston
for a conference and felt like skipping out early. Lots of reasons."

"You're on your way here now?"

"That's right. Just driving over the bridge and thought I
should call to warn you. Lots of traffic, but I should be there in
about half an hour."

Her heart inexplicably thudded in her ears as if she had been running or climbing a mountain. She could barely catch her breath while trying to sound casual about the whole thing.

"I guess I can't say no then."

"Didn't want to give you the chance to say that again."

"Okay, I'll see you when you get here."

It took less than a half hour. Paul usually did everything a little too fast. He came breezing in, his tie and conference badge still on. He looked the same: short brown hair, hazel eyes behind wire-framed glasses. With a long, thin nose and a line for a mouth, his face was all right angles. He wore a light blue shirt and tan chinos while blending into his environment almost as well as a jellyfish. It had been years since they'd seen each other and he hadn't even had the decency to put on any weight.

She stumbled up from her desk. Her foot had fallen asleep at some point and she felt like Quasimodo as she dragged her leg along while moving toward him.

He chuckled at the scene. "You seem the same."

"Is that good or bad?"

"Good, of course."

They walked out toward a park bordering the ocean where a sculpture of a whale's fluke dove into rippling grass. Children hung from the fluke and used it as a slide. Paul smiled and watched as if they could be his own kids. Ellen looked out toward the waves.

"So what made you come down here?"

"I told you. I had a conference in Boston and wanted to see you."

"We haven't seen each other in what? I'm not even sure how long it's been."

"Years. Too many years. I guess that's what happens when we're always working. Before we know it, we'll be retired."

Ellen couldn't imagine ever doing such a thing. But then if she couldn't find more funding, she'd have to retire at thirty-five. She ran her hand through her hair, hoping she didn't look as disheveled as she felt.

"What's that on your hand?"

Ellen looked at her palm and tried to laugh it off.

"Oh, a jellyfish sting. It happened a while ago. It's mostly gone now."

"I guess that must be part of the job. Does it hurt?"

"A little. Not so much anymore. It kind of burns every once in a while, but that's about it." Just another reminder of a messed up life. She felt the pain ignite at the thought.

"Did you get that from the jellyfish around here?"

She nodded. "There was a swarm of sand jellies right off the coast. The whole thing's pretty strange. Sand jellies aren't normally found in the Atlantic at all. Jellyfish swarms of most species are pretty rare around here anyway, but if they do appear it's usually only in the summer. We just found these a little while ago. Not only that, but the sand jellies were much larger than normal. None of it makes any sense."

"It sounds like you'll have a lot of interesting data to go through."

She tried to change the subject. "How do you like the job out there? Is it as perfect as you thought it would be?"

"I love it. Every day is different. I never know what's going to happen from one day to the next."

Ellen felt the buried rage ignite again. She should be the one living out a dream in San Francisco, not him. It was her research that brought him there. He didn't even have to find his own funding: how nice that would be, to be able to concentrate on the research without the constant worry that it could end at any time.

"That's great. I'm glad it all worked out for you. I should really get back to work."

"Wait. I know I'm probably the last person you want to see these days. But I wanted to see you, to find out how you were doing, and I wanted to say I'm sorry for everything. I should have given you the credit you deserved. I see that now and I'm sorry."

Ellen felt herself melt in his general direction, but she couldn't let that happen.

"Why bother apologizing now, after all this time?"

"I still feel horrible about it, that's why. You might think everything's great for me out there, but it's not. I lost you along the way. I'll always regret that."

She wanted to kiss him. She wanted to pull him closer. She wanted to leave and never look back. She wanted to run.

"That's okay. I'll try not to go on hating you forever."

"Thanks. I appreciate that." Paul gave her a quick hug, then pulled away. "I also wanted to offer you a job. There's an opening that would be perfect for you."

"Is that the real reason for the apology? Because you wanted to offer me a job?"

Paul shrugged. "Not really, but the job opening made me think of you, so that's why I thought it would be good to see you."

They turned down a side street and walked by a stone building that was once used as a warehouse for slaughtered whales. The building always made her wonder about the mentality of those who act as if everything is there for the taking.

She glanced over at Paul and wasn't sure what to think about the job offer. Maybe he wanted to use more of her ideas. He must be running out of them by now. Or this could be a peace offering. Either way, she couldn't do it.

"Thanks for the offer, but I can't leave everything here, even if everything here is a mess."

"I figured it was a long shot, but thought I'd ask anyway. How's everything going with your work then?"

"Well, my funding's about to run out so that's a big problem. Other than that, I keep hoping to feel like my work makes some kind of a difference. But I still don't feel that way. I don't know if I'll ever feel that way."

"But it does, you'll see."

"Sometimes I feel like such a fool for even trying. Maybe the world is too huge. Maybe there are too many people these days. It's really not very often that one person can be heard at all."

"That doesn't sound like you. You were always so sure your research would change the world someday."

"I was just young and too idealistic."

"I don't believe that," Paul said. "Never give up on your dreams."

As they walked side by side through a maze of research buildings, it reminded her of the walks they used to take through Boston back in graduate school. Paul insisted on getting away from their studies at least once a day for an airing. It would usually be early evening by the time they finally got around to it and they'd be in a daze from sitting at their computers all day.

She remembered drifting into a vacant courtyard made of white stone and hearing the trickle of a water fountain, then distant church bells dancing through the air. They ended up at a cathedral just as a chorus began to sing and fill the church. Mesmerized, they gazed up at the blue and purple petals of stained glass above the altar and listened. The sound was so overwhelming that tears filled their eyes. Then they turned toward each other and laughed. At that moment, she thought they'd always be together, that they'd keep laughing at their own ridiculousness.

Ellen tried to focus on the reality of Paul instead of her hazy memories.

"So is San Francisco as fun as everyone says it is?"

"It's great. Why don't you come out there sometime? I could take some time off and show you around."

She tried not to look as surprised as she felt. "I can't get away from work. I'm going on a research cruise soon and then there's the problem with the funding. There's a lot going on right now."

Paul's jaw tightened as he nodded. "Same old story, eh?"

"I guess. Then after the cruise hopefully there'll be lots of data to go through and I'll have to get more funding somehow."

"Sounds pretty busy. Where's the cruise going?"

"To the Atoll Islands. The whole thing should take about four weeks."

"Wow, that's a long time to be gone. I probably shouldn't have bothered you."

"No, that's okay, this is a nice break."

They wandered toward the aquarium and Ellen perked up at the thought of seeing the harbor seals. When they approached the outdoor tank, she was rewarded with the sight of a seal surfacing, blinking, and staring directly at her. His whiskers quivered, making her think of Jerry the Walrus. Then he plopped back down into the water and glided away.

"He was really staring at you there."

"Yeah, that was funny. I feel bad for him stuck in that tank though."

"Well, at least no sharks will eat him in there," Paul said as he watched the seal swim through the clear water.

"I guess. But wouldn't you rather take your chances and be free?"

"Oh, I don't know. Freedom is overrated."

"You only think that because you have freedom. If you didn't have it, you'd probably want freedom more than anything."

"Maybe. But I think I'd rather feel safe and happy with lots of fish around to eat."

"I guess that doesn't sound so bad."

Ellen wasn't sure if they were still talking about the harbor seal or not. She decided to change the subject with the first thing that popped into her mind.

"Any girlfriends out there in San Francisco?"

"Oh, just a few."

"What are they like?"

Paul laughed and shoved his hands deeper into his pockets. "I'm kidding. No girlfriends at the moment. Too busy, I guess."

"I would have figured you'd be married by now."

"Why's that?"

"Because you wanted to get married, I guess. I don't know."

"I wanted to marry you. I didn't just want to get married."

"I know. I'm sorry."

"Me too."

They ended up at a hard gravel parking lot. She didn't know what else to say and stood there hoping he'd say something.

"Well, I should get going," Paul said. "My flight's tonight."

Ellen stepped forward and hugged him for a little too long. His shirt smelled like sunshine.

"It was nice to see you," she said into his shirt.

"Remember, you can visit any time." Paul slid into his rental car. "Good luck with the cruise."

She waved goodbye and turned back toward work once he was gone. With every step, she wondered if she should have married him after all. She tried to imagine what a life with him would have been like. They probably would have had children. Somehow, she didn't think she'd be going off on a research cruise halfway around the world. Still, she might be happier as a wife and mother.

Maybe it wasn't a big deal that he stole her research. Maybe that's the way love is: a giving in, a surrendering of the self. But if that's the way love has to be, it seemed better not to love at all.

Her parents were disappointed when she called off the wedding. They'd been hoping for grandchildren. Sometimes she wished she could move back home to be closer to them. They were getting older now. They needed family around. They hadn't had any other children and they hardly ever saw her.

But she'd miss the ocean too much, which seemed a little strange after growing up nowhere near it. The Great Lakes did at least look like the ocean, complete with huge waves and sand dunes, but whenever she went back to visit it felt like something was missing. At the beach she would stop to breathe it all in, expecting to smell the tangy salt air, but it wouldn't be there. Then she would long for it, and long for the ocean.

Besides, there were no jellyfish in the Great Lakes to study, just regular fish and an invasive species of zebra mussels. The mussels had hitched onto a freighter at some point and managed to introduce themselves into the fresh water from their normal ocean environment.

Ellen had done the opposite, riding partway across the country in her rusty Volkswagen bug to colleges in the East. She had adapted to her new environment and never looked back. She wondered if those mussels now longed for the smell of the ocean air. She took a breath and filled herself up with it.

Sure, she had made a few sacrifices along the way. She did regret not having children, especially when she saw them laughing or playing or snuggling into their mother's arms. The look in Paul's eyes when he watched those kids play on the whale sculpture almost made her want to give up on everything and go back to San Francisco with him. Maybe someday, maybe soon, the sacrifices would all be worth it.

CHAPTER 12

J UST AS RED and yellow bled into green and wood smoke replaced the scent of suntan lotion, summer burst through
again for the weekend. The air felt warmer and softer than
it had for the past few weeks. No clouds could be seen, only
blue sky and sunshine: the kind that should be soaked up and
enjoyed.

Ellen realized no matter how much work there was left to
do, for this day it shouldn't matter. She didn't want to think
about Paul or work or the jellyfish catastrophe and her lack of
funding. She needed an escape.

She changed into shorts and a tank top, put her baseball cap
on, and started to get the boat ready. *Soliton* hadn't been out for
a while, which seemed almost cruel now, as if she could be a dog
that needed to be taken out for a run. Ellen didn't want to keep
her leashed up to the dock any longer.

The sunlight gave its gold away to the rustling trees and water. She wanted to be out there in the middle of it, surrounded
by the light so that it would seep into her bones and keep glowing
there all winter long.

She disconnected *Soliton* from the dock and waved goodbye to the ducks. *Soliton* puttered out, unsure what to do with herself now that she could really move again.

Ellen steered underneath the drawbridge into the ocean. The deep harbor that allowed research ships to dock near land caused tricky currents and swells knocked her little boat around everywhere. With the motor full on, she plowed through it all.

Scrub Island loomed low off to the side. Only a few stunted trees grew there, looking like hieroglyphics spelling out stubbornness while facing the constant ocean wind. The scrubby trees bent and stretched and became permanently slanted in one direction.

In the 1700s, pirates were known to hide out on Scrub Island. They used it as a base to attack merchant vessels or nearby farms, where they'd scout around and take an occasional pig or goat before retreating back to the island. Ellen imagined pirate ships surrounding her along with their chants and songs and raucous laughter. She tried to listen as the waves sloshed with their stories.

Once Scrub Island slipped by, they entered the open ocean. *Soliton* immediately began to bounce with a reckless joy. Ellen gripped the steering wheel and accelerated into sea sparkle, causing ocean water to splash in her face. She licked it off her lips, tasting the salt and something else she couldn't define.

Martha's Vineyard came into view with its white church steeples and sea captain homes standing against the sky much as they had for the last few centuries. Ellen slowed the boat to maneuver closer and steered toward a jetty made of boulders.

Soliton puttered past the jetty into a marina where they could dock and pay a meter as if parking on a city street. They found a spot and pulled in. After tying *Soliton* up to her new resting place, Ellen felt exhausted but exhilarated. The splashing sea had drenched her. She went below to change into a drier tank top while trading boat shoes in for sandals and sunglasses. Her legs wobbled as she stepped off the boat onto a boardwalk that paved the way toward vacant restaurants and bars. It was still too early for lunch so she decided to wander.

She took a few steps on the echoing wood and looked back at sea sparkle before turning down a side street into town. Cobblestones curved past gas lamps and storefronts. Ellen glanced into the display windows. She never really liked shopping, especially when it had to be done in a mall or closed-in area. Strolling outside in the open air and occasionally peeping into stores felt much more civilized. In one window, a metal contraption with octopus arms pulled globs of pink saltwater taffy in all directions. She told herself to stop on the way back to get some fudge for her parents.

The cobblestones led to a town square lined with gingerbread houses. Each house painted with bright purple, pink or yellow trim took on the appearance of candy. Ellen suppressed the urge to lick them. Fences and porches had been carved into delicate white swirls and points as if they could be made of sugary lace instead of wood.

The gingerbread houses all gathered around an outdoor church with a tent-like sloping iron roof. Ellen took a few steps toward the church and looked right inside. There were no walls, just metal poles holding the roof in place.

A plaque let wanderers know that church services had been performed in a tent at this location in the early 1800s. Before the gingerbread houses were built, families pitched tents here for the summer so they could attend church meetings every day and night. Gradually, small wooden shacks and then cottages replaced the tents, with most owned by the same families for generations.

Ellen didn't think it would be much of a summer vacation if they went to church every day and night. As soon as the thought entered her head, a low moaning noise erupted from the iron roof. She felt a tremble travel down her spine. It must be the wind. Still, she backed away and decided not to think any more derogatory thoughts about the church while standing so close to it.

She walked toward the bright gingerbread houses to shake off the creepy feeling, but now even the cheery cottages took on a sinister appearance, the carvings suddenly dripping with gothic overtones.

Ellen headed toward the boardwalk and the sun and the possibility of lunch. More people now meandered through town. For once, she felt grateful for the crowds. They made her feel a little more normal while helping to shake off the creepy chill.

She chose an outdoor restaurant called the Sand Castle since it looked like the sunniest spot. Picnic tables settled into the sand around a wooden bar. Ellen figured she might as well sit at the bar instead of occupying a whole table by herself. She managed to hop up on the barstool without falling, then took her sunglasses off and squinted.

"And what can I get for you to drink on this beautiful afternoon?" The bartender asked in a Jamaican accent.

"Just a lemonade I guess."

"If it has to be just a lemonade then I will get you the best lemonade. Freshly squeezed by my own hands."

He walked away and returned with an icy glass and a menu. Ellen took a sip. It tasted sweet and sour all at once and cooled her off right away.

"You like the Tigers?" He asked, nodding to her baseball cap.

"Oh, I did when I was little. They were always the underdogs."

"And why do you like these underdogs so much?"

"I guess it's because you don't expect them to win. So when they do win, it's more exciting. The only thing is they'll break your heart at some point."

"Ah, very true. Those underdogs can be sneaky in that way, but they are still the most fun. My name is Andrew," he said while wiping the bar. As if on cue, steel drums started playing a Caribbean tune off in the corner. "I am only here for one more week and then I must go back home to Jamaica so be sure you do not get too attached to me."

He wore a blue and white flowered Hawaiian shirt. A constant smile embraced his face. Ellen thought he must be used to charming anyone who happened to sit at his bar. She was glad for the distraction.

"Why do you have to go back?"

"I only stay here for the summer. This place closes in another week since it is no good to sit in the sand when it is cold and rainy and snowing. And I am very afraid of the snow."

"Afraid of the snow? How could anyone be afraid of the snow?"

"Easily. I have only been out in it once in my life. And that was enough." Andrew shivered and rubbed his arms, reminding her of the chill from the outdoor church.

"Do you know anything about that outdoor church with those little gingerbread houses all around it?"

"Yes, but what I do know you do not want to know."

"Oh, why's that?" Ellen couldn't help but be curious now.

"Okay, I will tell you," Andrew leaned forward and whispered, "Some say there is a ghost hiding away in that church."

"A ghost? Do they say that so more tourists will go there?"

"No, I believe it. The place has a feel to it, you know?"

"I guess." Ellen took a sip of her lemonade.

"Did you see the ghost?"

"No, I was just over there a little while ago. Maybe ghosts don't show themselves in daylight, I don't know. But it did have a strange feel to it."

"Yes," Andrew nodded. "Yes, we are always dismissing these things, these feelings, but they are still there. The world is filled with spirits whether we want to recognize them or not."

Ellen felt goose bumps rise up on her arms and tried to rub them back down.

"You see?" Andrew said. "Maybe you carry the spirit with you now."

"I hope not." She started to feel very creeped out by the whole thing. If there had been a spirit there, for some reason she pictured it as a scraggly minister with long white hair and yellow teeth.

"It would be a good thing if you carried the spirit. There would be a reason for it. The spirit would help you."

"I guess that's okay then," Ellen said. "As long as it helps me, that is. I could use all the help I can get."

"I will try to help you then too. But first, you must eat something good."

Ellen decided on a bean burrito. Andrew left to place the order, took an order from a couple sitting at the other end of the bar, then came back carrying a huge conch shell.

"This is my magic shell."

Ellen looked at him in total disbelief. He rubbed the shell until she expected to see a genie pop out.

"It is magical," he said. "We forget there is magic all around us, just like spirits. Look at this here, it was once a home; it protected a life. And now it is a work of art. Look at how the colors and shapes all swirl together."

The shell held a sunset of soft sienna and rust stretching toward a smooth pink center. White and pink twisted up to a spire. It could have been a sculpture carved with the finest detail.

"And it is a horn." With that, Andrew raised the shell to his lips and blew, creating a loud groaning noise that sounded like a sick bull. The couple at the other end of the bar turned away from each other to look at him.

"But most important, it is a tool for us to listen to the ocean. There is a little ocean inside. Here, listen to the ocean; listen to what it has to tell you."

He held the shell up and Ellen pressed it against her ear. She knew there was nothing in there but air and possibly the remnants of what once lived inside, but she listened and heard the ocean.

Andrew covered her hand with his to help hold the shell up. He gazed into her eyes as if the whole thing could be a religious experience.

"You hear it? People say the ocean roars. I say it pulses. It is a living, breathing thing with a heartbeat. We need to remember to listen to it always."

Ellen nodded and kept listening to the heartbeat, wondering if there was a little ocean buried inside after all. Andrew left to get her food and set it in front of her. Her burrito was smothered with tomatoes, red peppers, onions, and guacamole. Plunging into it became another sort of religious experience.

After lunch, Ellen thanked Andrew and felt the urge to hug him goodbye but the polished wooden bar stood between them. She settled for squeezing his hand. His eyes smiled back at her.

She left the Sand Castle and went to the candy shop to buy the fudge for her parents, figuring she might as well walk off her lunch before getting back into the boat, even if the end result would be the temptation to eat some of that fudge.

On the ride back home, *Soliton* bounced more than on the way there and occasionally flew through the air. Now when Ellen licked the saltwater off her lips, she tasted all the life that the ocean harbored, from the tiniest plankton to starfish and jelly-fish, right on up to whales and dolphins. She heard their songs, felt their struggles for survival, and listened to the echoing heart of the ocean. And she felt the pulse of the ocean giving its life to all those lives it held.

CHAPTER 13

E VERY MORNING AND every evening before dark, Kalani wandered the shore. She walked the line between her world and David's and took no joy in it. She knew he was out there. She could feel him, but she could not find him.

She kept thinking she would see him in the distance on one of these walks. They would run toward each other with arms outstretched like actors in a bad movie. Then they would embrace, hold onto each other, and they would be whole again. Until then, she would be a castoff piece of driftwood. A bit of something that could not fit together with anything.

The children looked to her for clues as to how they should act. She tried to be brave for them. She told them their father would be back and they believed her. But she felt herself turning into shadow, and every day with no David made the shadow smaller. Soon she would be nothing but a wisp of an idea.

David had always watched out for her. They grew up together. The other children used to tease her because she looked different, with green eyes and wavy, uncontrolled hair that flew around everywhere. They said she didn't belong on the island, that a mistake had been made. She started to believe it herself.

But David put a stop to their teasing. He said it was a good thing she was different, that it made her special.

When they were children and everything was new, they would sneak off and explore the island together. There was a secret place, a field of wildflowers. David would drape her in necklaces and crowns made of flowers. She would come home smelling sweet and smiling. She knew him as well as the island, every mood, every rocky place, every burst of light.

Kalani dipped her toes into the water, then trudged deeper. She gathered her dress around her legs and walked in up to her knees while standing against the waves. She kept willing the ocean to take her and bring him back. She stood and waited and half expected the ocean to reach out and grab her. But it never did.

Still, she could feel David. Sometimes he was very close. She felt him in her head, buzzing there, almost as if he could talk to her. She wished he would tell her what to do. More than anything, she wanted to go deeper into the water and immerse herself in his world. Sometimes she could hear David calling out to her. He wanted her to join him. But she stayed at the edge of his world, knowing their children needed her.

Now she walked farther than usual, out of the water and up a hill that soon became a cliff of loose rocks. She heard the stones scatter and fall with each step. They made her slip but she kept climbing. She felt her heart travel to her head. Her breath came faster and faster. When she reached the top, she swerved and almost fell all the way back down to the boulders and crashing sea below. At this point, she wouldn't care if she did. She moved away from the edge and looked down.

The cliff jutted into the ocean and from there she could see the Man in the Rock. She stared at the hideousness of it. The people were forbidden to talk of the Man in the Rock. Talking of him brought bad luck. She knew David liked to think of him as a protector, but Kalani despised the screaming face. To her, he looked like a prisoner, trying to break free of all that rock while screaming in pain. The thought of it gave her nightmares. It had always been there. It had always been the same. Whenever she happened to be near it, she tried not to look. Now she stared. The face had changed. The mouth was still open in what could be called a scream, but it curled into more of a leer. The Man in the Rock did not look as frightened as he had for her whole life. He looked somehow satisfied.

Kalani turned away and stared into the churning water, searching for David.

CHAPTER 14

⁓

THE LAST WEEK before the cruise became a whirlwind of organizing, packing, and labeling everything from scuba and lab equipment to foul weather gear. Clothes were a secondary concern, but Ellen was glad she remembered them only after everything else was finally done and ready to go.

The ship arrived in port two days before the cruise. It docked behind her red brick work building and dwarfed it entirely, even though the building had often swallowed her whole. The *Eagle* resembled a small offshore city complete with smokestacks, flashing lights, and towers reaching into the sky. Crew members scurried around on deck like puppets on an oversized stage.

The *Eagle* also hummed. Ellen could hear the metallic humming from inside her office, a constant whirring reminder that she'd better be ready soon. She had seen a few crew members walking through town with their uniforms on, clean cut and fresh faced, all wearing the same stunned expression upon discovering that their ship was actually larger and more exciting than the town. They looked about ready to go.

She saw Ryan here and there, always in a hurried passing as they both began to load their gear onto the ship. Each time Ellen went aboard to dump more supplies in the storage area, she felt a surge of excitement at the thought of going off on an adventure. She kept peeking in at the ship's empty laboratory while imagining all the work to be done and the discoveries yet to be made.

Most people had never been to or heard of the Atoll Islands. This would be the closest she'd ever come to discovering a new world or traveling to another planet. Ellen supposed the early explorers must have felt this way. She had no idea what to expect from the uninhabited and mysterious area, and yet it held such promise.

Her previous research trips had either been to Bermuda or open ocean locations in the North Atlantic. It only took a few days to get to Bermuda and those cruises would usually last for about a week.

In contrast, it would take a full week just to get to the Atoll Islands. The islands were so far from everything that they weren't really near anything, but they were closer to Hawaii than anything else. A few more island chains hovered nearby. Ellen thought of them as scattered unreachable mountaintops. And the *Eagle* would fly through the blue ocean sky to bring them there.

Bolted metal shelves lined the walls of the ship's storage area. Ellen lugged another container in and plunked it down. The area designated for their things was filling up. She slid a few plastic bins closer together and told herself to remember to get some bungee cords to anchor everything in place.

She backed away from the shelves and right into Ryan. He held another container and reached around to slide it onto a shelf. His arms brushed against her side.

"Sorry I keep running into you," she said.

"No problem. Everything all packed and ready to go?"

"Yeah, sure. That'll probably only happen a couple hours before we leave. If we're lucky."

"Think we're done for today though?"

"Maybe. Have you brought everything you'll need on board?"

"The wetsuits and my supplies are all here," Ryan said. "I'll just bring a bag of clothes tomorrow morning."

"Okay, I'll go get some bungee cords for now but you can go. Make sure to get lots of sleep since you might not get much on the ship."

"I don't have to go yet. I can help with the bungee cords. Where are they?"

"Oh, I've got a few back on my boat if there aren't any more in the lab."

"Great. I've always wanted to see your boat."

Ellen wasn't so sure about bringing Ryan onto her boat. She rubbed her sweaty hands on her jeans.

"Okay, but it's no big deal or anything."

"No big deal? I'd love to live on a boat."

"That's good, let's see if you still feel that way after the cruise."

They left the humming research vessel while nodding to a few crew members on the way out. The bouncing gangplank that connected the ship to the dock made her feel shaky and unstable.

"Don't you like living on a houseboat?" Ryan asked.

"Yeah, it's a lot of work and there are inconveniences here and there, but it's worth it for the view. It's definitely not the same as being stuck on a research vessel for weeks at a time though. Some people go a little stir crazy and start to think of the cruises as prison terms."

"I don't think I will. I'm really looking forward to spending all that time on the ship."

"Like I said, we'll see how you feel after the cruise."

They crossed the empty street toward Snake Pond and the marina. The dock at the marina narrowed to a single-file pathway, forcing Ryan to walk behind her. Ellen thought she could feel his breath on her neck. Maybe it was just the sea breeze tickling her skin. She almost wanted to stop walking so that he'd run into her again.

They climbed aboard. Ellen motioned toward the boat. "Here she is, exciting, eh?"

"Yeah, it really is." Ryan scrutinized the deck with its built-in sloping bench seats. He looked like he'd never seen plastic before in his life.

"I named her *Soliton*." She felt like she was introducing Ryan to a lifelong friend and figured she might as well provide a few more details. "A soliton is a rogue wave that's not affected by any other waves. Usually, waves are constantly interacting with each other but not solitons. They always behave independently from other waves. I liked the sound of it."

"Of course." Ryan nodded his head, causing his light brown hair to fall over his eyes. He brushed it back with a stroke of his hand.

"I'll go find the bungee cords, they're down there somewhere." Ellen waved to the ladder that led below deck.

"Mind if I go with you? It'd be great to see what it's like down there."

"Okay, but it might be messy. I've been pulling things out all over the place to pack for the cruise." She hoped she hadn't left any underwear out at least.

"That's okay, I'm messy too."

Ryan followed her down the ladder. Once they reached the floor, he surveyed her cramped living quarters. He looked at home on the boat with his khaki shorts, sneakers, and t-shirt, as if he might go out fishing at any moment.

"This is so cool."

"Yeah, I guess." Ellen looked around, trying to see it all through his eyes.

Her bed was tucked away in the far corner, unmade of course, but that looked like the only real mess other than a few pieces of scattered clothes. Books filled the built-in shelves along the bed and Ryan squinted toward the titles. The kitchen area to the side featured a tiny stovetop, sink, and microwave all built into the wall near the ladder. Mostly, cabinets and shelves lined every inch of space and that was a good thing because if she didn't have the cabinets and shelves everything would be much messier.

She walked over to the cabinet where she thought the bungee cords might be and opened it with a jolt, causing bottles of never-used cleaners to tumble out and clatter all over the floor. Ellen picked them up, moved more containers around, and finally found the bungee cords hidden behind everything. They were all tangled together in one lump. She took the jumbled mass out and held it up for Ryan to see.

"Here they are. Guess I'll have to untangle them."

"Oh, I can do that." He reached over and took them, leaving her with nothing to do but wonder if she should offer him dinner.

"Want something to eat? I don't have much left, but there must be something."

"Sure, that'd be great," he said, already distracted and fumbling with the bungee cords.

Ellen opened the mini refrigerator. "All I have is water."

"Sounds good."

She pulled out two bottled waters, opened them, and handed one to Ryan. He disentangled one hand from the bungee cords long enough to take the bottle.

Ellen looked through a few cabinets, then back in the refrigerator and freezer. "I'm afraid the food selection is even worse. There's some canned soup and macaroni and cheese."

"I don't want to eat all your food but macaroni and cheese sounds good."

She took the packages out of the freezer, unwrapped them, and plunked one into the microwave. "Might as well eat all the food since we're leaving tomorrow."

"I can't believe it. Even though it feels like we've been preparing for forever, it still kind of snuck up on me."

"Same here. There's never enough time to prepare. So we're just going to have to go and forget about any more preparing."

"That doesn't sound like you."

"It doesn't?"

"No, I mean, I would think you'd want us to make sure we're really ready and that we haven't forgotten anything."

"I guess, but there comes a point when you can't do any more so hopefully we're there now because, I don't know about you, but I'm tired."

"Yeah, me too," Ryan said as the microwave dinged. Ellen took one platter out and threw the other frozen block of mush back in its place.

When the microwave dinged again, Ellen gave a dish to Ryan and together they climbed back up the ladder to eat outside. Ryan somehow balanced his water, dish, and bungee cord mass without dropping anything as he followed her up.

Just her luck, the sun hid below the horizon, leaving a glowing orange sky with cloud streaks in its wake. Water lapped against the side of the boat, causing a slight sway. It all felt too uncomfortably romantic. Ellen cleared her throat and searched for something to say, but the soft glow was all she could think of and calling their attention to that didn't seem like the right thing to do.

"So do you eat out here all the time?" Ryan asked while plunging into his macaroni and cheese.

"Pretty much, except in winter or when it's raining."

"What do you do in the winter?"

"I stay inside. I have a space heater in there so it can get pretty warm. But if it ever gets too cold, I can always stay in the office."

"You've had to do that?"

"Only a few times so far."

"Don't you ever get lonely living out here by yourself?"

"No, not at all," Ellen said, denying what she hoped wasn't all that obvious, redefining herself from possibly lonely to independent. "I've got my laptop, my work, and I've even got a seagull for a pet. That's all I need."

She nodded toward the seagull perched on the boat railing. She should probably give him some food or a least a treat. If he were a real pet, she'd have to. The seagull studied them, then jumped up and flew away all in one white-winged motion. Ellen felt a sudden chill.

She finished her macaroni before it could morph into cold mush. Ryan chewed his last bite, licked his lips, then looked at her as if he might want something more.

"Guess I'd better get going." He reached for the bungee cords at his feet. "I'll bring these home to untangle them."

"You don't have to. I can do that."

"No, just make sure to get lots of sleep. Big day tomorrow and all that." He turned toward the boat ramp to leave.

"Okay, goodnight."

Ellen felt a splash of reluctance that he hadn't tried anything while they were alone on the boat together, especially now that the light faded into dark swirls of bold romance. But if he did, she'd have to force herself to push him away and then the cruise would be awkward. So it was a good thing that nothing happened. She had to focus on her work. Still, as she watched him walk down the dock, she couldn't help but feel as if they had missed out on something.

She scoffed at herself as she gathered up her things to go back inside. She could only hope he didn't think of her as some creepy old person sighing all over him, even if she did just that as she watched him walk away.

~

He had never seen anyone so lonely. It seemed to have settled beneath her skin. She didn't come right out and act that way but he could still see it for some reason, aching away beneath the surface. It made him want to help. But he didn't know how.

Ryan walked to the house he rented with two other guys. The front porch sagged. Bare wood could be seen beneath flaking white paint while rot ate away at the edges. He couldn't believe the house hadn't completely fallen apart by now. College students usually rented it so the landlord didn't really care. But he wasn't in college anymore. He shouldn't still be living this way. He wanted to start living a real life, whatever that meant.

He sat on the beat up old couch that sagged out on the saggy porch and tried to untangle the bungee cords. The house sounded quiet. His housemates must be out. If they were home, he'd hear music pounding through the rotting walls. He shook the mass of cords so that they loosened a little, then moved a piece back through a loop, hoping he could change the mess for the better and not make it worse.

Here he was, in his late twenties already and still living with roommates like in college. He didn't necessarily want to get married and have a family and all that, not yet anyway, but maybe he should have done some of those things by now. He hadn't even been in very many serious relationships. A few here and there, but nothing that had been any kind of a big deal. At least he finally had a good job so maybe his family wouldn't think of him as a complete loser.

He wondered why Ellen seemed so lonely. Didn't she have a family or friends? She always looked distracted or flustered while her ponytail swung around in a life of its own. She made him think of Audrey Hepburn. They both had that same kind of lost, frantic look while their eyes showed a certain kindness. He didn't see how Ellen could be so many different things at once. She was graceful and awkward, determined and shy, lonely and independent, all things that shouldn't really fit together in one person and yet somehow did.

His housemates walked over the brown lawn toward him. For some reason, they kept their hair shaved down to the point of practical baldness. When Ryan first met them, he assumed they'd have military-type personalities because of their haircuts, but it turned out that they didn't at all. They didn't even make their beds.

"Hey, want to go to the Pirate?"

Ryan didn't look up from the bungee cords. "Nah, I was just there the other day."

"So you'd rather play with bungee cords?"

"I'm doing this for work, but yeah."

"Looks like a challenging project."

Ryan looked up. "You guys go ahead. I've got to get ready for the cruise anyway."

"Since you're going off on a four-week cruise tomorrow, you'd think you'd want your last night of freedom to be a wild one."

"I've had enough wild nights."

"There are never enough wild nights, my friend, never enough. You'll regret this when you're stuck out on that ship in the middle of nowhere."

Ryan waved them off. "Yeah, probably."

He didn't think he'd regret not going out though. He managed to get the right piece through another loop and felt a sense of victory as he freed an entire bungee cord. He held it up and placed it next to him. The others were still tangled but he knew if he was patient enough, he could eventually straighten them all out. It just took time.

CHAPTER 15

ELLEN BOLTED UP, thinking she'd overslept before realizing it was still dark outside. The alarm clock's red glow announced the insane hour of 4 AM.

She flopped back down before figuring she might as well get up. She'd been a little delayed by Ryan's visit and didn't want to do much after he left. She forced herself to click the light on. Mostly, she needed to pack. Then close up the boat. There should be enough time to do everything since the cruise didn't leave until 10. But before anything else, she needed coffee. Lots of coffee.

She dragged the metal can out of her bare cabinet, opened it up and sniffed the trapped coffee air, hoping the smell would wake her up. Her eyes opened a little more, but that was about it. She'd need much more of a coffee infusion than that. She scooped some extra heaps into the filter.

While the coffee dripped and dribbled all too slowly, Ellen wandered over to her cabinets and pulled out bunches of clothes: sweatshirts, tank tops, shorts, socks, bathing suits. They'd mostly be in the tropics, but they'd also be cruising along the eastern seaboard and could run into some cold weather. She had to make sure to pack enough rain gear and a few baseball caps. Baseball caps kept her hair out of her eyes during the constant wind and helped make showers not quite so necessary. Not that she ever had time to worry about her hair anyway, but at least she really didn't have to worry about it with her baseball cap on.

Her main wardrobe of tank tops and shorts didn't take up much space in the duffel bag. Ellen scrunched in a rain jacket and more foul weather gear. Once it was all zipped up, she sat on her bed and leaned against the packed bag while inhaling her coffee. Through the tiny porthole, she watched the gray light of morning change everything.

When it was time to go, Ellen hauled her duffel bag and laptop to the research ship and sought out the sleeping quarters. No one was there yet so she plunked her load onto one of the lower bunks and wandered down to the storage area.

Their gear sat on the metal shelves with bungee cords strapping everything in place. Ryan had gotten everything untangled somehow. She touched the cords, making sure they were all secure. He must have done it last night. Then she started thinking about his hands and wondered what else they could do before she could once again stop herself from thinking such things.

She had already closed up *Soliton* so there wasn't much else that needed to be done before departure. She went outside, bounced down the ramp that stuck out from the ship like a wayward tongue, and thought she might as well get some more coffee. She looked back as soon as her feet touched stable ground. The ship loomed over the huddled clapboard buildings while promising certain adventure.

The coffee shop felt warm and cozy as soon as she walked in, with cinnamon, chocolate, and coffee scents enveloping her. She took a deep breath of the sugar-laced, caffeinated air.

The workers behind the counter stretched up and bent down all at once, pulling jars from shelves here and there, adding all kinds of ingredients for all kinds of potions. They worked to the rhythm of a song that played in the background, a crazy mix of bongos and flutes, and the three workers became one animal with six arms stretching everywhere.

While waiting in line and watching the six-armed animal, Ellen looked at a scrap of newspaper tacked to the wall by the counter. She found Aquarius, then read:

"Every time you think you finally have yourself figured out, you realize that you are once again completely off base. It can take a lifetime to really know yourself, but to know yourself well enough to succeed in the moment is a much simpler thing."

It sounded more like a fortune cookie than a horoscope, but part of it was true. She hadn't figured herself out yet. She'd probably never figure herself out. She kept drifting, occasionally propelling herself toward something without really knowing where she might be headed. Her dreams guided her, but would they send her off in the wrong direction? Would this cruise turn into another disaster? At least her horoscope mentioned succeeding. Not that she believed in horoscopes or fortune cookies.

Ellen ordered her coffee and bagel, thinking she should have brought her laptop since everyone fiddled around with theirs and looked productive. Then the door opened with a jingle and Ryan walked in, laughing with some pretty blond girl. Of course he had a girlfriend. She should have figured that he did. They looked like they could be on their honeymoon: both tanned and athletic and perfect for each other. They practically blended into each other right there in front of her. She forced herself to try to be happy for them.

"Hey Ellen," Ryan said, looking surprised. "I'm glad you're here."

"Hi," she said as she paid for her coffee. How she wished she never liked coffee. She started planning an escape route. She could pretend there was more to do back in the office. Come to think of it, there must be more to do in the office.

"This is my sister, Emily, she came to see me off," Ryan said while gesturing to the girl on his arm.

"Oh, hi," Ellen said again, feeling even more foolish than before. "That's nice of you."

"Well, I'm going to miss him." His sister cradled his arm and held it closer. "I can't believe he'll be gone for four whole weeks."

"Yeah, it's a long time. Even for a cruise."

Ryan ordered their coffees, then spun toward Ellen. "Want to sit with us? We still have some time before the ship leaves, right?"

"A couple hours, but we should be aboard at least an hour before."

"Sounds like we can all have a few leisurely cups of coffee then."

"Sure. Then we'll be jumping around on the ship like caged animals."

They wandered over to a vacant corner where a faded green couch and two yellow chairs huddled together. Ellen chose one of the chairs. It immediately felt too much like a throne. Ryan and his sister sank into the green cushions across from her.

"I may never get out of this couch," Ryan said, looking suddenly sleepy. He put his arm up along the back, again making it look as if his sister might really be his girlfriend.

"I'm so glad to finally meet you," Emily said. "Ryan talks about you all the time."

Ellen felt her face start to flush. She tried to mask it by taking a sip of her coffee, but the hot coffee probably only made her face redder.

"He does?" She managed to choke out. She looked at him but he just sat there. She coughed a few times; hoping they'd think her red face was due to a sudden lack of oxygen rather than complete embarrassment.

"Oh yeah, mostly about your work," Emily said. "It sounds fascinating."

Ellen almost let a little snort escape in response, but held it in. "I guess it can be. Sometimes."

"There are so many different types of jellyfish though, right? And you probably haven't been able to study them all yet."

"That's true, I haven't been able to study them all yet. There are about two thousand known species of jellyfish and some are in places that I haven't been able to get to like the Arctic or the area we're traveling to on the cruise."

"And you've been researching jellyfish for so many years. Imagine that. That there's still so much more to know after you've been researching them for so long."

Ellen wondered what Ryan had been telling his sister. She thought she must seem like some sort of jellyfish spinster, holed up in her office day and night dissecting bits of jellyfish flesh, searching for answers that never revealed themselves.

"I guess it can be pretty daunting," she said. "There have been lots of times when I've wanted to give up on the whole thing, but then something happens, usually one little flicker of something that hadn't been thought of before, and then I get excited about everything all over again."

"That's great. I can see why Ryan admires you and your work so much."

"What about you?" Ellen asked. "What kind of work do you do?"

"Oh, well I'm a waitress. For now, that is. It's not my life's ambition or anything. But it is a way to earn some money while I'm trying to be an artist."

"You are an artist," Ryan jumped in. "Her work's really great. You should see it sometime."

"It's not that great," Emily said. "I mean, I do like some of it. But I keep changing most of my stuff around all the time. I'll like it for a little while, and then it seems like it needs something else so I'll change it completely around. I work mostly with acrylics so luckily it's easy to change those kinds of paintings by piling the layers on."

"What kinds of things do you paint?"

"Oh, I don't know, I'm looking forward to seeing some of the pictures of jellyfish that you and Ryan will be taking on the cruise. It would be a real challenge to try to paint something like that. But mostly I like to paint everyday things and make them look different. It's semi-abstract so that makes it hard to tell when it's really done."

"That reminds me of a quote," Ellen said. "Something like a painting is never finished, it just stops in interesting places."

"I hope that's not true." Emily scrunched up her face. "I'd like to feel as if some of it is finished someday."

"I know what you mean." Ellen turned toward Ryan. "I should go wrap some things up in the office before we leave. I'll see you on the ship."

"Okay, see you on the ship," Ryan said while looking like he'd never get up off that couch.

"It was nice meeting you," Ellen said to Ryan's sister, then grabbed the leftover coffee and bag of uneaten, hardened bagel and turned to go.

"Nice to meet you too. Take good care of my brother now."

Ellen didn't know what to say to that so she just waved good-bye and hurried out, feeling the need to disappear to her office. The drawbridge chose that particular moment to rise up ever so slowly, temporarily blocking her destination. Cement and metal squeaked as the chunk of road that formed the bridge rose straight up in the air.

Once the bridge pointed all the way up and hovered there, Ellen could see the scrawled and spray-painted messages left by kids who had decorated the underside, anticipating moments like this. While standing around waiting for the drawbridge to go back down, everyone found themselves faced with philosophical phrases to ponder like: "Stop the Madness" or "Who Even Are These People?"

A sailboat slipped through the opening created by the raised drawbridge. As the boat made its escape to the open ocean, Ellen couldn't help but think it would have been nice to grow up with a sister or a brother, someone to depend on, someone to laugh and play with. She would have liked to feel that kind of a connection with someone. Who even are these people? Who is anyone, really? And even if you think you know someone, how do you know for sure?

CHAPTER 16

ELLEN STARTED TO panic as she walked and then ran around the deck. She couldn't find Ryan anywhere and the ship would be pulling away from the dock in about two minutes. She could only hope he'd made it aboard. He must be there somewhere, but she'd feel much better about the whole thing if she could see him and confirm that he really was there. She blamed the coffee shop couch for swallowing him up.

The ship gave out three short, bone-rattling tuba blasts before extricating itself from shore. She looked down the length of the dock below, expecting to see Ryan there running toward the departing ship. A crowd of people gathered on the dock instead. Then she did see him, farther down on the ship's deck, practically hanging off it while waving good-bye to his sister. Ellen let out a sigh of relief and swayed down the deck to join him.

"So what do you think so far?"

"It's great, I love it," Ryan said, still waving back toward his sister. "I guess it'll be hard to be away from my family and everyone, but I think it'll be worth it."

"That's good. I'm glad your sister didn't try to abduct you or something so that she wouldn't have to be without you for four weeks."

"Yeah, she wanted to. Well, both my mom and sister wanted to but I fought them off earlier."

"So your family's pretty close then?"

"Yeah, of course, aren't all families?"

"No, not all," Ellen said into the wind.

"Well, even if some people don't think their families are close, I bet they are in some way, whether they realize it or not."

"I guess."

The smell of the ship's greased metal competed with the ocean air. Ellen looked out at Scrub Island, at the harbor and waters where pirates and sea captains once roamed. She wondered if the waves still told their stories or if they had forgotten all about them.

From way up on the research ship, the island looked even smaller and scrubbier than it had from *Soliton*, the dark trees twisting and bending into unnatural shapes from a lifetime of being out there in the open, facing the wind alone.

"I think I'll go unpack," Ellen said as she pushed away from the cold metal railing.

"Okay, I'll be out here if you need me." Ryan leaned into the wind, letting it ruffle his hair from his forehead. "Unless we need to do anything work-wise for now."

"No, not yet, enjoy it while you can."

Ellen decided to take her own advice. After unpacking, she grabbed a paperback book, stretched out on her bunk and read for pleasure for the first time in years. The book, about an Old West mining town, described a place that couldn't be more opposite than the place she found herself in now. As she turned the pages, the two places began to converge so that she rode along on the waves as if on horseback.

The *Eagle* soared, stopping to roost at a few eastern ports, but never for very long. At one point Ellen went out to get some air and thought she saw a gorilla board the ship. She decided she must be hallucinating and went back to rest and read. She tried to remember all the stops: New York, New Jersey, North Carolina, she thought there might be others in there somewhere but couldn't be sure. The ship took on more researchers at each one. A few trickled into the women's quarters, but most only stayed long enough to dump their luggage off onto a bed. One older woman went right to sleep as soon as she arrived and now snored lightly. Another woman had seen Ellen reading and opened a book of her own to read. She yawned occasionally over in her corner. Ellen thought of all this as a slow introduction to living so closely with others again, the snoring and yawning, the light breathing of humanity as it continued to close in all around.

Then a hurricane burst through the door. "Hey y'all, how's everyone doin' in here?"

There were murmurs in response, the readers reluctant to drag their eyes away from their books. A snort of surprise escaped from the snoring bundle. Their lack of enthusiasm didn't bother the invading force of nature one bit.

"What is this, a library or a dormitory or what all?"

Ellen slipped her eyes from the page where Native Americans were about to attack and looked at the source of the noise. Must be a student, fresh and glowing all bright and pink, with shiny red hair slicked back into a ponytail like hers, but at the same time not at all like hers, because everything about this girl seemed too perfect and so she would never pull her hair back in a haphazard way like hers.

"It's a research ship," Ellen answered through a yawn.

"Well, I know that, silly." The girl waved her hand at her. "What's everyone bein' so quiet about? Shouldn't we all get to know each other or something?"

"We're trying to read for now because pretty soon we'll be too busy to read, or sleep as the case may be," Ellen glanced over at the woman who somehow kept snoring through it all. "And don't worry, we'll have four weeks to get to know each other."

"Well, okay, sorry for interrupting you all. My name's Maddie, by the way, short for Maude, can you believe my parents named me *that* of all things? They loved the show, that and The Golden Girls. So they named me after Maude, even though that's not even her real name. And even if it was, why would anyone name a little baby girl after an old lady? I mean, maybe my face was wrinkly and all, but still."

"You were born after The Golden Girls?"

Ellen remembered watching reruns of the show in her college dorm room. Her friends would each select a character to be, then they'd have to drink whenever that character's name was mentioned. She was always amazed by how often they said each other's name on that show.

"Well, I guess it was while the show was still going on or something, I don't know. I just know I was born back in 1986."

Back in 1986? Ellen remembered 1986 like it was yesterday. She had followed every detail of the Iran-Contra affair, running home from school to click on the news and jot down the latest in her spiral notebook. Anyone born in 1986, in a time she could so clearly remember, must still be a baby, a child in a stroller. Not someone like this person standing before her, looking mostly grown up and able to walk and talk and apparently even graduate college. She realized Ryan must be a few years older and felt incredibly foolish. She was tempted to laugh at Maddie and say it couldn't be true, that she must have mixed up the digits or something, because Ellen could remember feeling grown up in 1986, even if she hadn't been. But then she didn't want Maddie to know she was that old. So she didn't say anything.

"Anyway, I thought you might want to know it's dinnertime," Maddie said.

Which meant Ellen had read right through lunch. Had she fallen asleep at some point? She couldn't be sure. If she had fallen asleep, that would explain the gorilla sighting. She must have been dreaming. The motion of the ship coupled with the reading had been making her drowsy all along. Suddenly she wished for such a thing as room service on this cruise that wasn't really a cruise. She stretched and attempted to sit up.

"Thanks for letting us know about dinner. Are you from North Carolina?"

"South Carolina, pluheeze," Maddie said. "Don't you ever let my parents hear you suggest such a thing. They love the South so much, they think North Carolina isn't located in the true south because it has the word "north" in it. Well, that and all the Yankee spies and carpetbaggers. Course, you'll find those in South Carolina too. They just think there's more of that sort of thing basically anywhere north of where they are."

Ellen smiled and wondered if this girl had been a character in her book. She could have jumped out of the pages when no one was looking. At least she wore a sweatshirt and shorts and not some elaborate gown filled with hoops and fluff, not that anyone would ever allow her onboard dressed like that.

"I'm Ellen. What are you studying?"

"Coral, and you?"

"Jellyfish."

"Coral and jellyfish, well now those two kind of go together, don't they?"

"I guess. They're both in the same area of the ocean we're headed toward at least."

Maddie burst into a laughter song, making Ellen feel as if she could be a funny person, while at the same time knowing she'd never been that funny. Maddie chewed her gum with a vengeance whenever she wasn't talking. She smelled like bubble gum. The sticky sweet kind.

"Let's go eat," she sang out, as if the act of eating could be an adventure in itself. Her green eyes sparkled with excitement. Ellen tried to remember what that kind of ecstasy for life and dinner felt like.

CHAPTER 17

⎯⎯⎯⎯ ◠ ⎯⎯⎯⎯

T HEY OPENED THE heavy metal door that separated their sleeping quarters from the rest of the ship and walked through the bleak hallway together. Ellen learned that Maddie was a graduate student studying in Virginia. The ship had picked her and a few others up in Norfolk just in time for dinner.

"What do your parents think of you going to school as far north as Virginia, then?" Ellen asked.

"Oh, they absolutely hate it. They never come to visit me, even though I am technically still south of that Mason-Dixon line, but it's a little too close for them. Which is fine, really, I'm usually so busy anyway. But I still try to visit them whenever I can."

Ellen smelled baked bread and soup as they entered the mess deck, which was set up in a military buffet style. They each took a plastic tray, napkin, and silverware while getting into the line that marched by the food selections. Ellen decided on the bread and soup since it smelled so good. Maddie took a plate of roast beef with mashed potatoes and gravy.

"I never eat like this at home, but hey, we're on a sort of vacation, right?"

"You must not have been on a cruise before," Ellen said.

"Oh, well sure I have. Just never one like this, for so long. But I've been on ones that have gone like to Bermuda, for a few days here and there? That was a little like a vacation. We got to get off the ship and get some rum punch anyway."

"I don't think there's going to be any rum punch where we're going."

"Well, that's too bad now, isn't it? I could use a little rum punch."

Maddie pointed to a table half filled with middle-aged men. "There's my professor, Dr. Holbrook. Come on, I'll introduce you."

She led Ellen to the table and sat next to a man with short black hair. His head stayed bent down as he shoveled food into his mouth. Ellen noticed a few silver flecks that made her think of quartz on volcanic sand.

"Dr. Holbrook, this is my friend Ellen."

Ellen sat across from him and said hello. He glanced up and nodded. His face looked a little weather beaten but light eyes softened his overall appearance.

He turned to Maddie. "You can call me Michael. Now that we're on a cruise together, we're colleagues, not just professor and student."

"No, I don't think I could do that, silly," Maddie said. "You've always been Dr. Holbrook to me. It would be too strange."

"Well," he said while looking over at Ellen, "then you can call me Michael."

Ellen smiled in response.

"She studies jellyfish," Maddie said. "They kind of go together, don't they? Coral and jellyfish?"

"They're both in the same part of the ocean we're going to anyway."

Maddie burst out laughing. "That is the same exact thing Ellen said. Isn't that funny?"

Both Ellen and Michael plunged into their food instead of answering the question.

"In a way, they do go together," Michael said after a few minutes of nothing but slurping noises. "Coral and jellyfish are from the same group. They have quite a few similarities."

"I'm guessing it's probably better to study coral these days though, with climate change being such an issue," Ellen added between spoonfuls.

"Yes, I suppose so. Though, in my own defense, I did become interested in coral long before all the global warming hype came about."

"Oh? How did that happen?" Ellen figured she might as well ignore the "hype" comment for now.

"My mom. It's all her fault, really. She used to take me scuba diving starting from when I was about ten. I couldn't get over the fact that under the waves, down in the water, it might as well be another world. A place where stars swim and rocks are alive."

"That's great that you were introduced to all that at such an early age."

"Yes, she was determined to experience everything and I was lucky enough to be along for the ride. She introduced me to all kinds of things: scuba diving, karate, ballet, even hang gliding.

But scuba diving was the only thing that really stuck. And now here I am."

Ellen choked down a laugh along with her soup, picturing the man before her in ballet tights. "Luckily it wasn't the ballet that stuck with you."

"I guess so. Though I can still do a few of those moves."

Ellen looked up to see Ryan wandering around with his tray. She waved toward him. He stopped, then looked relieved and came right over. After the introductions, he sat close enough so that she could feel the warm heat of him.

Maddie perked up across the table, dipped her head down, and smiled at Ryan while suddenly acting demure or mysterious or something. Ellen surprised herself by feeling a rush of jealousy. She wished she could somehow stop her from smiling in such a provocative way. Maddie looked like one of those models, like all of those models who try to sell everything no one really needs with downcast eyes and a smile exactly like that one. Ryan didn't seem to notice. He was too busy attacking his roast beef and gravy. Ellen looked at the bloody massacre of his plate and felt a little queasy.

Michael stood up. "Sorry to eat and run, but there's always more work to do. It was nice meeting you." He nodded toward Ellen and Ryan.

Ellen wondered if he could be one of those professors who went from student to student, each year a new one, an everlasting harem full of ever so brief caresses and charms. She looked at Maddie. Though if they were together in that way, even just for the span of a semester, you'd think she'd call him Michael.

"Are you studying jellyfish too?" Maddie asked Ryan.

"I'm her research assistant, so I pretty much do whatever she tells me to do."

Maddie looked at Ellen in the same way that Ellen had just been looking at her, calculating all the possibilities. Ellen knew what it looked like: a woman scientist with a younger male assistant who just happened to resemble a teddy bear. She would have hired him even if he had been repulsive in some way. In fact, it would have been easier. But he was the opposite of repulsive and so people naturally wondered.

"Yeah, I guess it's the same with me and Dr. Holbrook," Maddie said. "I love it though. You get to learn so much from following people like them around."

"That's true, I've already learned a lot," Ryan said.

Ellen started to feel uncomfortable, like a rock star sitting there eating with groupies. She didn't know what to say to their praise, figuring that anything would sound hollow up against it, so she decided to follow Michael's lead and try to get some work done. Although part of her didn't want to leave them alone together, another part told her she might as well. She had finished her soup and bread a while ago, after all.

"I guess I'll get back to work," she said. "Have fun."

"Okay, goodnight," the two said simultaneously.

CHAPTER 18

THE NEXT DAY brought more stops along the coast. Additional crew members and researchers came aboard while some of the crew departed in an elaborate predetermined exchange. The ship seemed unable to completely disconnect from land. Ellen started to feel as if they would never truly be at sea. Then late in the day, they blasted off from Miami, the last port in Florida. The ship sliced through the mounting waves. It felt like the voyage had finally begun.

Dark lands sloped in the distance. The Fountain of Youth was supposed to be located on one of those islands. Ponce de Leon spent his life searching for it but never found it. Ellen could relate to that. She wondered if the same sort of thing would happen to her, if she might spend her life looking for answers that never revealed themselves.

During Ponce de Leon's time, people believed the New World was a paradise overflowing with gold, spices, and wonders including islands that floated in the air. Ellen figured some of the fantastical legends had been created so that people would want to see the magic for themselves, to make sure that waves of people would keep putting their lives at risk to cross the endless ocean in search of that magical unknown. Their searches weren't so different from her own constant quest for more knowledge. Just as the explorers did, she kept searching. And she would probably spend her whole life doing it.

At least she'd made a few discoveries along the way, but they weren't the earth shattering kinds of discoveries most people care about. Just once, she wanted to make that kind of a discovery. Something that would make her famous, even for a little while, so that she would know all her work hadn't gone completely unnoticed. Mostly, she wanted a little recognition. She supposed Ponce de Leon did too and look what he became known for: not finding something.

If she did discover something earth shattering, if she found the answers she searched for, she knew that doing so wouldn't exactly guarantee happiness. It was an easy thing to forget, but more than anything, it was the search that excited her. The mysteries and the not knowing gave her the energy that drove her onward. Suddenly knowing the answers might end up being disappointing or at least a bit anticlimactic.

Maybe some mysteries were better left alone. At one time, her parents tried to convince her that leprechauns were real. When she asked why she had never seen any, they said because all leprechauns live only in Ireland. From then on, she imagined what their lives were like and couldn't wait to go to Ireland to find them. She thought the rainbows would show her the way and practiced following them whenever they appeared. When she found out that leprechauns weren't real after all, the world didn't feel as magical. Yet, she ended up dedicating her life to figuring out the mysteries, to demystifying them. In a way, she was still chasing down the magic and following rainbows.

The wind picked up and became a constant force. She could no longer see land. The sun ignited the sky with a fiery red and yellow, causing the water below to reflect a soft muddled pink.

She stayed out on deck to watch as the sun slipped into the water. She wanted the ship to go faster, to somehow catch up with the sun so that the sunset colors would always be there. Then the sun disappeared into the waves and the colors became even more vibrant while streaking across the sky, mixing with the purple gray clouds, causing Ellen to think perhaps the best part of the sunset is after the sun is gone.

A flock of herons dipped so low overhead that she could hear the flapping of their wings and the surprising whoosh of the displaced air. They came up from behind, flew into the sunset and kept on flying by, hundreds of them flapping quietly together. Their slow moving wings blurred the sunset colors as they disappeared into the blur.

Ellen loved the feeling that came from not being able to see land or even a hint of it. She had heard some people became agitated by the feeling and couldn't understand that at all. Her body tingled. She looked out to see waves everywhere, surrounding her, beckoning her further into the unknown. Horizons felt limitless with no buildings or people or land to obstruct them. Anything seemed possible.

They would be seeing land soon enough though. The ship would be sailing by a few more islands, then on through the Panama Canal. After taking a full day to get through the canal and into the

Pacific, they would be out in the open ocean again before arriving at their destination, which was mostly open ocean in itself.

The trip back home wouldn't take nearly as long. The ship was due to arrive in Hawaii at the end of the cruise and they planned on sending everything back home from there.

It would have been better if the longer part of the voyage could have been on the way back, once they had data and samples to work with, but everything depended on the ship's schedule. So much depended on timing, but at the same time everything still seemed so random.

A door creaked open and Ryan walked up beside her.

"I figured you'd be out here."

"Good guess. Can't go too far and still be on the ship though."

"Yeah, I'm starting to see what you mean by the whole feeling like it's a prison thing. There must not be views like this in prison though."

"No, I guess not."

They looked out at the waves. Ryan leaned a little closer so that the bulky arms of their sweatshirts touched. Ellen tried not to think anything of it. It did feel a little chilly with the sun below the horizon and the wind picking up. She needed all the warmth she could get, even if it was only from a random sweatshirt touching her sweatshirt.

"Maddie seems nice," Ellen said.

"Yeah, I guess," Ryan rubbed his hands together. "Aren't you cold?"

"A little."

He leaned closer so that she could feel his arm underneath his sweatshirt. They weren't really touching, she couldn't feel his skin, but she was aware of his arm there under his sweatshirt and the warmth that radiated from his body.

"We might be dipping into the Bermuda Triangle right about now, just so you know," Ellen said in an attempt to think about anything else.

"Really? And you didn't want to warn me before this?"

"I didn't think of it until now. But don't worry, the chances of a ship like this disappearing are pretty slim."

"In a way, it would be exciting if that happened," Ryan said. "Then at least we'd know the answer to that mystery."

Ellen thought the real mystery at that moment was how Ryan kept reading her mind.

"Right, but if we did disappear we wouldn't be able to tell anyone we discovered the answer," Ellen said. "The only ones we might be able to tell would be the aliens who abducted us and they'd already know."

"You don't really believe in that stuff, do you?"

"Not really. I used to a little, or at least the mystery intrigued me enough to look into it some more. But then I found out that the ship and aircraft disappearances weren't all that mysterious. For one thing, the Bermuda Triangle is one of the most heavily trafficked areas for boats and planes in the world. And the Gulf Stream flows through the Triangle, which helps create erratic weather patterns like hurricanes."

"There must be more to it than that though."

"There are all kinds of scientific explanations," Ellen said. "Another one is the existence of methane hydrates in the seafloor right around here. If the methane hydrates erupt, they can create areas of water above them with so much dissolved gas that there's no longer enough buoyancy for a ship to float. If a large enough eruption occurred when a ship happened to be sailing by, it could cause the ship to suddenly sink. Methane eruptions can even cause airplanes to crash because they create less air density."

"Well, that explains it then."

"I thought so too, but then I found out that no large releases of hydrates have occurred in the Bermuda Triangle for the past fifteen thousand years."

"Too bad, that sounded pretty convincing. What do you think the causes for the disappearances are then?"

"Probably hurricanes, erratic weather patterns, and possibly freak waves coupled with the fact that it's a heavily trafficked area."

"Somehow that's not as exciting."

"I know what you mean."

Everything grew steadily darker as the colors faded from the sky. Soon there would only be the stars. A few flickered on at the thought. It felt as if everything conspired against her sane, rational self so that she would throw caution to the wind, turn and kiss Ryan, and let his mouth heat her body through instead of a sweat-shirted elbow. He acted as if he wanted her to do it. But then, maybe she read him all wrong. Maybe he only wanted to provide a little warmth.

Besides, there were rules against that kind of thing on the ship. They were here to do their work. No distractions, no romance allowed. If anyone saw them acting a little too friendly, she could lose her job. Even if her funding eventually came through, she was still jeopardizing her career by being out here with Ryan on a night full of stars. She thought it might be worth it for the chance to feel his arms around her.

"We should go back inside," she said. "There's going to be a few more days of downtime. I hope you brought some good books."

"Yeah, I brought a lot. I couldn't decide on just a few."

"That's good. Then around when we're tired of reading, we'll be going through the Panama Canal."

"That should be exciting. What's it like?"

"I don't know. I've never gone through it before."

"That's funny, I thought you'd done everything."

Ellen laughed into the wind. "No, not even close."

She took a step back and stumbled a bit from the motion of the ship. After opening the metal door, they walked into the startling yellow light inside and turned to go to their separate quarters.

She flopped down on her bed and picked up the Old West again, figuring she might as well see what the characters were up to. It didn't help that the story had deteriorated into a doomed romance between a cowboy and a Native American. She wondered why so many romances must be doomed before they had the chance to begin, but stretched out and read all about it anyway.

～

Ryan rummaged through his duffel bag and came up with a book about the ocean. He knew that reading it wouldn't exactly be any kind of an escape, like reading should be, but he wanted to learn more than he wanted to escape. If he knew more about the ocean, then maybe he could help Ellen more. So he read and even highlighted some pages, something he hadn't done since college.

After a while, his thoughts drifted out of the pages and down the hall. At first, he wondered what Ellen might be reading. He could picture her reading easily enough, but he had no idea what kind of a book it might be. She was becoming more and more of a mystery. That didn't make sense. People should become less of a mystery as you get to know them, not more of one. He could usually predict whatever she wanted done for work, sometimes before she even knew what she wanted, but everything else remained a mystery. Whenever he thought he'd finally figured her out, she'd say something that wouldn't seem right, like when she said she had a dog as a kid. He couldn't picture that at all.

He supposed it was because she didn't talk much about herself, so then whenever she did say something personal it sounded strange. But that wasn't all of it. He ended up thinking of her a little differently whenever she said something that didn't fit. So the result was that he became more and more confused.

It was as if she had become one of his sister's paintings, one that was continually repainted. Just when he really liked a painting, Emily would paint over it with completely different colors. Then he'd have to get used to the new painting. He'd always end up liking it just as much, but sometimes it took a while. Like paintings, people add more layers as they change. But when something is added, something else is usually covered up. What could Ellen be covering up? Did she have red or yellow buried underneath her cooler shades of blue?

She couldn't really have that many layers though. Sometimes she looked hollowed out, almost translucent, as if life had scraped her too many times while leaving only the essentials. He saw it in her eyes and in her hurried actions: a look of panic smoothed over by a thin veneer of control. She made him think of a kite held by a string, dipping and swaying with the breeze. He could only watch and hope the breeze wouldn't tear her apart.

The ship lurched and rolled, causing his stomach to do the same. He'd have to get used to it even if it did make him sick. The up-and-down motion made him remember that even if you think something is a certain way, it's really always changing. Nothing is ever fixed or certain. All anyone can ever do is hang on and ride the waves.

When he was ten years old, he thought he had the perfect life. He would play outside with the neighborhood kids every day after school until his mom called him in for dinner. After eating together, the whole family would relax and watch TV in the living room. His mom and dad sat on the couch while he and his sister sprawled out on the carpet in front of the TV. Maybe he didn't look back at his parents often enough during those times, because he didn't notice that after a while his mom and dad weren't sitting very close on that couch anymore.

Then the fights started. He would wake up to the sound of yelling or crying. Emily was six at the time. All he cared about was shielding her from it, protecting her in some way. He would sneak into her bedroom so they could sit together in the dark. They'd make a tent out of her comforter and stay huddled in there with the flashlight. Sometimes he'd put on a puppet show with her stuffed animals, giving each a funny personality. Sometimes he could make her laugh.

Eventually, his parents got divorced and became friends once they didn't have to live together anymore. So things and people were always changing. That's one of those things he'd always known, but for some reason it was still easy to forget.

CHAPTER 19

T HE OCEAN GREW more agitated as the night wore on. There was no escaping it. While trying to sleep, Ellen felt the mood shift from calm waters to mounting rage. By early morning, the ocean screamed and roared and howled.

The tossing ship caused her stomach to rise and fall. They might as well be on one of those amusement park rides that promised jostling in all directions. She struggled to get up while holding onto the metal bedframe. A few women ran to the bathroom as soon as they were able to stand. Ellen turned her attention to a nearby porthole. Normally, a circle of sky would be there but now only frothy water could be seen: a washing machine whipping suds around with ruthless determination. No light found its way through the rage. It seemed possible that the ocean had swallowed everything, including the sky.

The drawers in her dresser opened and slammed shut by an unseen hand. She grabbed her clothes while still gripping the bedframe, the only stable thing around because it was bolted to the floor, then sank back into bed to change. She didn't want to risk standing on one leg to put her jeans on. That action could be treacherous enough when the floor wasn't moving in every possible direction.

Ellen headed into the hall toward the mess deck. Food was the last thing her flip-flopping stomach wanted, but it might be easier to see what was going on from there. She staggered, then grabbed the railing that lined the wall.

The stark hallway morphed into a funhouse. It tilted in unnatural ways, giving it an almost liquid feel. The wall she clung to rose up until it almost became the ceiling, then dropped down while the other side lifted. She crept along the wall like Spiderman. Then the ship turned, causing the hallway to dip toward her destination. The motion of the ship propelled her forward until the floor tilted back into a hill. She hiked the hill and pulled herself up along the railing before reaching the door to the mess deck.

While hoping things would look a little more normal in there, she swung the door open to semi-darkness. Only a few blinking and buzzing overhead lights stayed on. A handful of researchers hunkered down at the swaying tables.

Michael sat there eating a full breakfast while looking unfazed by it all. His black hair was a little disheveled but that was about it. He seemed completely at ease while everything around him shifted and swayed. Ellen wasn't sure about bothering him but she had to talk with someone. Nothing like a vicious thunderstorm to break the ice. She staggered over and fell into a chair across from him.

"Okay, I have to know. How can you eat during all this?"

"This? This is nothing. I've been in worse than this before."

"I don't see how that's possible." Ellen felt overcome by the urge to plop her head down on the table.

"It's a little tropical storm. Not even a hurricane yet. The captain tried to go around it. So for now, we're only on the edge of it."

A scientist sitting near them jumped up and ran out of the room. A few more followed.

"We're going to be the only ones left in a few minutes," Ellen said. Lightning flashed an exclamation point.

"It's still pretty early and dark out because of the storm. Maybe everyone's sleeping in."

"Anyone sleeping right about now would have to be able to sleep on a bucking horse. The ship practically tossed me out of bed, even with that metal bar there to hold me in. Do you think Maddie and Ryan are getting sick?"

"I hope not. We're going to need them pretty soon."

A loud cracking noise shook the ship.

"What was that?" Ellen asked. "Did the ship just crack in half?"

"Just lightning. No big deal."

The rocking became more violent. The surrounding walls groaned and creaked, making it obvious that the ship consisted of separate metal pieces. There was no guarantee that the pieces would stay together. Ellen felt her stomach threaten to erupt. Whenever the ship dropped, it gave the sensation of spiraling down an elevator shaft. Tables and chairs were bolted to the floor but the chairs swiveled erratically. The flickering lights added a disco feel.

"I'm going to take a peek outside to see what's going on out there." Ellen stood while holding onto the table for as long as possible.

"Okay, but I wouldn't actually go out there if I were you. The waves must be getting higher. One of them could leap up and grab you."

"I guess I'll have to take my chances." Ellen swerved while attempting to walk to the door. She made it to the window but could only see the murky sky in between splashes of water. The horizon came into view, then one side of the ship dropped into a wave and the angry ocean surface filled the window. A porthole view of the world felt too limiting.

Ellen opened the door. The wind took her breath away as if it needed all the air that could be found. She stepped outside, slammed the door shut, and held onto a metal staircase. The water poured down, from the sky or the ocean, it was impossible to tell. She swung around underneath the staircase while keeping a hold on it. Mini-waterfalls gushed down each stair to transform the entire structure into a xylophone. She listened to the music and turned to face the angry ocean.

She had never felt such fury. The ocean kept trying to hold her back, to push her away. All her life, whenever she thought she'd come close to figuring anything out, the ocean always turned everything around. It would never want its mysteries solved. It only wanted to perplex those who tried.

She wanted to yell, to howl at the wind and the waves. Instead, she laughed. Her laughter released something inside, something heavy she'd been carrying around, something unacknowledged.

She felt lighter. Soaring seemed possible all of a sudden, and not just because she held onto a ship that flew through the air.

A lightning bolt sliced the sky, ripping everything open, followed by another loud cracking noise left to wander off in the dark. With the flash, Ellen saw red off in the distance where the bolt touched the ocean.

She waited for more lightning and for the chance to see the red puddle again, but there was nothing. She stared at the seething sky. It could have been her imagination or a reflection from the lightning bolt. Still, that flash of red on the water felt more unsettling than the churning storm.

CHAPTER 20

O NCE THE STORM died down, Ellen brought her laptop to the lab, hoping to reserve a section before the invasion of the sweaty bodies began. But when she opened the door, she saw the invasion had started without her. People sat huddled along the counters with their laptops, virtually connected and plugged in.

Ellen moved through the thick air to a vacant corner area. Her ponytail swung behind like a wagging tail. She brushed a few escapee strands away from her eyes before plunking her laptop down on the counter to mark the spot.

It would be even more crowded once they reached the Atoll Islands and the research could truly begin. Until then, she hadn't expected this many people. Since so much could be done virtually these days, some must be tapping into libraries, testing instruments, or checking data from buoys back home. The rest were probably just bored, like her.

She set her laptop up and logged into email first. Hundreds of unread messages flooded the screen, enough to make her want to close right out again. She started clicking anyway: there were the emails that the institute sent out every day, talking about all the newsworthy things other scientists did, then there were emails from people she worked with asking administrative questions that didn't really matter. Most of the messages were from colleagues at other research facilities asking if she could keep her eye out for and perhaps take samples of certain types of jellyfish or even other organisms that she didn't study. She responded to some while being careful not to promise too much.

After going through all the messages, she decided to do some actual research. She hunted through virtual libraries and pulled up half a dozen recently published articles. She began with one that detailed how jellyfish blooms coincide with peaks in microbial activity. This seemed like an obvious thing, since the jellyfish eat the microbes and the microbes feed off the mostly carbonic waste of the jellyfish, but she read all about it anyway.

With a glance at the tiny clock on her laptop, she saw it was past time for lunch. She hadn't noticed. For some reason, reading about jellyfish waste products hadn't made her very hungry.

Ellen wandered to the mess deck and saw Ryan and Maddie seated at the far corner with a few students and engineers. Well, good for them. She hoped they would be happy together. She couldn't have him following her around for the whole cruise anyway, at least not until the real work started.

She chose a salad and walked to the other end of the room without looking toward them, even while knowing she should be past that sort of junior high school behavior by now. She sat by herself and fiddled around with her salad while wishing she had brought her book. Someone carrying a tray paused across the table. She glanced up to see Michael looking like he might be trying to decide whether or not he should sit with her.

"Hi, go ahead and sit if you want. I was just thinking I should have brought a book but now you'll have to entertain me instead."

"Thank you," he said as he sat down. "I'm glad to see you survived the storm. Right after you went out there, an announcement came through from the captain asking us to stay inside."

"Oh, I didn't hear that."

"I'm not surprised. What was it like out there?"

"Pretty vicious. I just wanted to make sure the ship wasn't going to sink. It was too hard to tell what was happening from inside."

"I don't know about that. I could pretty much tell there was a crazy storm out there. That was all I needed to know."

"I guess." Ellen wasn't sure what else to say so she turned her attention to her food. Michael did the same. An awkward silence reared its head until Michael cleared his throat.

"So is all this downtime getting to you too?"

"It's starting to," Ellen said. "At first it was great to be able to read something for fun. But now I just want to get out there and start the real work. I must be a sadist or something."

"Me too. I even read through some journal articles this morning."

"That's what I was just doing."

"No. Really?"

She nodded. "I didn't see you in the lab but I guess I could have missed you. It was pretty crowded in there."

"I used my laptop in my room. I'm not that much of a sadist that I'd go work in the lab yet."

"Yeah, it was a pretty silly thing to do. I thought I'd carve out some space or something, but I guess we don't want to get too sick of it yet either."

"True, there's plenty of time for that."

They paused and chewed for a while again. Ellen looked around. At the next table, two Russian scientists talked with others from China and Japan. They bent toward each other as the conversation became more intense. A few raised their voices and shook their heads. Most bystanders would assume they were talking politics, but Ellen knew better. She figured they must be talking science.

"It was pretty hot in the lab," Ellen finally said for the sake of saying something.

"If it's going to be more than a hundred degrees outside as we get closer to the equator, imagine what it'll be like even if the air conditioning happens to be working."

"Scary. Our computers might melt."

"I'm more concerned about me melting," Michael said.

"And yet the other day it sounded like you might be a global warming skeptic."

"What made you think that?"

"I think it was because you used the words 'global warming hype.'"

"Well, we are still at the data collection phase of the whole thing. I don't think we can be definite on it one way or the other. We've got to keep collecting and examining the data for now. Then we'll see."

His words stunned her. "But there's so much data in favor of it. Not even just data, everything we're seeing now points to it: the polar ice caps melting, jellyfish blooms, coral bleaching." "Right. I should have been more clear. The Earth may be warming slightly, and we do see evidence of that around us, though coral bleaching and jellyfish blooms do have other causes. I'm just not one-hundred percent convinced that it's all due to the climate change threats we hear of, meaning that it's because of man's evil nature and the carbon dioxide we pump into the air. I think there's a certain amount of arrogance in believing humans can have that much of an effect on the world."

"The overall rise in temperature must be due to the increase in anthropogenic carbon dioxide. What other reason could there be?"

"Well, the Earth does have natural warming and cooling cycles."

"Yes, but not on this kind of a scale, where the warming period has been so sudden in such a short time period."

"Okay then, prove it."

"I will. I'll prove it to you." Ellen was glad to have another challenge on her hands.

"I believe you will. And that would be quite a feat. Most of my colleagues have been trying to prove it to me for years now. It has to be irrefutable proof that humans are actually causing it though. I guess I am a skeptic, one of the last holdouts. But when you think about it, we've already lived through all kinds of disasters that were supposed to be the end of the world. Back in the eighties, everyone was convinced that the entire world would blow up at any moment or that there'd be a devastating nuclear disaster and that didn't happen. Remember the hole in the ozone layer? I'm thinking global warming might turn into something like that, one of those old memories like learning to crouch under your desk at school for a bomb scare."

"I hope you're right. But there were nuclear disasters in the eighties so it wasn't all just hype."

"They just weren't the kind of disasters that everyone was so afraid of."

"Unless you happened to live in or around Chernobyl or Three Mile Island."

"Right. I hear Chernobyl is a wilderness area now. Deer can be seen hopping through the forest where there was once a city."

"Yes, but do the deer have two or three heads?"

Michael grinned, crinkling his eyes. "Well, that would be an interesting trophy for a hunter then, wouldn't it?"

"Do you always look on the positive side of everything? Even if it means ignoring all the evidence?"

He cleared his throat and smiled. "For now, there's no other side to look on. Until you prove it to me, that is."

CHAPTER 21

———— ∿ ————

E LLEN SPENT THE next two days researching everything from ocean acidification to ice cores to global measurements of carbon dioxide.

She marveled that she hadn't researched some of these things before, since all of it did have links to climate change and the apparent increase in jellyfish populations. But all too often, she continued to study her own specialized area without branching into others. Then again, with two thousand known species of jellyfish in the world, it would take a lifetime or possibly more than a lifetime to fully study jellyfish.

At least conferences and research cruises helped bring experts in their fields together. Because if one person spent a lifetime studying something, it would only follow that talking with another who spent a lifetime studying something else could be beneficial to both; especially when everything is part of the whole. The more Ellen researched, the more she began to think of the Earth, everything and everyone in it, as one organism.

Still, she didn't want to approach Michael with any information until she felt absolutely sure of it all. It amazed her how much knowledge could be gained with the use of a laptop and an internet connection. She could visit libraries all over the world. She could pull up hundreds of scientific journals, each overflowing with studies. Luckily, the world hadn't blown up in the eighties so that the information age could begin. Now everyone has the chance to learn so much.

It would take many lifetimes to scratch the surface of so much accumulated knowledge and here she was, merely sifting through it all hurriedly, cupping a tiny portion in her hands and studying it while an ocean of truth spread out before her and trickled between her fingers.

She thought she heard steel drums playing off in the distance at one point and imagined the ship sailing past some tropical island or other; either that or the drums were pounding in her head as she continued to sift through all the knowledge.

She had found a quieter area off the main lab where this kind of research could be done without too many distractions. The only sweat in the new lab was her own. It was really more of a closet but it embodied that cozy feeling of being tucked away. She used to love to hide in closets as a kid, and being in a lab always felt like playing, so it made sense to play in a lab closet.

On the morning of her third day of straight research, the ship stopped humming. Ellen stood up and listened. She couldn't hear the monotonous mechanical noises or feel the constant motion of the ship. Something must be wrong.

Her closet door squeaked when she opened it, but everyone in the main lab stayed clustered with their computers and whirring fans and didn't seem to notice. Ellen hurried out toward the door to the deck. As soon as she opened it with a whoosh of heat and humidity, the horizon dropped. Her stomach somersaulted. She reached out to grab the railing. Only then did she realize they must be at the Panama Canal.

It would take all day to get through the forty-eight-mile canal with its locks and separate passageways. It looked like they were already situated in the first lock. Water poured in around the sides and the entire ship moved up as a result. Once the ship finished maneuvering through this set of locks, it would climb eighty-five feet up with the power of water and engineering.

Low lying white buildings with red-tiled roofs held the jungle back and made Ellen think of the miniature buildings that came with train sets. Then she looked further over the railing, all the way down the metal slant of the ship, and noticed a tiny train to complete the picture. Seeing it there made her want to stretch out on the living room rug and play again.

She swayed toward the bow as the horizon continued to sink. A group of researchers gathered there to witness the spectacle of the locks. From this vantage point, Ellen could see two separate waterways running straight ahead and parallel with a strip of land in between.

The steel doors in front of the ship swung out, opening the lock they were in so that they could creep into the next area once the water levels in both were equal. Once they were situated in the second lock, the steel doors eerily closed behind them and the process began all over again. More water gushed in and the ship moved up and up as if climbing an elaborate staircase.

A shadow appeared next to her. Ellen looked over to see Michael standing there with his arms folded. He squinted off into the distance. Black and white stubble on his face made it look like he hadn't shaved since the start of the cruise.

"Amazing, isn't it?"

"Yes, it really is," Ellen said. "For some reason I didn't stop to think it would be this involved."

"Good ole Teddy Roosevelt. He wouldn't let anything get in his way. Even thick, tangled jungle, venomous snakes, one of the world's most volatile rivers, lots of heavy mud, and a mountain."

"And it only took ten years and thousands of lives."

"And a revolution," Michael said.

"Right. What's a revolution when you're cutting through a mountain?"

"Not much in the grand scheme of things. Have you had breakfast yet?"

"No, I usually forget about details like that while researching."

"Would you care to join me? All this puts me in the mood for some Columbian coffee."

Ellen smiled at the thought of coffee. "Sounds good."

Michael grilled her all through breakfast on what sort of irrefutable climate change facts she'd been able to dig up so far. Ellen remained evasive through the interrogations. She didn't want to leak little bits out too soon and have him jump all over the jumbled pieces. She'd rather wait for everything to build up inside until it reached the point of combustion. Then he wouldn't be able to refute it. He'd have to nod and agree that she'd been right all along.

After breakfast and coffee, and a debate concerning whether their coffee was Columbian or Panamanian or Nicaraguan or even American coffee, they went out to check on their progress through the locks in time to see the last set of steel doors open to a silver lake.

The ship released from the lock and glided into the open. Orange mud and dense jungle rimmed the lake. Scattered islands hovered over the gray water haze.

"Back when the canal was built, this was the largest man-made lake in the world," Michael said.

"What are you, a tour guide?"

Michael's low laugh blended in with the chirping and squawking noises erupting from the jungle.

"No, I've just been through here on other cruises and my curiosity got the best of me so I researched it. Shall I enlighten you some more?"

"Sure, why not?"

"Okay then. A river basin was flooded to create this lake. The water is used to fill the locks and every transit across the canal uses millions of gallons. And these islands aren't really islands. They're mountain tops."

"It's strange to think of the trees and villages and everything else that would have been covered up by all this water."

Silence fell out on deck as the lake opened up around them. Almost as soon as the silence descended, chattering began. The chattering became louder. Someone pointed to a tree drooping over the shoreline.

"Look! A monkey!"

Everyone turned and sure enough, a monkey jumped up and down on a branch and taunted them. As Ellen's eyes grew accustomed to the thickness of the jungle, she noticed a dozen or more chattering and screeching monkeys climbing through the shadows. Tropical birdcalls combined with the monkey noises and echoed through the trees.

"Certainly wild, isn't it?" Michael asked.

"Yes, it is." Ellen felt the urge to run through that jungle and be wild herself, to keep running with monkeys jumping and brightly colored birds flying all around.

Ryan walked up next to her on the other side from where Michael stood.

"Hey, I was wondering where you were," he said as he joined them.

"Here I am. Where were you?"

"Over on the other side. This whole thing is so cool. I loved feeling the ship rise up in the air like that. Now I can't wait to go back down again. It's like a really slow roller coaster ride."

"I guess we're going to be in this lake a while longer so I'm going to take the chance to get a little more work done," Michael said. "See you both later."

Ellen surprised herself by thinking she didn't want him to leave. He had become so familiar in such a short time. That didn't happen with most people. But then, she guessed she'd see him again soon enough. As long as they were all trapped on this ship together, they'd have to keep running into each other.

A crocodile slid through the water over by the orange shore. She wondered if crocodiles ate monkeys. Ryan fit right in with the exotic scenery. His tan had deepened in the last few days and his ruffled hair looked lighter in the sun. He caught her looking at him. She tried to think of something to say.

"So you're getting to know some of the other researchers?"

"Yeah, mostly students. A few engineers, most of them divers. So if we need extra divers when we go out we could always ask some of them."

"That's good. We'll need at least one more to act as a safety diver for the deeper dives and the night dives. I should start planning it more at some point."

"But we don't know what it'll be like when we get there, so how can it all be planned out?"

"Good point. I guess it can't be," Ellen said. "Might as well watch the monkeys instead."

"It's so much better seeing them out here than in a zoo, isn't it? Here they can be themselves. They can run around and be free like they're supposed to be."

"That's true, it's much better this way."

Ellen felt hotter by the minute. The tropical humidity must be getting to her. She tried to take a deep breath of air that had become more like water. It invaded her lungs, making them feel like saturated sponges.

She patted her neck to cool herself off and felt drenched skin. Strands of hair that had come loose from her ponytail stuck to her neck and forehead. She drooped a bit and looked over at Ryan. He didn't look as drained as she felt. A few drops of sweat glistened on his brown neck. He smelled like sweat and salt water and something sweet, all of which combined to smell much better on him than it did on her.

"It's getting hotter," Ryan said, echoing her thoughts like usual.

"Must be close to midday."

"Yeah, it would be tempting to jump into this lake if there weren't crocodiles in there."

"They probably wouldn't hurt you," Ellen said. She wiped some of the sweat from her forehead before it trickled into her eyes.

"Yeah, right. Don't know if I'm willing to take that risk."

"We'll be diving soon. Then you'll probably end up getting sick of swimming."

"No way. I love swimming. I don't think I could ever get sick of it."

"That's good since we'll be going out on a lot of dives."

The heat continued to sink in until it made her feel translucent, as if the sun could reach in and burn her internal organs along with her skin. She felt too exposed and dizzy out there in the open. Time to retreat behind a few closed doors.

"I guess I'll go in to try to cool off. Maybe take a shower or something."

"Okay, I'll let you know if you miss anything."

A cold shower, that's what she needed. A freezing cold shower. Too bad the water wouldn't be able to get cold enough. She couldn't be sure if she felt overheated from the weather or from standing so close to Ryan. Whenever questions like that popped into her head, she realized the ultimate answer was: probably both.

CHAPTER 22

A FTER HER LUKEWARM shower, Ellen stayed in her quarters to read while hoping it would magically cool down outside. She opened her book and the romance continued on even though it was clearly impossible.

What made love so impossible? It should be easy. It looked easy for most of nature. Humans were the only ones who complicated everything. Not that she was in love with Ryan or anything like that. She was just inexplicably attracted to him even though she had given up on love.

Her thoughts spiraled into puzzles, mysteries, impossibilities. She considered napping as a means of escape, but then didn't want to miss out on anything else as the ship maneuvered through the canal. She forced herself up to face the elements.

As soon as she opened the metal door, a rush of heat and humidity slammed into her. Even though the onboard air conditioning barely worked, it still made a difference. The temperature change made her think of the people who endured working in this area for years while chopping back brush, digging ditches, and hauling away tons of mud and rock without the reprieve of air conditioning.

She could see the hot air hanging there over the horizon, but it didn't seem as oppressive as it had earlier in the day. It didn't feel as much like a gorilla perched on her shoulders while weighing her down like before. Now the gorilla felt more like a monkey. The shower must have helped. She felt a little more awake and not quite as clammy and dizzy.

She found Michael walking around outside.

"So where are we now?"

"Still in the canal," he said. "Surprise."

The ship floated through the gray lake and headed right toward a massive rock barrier.

"You're just in time," he said. "This is one of the more dramatic parts."

"Crashing into that cliff? That would be dramatic."

The ship continued straight toward the wall of rock. Ellen began to doubt the abilities of the ship's captain. She closed her eyes. Visions of open crocodile jaws filled the darkness. Her fingers clenched the sticky railing until the ship lurched and turned. She opened her eyes to see a narrow canal up ahead.

"Another mountaintop. We're going to go right through it," Michael said.

"I guess I'd rather go through it than crash into it."

"We're going through the continental divide right now. It took seven years to blast through all this, so this part used up most of the time spent on the entire project."

As the ship pushed through the channel, Ellen looked up along the jagged rock walls. They stood so close together that the ship could easily scrape against them while curving through the dynamite-blasted path.

She tried to imagine what it must have been like when they were blasting this out, turning a mountain into a waterway, and all the work that went into it more than one hundred years ago. She thought of the yellow fever and malaria, the letters written home, the heat and sweat, the avalanches, injuries, and deaths. So much had been given in the name of progress. Now that the world had progressed at least a little, she could only hope it had all been worth it.

She thought all this, but said only, "Seven years to blast through this part? Wow, that's incredible."

"You can almost imagine the people and the work that went into it by looking at all this chiseled rock."

"I was just thinking about that. It's amazing that they were able to plow through so many obstacles."

"It must have felt like they'd never finish. There were so many landslides that some of the workers had nervous breakdowns because of them. Altogether, ten years isn't bad for the entire project when you think of all they had to overcome, though I can't imagine working under those conditions for years on end. So many people died. If you include the earlier years from when France worked at it, more than twenty-five thousand lives were lost."

Ellen tried to fully comprehend all those people, all those who gave their lives to make things easier for future generations.

"Wow. I had heard it was thousands but twenty-five thousand? Do you think it was worth it?"

Michael squinted into the distance. "That's the question, isn't it? I think the answer to that still remains to be seen. It all depends on what we do with the future that's been given to us by those earlier generations."

The ship curved through the waterway while managing not to scrape against the rock walls before entering more locks. Steel doors closed behind them. This time, water was drained from the lock so that the ship started dropping and the horizon crept up. Ellen felt her stomach turn over again.

"After this, we go into another lake and then more locks," Michael said.

"When will it ever end?"

"When we get to the Pacific. It's as if we're being lifted up and dropped down on the other side of the world."

Once they arrived on the other side of the world, the ship drifted into Balboa Harbor and docked so that the canal pilot could leave the vessel. The ship's regular captain took over from there.

Ellen felt a jolt as the ship left the dock and then they were off again. She could still hear monkeys screeching back in the jungle. On the horizon ahead, the gray and white shapes of Panama City's skyscrapers made her think of clenched teeth.

The ship neared the Bridge of the Americas, a labyrinth of steel uniting lands the canal had separated. Ellen looked up to see cars zooming back and forth like tiny excited animals.

Down below, tourists in splashes of Hawaiian shirts and Panama hats dined at an outdoor café. Ellen caught a whiff of fried food. The people at the café raised their glasses and tipped their hats in a toast to the ship as it glided by.

After sailing under the bridge, the ship wandered off into the Bay of Panama and they instantly felt a cooler, drier ocean breeze greet them. They sailed by other ships and tankers anchored in the bay, waiting their turn to travel through the canal to the Atlantic Ocean. As their ship continued into the Pacific, the sun started to set in a pink and purple celebration of their arrival.

Ellen felt the immensity of the Pacific Ocean before her. She knew it covered twice the area of the Atlantic Ocean and extended over an area far larger than all the dry land on the entire planet. She looked out and saw only water and sky, blending together and giving the impression that they could be sailing over the edge of the world or off into nothingness. She felt prepared for anything. There were about twenty-five thousand islands scattered throughout the Pacific. She couldn't wait to get to the few they'd be exploring. They were out there somewhere within all that blue.

CHAPTER 23

R OBERTO PLOPPED ONTO the hot sand. He let his hands and feet sink in to feel the cool damp underneath. If he kept sinking in like this, he might disappear just like Papa.

He propped himself up to stare at the waves that took Papa away. They flashed bright white like teeth, hungry for more. The teeth bit into the sand, pretending to be harmless while eating bits and pieces of the shore. They inched closer. Soon they would bite into him.

Nothing had been the same since Papa went away. Everyone used to be happy and laughing all the time, but not now. Not anymore. Mama kept turning away to cry. She thought Roberto didn't see, but he did. They were all pretending. He promised himself that he'd never pretend once he was all grown up. Pretending only turned you into someone else.

Roberto listened for Papa's voice in the grumbling waves. He leaned back, hoping the waves would grab him and take him into the ocean to visit Papa. They told him it wouldn't be long now, he'd be there soon.

Something touched his leg. Roberto leapt up from the sand.

"Papa?" He yelled out, sounding too much like a child.

But it wasn't Papa. It was only a bottle rolling back and forth with the waves. Roberto scooped it up, drained the water out, and looked for a message inside. Instead, he found only emptiness.

He examined the markings and scratches. It looked like Papa's yaqona bottle, but they all looked the same, with seaweed designs crawling all over the outside. The bottle felt as cold as it always did. Roberto kept it in his hand and felt the freezing weight of it as he ran home through the sand.

His mother stood outside of the house with her arms crossed over her blue dress. Her dress flowed all around like water, making her look like a mermaid. She was talking with a neighbor and with her arms crossed like that, it looked like she might be holding herself together. Roberto wasn't so sure he should bother her, but ran up to her anyway.

"Look what I found on the beach." He held the yaqona bottle up for her inspection. "Do you think it's Papa's?"

She stared at his offering like she might be scared of it, then took it in her hands and searched the markings. When she found what she was looking for, she sighed.

"Yes, this is your Papa's. See this part? He carved our initials into the design when we were first married." Her eyes fluttered, blinking away tears. Their neighbor, Karina, reached out to rub her arm. Mama looked into her friend's eyes with gratitude and tried to smile her tears away.

Then she turned to Roberto. "Show me where you found this."

Roberto reached up to take her hand and they walked back along the slippery path to the beach.

"Since his bottle found the way home, that means Papa will to, right?"

Mama's eyes fluttered again. "I hope so. Yes, that must be true."

"All he has to do is follow it. It's too bad he couldn't put a message in there for us, to let us know he'd be right behind it."

"Maybe Papa didn't have anything to write with."

"He never brings anything to write with when he goes out fishing. So he must have sent the bottle as a sign that he'll be coming home soon, right?"

"I think so. That must be it."

Roberto stopped and pointed. "It was right over there. Maybe we should wait there for Papa then?"

Kalani looked everywhere, searching the sand for something more. A scrap, a remnant, a faded memory. When nothing could be found, she sat down on the sand and pulled Roberto onto her lap. She kept her arms around him. Roberto wiggled for a second before leaning back into her softness.

"Don't worry Mama, he'll be back soon."

Her arms squeezed harder around him. They both searched the horizon, imagining Papa out there somewhere, finding his way back to them. The waves carried nothing but emptiness and they echoed with a lonely song as they brought nothing to shore over and over again.

CHAPTER 24

As they pushed ahead into the Pacific, the ocean greeted Ellen with more breezes. They encircled her clammy arms and tickled like the hug of a long-lost love. She eased into the embrace while hoping the ocean would show her its secrets after all.

She hadn't eaten since breakfast. The heat and humidity filled her up as if air could be food and made her feel like she'd never want to eat again. Now the cooler wind reminded her that air wasn't really food, even thick, humid air. Tomorrow and the next day would only get hotter as they continued to advance toward the equator. She might as well fill herself up with something other than hot air before that happened.

She turned toward Michael. "Hungry?"

"Sure." He looked as if he had forgotten all about her but disconnected himself from the railing and stretched through his perplexity.

Ellen gravitated toward heaping portions of curried tofu and jasmine rice with peanuts sprinkled on top. Michael chose the same and they found an empty table in the corner. She didn't see Ryan or Maddie around anywhere.

The meal consisted mostly of yellow slop but melted in her mouth with subtle flavors of spice and a creamy sweetness. She tried to eat it slowly, to fully savor it, but gobbled it down instead.

Their silence didn't seem to matter at first because they were both too busy eating. Ellen looked away from her food and tried to think of something to say.

"So how do you like living in Virginia?"

"It's all right. It helps living so close to DC because of all the meetings. The heat and humidity can get to you though. But it's nothing like this."

DC made Ellen think of Marcus and her threatened funding. She tried to shrug it off while pretending she still had a future. Maybe silence was better after all.

She swirled her food around with her fork, then added, "I guess we'd better get used to the heat and humidity since it's going to keep getting hotter as we get closer to the equator and all that."

"Can't wait."

"I can't wait to get out there. It's hard to believe no one's been able to do any research in that area yet."

"We probably should have examined the coral there by now, especially given that there's an extensive amount of it. But it's always been pretty inaccessible. The island governments didn't want any outsiders coming in. We're fortunate to be the first allowed to research the area."

"I wonder why they've changed their minds about it."

"It could be that they've seen some changes happen. Some of the reefs might not be as healthy as they once were and the people living there could have noticed a reduction in the amount of available fish. I think they've realized even though we are outsiders, we're here to help. And the things we learn there may not only help their community but could in turn help other communities. As it is though, we still have to ask permission to dive once we get there."

"I thought that had been worked out already." Ellen drooped a little while hoping this wouldn't delay them too much.

"In a way it has since they know the intentions of this cruise and they know the experiments will include scuba diving. But when we do arrive, anyone who wants to dive in the area will have to get permission from the island chief first."

"So it'll be like a field trip for everyone to go see the chief?"

"I guess so. Maybe they recently decided they want to take a good look at us. That's all I've heard. I don't know what else it'll entail."

"Tribal dancing?"

"I hope not," Michael said. "But the smoking of a peace pipe or something like that might not be so bad."

"I hope we won't have to eat or drink anything too strange."

"Probably not. The whole thing sounds like it's just a formality. Still, it's much better than the usual formalities of filling out government forms and having to get officially recertified in another country."

"In that way, island life does sound more appealing."

"More human, less hectic and annoying. I'm all for that."

"We may never want to leave."

"That's highly possible." Michael smiled as he put another bite in his mouth.

"What kind of shape do you think the coral will be in?"

"That'll be interesting to see since some of the islands are inhabited and some aren't. Because of that, we should be able to determine if there is a direct human impact on the coral by observing any differences."

"Right, but it can't be that simple. There are all kinds of factors affecting coral including climate change. And if that is a major factor, you'll probably find coral bleaching everywhere."

"There are also a number of things affecting coral health on a regional basis. Things like over fishing and silt runoff from nearby rivers. Even natural events like hurricanes can cause coral bleaching. Unfortunately, the algae that keeps the coral alive is sensitive to all kinds of environmental changes, not just warmer ocean waters. When the algae dies, the coral dies."

"Do you think you'll find much coral bleaching out there then?"

"There could be a slight impact near the inhabited islands because of the farming, but since there aren't large human populations in the area, I'm hoping there won't be much."

"That would be great if any damage could be contained regionally. It's better than thinking we're constantly messing everything up and causing worldwide disasters. I hope you're right. But I don't think so. It's hard to believe you don't think humans are to blame for climate change when we're seeing evidence for it all around us."

"Oh, we're certainly to blame in some ways. But how much are we to blame and in what ways? How much of an overall effect do we really have, meaning is it primarily regional or global, and are some of these changes simply part of natural cycles that have gone on for thousands or billions of years?"

Ellen suddenly felt like one of his students, as if she had been sitting in his class daydreaming when he pointed to her for the answer.

"You're not going to get it out of me yet. I'm still researching."

Michael involved himself with using his bread to mop up the last of his sauce.

"Well, let me know when you're ready. I'll be looking forward to the enlightenment."

"Hey there, you two," Maddie said as she sat next to Michael. Ryan trailed along behind her and edged in next to Ellen. "So what do you think it'll be like when we finally get to where we're all going?"

"We were just talking about that," Michael said. "We're looking forward to the tribal dancing."

"Tribal dancing? Now you're being silly."

As they talked and joked around, Ellen's thoughts circled back to her research. She caught herself thinking of the relationship between jellyfish and coral and climate change and realized she had no idea what Maddie and Michael had been saying to each other for the last ten minutes. She didn't think Ryan had said much, but she couldn't be sure. All she heard were her own thoughts, her own incessant questions and theories.

Just when she thought she must need more excitement in her life, a gorilla walked over with his tray and nonchalantly sat next to Ryan. Maddie and Ryan both started laughing hysterically. Michael looked at the gorilla as if he could be insane. Then the gorilla lifted his hairy arms and jerked his own head right off to reveal a grinning kid with damp curly blond hair and wild eyes.

"Hey everyone, this is Jake," Maddie said while still laughing. He's a student from NYU."

"Nice to meet you," the gorilla said.

"Aren't you hot in that thing?" Michael asked.

"Yeah, but I like wearing it so I'm used to being hot in it."

Michael turned to Ellen with a questioning expression. Ellen didn't have an answer so she just shrugged.

"I sort of became attached to it while I was at school," Jake said as if the gorilla suit could be a pet of some kind. "It all started when I ended up as the football team's mascot. I still don't know how that happened. But then it was so much fun dressing up like this that I started wearing it to classes and around the dorms. So I thought might as well bring it along. You never know when you might need it."

Maddie kept giggling. "You kind of scared me at first, but then I figured it must be you. That's so funny. But if I ever see you out on deck at night in that thing, I just might scream and jump overboard."

"Good idea, I'll have to start stalking the decks at night."

"Oh, no you don't. If you startle me enough out there, I might push you overboard instead."

"I'll take my chances," Jake said with a grin that looked suspiciously like a gorilla, even without the mask on.

Ellen watched as Jake slurped his food while thinking he must be getting sauce on the gorilla suit. He wouldn't know it if he did, it was so thick with hair. The thought made her feel a little queasy. There could be all kinds of crumbs and sauces and half eaten bits of food stuck in there. How do you clean a gorilla suit? The question had probably never occurred to him. Ellen realized she was done eating and decided to run away from the gorilla, get back to her research, and maybe even get some rest. That is, if she didn't have gorilla nightmares.

Michael announced he had to get back to work before Ellen had the chance to say the same, causing her to chime in with a lame, "Me too."

"See you tomorrow," she said to Ryan as she left the table.

Ryan nodded but looked more interested in talking and laughing with Jake and Maddie. Hopefully the gorilla wouldn't keep him up all night.

~

Ryan watched Ellen as she walked away with Michael. Maddie watched Ryan. Jake kept slurping his sauce-covered food.

"What's with her, anyway?" Maddie asked. "She looked at Jake like she was disgusted with him or something."

"It wouldn't be the first time a woman's looked at me disgustedly," Jake said while chewing.

"She's always thinking about her work," Ryan said. "She probably wasn't even thinking anything about Jake."

"That's even worse," Jake said. "I'd rather have them be disgusted than think nothing of me at all."

"Well, I think the whole gorilla thing is funny," Maddie said.

"It is kind of hard to eat with the suit on though. Might as well take it off now that I've stunned and disgusted everyone."

Jake stood up, unzipped himself, and stepped out of all that fur. He breathed a sigh of relief to be in a t-shirt and shorts again and carefully placed the limp fur on an empty chair. He propped the gorilla head up on the table. The blank gorilla eyes stared out, observing everyone.

"You kind of like her, don't you?" Maddie asked Ryan. The question made Jake look up from his plate for a full second.

"Sure I like her," Ryan said. "We work together. I try to help her out as much as I can."

"That's not what I meant," Maddie sang while playing with her food. "But never mind, none of my business anyway."

Rather than go into any more details one way or the other, Ryan figured it would be best to change the subject.

"So Jake, you think you'll be able to act as safety for us?"

"Yeah sure, no problem."

"We won't need you for the shallow dives. But we'll need you later for the night dive and the deeper dives."

"I can't wait to go diving," Maddie chimed in. "It's so beautiful out in the crystal clear water, especially when you're studying coral. The coral's so intricate and there are so many different kinds, there's always something that we haven't seen every time we go out. It surprises me every time. Don't you think so, Ryan?"

"I've never gone diving in tropical waters, just in the ocean back home."

"Well then, you're in for a real surprise."

"Yeah, I guess. What made you want to study coral anyway?"

"Oh, I don't know. We lived near the ocean in South Carolina and I'd always be out playing in those tidal pools whenever I had the chance. Sometimes little pieces of coral would wash ashore and they'd be such bright colors. Like pink and purple and orange. So then I'd imagine the places those things could have come from, like they were different planets, all glowing with those strange colors. Then I found out they're not really just pretty rocks, that they're actual animals, and that they're not from other planets but from this planet, and that just made them all the more exciting, you know?"

Ryan nodded. He could picture her bent over the tidal pools as a kid; her wet hair the color of the coral as she picked the pieces up and examined each one.

Maddie kept talking. "They're so diverse too. They can look like trees or bubbles or brains. And really, the reefs are brains when you think about it because they record the ocean's chemical composition and temperature for as long as they grow, which can be for centuries. That and all kinds of medicines come from coral. Things like treatments for cancer, Alzheimer's, heart disease, all kinds of viruses, and who knows what else could be derived from them in the future. I mean, they've been called the medicine cabinets of the 21st Century even though people have been finding ways to use them as medicine for thousands of years."

Ryan watched her as she talked on. She actually smiled while she talked, something he had never seen anyone do except maybe for television newscasters. She was pretty in a cheerleader kind of a way. She had a lot of energy, the kind of energy that might repel some people at first when really it was a good thing to have so much energy. He wondered if she had been a cheerleader. Even though he played every possible sport all through high school, he never really went for the cheerleader type. He usually liked the quieter ones. But the cheerleaders weren't so bad. At least you pretty much always knew what they were thinking.

"Hey, will you guys have time to help me with an experiment tomorrow?" Jake asked when Maddie paused for a breath.

"Sure," Ryan said. "There's not much for me to do until we get to where we're going."

"Yeah, okay," Maddie said. "What kind of an experiment is this, anyway?"

"It's an experiment that defies all reasonable explanation. You'll have to see it to believe it."

CHAPTER 25

SINCE CROSSING THE Panama Canal from one ocean to another, Ryan noticed the water surrounding and buoying them felt calmer. So far, the name "pacific" seemed fitting. The ship had stopped tossing around and now glided along on a shining surface. He stood at the bow and looked out at what could have been ripples in a pond instead of waves.

After making life-threatening journeys around South America, the explorers must have felt a similar sense of relief at finding this body of water so truly pacific. But just when you start to think something like that and possibly underestimate its strength, a tsunami or tidal wave comes roaring up from the depths.

Jake walked up behind him. "Ready for the experiment?"

"Ready. As long as you're not going to be experimenting on me."

"Would I do something like that?"

"I don't know, but if I had to guess, I'd say yes."

Jake turned to Maddie once she trotted up beside him. "Where do I get this kind of a reputation?"

She put a hand on his shoulder while pretending to console him. "Well now honey, I hate to break it to you but you just might have something to do with it."

"Okay, I've got everything we need right here." Jake swung a backpack off his shoulder and opened it up. He reached in and handed them each a pair of safety glasses.

"This keeps getting scarier and scarier," Ryan said as he took the bulky glasses.

"It's not very scary," Jake said. "But then again, you never really know until something scary suddenly happens."

He reached back into his bag of tricks and took out a handful of plastic film canisters, antacid tablets, and a bottle of water. He lined them all up on the deck and looked over at Ryan and Maddie.

"So what do you think we're going to do with these?" Jake asked while squinting into the sun.

Ryan shrugged. "It doesn't look like we could do much with them."

"Wrong, we're going to build a rocket."

"Sure, but I think you forgot the rocket fuel," Maddie said. "Oh, and the rocket too."

"Nope, it's all right here," Jake brushed his hand through the air to show off the potential of his supplies. "This is all we need."

"Okay then, what are we supposed to do?" Maddie asked.

"Put your safety glasses on. Mostly I just needed an audience."

They shook their heads and complied, feeling a little ridiculous to be wearing safety glasses when no real danger could be found.

"I've always wanted to try this," Jake said. "But it's hard to find the right kind of an audience. And if you don't have an audience, well then why bother."

"So all we do is watch?" Maddie asked.

"Just watch and possibly run for cover."

Maddie giggled and pulled the safety glasses over her eyes. "Okay, we're ready. Let's see your magic trick."

Jake gave her a serious look. "Experiment."

"Yeah right, experiment."

Jake opened the bottle of antacids, took out a pocket knife and sliced the tablet in half. Then he opened the plastic film canister and dropped half of the antacid inside.

"Okay, stand back."

He hovered over the canister with the water bottle and let a drop of water out. It plopped into the canister. Then he snapped the film cap on, turned it upside down, and ran back to where Ryan and Maddie stood.

Before Ryan could say anything about these strange antics, a tremendous pop made everyone jump. Maddie grabbed onto his arm and kept holding on even after the surprise had died down.

The film canister soared through the sky just as a rocket would. Well, a rocket for ants anyway. It went up a good twenty feet and hovered for a second before dropping back down from the sky.

"Try to catch it," Jake yelled out. He ran underneath and teetered, looking like a baseball player waiting for a fly ball.

Ryan trotted over and got ready to make the catch. The only problem would be if Jake or Maddie ran into him while trying to catch the canister themselves. He figured they must look like the Bad News Bears already, with everyone staring up into the sky and swerving in different directions. Ryan reached up and made sure to catch the thing before they all ran into each other and ended up in a mangled heap on the deck.

"Good catch!" Jake yelled out.

Ryan looked into the canister. It was empty. The antacid had turned into rocket fuel.

Jake took the canister and retrieved the plastic top from the deck. "Okay, now, for the true experimentation part, what do you think would happen if I added more water? Do you think it would go farther?"

"I don't think so," Ryan said. "More antacid, sure then maybe, but not just with more water."

"I can't believe people take those things for upset stomachs," Maddie said. "Imagine what these pills do in there. Why don't they cause holes or something?"

"There isn't as much of an explosion when there's no film canister involved," Jake said. "The canister compacts the whole thing, making it more powerful. The antacid and water together generate carbon dioxide. That builds pressure inside the canister. The more carbon dioxide, the more pressure, until the rocket blasts up."

"Still, I don't think I'll ever in my life take an antacid tablet after seeing that," Maddie said.

"We drink carbon dioxide all the time whenever we drink soda, and we haven't exploded yet," Jake said.

"So if we didn't burp, we'd explode?" Ryan asked.

"Possibly. Now that would be a fun experiment."

"Hold on right there," Maddie said. "I'm not sacrificing my stomach to your crazy experiments."

"Okay then, let's try putting more water in the rocket to see what happens."

Ryan saw how this kind of thing could go on all day. He noticed a light in Jake's eyes that hadn't been there before. He could see why Jake wanted to be a scientist. Probably, it had been there all along. He pictured Jake as a kid mixing different household products together, like baking soda and vinegar, and the explosions that would have resulted. Jake wanted to know what might happen just for the sake of gaining more knowledge, even if the thing he wanted to know was how high a little plastic film canister could go under the right conditions. Ryan envied him. He couldn't imagine always knowing what he wanted to do. For that matter, he couldn't imagine ever knowing.

CHAPTER 26

WHILE THE SHIP plowed on toward the equator, Ellen kept researching. The more she researched, the more questions surfaced. She dove deeper and deeper, down below the surfaces of things toward the pulsing heart of it all. There she hoped to find something, anything irrefutable. But in this world of shifting shadows and light, nothing could be truly irrefutable. So she kept diving deeper. As she dove, she traveled farther from the light and farther into the darkness of the unknown.

When the ship anchored near the Atoll Islands, she still didn't have her irrefutable proof but she had filled her laptop with data and felt close or at least a little closer. For now, it would all have to wait.

She thought it might be about time to check their equipment even though they wouldn't be diving right away. First they had to visit the island chief to ask permission to dive. Her stomach fluttered at the thought. She had no idea what to expect from it all.

Ellen wandered into the storage area and was surprised to see Ryan there, already checking the equipment and testing the oxygen tanks.

"Hey," she said. "You must have read my mind."

"I figured might as well start in on this stuff so you wouldn't have to boss me around about it later."

"I don't boss you around."

"That's because I read minds."

"Right, I forgot." Ellen pulled some equipment off the shelf. "I haven't seen you around much for the last couple days."

"Oh, I've been around. You're the one who's been holed up with your computer this whole time."

"I guess. So we're going to have to ask the chief for permission to dive. Did you know that?"

"I heard something like that but wasn't sure it was true."

"Yep. That would be crazy if we came all this way and he decided to say no."

~

Toward early afternoon, islanders rowed out in long thin boats to greet the giant metal ship. Ellen thought of Columbus and the Arawaks as the boats moved toward them. After landing in the New World, the explorers eventually enslaved and killed the Arawaks, wiping out their entire population and culture in the name of progress. Now, hundreds of years later, she visited a tropical island in another part of the world, also in the name of progress. Hopefully there wouldn't be any blood shed over it this time.

While looking out at the wooden boats, Ellen couldn't help but wonder if progress was worth all the trouble. Too often, progress came at the expense of nature. People could plow through mountains, dam up rivers, create lakes, wipe out entire populations. They could do everything except bring the world back to its natural state.

And after all that, did it create happiness? These islanders, these men who rowed toward them, looked like the happiest people Ellen had seen in a long time, maybe even ever. They looked comfortable, as if they never doubted themselves. Though there were many of them, they rowed together as one. As they drew closer to the ship, Ellen could hear singing. A long, low-pitched tune flowed along with their boats and mixed with the sound of the waves and the ocean breezes.

Ellen had grabbed a light jacket in case they were going to be out there into the night, even if the night would likely be warm. She tied the jacket around her waist and felt a little ridiculous since it had been manufactured with some kind of high-tech material that was supposed to breathe and keep out the rain, all while half-naked men rowed toward them. At least she was supposedly prepared for anything, even if she did look out of place. Luckily, she had decided to leave her baseball cap back on her bed.

Ryan stood next to her. He didn't look as silly as she felt, even though he also seemed to be overdressed in shorts and a golf shirt. He caught her looking at him again so she dropped her gaze and watched the men rowing the boats. The crew members slid a metal door open near the water's surface and the men rowed toward it.

Ellen walked with Ryan down the stairs to wait with a group of scientists. Some were more dressed up than she had thought to be, wearing chinos with collared shirts and occasional leather belts. Most also wore either rimless or thick-rimmed glasses from years of staring at computers. A few exhibited tense faces as if they kept their teeth clenched at all times.

The island men rowed up alongside the open door. Ropes were thrown out from the research ship, and a couple islanders stood and held onto the ropes to bring their boat up against the steel ship. Then the rowers in the middle reached out and grasped the hands of people from halfway around the world. By now, the men had stopped singing but greeted them with wide open smiles.

Ellen stepped aboard, grateful for the smile and the callused hand that steadied her, then half sat and half fell onto a wooden seat. Ryan followed and sank down beside her. Their legs briefly touched. She felt the soft hairs for a second before the rocking of the boat pulled them away again.

A few more researchers stumbled aboard. Once everyone was seated, their boat glided away from the hulking metal ship and turned toward the island. Another boat took its place next to the open hatch to pick up more researchers. Ellen saw Michael lean out to board a rowboat. He looked as silly as she felt.

The rowers took up their paddles and began singing the low-pitched tune again. Their smiles never faltered. Ellen smiled back but hers felt weak and inadequate in comparison. Her body pulled up and back with each paddle stroke. She contented herself to settle into the rhythm of the boat and the song. The boat sliced through the waves easily, feeling much faster than the research ship now that they were closer to the water's surface.

The island they rowed toward overflowed with vegetation. A thin strip of bright white sand could be seen around the edge. Immediately beyond the sand, palm trees bent toward the water and grew so close together that they twisted around each other as if dancing the tango.

"How are we going to get in through all those trees and vines?" Ellen asked mostly to herself.

"Good question," Ryan answered.

Off to one side, a rock formation towered out of the waves. With each paddle stroke, the rocks came into focus a little more until Ellen saw the unmistakable face of a man leering. She shivered despite the heat.

"Look at that rock," she said. "Notice anything strange about it?"

"Yeah, it looks like a really creepy face."

"I wonder what kind of an effect something like that would have on the people who live near it."

"I wouldn't want to see that every day, that's for sure," Ryan said. "But at least it doesn't stop them from singing."

"That's true. Maybe they have to sing to it to keep it calm or something."

Ryan looked over his shoulder at the face again. "It's not working."

They rowed past the rock and could no longer see the chiseled face, but the vision remained in Ellen's mind. The face looked so evil. But there was something else. It also looked strangely satisfied.

The boat pulled up onto the sand with a rush. Ellen bent down to take her shoes off before stepping into the water. Unhampered by shoes, the rowers jumped out first. One of them held out his hand to help guide her.

The rowers wore cotton shorts cut off above the knee. Instead of shirts, necklaces made of tiny blue and white stones circled their necks and jingled as they moved. The men stood and sang out to the other boats as they made their way to the island. Once all the boats floated to shore and everyone staggered out, the rowers dragged the empty hulls inland so that they rested partly in the jungle and away from the waves.

Then one of the men turned to the group and said, "Welcome. We will go to the village now."

Before Ellen could fully comprehend what was happening, the jungle opened its mouth and swallowed the rowers. They disappeared into green leaves.

CHAPTER 27

E LLEN HUNCHED DOWN to put her shoes back on while thinking it all must be a dream. She'd wake up soon, back in Deep Harbor where she was supposed to be, in a place surrounded by buildings and roads.

She followed the other researchers. Everyone walked up to the place where the men disappeared. Then she saw that a narrow path did unbelievably exist where it seemed there had only been jungle. Drooping palm tree leaves and vines covered the path, but it was there.

They started to move single-file down the path. The researcher in front of Ellen, she thought his name might be something like Bill, turned his head back and said in her general direction, "I can't believe we have to go through all this. They're obviously going to give us permission to dive. Why not just give it to us then? I'd like to get to work."

Bill didn't look happy. He happened to be one of the ones wearing long pants. He probably thought it might help as a sign of respect, but now he sweated through his shirt because of it. Ellen looked at the armpit stains and the darker patch beginning to form on his back. She slowly nodded her head in agreement.

She wanted to get to work too. Looking at those sweat stains was the last thing she wanted to be doing right about now.

They walked on through the jungle for either an eternity or a few minutes. She let Bill get ahead of her when she couldn't stand to look at him anymore. Now she saw nothing but green leaves with occasional flickers of the blue dress shirt and sweat stains in front of her. Strangely, Bill carried a laptop. It bumped against his side. Ellen couldn't help but wonder what he thought he'd accomplish with a laptop in the jungle.

Screeching and scattering erupted from the darkness beyond the leaves. The noises sounded a little too close. Ellen glanced back at Ryan after a particularly loud screech but he acted unfazed by it all. She wasn't so sure about running through the jungle for wild fun anymore. An image of that leering face trapped in the rock popped back into her mind. At the moment, she wanted to run toward any kind of civilization.

A village appeared when she least expected it. Buildings made of corrugated metal could be seen off to the side, sprouting out of the sand, transplanted from another world. Hard-packed sand served as a road through the village. Chickens plucked at the ground while goats watched from the shade of a few palm trees. Most of the homes were made of plywood and thatched palm tree leaves, some with front porches. People came out of their homes to greet them when they saw the strangers arrive from the jungle. Children ran up to them.

The rowers led the group to the village center where flat rocks circled a large fire pit. They beckoned to everyone, scientists and villagers, to gather around. A low fire crackled. Ellen took a breath of wood smoke, ocean air, and something nutty. She looked into the fire pit and saw a lump of seaweed with smoke leaking out of it.

After everyone sat on the ground or on scattered rocks, a rower stood up. "Welcome to our village and welcome to our seas. Our chief Manato welcomes you."

With that, a man strolled out of a nearby home. As he stepped onto the front porch, he might as well have been stepping onto a stage.

He looked completely different from the other men while wearing flip flops and a flowing gold robe made of some kind of silk. He was also bald, contributing to an overall shine, while most of the others had straight black hair. Everyone stood as he walked toward the fire. He nodded toward them and made a motion with his hands so that they would sit down again.

"Welcome to Mala and to the island chain you call the Atoll Islands. I know you are all here to do the work of the creator and protector, to learn from our islands, and to help our coral and sea life grow ever more and stronger. I welcome you to our seas and you may now dive in our oceans."

The researchers looked at each other, wondering if that was it.

"But first, we will celebrate your arrival and I will tell you some of our great legends so you may better understand our islands and the places you will be diving."

He walked toward to the fire and sat in front of it, then took his time while looking into the eyes of every villager and visitor gathered there. After scrutinizing each one, a smile came over his face as his voice took on the tone of a ghost story.

"One of our gods in Mala legend is the fierce sea monster Minawaka. He was once the guardian of the reef entrance to our island. He would change himself into a shark and travel through the reef, challenging others to fight. But whenever he fought as a shark, great waves would form, valleys would flood, and there would be much suffering."

The fire crackled and popped, adding an exclamation point to the story.

The chief continued, "Until one day a giant octopus grew tired of the waves and the suffering caused from all this fighting. This octopus snuck up behind Minawaka and coiled his tentacles around him. The octopus began to squeeze. Minawaka begged for mercy and agreed to never fight again or harm anyone from the island of Mala. And so we have no fear of sharks when we are out fishing or swimming. Even today, fishermen pour yaqona into the sea as an offering to Minawaka before they fish in his waters. We will now have some yaqona so that we may feel closer to Minawaka before diving into his home."

With that, two rowers stood up, walked into a nearby house and came out carrying large clay bottles. One of the men brought his bottle to the chief so that he could take a sip from it. When the chief was done, each of the rowers took a brief sip and handed the bottles to others. Ellen felt like she had wandered into a church, even though she was sitting on the ground around a fire pit that kept smelling better and better.

Ryan handed her one of the clay bottles. The weight and freezing feel of it surprised her. She took a sip of something spicy, earthy, and very cold. She wanted to try another sip to figure out what it could be, but passed it on instead.

"Now I will tell you the legend of the Fire People," the chief said. "Many generations ago, a warrior went fishing for eels. As he walked along the tidal flats, he felt an eel in the mud with his feet but when he pulled it out of the mud, it assumed the shape of a spirit god. He knew catching a spirit god was much better than catching an eel, so the warrior kept a firm grip on his catch to bring it to his chief. The spirit god pleaded for his freedom and offered gifts to the warrior in return. The warrior refused. Then the spirit god offered him power over fire and spirits and the warrior became more interested. But the warrior did not believe the spirit god could give him this.

"To prove his gift, a pit was dug and lined with stones. A great fire was lit. Once the stones were white with heat, the spirit god told the warrior to put his hands and arms into the fire. The warrior did this only to show his bravery but then he did not feel the heat or suffer any burns. To this day, his direct descendants still have power over fire and spirits. We will show you this, but first we must eat."

A few of the men stood up, retrieved wooden platters and tongs, and walked over to the fire pit. They picked the seaweed up with the tongs and arranged it on the platters. Then they placed pieces of smoked fish next to the seaweed and passed the servings around.

The chief sat down and started to eat, which seemed to be the signal for everyone else to join him. Ellen shared her platter with Ryan and Bill the sweaty guy. She picked up some of the seaweed with her fingers and tried it. To her amazement, it crunched with a nutty flavor. She didn't think seaweed looked all that appetizing and never would have thought it could taste so good. She let Ryan and Bill devour the fish while she snacked on more seaweed. She'd have to try this kind of seaweed cooking at home: cheap food and she could clean up the beach at the same time.

No one talked while they ate. When everyone finished, the clay bottles were passed around again and again. Ellen took a sip and still couldn't figure out what the ingredients might be. Goose bumps rose up along her arms after drinking it even though the tropical heat still weighed her down. Her usual desire to solve any mystery came creeping in as she tried to determine how the drink could have such a bone chilling effect.

The fire picked up and didn't smoke as much without the seaweed. Sparks joined the stars as palm tree leaves swished with background songs.

Villagers gazed into the fire and started to sing. This didn't sound like the low moaning song that greeted them on their arrival. It was the opposite, filled with high-pitched tones that echoed through the air to wake something up. The flames grew in response.

Two men stood and took sips from the clay bottles. They walked over to the fire while staring at each other through sizzling flames.

Once the singing had risen to a particularly high pitch, they reached into the middle of the fire with their bare hands. They didn't draw back in pain like anyone else would have done. Instead, they kept their hands in the fire and began to move as if massaging the flames or dancing with them.

The fire popped and sizzled. Ellen prepared herself for the nightmare of charred flesh. Still, the men reached in further as the flames grew more powerful. With a roar, the fire sent a cough of sparks into the air.

Ellen watched as bits of light sprouted wings and began to fly. The sparks turned into butterflies the color of fire. Yellow, orange, blue, and purple wings hovered like a strange cloud before disappearing into the night.

The villagers sang in rejoicing tones as the two men stepped away from the fire and walked back to their seats. Ellen couldn't see any burns or redness on their arms or hands. Some of the butterflies lingered near the flames while a few rested on the shoulders of villagers.

"They are the souls of our loved ones," the chief said. "They are with us always but sometimes we forget when we cannot see them. We must remember to feel them always, feel their love and give our love in return. They like to visit in this way to remind us of this."

A purple butterfly zig-zagged through the air before landing on Ellen's knee. It looked at her. Ellen stared back. Streaks of silver, black, and yellow lined the purple. A surge of happiness filled Ellen's body. For the first time in years, she felt whole again.

The chief looked surprised and pointed toward her. "You have a loved one with you now. You and this loved one were very close."

Another butterfly, a black one practically invisible in the night, rested on her other knee. She felt an overwhelming love from the purple butterfly but only a strange tingling chill from the other one.

None of this could be true. This was the stuff of legends and legends had been made up to explain the unknown. Legends weren't needed these days, in the midst of the information age, now that explanations for almost anything could easily be found. She stared at the butterflies while wondering how they could have flown out of the fire. Their wings flapped with the colors of flame. She looked back at the arms of the men and saw no signs of injury. But there were explanations for everything, weren't there?

CHAPTER 28

A FTER THANKING THE chief and saying goodbye, everyone trudged back through the jungle and reached the shore right at the peak of sunset. While standing there on the tropical beach, looking over the turquoise ocean and all the colors made by the sun's departure, Ellen couldn't help but feel as if they were on some kind of an adventure cruise: take part in a traditional fire ceremony, run through the jungle, then return home to watch the sun set over your own tropical paradise. Something like that.

Singing erupted from somewhere behind them. Ellen turned to see the women from the village standing in a line while gazing out at the ocean and singing to it. Their blue and white dresses flowed with the breeze. Everyone looked back at the waves. Ellen almost expected a sudden tsunami to come roaring up at them. She hoped the purpose of the song was to say goodbye to the sun or something instead of calling up any powerful natural forces.

The ocean frothed in response. A rock emerged from the water between the horizon and the shore. Waves lapped over the giant rock. Then another rock appeared near that one, and another one.

"I've heard of this," Michael said while walking up to her. "Their song is calling the sea turtles."

She looked at him with complete disbelief. "How can they call sea turtles? How can anyone call sea turtles?"

"I don't know, but that's what they're doing."

Ellen examined the ocean again. The rocks moved slowly toward them. "Okay, if that really is what's happening, why are they calling the sea turtles?"

"It's another legend."

"Why are they showing us all these legends? Do they want us to think they have magical powers or something?"

"Well, don't they? Those butterflies were amazing. And look, the sea turtles are heading this way."

The sea turtles looked larger and larger as they slid toward them. There were about eight all together now, maybe more.

"According to the legend, one day long ago a woman and her daughter were out fishing when members of another island snuck up on them and captured them," Michael said. "They tied the women up and kept them as captives on their boat. The sea gods heard the women's pleas for help and sent a storm out to them. While everyone was busy trying to make sure they wouldn't capsize, the women turned themselves into sea turtles and slipped over the side to escape into the ocean. It's supposed to be the descendants of those sea turtles who rise up whenever the women of their village sing to them."

"Wow. That's truly unbelievable. There must be some other reason for this."

The sea turtles continued their slow approach. Ellen started to feel like they could possibly be under some kind of an attack.

"Oh, another funny thing is that only women from this particular island can call the sea turtles. And if someone from Namuna Island, the island of their captors, happens to be around at the time of the singing, the sea turtles won't appear at all."

"I guess no one around here is from Namuna then. I'm starting to wish they were though. Is it just me or does it feel like the sea turtles might come out and bite us?"

Michael laughed. "I wonder if this is what it feels like to them when we invade their territory by diving. Might as well get friendly with them now. We might be swimming with them tomorrow."

Just as he said that, the singing stopped and the sea turtles sank back into the waves. So they wouldn't be attacking after all.

"They wanted to listen to the song." One of the rowers explained. "To feel close again to family and friends."

As the sea turtles disappeared into the waves, one of the women put her hands over her face and began to cry. The villagers turned toward her and tried to comfort her. A few rowers murmured something to the women, then one came back to explain.

"Many days ago, the ocean took her husband. He went out to fish and never came back. She keeps hoping their songs will call him back like the sea turtles, but so far no good."

Ellen walked up to her. She wanted to help somehow but didn't know what to say. The woman looked so distressed, so lonely, so empty. Ellen recognized the look of loneliness and helplessness and felt powerless against it. She reached out to hug the woman and kept holding on.

"He'll find his way back. Don't worry."

"No, I knew this would happen. The ocean kept calling him, whispering to him to go farther and farther out and away. It took him and it will never give him back. But now he knows everything. Now he knows all its secrets."

Ellen knew it couldn't be true, but then how could any of the things they had seen be true? Had he really discovered the ocean's secrets, all its mysteries? Could anyone ever do such a thing?

The rowers dragged the boats into the water while acting a little wearier than they had earlier in the day. Ellen couldn't blame them. She felt tired too and she hadn't done anything but watch the whole spectacle unfold from one astonishing legend to the next.

Everyone eased back into the boats. The rowers pushed and pulled at the oars until they released from shore and slid toward the research ship, their temporary home. Ellen closed her eyes so she wouldn't have to see the face leering through the rock again. Still, it loomed up in her mind, probably even scarier than in real life. She hoped the cooks on board were in the middle of making something good. Seaweed for lunch didn't quite cut it after all.

Dinner turned out to be spaghetti, which reminded her of the seaweed but tasted completely different, almost too different. It didn't fit with the sunshine and the tropical breezes in the way that the seaweed had.

She ate with what had become the usual crowd of Ryan, Michael, and Maddie. This time she observed them as she might observe jellyfish. It was a strange contrast in people. Maddie slurped her spaghetti joyously and hummed while Michael and Ryan solemnly swirled their spaghetti around forks and took regular bites. Michael separated out any tomato chunks and wouldn't eat them. Maddie and Ryan scraped their plates for more. They all ate at about the same pace. For whatever reason, the eating habits of humans didn't seem as fascinating as the eating habits of jellyfish.

Bill the sweaty guy wandered over and plunked himself next to Michael with the clang of a tray on the table.

"So what was that all about?" He gave the group a little sneer, revealing teeth that strangely resembled barnacles.

"Well, she was pretty upset," Ellen said while twirling her spaghetti.

"I don't mean the woman. I mean all those legends and that ceremony."

"Oh, I thought that was nice."

"Nice? We finally get here and we can't do the work that we're here to do. Instead, we're subjected to some kind of tribal voodoo."

Maddie jumped in, "Yeah, but it was a fun kind of voodoo. At least they didn't make us stick our hands in that fire."

"We wouldn't have been able to. We're not direct descendants of Hoochie Coochie or whoever that was with the special powers."

Michael looked at him for the first time since he sat down. "The whole idea behind the ceremony was so that we'd respect their land and their ocean while we're here. It's funny that you seem to have missed that completely."

"Yeah, I didn't quite get that. I was too busy sweating my ass off and eating seaweed at the time."

"Well, the whole ordeal is over now," Michael said. "You can relax. We'll be able to get to work tomorrow."

"Thank God for that," Bill said.

Ellen considered whether she seemed that dedicated to her own studies, to the point where she'd rather work than do anything else and wouldn't notice or take part in the fun things going on around her. But then maybe that explained her life.

CHAPTER 29

T HE FIRST DIVE was scheduled for 9 AM. About an hour be-
forehand, Ellen peeked into the storage area that had become their office away from the office. Ryan was already there
testing air tanks and lining everything up so that it would be
ready to go.

"I haven't seen the gorilla around lately," she said while
reaching out to help. "Has he been stalking the decks and I just
haven't noticed?"

"No, he got out of that thing right away after that first night
and hasn't worn it since. Whether he wanted to admit it or not, I
think he got pretty hot wearing it."

"That was a lot of fur to be wearing in the tropics. Were you
able to convince anyone to dive with us as safety?"

"Yeah, Jake."

"Jake the gorilla?"

"Why not? He's not going to wear the gorilla suit while diving or anything."

"But he doesn't seem to be taking this whole thing very
seriously."

"Sure he does. He's really into all this stuff. You'll see."

"Okay," Ellen acquiesced. If they didn't have a third person to act as safety for some of the dives they wouldn't be able to go as deep as she wanted to. "We won't need him today but we'll probably need him tomorrow and we'll definitely need him for the night dives."

"That's what I told him."

"Ah, reading minds again I see."

"Of course," Ryan said as he pulled out the scuba gear. "Figured you wouldn't expect any less."

Ellen didn't know what to say to that so she busied herself with the air tanks.

"I thought we'd mostly stay in the lagoon for this first dive," she said after a while. "Hopefully it's the kind of area that would attract a lot of jellyfish."

"Do all of these islands have lagoons?"

"Most of them. The ones that used to be volcanoes have them. The lagoons are usually what's left of the volcano centers."

"That's pretty cool. So in a way, we'll be diving into a volcano."

"I hadn't thought of it that way, but at least there's only water in there now. No more fire or molten lava to contend with."

"Sounds pretty tame in comparison."

"Who knows, there could still be something bubbling beneath the surface. There's usually something happening or changing even if it doesn't look like it. If coral hadn't built up around the edges of the volcanoes, these islands might have completely vanished by now."

"That's funny, I was thinking about that earlier," Ryan said. "About how much things are always changing even if it doesn't seem like it at the time. We look around and we think things are stable, but they never really are."

"That's true. Nature can be pretty tricky in that way."

Excitement tickled Ellen at the thought of diving into the unknown. She couldn't wait to explore the interior of the lagoon, then the ocean outside the atoll so the two could be compared. A few days after that, they would go on to the uninhabited islands and compare everything once again. If looking for the human impact on the world, what better way than to compare the inhabited with the uninhabited? Comparisons like that could work for jellyfish habitats as well as coral. But then there was always the lurking fear that humans might be impacting everything, even remote uninhabited and often forgotten areas.

Ellen grabbed her floppy wetsuit and hurried to her quarters to change. They had to be ready to board the inflatable research boat soon or they'd lose their diving slot.

Over by her bed, she pulled on her bathing suit first, then tried to squiggle into the scuba suit. The experience reminded her of trying to fit into designer jeans that were two sizes too small as a teenager. When she was finally able to zip the whole thing with one zip that went up to her neck, it felt comfortable. Much more comfortable than those designer jeans. She glanced into the mirror and saw that all the struggling was worth it. The suit hugged her body while sucking in and smoothing out any unwanted jiggling.

Ryan had already changed into his wetsuit and waited with their equipment. He looked her over quickly. She tried not to look too closely at him. The suits were definitely formfitting.

Ellen occupied herself with her flippers, mask, air tank, weight belt, and underwater camera as the hatch door opened and their pick-up boat appeared.

Their boat was basically a rubber floatation device equipped with a motor. No rowing or singing to accompany it, just some regular old crew member. He sat back with his life jacket on and piloted the outboard motor a bit possessively.

Two more researchers piled in and asked to be dropped off in the ocean area outside the lagoon. It looked like she and Ryan would have the lagoon all to themselves.

Ellen pulled on her flippers and air tank during the boat ride. The rubber boat bounced along on nonexistent waves, causing her to fall into Ryan a few times as she struggled with the gear. He reached out to steady her while helping to pull the air tank over her shoulders.

As soon as the tank was on, it weighed her down, making her slouch back into the seat. Diesel fumes invaded the air as the taste of gas filled her mouth. She breathed it in and imagined herself spontaneously combusting in the heat.

The boat drew closer to the lagoon opening and the water blurred from purple to turquoise. Ellen peered over the edge to see coral waving below. Tiny bright orange and yellow fish flickered in the light.

"You'll have to get out here," their guide said as he turned the motor off. "We don't want the boat to get too close to the coral."

Ellen nodded. She and Ryan finished getting their equipment on and regulators ready. They perched on the rubbery edge of the boat and plopped into the clear blue green.

Everything felt instantly different. Bubbles surrounded her. At first, a gurgling noise was all she could hear along with her Darth Vader breath. She concentrated on her breathing as they dove deeper. Once fewer bubbles appeared, she could investigate and adjust to what always felt so much like a different world.

While down below the surface, swimming somehow turned into flying. Ellen put her arms to her sides and propelled herself forward with a few kicks.

Stars clustered together on the ground rather than in the sky and any light took on an ethereal glow. Everything from the water to coral to sea life all boasted the brightest of bright colors as if only fluorescent crayons could now be used.

Ellen's mask filled up with water and her view turned murky and abstract. She stopped to clear it by pressing on her mask and blowing out through her nose. Once the bubbles trailed away, everything became clear again.

Ellen flew over to Ryan. She was tempted to linger around the outer coral edge of the lagoon opening, but also wanted to check out the lagoon. She pointed to the opening between the masses of coral and Ryan followed her through as the seafloor rose and the water became shallower.

She looked around for Minawaka. According to the island legend, he should be guarding the lagoon's reef entrance. They hadn't brought any yaqona to please him. She knew not to be afraid of sharks but couldn't help wishing they had brought some yaqona just in case.

As they drew closer to the pink coral opening, Ellen felt an overpowering current push and carry her away. She forced herself to relax and enjoy the ride, especially since the undersea river took them right where they wanted to go: through the coral and into the shallows.

Once in the lagoon, the current slowed and then dissipated. The water was so clear it was almost white, so white that it practically matched the sand below, which was a little disorienting. They had somehow found an underwater cloud to swim through. Ellen brushed her arms through the water while seeing nothing but foggy patches everywhere. The lagoon sloped and they swam farther down, traveling just above the seafloor and out of the clouds. Shadows and light played on the sand as fluorescent colors streamed through the watery haze.

The sand below looked bumpier than usual. As she swam closer, the bumps took on the form of gigantic clams. Most were enormous, about the size of watermelons. They clustered together in a tight community as their mantles or lips tipped up toward the sunlight.

Each mantle displayed a completely different blue pattern that showed like teeth between the partly opened shells. Some contained dark blue zigzags against light blue, others boasted polka dotted or swirled patterns. It was as if each wore different clothes, all with the same light and dark blue colors.

The clams worshipped the sunlight. They cracked their shells open to let the light in and perhaps something good to eat. Maybe their shells stayed open so they could recognize each other by their own distinct patterns. They could be talking in some way or joking with one another. With their mantles showing, they did look like they were smiling or laughing. Ellen figured they must enjoy each other's company since they were all clumped so closely together.

Schools of tiny bright purple fish flew by, grouped together to disguise themselves as one big fish. Was it all for protective reasons or were they enjoying each other's company too?

While witnessing these communities that could be part of each other instead of separate, individual animals, Ellen couldn't help but feel more alone.

She remembered seeing sea otters hold hands while they slept so that they wouldn't drift away from each other. The thought only made her feel worse. She had somehow drifted away from everyone in her life. She tried not to think about it and took a few pictures of the clams, mostly because she had never seen anything like them. Who knows, she might be able to find a clam expert to send the pictures to eventually.

Still on the hunt for jellyfish, she swam a little closer to shore. She stared sideways into the water with its shifting light blue and green. It almost seemed as if the light and shadows and colors purposely tried to confuse her as they continued to change and move.

Then off in the distance she saw one. A jellyfish. She felt the adrenaline pump through her body. She couldn't believe she noticed it at all. It was practically invisible: just a hint of something like a pink or clear bubble. She could look right through it as it drifted along on the currents while letting its tentacles trail out and billow behind. It held such a delicate beauty. She swam underneath it, ready to get the camera out while wondering what type of jellyfish this could be. Then as she drew closer, she realized this graceful, willowy shape was just a partially submerged plastic bag.

Looking down at the seafloor, Ellen saw a few more discarded items: an old tire, a rusted soda can. Well, this was an inhabited island after all. Out of sight, out of mind. The problem was whenever many people thought their actions had no effect. Then the trash really piled up.

Ellen surveyed the area. Algae grew on the tire. Tiny fish hovered over the algae, plucking at it. Another fish poked its head out of a muddy sneaker. At least some of the trash had come to serve a useful purpose in the lagoon. She swam over, grabbed the plastic bag, and stuck it in her mesh sampling pouch. Sea life or birds could get entangled in or try to eat that kind of garbage and die. She knew she was fighting a losing battle, but it was better than doing nothing at all. Besides, ocean life already struggled to survive. Those lives needed all the help they could get.

While feeling a little pathetic because her only catch so far turned out to be a plastic bag, Ellen swam closer to the surface. Schools of fish darted by, some with yellow and blue stripes, some silver. She looked into the deeper water. Still no jellyfish even though this seemed like a perfect environment for them. She took a few pictures of the colorful fish anyway. Ryan followed and took some pictures of his own.

Ellen floated through the water and stared into the haze. Jellyfish were difficult to see unless you happened to be right near them. So while hoping to get close but not too close, she drifted and floated as aimlessly as a jellyfish would, letting the ripples and currents transport her.

As she relaxed, she began to breathe less and create fewer bubbles. The fish swam closer, trying to figure her out. Some nibbled at her arms and fingers. She felt herself easing into a state of utter relaxation while remaining aware almost in an extra sensory way.

A grip on her arm jerked her out of her trance. She screamed, creating a flurry of bubbles. Ryan squeezed her arm tighter and pointed to a moray eel slithering below them. The eel was a thick one, mostly light brown, and could be seen sliding out of a coral area where it had been hiding. They couldn't see the end of the eel so they had no idea how long it could be.

Ellen patted Ryan's arm and gave him an "okay" signal while trying to reassure him. The eel wouldn't do anything to them, even if it did look a little sinister while slowly looping around beneath them like that. But it also looked to be on a mission.

They watched as the eel continued to glide out of the hole, acting like it didn't know they were there though Ellen thought it must know, that it could feel them even if it didn't happen to be looking directly at them. The end of the body finally appeared out of the coral so that they could see the entire length of it. The eel looked to be at least seven feet long as it swam and slithered off and away.

Since the eel was so incredibly long, Ellen knew it must be pretty old. The eel would also be female since members of its species begin life as males and change into females later. Ellen was tempted to swim after her, to glide alongside and find out what her mission might be. But it was time for their boat pick up and the eel had gone off in the opposite direction. She motioned to Ryan and pointed toward the open ocean to let him know it was time to go.

As they swam back toward the pick-up point, Ellen kept watching out for jellyfish. It would be a shame, not to mention a huge waste of time and effort if they never encountered any jellyfish at all on this research cruise. She couldn't let that happen. She couldn't let this cruise become a failure. There was too much to lose. At least there would be other dives. Then again, the lack of jellyfish could mean something.

CHAPTER 30

———— ∽ ————

Back on the ship, they rinsed out their gear even though they were scheduled to dive that afternoon. The afternoon dive would be in the ocean outside the lagoon. Ellen figured they would see some extensive coral formations. Hopefully jellyfish would be there too.

Too often, she felt the futility of conducting jellyfish population studies. It sometimes seemed similar to counting mosquitoes or flies in a backyard. Even if she could find and count them all as they flew around in their erratic zigzag patterns, it would still be impossible to be sure of the population in any area outside of that limited space of a backyard. If Ellen ever heard of anyone doing such a thing, she would laugh. Yet, isn't that what she was doing?

Of course, her purpose in life wasn't to count jellyfish. She wanted to study them. But the funding agencies were mostly interested in the numbers and so she tried to work her research in while counting them. Well, so far the counting had been easy: zero.

"I couldn't believe that eel," Ryan said as they finished rinsing out their gear. "I mean, that thing was huge. He was like a sea monster."

"It must have been pretty old since it was so huge, so I'm guessing it was female. Those eels start out as males and turn into females later in life."

"Wow. That's really weird."

Ellen nodded. "She could have been seventy or eighty years old. You can judge their age by their length. They can grow up to ten feet and live as long as a hundred years, maybe more."

"I wonder why they get to live so long."

"Maybe they've found a way to successfully adapt to their environment. After all, it's mostly environmental effects that kill us."

"I guess. Too bad there were no jellyfish out there though. Do you think that's because of some kind of an environmental effect?"

"I don't think so. Jellyfish are usually easier to see at night so hopefully we'll be luckier with the night dives. There probably should have been at least a few around, especially in a place like the lagoon. But you never know what you'll find when you go diving. Jellyfish can get tangled in fishing nets and since this is an inhabited island, that could be one reason for a lower population. Or maybe there's not really a low population here and they're just congregating in some other area. There's not much plankton around for them to feed on so that could be another reason."

"I hope we'll see some this afternoon. Imagine if we didn't see any for the whole cruise?"

"I've already imagined it. Then the paper would have to be on the lack of observed jellyfish populations."

"Not as exciting though."

"No, not at all."

And if that happened, she would probably have to find another job right after the cruise. She didn't have the heart to tell Ryan.

~⁹

After a quick shower, Ellen made her way to the lab. The sweaty air contained a tinge of exhilaration now that the research was underway. Wires twisted on endless journeys from the ceiling to pieces of equipment to power strips lining the counters. Researchers looked connected to their laptops while watching data stream in from sensors and remote cameras.

Handheld fans whirred in every conceivable space. Ellen moved through the heated gusts. Thomas Edison would be pleased. The air was filled with nothing but inspiration and perspiration.

Maddie slumped in the same position as the others, but her hands held her forehead as she leaned on the counter. Her forehead looked a little too heavy.

Ellen sat next to her. "What's wrong?"

"Oh, I don't know. I mean, nothing."

"Sounds real convincing." The smell of bubble gum made Ellen think of more carefree days as Maddie halfheartedly chewed.

"Every once in a while, I just think I have no idea what I'm doing here. You know? Do you ever feel like that?"

"All the time."

"But you always look like you know exactly what you're doing."

Ellen almost laughed but managed to hold it in. "The funny thing is I never feel that way. But you always look like you know what you're doing too."

"Yeah, right." Maddie rolled her eyes. "Now I know you're just fooling with me."

"No, I mean it. I'm willing to bet most of us think no one else has those same kinds of doubts, and the crazy thing is we all do. We all question ourselves and wonder what we're doing, if we're doing the right things, and what those right things even are."

"Most of the time though, you look so determined. Like you're chasing a dream and you're about to catch up with it."

Ellen smiled. "I hope we'll both catch up with those dreams, but the only way we're going to do that is to keep working at them."

"I guess you're right. Still, sometimes I think maybe I'm chasin' after the wrong dream here."

"That's what it always feels like. It's like searching through the dark with a tiny flashlight. You know everything's there in the dark somewhere, but you can never see all of it at once."

"That's exactly what it's like. Sometimes I can't see anything at all, even though it's right there in front of me."

"Sounds familiar."

"Well, I never would have thought it, but I'm glad you know what I mean. Believe it or not, sometimes I think I should go back home and marry that high school sweetheart of mine after all."

"I have those same kinds of thoughts too, about someone from graduate school."

"Really? Now that's funny. When I first met you, I thought we were so different. But I guess we're not after all now, are we?"

Ellen looked at the glossy red hair, the fresh face, the smile. Maddie glowed like a fiery sunset. Light eyes peeked through, fragments of sky holding onto the day. She recognized the excitement of discovery in those eyes.

"No, we're not so different."

She didn't think it could be true until she said the words. Then for some reason, they sounded right.

CHAPTER 31

E LLEN SOON FOUND herself flying over pink and orange coral mountains with Ryan by her side. Fish fluttered along with them, acting as escorts to their world while occasionally peering at them with a wary curiosity.

Life in all its shapes and sizes either darted by or peeped out of the reef. Ellen saw a tiny octopus hover over the coral. He searched out food by flopping down and converting his body into a tent to draw any organisms out and into his mouth.

Yellow fish packed together while dipping and diving and nibbling at the reef. Strangely, this was a good thing. The fish protect the reef by eating the seaweed that builds up there. If the fish didn't eat the seaweed, the coral would eventually die. While the fish help the coral in that way, the reef provides a home.

It was easy to get distracted with so much life and beauty waving all around. The fish breezed by, each group so colorful and graceful. Then the hypnotic beauty of the lacey, swaying soft coral took over and drew attention to all the life that hid in its shadows. Ellen found it easy to forget why she had entered this world and wished she could keep floating aimlessly through it.

A seal swam underneath her, close enough to touch. His whiskered face smiled for a second before he spiraled up to the surface. A smaller seal followed, spiraling in the same way. They kept spinning up in a slow motion dance. Then Ellen noticed a baby seal between them trying to mimic their movements. His parents looked proud and wouldn't let him out of their sight. The family mesmerized her as they swirled around her. They projected such a feeling of peace and happiness. She wanted to watch them forever.

Ryan looked like he could be in a trance brought on by the seals too. She motioned to him and swam off to the side, leaving the family to play together.

After swimming away for a while, an overturned rowboat came into view. Ellen couldn't help but wonder how it ended up there. She didn't see any holes or signs of damage that would make the boat sink.

A painting of a silver fish on the hull shimmered in the wavering light. It sparked her curiosity. If she could see what was under the boat, she might be able to figure out how it got there. A faint red glow seemed to emanate from somewhere underneath the hull.

She swam down to the rowboat, grabbed one side, and pulled up, but the weight of the water above held it in place. She looked around for Ryan and didn't see him anywhere.

A manta ray soared overhead. It decided not to make a landing and continued to flap away with the current while rippling its pancake body. Ellen abandoned the rowboat to look for Ryan.

With a few kicks, she flew off in the direction they had been headed toward. He wouldn't have gone far without her. He knew they were supposed to stay in each other's sights at all times. She kept swimming and searching and still couldn't see him. Everything felt suddenly colder without him there. Nothing but dark water surrounded her. It pressed in from all sides, causing a chill.

Yellow lights flashed up ahead. Ellen swam toward the lights and watched as they morphed into Ryan's kicking flippers. She wanted to hug those flippers and keep hanging onto them for the rest of the dive. Instead, she swam up closer and stayed by his side. At this depth, the sun streamed through the water as through a dusty windowpane. She stared into the murkiness while making sure not to lose Ryan again.

A huge shadow moved toward them, a shadow as large and looming as a whale. As it closed in, Ellen realized it was a school of gray reef sharks. They were young and small and packed close together for protection. They swam overhead and didn't bother them, but the shape of their torpedo bodies did look a little menacing. She glanced at Ryan and saw that he was looking toward them with some amount of panic. She probably should have told him not to worry too much about sharks.

The sharks were another sign that this was a healthy reef. The more diversity found around a reef, the better off it would be. If there were only smaller fish around, the reef wouldn't have as much of a chance. In this way, Ellen supposed, the sharks protect the reef in real life just as they do in the legends.

As she watched the reef sharks disappear into the blue, a jellyfish appeared off to the side. It looked like a Nomura, with a blood-orange, mushroom-shaped body trailing noodle-like tentacles. This one was small, about the size of her fist. They were known as the world's largest jellyfish and could grow up to six feet in diameter, with the largest one ever found weighing 450 pounds. On top of that, they were poisonous, with tentacles ready to sting any prey or humans who ventured too close.

Ellen waved her arms to attract Ryan while trying to remain in the same area without floating off on a stray current. Ryan looked up. She pointed to the jellyfish and beckoned to him to come closer. He took out his camera.

The Nomura scrunched up to suck water in, then pushed its tentacles out, propelling itself through the water. Ellen didn't see any others around and almost didn't want to take it.

Since their only catch so far turned out to be a plastic bag, they needed real jellyfish samples. She fumbled around for a jar from her collection bag. The jar had been fastened to the end of a stick so they wouldn't have to get too close to the stinging tentacles. Now she realized to be at a completely safe distance, the stick wasn't nearly long enough. She swam closer. It didn't seem to care that she hovered near.

While balancing in the water enough to get the sampling jar underneath the jellyfish, she made a swift upward motion to catch it but it propelled away. She swam closer to attempt the whole thing again, taking more precious moments to balance herself in the water. She managed to get the sampling jar in place and tried the upward motion. This time it worked. The jellyfish ended up in the jar, tentacles and all.

She clamped the top down as if it could be a grasshopper or firefly and she was eight years old again. A feeling of victory swept through her. She turned to Ryan. Hopefully he had finished taking pictures. She tucked the jar into the collection bag.

Lately, Nomura jellyfish had become famous for appearing in Japanese waters in annual swarms. The jellyfish in those swarms numbered into the millions and could stretch out over the ocean for hundreds of square miles. Fishermen caught so many in nets that their boats actually capsized from the weight.

The Nomura swarms off Japan had always been considered a rarity, occurring once every forty years. But recently the swarms started to appear every year. Jellyfish populations increase in warmer waters so climate change probably had something to do with it. Another reason could be increased pollution and more plankton for the jellyfish to eat. At the same time, overfishing reduces predators like sea turtles and swordfish. All of it contributes to the perfect scenario for huge Nomura invasions near Japan.

Ellen kept looking in all directions, hoping for a possible swarm. If there were larger Nomuras around, they wouldn't be able to fit in the sampling jars. She didn't want to encounter a 450-pound one, but another smaller one would be good to see. She decided to swim in the direction that the jellyfish had come from in case it had been part of a swarm. As she kicked through the water, she studied the wavering light shafts while expecting to see more jellyfish at any moment.

Nothing. Only one jellyfish after two dives. She let out a bubbling sigh. Why did she study something that was so hard to find? It was almost as if she unconsciously placed impossible hurdles or barriers on the path she had chosen.

She suddenly felt tired for always taking the difficult route, for continually challenging herself while others sailed happily and easily along. But then everyone must feel that way. Most people who didn't know any better would think of her life as the easy one since she was able to scuba dive in the South Pacific for work. If only they knew the aggravating truth of it all. Then she glanced over at Ryan swimming there next to her. Maybe some parts weren't so bad.

CHAPTER 32

A S SOON AS they were back aboard the research ship, Ellen took their one jellyfish sample to the lab. She wanted to freeze it right away so it would be preserved for a few days while they continued to dive.

Once the diving was over, there should be time to examine the tissue more thoroughly and do some DNA sequencing on it. She figured it must be a Nomura, but couldn't be completely sure until the tests either verified or proved otherwise. It was small, when its type was known for being so large, so it could be some other kind. She felt a little sorry for it as she placed it in the cooler and closed the lid.

While washing up, Ellen remembered how nice it had been to glide through the underwater world with Ryan by her side. His presence felt reassuring. She wondered if that was what marriage felt like. A constant presence. Someone who would always be there. A sudden uneasy feeling if that person wasn't around.

Not that she could ever have that kind of a relationship with anyone, especially Ryan. He was probably infatuated with Maddie by now anyway. Of course, she didn't know what his thoughts were. She didn't really know him. She couldn't look through his skin, the way she could with a jellyfish. She couldn't see whatever might be hiding inside. Not that it mattered.

Ellen dried her hands while realizing she still needed to rinse off the dive gear. She had been more concerned with her one jellyfish than anything else and had left it all in a heap in the storage room. As she reached the storage room, the door jerked open and Ryan stepped into the hallway.

"All set, everything's rinsed and put away."

"Thank you, I guess I owe you a dinner after all that."

"Sounds good. I'll go jump in the shower first."

"Yeah, me too," Ellen said. "Hopefully we'll run into the gorilla at dinner. We should go over some of the procedures for tomorrow's dives."

"Gorillas have to eat too. I'll look around and drag him in if I see him."

"Okay, thanks. By the way, I thought I lost you out there for a second."

"Weren't we together the whole time?"

"No, I stopped to look at an overturned rowboat and then couldn't find you for a little while."

"Really? I thought you were right behind me but I should have kept checking to make sure."

"We've got to remember to stay in sight of each other at all times when we're down there. Something could have been wrong. I could have been stuck somewhere instead of just looking at a rowboat."

"Sorry about that. I'll make sure to keep checking next time."

"Well, I should have stopped you from swimming but I was too distracted by the rowboat. It looked pretty mysterious sitting there on the seafloor."

"I wonder what happened to make it end up there."

"I didn't see any holes or signs of damage. If a storm or something like that put it there, it shouldn't have been so perfect looking. It's a mystery, I guess."

Back in her quarters, all Ellen really wanted to do was belly flop down on her bed and sleep. Visiting another world could be exhausting, especially when that world was so completely different from anything else. It had already started to seem like a dream, something felt much more than remembered, something that crept in at the edges of the real world. She tried to recall every detail, every color and feeling, even as it all began to fade away.

Dinner turned out to be some kind of chicken and some kind of eggplant, both looking suspiciously alike in their mushiness. Ellen chose the eggplant and took a salad for added crunchiness.

Ryan and Jake sat at a nearby table eating ferociously together. Ellen joined them, even if doing so risked being bombarded with food particles.

"No gorilla suit today?" She asked as she sat down.

"Nope, didn't have the energy. He'll make another appearance when you least expect it."

"Sounds scary."

"Yes, be afraid," Jake said as he sprayed some sauce in her direction. "So Ryan was saying you guys got a jellyfish today. Good job."

"Thanks. It would have been better to get more, but you can't always see them very well during the day. Too bad we're not scheduled for a night dive until tomorrow."

"I know what that's like," Jake said. "I've been studying salps."

"Really? Well then you know. They're even harder to see than jellyfish."

"Yeah, they're out there though. Want to know how many samples we got today?" He asked with a gorilla-like grin.

"I don't think you want to know," Ryan told her.

Ellen prepared herself. "Okay, how many?"

"Hundreds," Jake said with wide-open eyes as if telling a ghost story. "Give or take a few. So if you want some samples, the scientist I work for might give you some."

"Great, but I don't study salps."

"But why not? They're so much like jellyfish."

"Right, but they're not. They're more closely related to vertebrates."

"So salps, which look just like gelatinous, transparent jellyfish, are supposedly more closely related to us and so you don't study them?"

"That's right."

Jake laughed. "Are you sure you're not a little bit crazy?"

"Never said I wasn't," Ellen said while taking a bite of her food.

"Why are salps more closely related to us?" Ryan asked.

"At a certain stage in their development, salps have vertebrae," Ellen said. "It goes away as they develop and then they become more like jellyfish, but briefly they're more human."

"Cool," Ryan said. "It's like they're trying to figure out what to become."

"I know the feeling."

Ryan looked into her eyes, searching for something. Ellen turned toward Jake. "How did you catch so many?"

"Oh. We towed nets," Jake said. "At first there weren't that many but then we hit an area where there were tons."

"Where was that?"

"Pretty close to where you guys were today, maybe thirty meters to the south. But even though there were lots of salps, we didn't bring in any jellyfish."

Ellen figured that was good and bad. If they had brought in jellyfish she might have been able to convince the scientists to let her have a few samples, but then she'd be kicking herself for not being in the right area today. Mostly, it seemed to be bad news since they should have found at least a few jellyfish with those nets. The whole region should have more jellyfish than it seemed to so far.

"Why don't we tow nets to find jellyfish?" Ryan asked.

"Mostly because if we found any the nets would turn them into jellyfish soup. I'd rather find the kind of samples that stay in one piece."

"Right," said Jake. "Even salps are pretty fragile for net collection, but at least it can be a good way to get an idea of how many are out there and the different types that are there. But yeah, we don't end up with great or reliable samples."

Ellen nodded. "Besides, if we towed nets and found a Nomura swarm, they could weigh the nets down and make us capsize."

"Good thing we didn't find anything like that," Jake said as he shoveled more food into his mouth. "Other than the salps, all we caught was a little octopus. We let him go, he was so tiny."

"Isn't there anyone studying them around here?"

"Probably, but he was so tiny that I couldn't bring myself to take him."

"But salps are even tinier," Ellen said. "And they could be more important ecologically since they remove carbon and carbon dioxide from the surface waters."

"Well, that may be true but I wouldn't be able to bring myself to take larger animals. They're struggling to survive as it is. Then we come along and scoop them up and away. It doesn't seem right."

"So you don't think of salps in the same way as an octopus?"

"No, not really. Call me silly, but they don't seem the same to me."

"They can be pretty similar though. Salps are just smaller."

"Yeah, a lot smaller. Most of the ones we caught today were as big as the fingernail on my pinky. And there are more of them to go around."

"Let's hope so," Ellen said, smiling at him now.

"Oh come on, you can't make me feel guilty for taking *salps* of all things. You're the one taking jellyfish."

"Sounds like I did make you feel a little guilty. And we only took one jellyfish. How many salps did you say you took? Hundreds?"

"Wow, she's good," Jake said, glancing at Ryan. "She really turned that whole thing around."

"Yeah," Ryan said, "Told you."

"What's that supposed to mean?" Ellen held her forkful of food up as if it could be a weapon.

"Nothing," Ryan said. "I mean it in a good way. I only told him good things about you."

"Oh, of course." Ellen rolled her eyes. "Anyway, we should talk about the dives tomorrow."

"Back to business already?" Ryan asked.

"That's what we're here for after all."

"Wait, haven't we been talking business all along?" Jake asked.

"Impossible to tell, isn't it? Okay then, let's talk about the dives," Ellen said. "So Jake, you've been a safety before?"

"Yes, millions of times."

"Yeah, right. And how old are you?"

"Okay, more like ten times. But it seems like millions."

"You're going to take this seriously, right?"

Jake took a breath and tried to settle his grin down to a straighter line. "Of course."

"And you know that our lives will be depending on you?"

"Yes." This time he looked a little more serious. "Don't worry, I'll be professional and all that. You can ask around if you don't believe me."

"Okay, not that I don't believe you. So the scientist you work for doesn't mind that we're stealing you away for a while?"

"No, I told him I'd be on the lookout for salps while diving. But don't worry, I know the priority will be to act as safety."

"He's not going to expect you to collect them or anything, is he?"

"No, if I do see any I just want to study them to see if they're acting any differently in the open ocean around here than in the tanks, and to see how they interact with whatever else might be nearby."

"Okay, I guess," Ellen said even though she wasn't one hundred percent sure. She didn't want to end up drifting off into the ocean on some sudden current because Jake was busy watching salps. But then, she didn't have a choice at this point.

CHAPTER 33

———— ～ ————

RYAN WENT UP to get more food once Ellen retreated to the lab. The food looked sloppy and reminded him of home. His mom usually cooked meals like this when he was a kid, with all the ingredients blended together in a heaping mass of warmth. It was the kind of meal that kept cooking all through the afternoon while he'd be outside playing baseball or tag, the kind of meal that would make his mouth water as soon as he stepped into the house to smell the tomatoes and onions and green peppers all stewed together.

"So what do you think of Maddie?" Jake asked while plopping a mound onto his plate.

Ryan shrugged. "She's okay."

"Okay? She's gorgeous. Unfortunately though, we're too friendly for intimacy. We don't want to risk the friendship. That's what we say. So just a warning, don't get too friendly with her or you'll never stand a chance."

"That doesn't make any sense."

"I know, but neither do women. You must have figured that out by now at least."

"I'm sure some of them make sense."

"You might think they do, but that's just them fooling you. That's been my experience so far. Not that I've had nearly enough of these kinds of experiences. It's like with the whole friends thing, you try to be all charming and make them laugh and everything. Then you find yourself becoming friends and you think that's a good thing because the two of you are getting closer. But if you pass a certain friendship point where you're really good friends, forget it. Then you'll just be friends and that's it."

Ryan tried not to think of Ellen. But when they sat back down at the table, Jake started talking about her and so he found it impossible not to think about her.

"Now take Ellen on the other hand, she seems like one of the ones who might make sense. But then, no one has a chance with her anyway."

"What do you mean?"

Jake looked up from his food and grinned. "I don't know. She seems kind of tough or serious in a way, don't you think? She's a bit of a mystery. All she talks about is work, so then you can't really get to know her, just her work. Or maybe that's all there is to her. It's hard to tell."

"I guess. But then I don't know her all that well."

"Exactly. Think about what she studies, for one thing. Jellyfish are beautiful and lethal. That alone should serve as enough of a warning."

"She kind of reminds me of jellyfish in a way. Maybe because she seems fragile and not so fragile all at once. She'll go along with the current for a while, but then she'll suddenly turn and propel herself against it."

"See? That's what I'm talking about. That kind of thing can be pretty deceptive."

"She's not trying to be deceptive. I think she's just trying to hold herself together and figure everything out at the same time."

"You're just blinded by love or lust or whatever it is."

Ryan tried to laugh that one off. "Just because I want to help doesn't mean I'm in love with her or anything."

"Well, why do you want to help her then?"

"Because I work for her. I'm supposed to help her."

"Yeah but it seems to be going a little beyond helping in a work capacity. At least to me. But maybe I'm just crazy."

"Can't someone want to help someone else without having any ulterior motives?"

"If it's true that you have absolutely no ulterior motives whatsoever, then I'm impressed. You're a true boy scout. I didn't think there were any left these days."

"Come on, don't be so jaded. Of course there are boy scouts left. We just have to grow up at some point."

"I think I'd rather not grow up and remain jaded. That's what our generation's all about. That and apathy."

"That's not true. You care about things."

"Yes, unfortunately I suppose I do. Sometimes I care too much. Which is why at times it becomes necessary to put that gorilla suit on. Even in the tropics."

"Once again, you're not making any sense."

"Nothing makes sense. Might as well give up trying to make any sense at all. All I know is the gorilla is really going to have to sneak up on Ellen one of these days. Just to make sure she doesn't keep taking herself too seriously."

"Don't go giving her a heart attack or anything. I get the feeling she's not as tough as she seems."

"I'll try not to, but I can't make any guarantees. Once the suit goes on, the true animal in me comes out."

Once they finished eating, it was about time for the movie to start. Ryan decided to watch it with Jake since he didn't feel like reading and possibly letting his thoughts wander all over the place and back to Ellen.

He couldn't believe Jake had basically accused him of being in love with her, even if he had been sort of kidding. Hopefully he hadn't been going around acting like he could be in love or anything like that. He admired her and that was it. Jake just wanted to turn it into something else for his own entertainment.

As the colored lights flashed on the movie screen, Ryan forced himself to think of anything else. He imagined his sister working on a new creation glowing with purple and gray and yellow, all swirled together into something he couldn't figure out.

He loved every one of her paintings. They projected feelings more than anything else. Each one made him look at the world in different ways and gave him another insight into his sister, someone he already knew better than anyone. It made him think that maybe far in the future, people wouldn't use words to explain themselves, only thoughts, feelings, and paintings.

They never needed words when they were growing up together. They would play for hours with his trucks or Star Wars action figures. Sometimes they would climb trees or venture out onto the roof for fun. Whatever they found to do, they would end up doing it without the need for any discussion or figuring things out first.

Words, he discovered, were completely inadequate. They defined and limited things. People relied on them too much as a tool for understanding each other and when the tool itself is flawed, when you can never think of the right words to say, then the goal of understanding can never be accomplished.

It seemed much better to experience the feelings instead of having to express or explain them all the time. Maybe someday someone else would feel his feelings and understand. So far, that had only happened with his sister.

CHAPTER 34

A FTER HOURS OF lab work, Ellen discovered she could no longer see straight and ended up practically sleepwalking back to her quarters.

She collapsed onto her bunk. Soon too many thoughts started swimming through her head. They swam too fast, bounced off each other, and wouldn't let her sleep.

When she first stretched out under the scratchy blankets, she thought it would be nice to feel someone's arms around her while drifting off to sleep. She wasn't sure how long it had been since feeling anything like that. The months and years had a way of blending into each other as they sped on by.

She thought of Paul and all the love she'd felt for him back in the early days. She tried to go back in time while willing his arms to form out of the air or blankets, to imagine that feeling again and snuggle into it. She'd been happy with him, happier than she thought possible, until it all came crashing down.

Ellen wondered what her grandmother would have thought of him. Soon after her jellyfish book arrived in the mail, her grandmother died of a heart attack. Ellen never saw her again.

She remembered sitting in the car while her parents attended the funeral. She stayed out there in the freezing cold, letting her toes and fingers go numb, feeling more alone than ever. But she didn't want to go in and see her grandmother in a coffin. Anything was better than that. At least in her memories, she would always be sitting on a beach wearing a bright pink floppy hat, waving out to Ellen and watching her dive through the ocean waves on a perfect blue-sky day.

At the very least, she wished her grandmother could have lived to see the effects of her jellyfish book. Ellen imagined looking through the book with her, pointing at the pictures and showing their favorites to each other, even laughing at the more spectacular ones. She longed to tell her all she had learned. She wanted to tell her about her life, about Paul and her decision not to get married. Somehow, she would understand all of it.

Her grandmother was the only one who truly understood her. Ellen felt hollow without her. Hollowed out and empty and lost. All she wanted to do was to see her again, to hug her and laugh with her.

Life didn't make as much sense without her. And without her, Ellen drifted. She went through the motions of school and studying and lost herself in the ocean. She could see why the islanders wanted to believe the spirits of loved ones came back as butterflies. That thought was much better than feeling so alone.

Her parents were now around the age that her grandmother had been when she died. Ellen tried not to think about it. They wanted her to come home for Christmas. Ellen tried not to think about that. It would be hard to get away. With the timing of this research cruise, by Christmas there should be an overload of data to sift through. But she should go see her parents. She should find a way. Then again, if she didn't find more jellyfish or funding she might have to move back in with them.

Home. She hadn't lived in a real home since she moved away. Home made her think of Silver, her golden retriever. She named him after Long John Silver from *Treasure Island*. At the time, it was her favorite book. She read it to him often. Silver always perked up whenever he heard his name.

She still dreamt of Silver and tried to dream of him now. In her dreams, he always licked her face until she laughed and shrieked and fell over backwards.

Instead, an imaginary friend from around that time crept into her dreams. Irving the Giant used to pick her up while she played in the backyard, plop her on his shoulders, and show her the world. He always said he was preparing her for a life of adventure.

Her grandmother believed in Irving and even pretended to talk to him at times. Whenever Ellen visited, her grandmother would leave food outside for him because he was too big to fit in the house.

Now Irving lifted Ellen onto his shoulders like in the old days and together they flew out over the ocean. She could feel the wind on her face as she looked down over the turquoise surface with spreading fingers of indigo. All the shifting, whirling colors of the world spread out before them as they flew over the ocean and islands, mountains and jungles. Everything looked so vibrant and alive. She felt a surge of love for the world.

In the distance, a dark red patch covered the ocean surface and started to pulse.

CHAPTER 35

B LUE-WATER DIVES STILL scared her. The seafloor couldn't be seen in a blue-water dive. It usually felt wrong and disorienting with nothing but water everywhere.

Even though they'd be going about one hundred feet down, they wouldn't see a hint of the seafloor on this dive. While Ellen had never drifted in outer space, she figured an astronaut must feel about the same as she did on blue-water dives.

The designated safety held the tethers connecting divers to the outside world. He kept track of their depth and would bring them up slowly if they encountered any problems. Since this role was such an important one it wasn't normally filled by someone who liked to joke around and wear a gorilla suit.

Night diving could be even more dangerous. Everything would be dark except for the bioluminescence in the animals and the water. It would be much easier to get lost in the black water than the blue. So in a way, the morning blue-water dive would be a test for their new safety diver. Ellen hoped he wouldn't fail.

She changed into her bathing suit and wet suit and walked down to the storage area. Ryan was there in his wet suit checking the air tanks. His hair still looked damp from his shower and it stuck to his forehead as he concentrated.

"Anything I can do to help?" Ellen asked.

"Nope, all set. We're ready to go."

"Great, looks like we're a little too early for our early morning dive. Where's Jake?"

"He'll be here."

"Did you see him at breakfast or anything?"

"Nope, but he'll be here."

Just as Ryan finished talking, Jake appeared with his scuba gear.

"We're okay to go," he said with his gorilla-like grin.

"In that case, I'm going to grab something quick for breakfast before the boat shows up," Ellen said while doing a fast trot down to the galley.

It wouldn't do for her to throw the whole boat schedule off for the rest of the day by being late, but she couldn't imagine waiting until after the dive to eat either. She rarely ate breakfast. All this diving must be making her hungry.

She hurried in and grabbed a chocolate chip muffin. Hopefully the chocolate bits would provide extra energy. She bit into the muffin while walking back to Ryan and Jake and was licking her fingers by the time she joined them again.

"Wow, that really was a quick breakfast," Ryan said. "Probably about a minute."

"Did you time it with your dive watch?"

"No, of course not, these things aren't toys. But that was definitely a minute, and not a minute more. I bet you even beat some world record somewhere."

"I doubt it," Ellen said. "I used to try to beat those world records when I was a kid just for the chance at being famous. I never could do it, so I gave up on all that fame and fortune stuff. If it hasn't happened yet, it's never going to happen."

"Which world records did you try to beat?"

"Oh, I don't know. Pogo stick bouncing, longest amount of time roller skating, that kind of thing."

"That's so funny, I can't imagine you doing all that stuff," Jake said. "You should have tried being the youngest scuba diver or the youngest person to stay under water for the longest amount of time or something."

"I didn't really start scuba diving until later. Anyway, I'm sure some parent somewhere brought their baby scuba diving. Can't beat that."

"I guess," Ryan said. "But you never know. You could still be famous someday."

"Yeah sure," Ellen said as their boat pulled up. "I've given up on all that by now. Now all I really want to do is learn as much as I can about jellyfish."

"But you've learned so much already."

"I haven't learned enough. I'll probably never learn enough."

Ellen piled her gear into the little boat and jumped in, ready to search through more of the great blue unknown. Once they were all in, their driver swung everyone around toward the open ocean. The boat bounced higher and harder on the waves. They held onto anything that seemed stable to keep from bouncing out.

After zooming away from the hulking research ship and any possibility of land, they arrived at their destination: a bobbing buoy planted in a field of waves. This served as a marker for their boat driver. The dive site had been chosen because they knew the ocean depth was approximately 600 feet or 183 meters at this location.

Jake brought out the safety lines and connected Ryan and Ellen. Ellen yanked her flippers on, adjusted her air tank, weight belt, and collection bag, and put in her regulator. The others did the same, then pulled on their masks and gloves before jumping into the waves. Jake stayed in the middle so that they were each tethered off to one side. The idea was to form a triangle. They made an attempt while the currents pushed and pulled.

According to the dive plan, they wanted to get down to one hundred feet. Ellen didn't want to waste any time. Their triangle began to sink down, with Jake always above and Ryan off to her side. As they descended, the water turned from sky blue to light green to emerald, then a darker and darker blue. Ellen kept checking her depth gauge. Most divers can only venture down to about 130 feet without some kind of submersible or special diving suit to protect them from the extreme ocean pressure. That pressure could make anything not built for it, like a human body, implode.

Ellen couldn't help thinking about the weight of the water as it increased over her head. When considering the entire surface of her body, with every foot they descended an added load of almost half a ton pressed down. As they dove deeper, they had to make sure their air pressure automatically increased so that they would be, in a way, inflated with enough compressed air to offset the increase in pressure. With numbers like that, plus the threat of getting the bends if they returned to the surface too quickly, Ellen wanted to make sure they wouldn't go below one hundred feet.

The whole thing was far from natural for humans. When breathing compressed air, nitrogen and other gases entering the lungs dissolve in the blood and tissues. Just the thought of what the bends really is – gases bubbling up in your blood – was enough to make Ellen consider staying in the lab and never leaving. But if she did that, she wouldn't be able to observe jellyfish in their natural state.

Now that she had gone diving hundreds of times, it seemed worth the risk. Scuba diving allowed her to become part of the jellyfish's world. Besides, there was no real risk of getting the bends as long as they made frequent safety stops on the way back up to the surface.

At twenty feet, pain stabbed her ears. She swallowed over and over again. The pain was the same kind that happened on airplanes because of the change in pressure. She kept swallowing and felt the pain ease away.

She knew there were more, perhaps many more, strange and exotic species below their search area. She felt so limited while considering that the ocean is 35,800 feet or about seven miles at its deepest point. Yet, they could only descend through a tiny portion of that great expanse without a submersible built for such depths and even that could be risky.

Ellen looked off to the side as they swam down in case she might happen upon a stray jellyfish. She didn't see any but figured the real investigating would be during the slower trip back to the surface. Distant shadows loomed here and there. The shadows turned into large fish as they slithered closer. Some stared, trying to figure out what type of fish she might be.

Finally at close to one hundred feet she stopped and motioned for Ryan to do the same. She looked up toward Jake and saw that he had stopped too. They searched through the gloom. Now that they weren't moving as much, more curious fish came up to them. One large gray fish banged his head against her mask. She couldn't tell if it was a sign of aggression or the way this particular type of fish said hello.

Ryan looked as gray as the fish. At this depth, most colors turned into gray or blue. He became a shadow while pointing off into the watery distance.

Ellen swam closer to see a dark gray blob propelling itself through the water. She struggled with her camera while following the blob. It turned out to be a jellyfish. She took pictures while Ryan shined his flashlight. Then she put the camera away, opened the collection bag, and grabbed a sampling jar. Every simple action took quadruple the amount of time as on land. She readied the sampling jar, then looked up and couldn't find the jellyfish anywhere.

Ryan pointed into the distance again to show her where it had gone. All she could see was dark blue water. The jellyfish had propelled too far away. She didn't want to go after it and risk getting everyone tangled in the safety lines, so she waved it off to let Ryan know they'd be giving up on that one.

She put the sampling jar back in the collection bag and gave Ryan the thumbs-up sign to show it was time to move up a little for now. She slowly swam up and to the side, hoping they'd double their chances of finding anything if they were a little farther apart.

Ellen stopped after ascending fifteen feet. She looked up and saw that Jake had also stopped or else she had forced him into it when he felt the tug on the line. As long as they had to perform this safety stop, she stared off to the side.

She was so distracted by the eerie darkness surrounding her that a jellyfish swam right by before she actually saw it. This one was semi-translucent. At least she had that excuse for letting it sneak up on her like that. Out of the water, it might be pink but in the shafts of gray light it also looked gray and practically invisible.

Ellen motioned to Ryan to take pictures while she tried to get the sampling jar out. She grabbed an empty jar, then fumbled while trying to open it with her gloves on, dropped it, but caught it just in time before it started making its way down to a seafloor that couldn't be seen.

With a few kicks, she glided over to the jellyfish. She looked at Ryan to make sure he'd taken enough pictures. He nodded. She put the sampling jar underneath the jellyfish and tried to bring it up swiftly, but like usual the water made her arm travel slower than intended and the jellyfish propelled itself away with one thrust. She followed while the jellyfish kept propelling away. Finally, she swept her arm up and the jellyfish stayed in the jar. She felt like cheering but the water made showing any emotion difficult so she kept the cheer inside.

Ryan gave her an "okay" sign so maybe he was cheering inside too. Ellen added the jar to the collection bag around her waist and drew it closed.

She looked off into the dark water again and didn't see any other nearly invisible jellyfish so she gave Ryan the sign to let him know they might as well swim up a little more. She checked her air. She still had plenty, which was good since they had to keep making safety stops. She forced herself to take long, slow breaths so that less air would be used just in case.

On their trip back to the surface, they found and caught two more: a small comb jellyfish and a dark gray one. Ellen kept checking her depth to make sure they wouldn't ascend more than thirty feet or nine meters per minute. She noticed that Jake's pace above them seemed in line with that rule so she forced herself not to worry.

At about fifteen feet, Jake stopped for the final safety stop. They'd have to stay at this depth for at least three minutes to let their bodies adjust to the change in pressure. She tried to relax and looked into the now light blue. Sunlight filtered through the water, creating a welcoming glow. There were plenty of fish flitting around, but no more jellyfish that she could see.

Once the team surfaced, Ellen couldn't find the buoy and dive flag marking their pick-up spot. She inflated her vest, took the regulator out, and pulled off her mask in an effort to see more clearly, but still nothing. Nothing but mounting waves and water. No land and no slimy buoy and no boat.

They couldn't be that far off course. They had only gone straight down and back up again while barely swimming off to the side. Did a current sweep them away somewhere? Ellen felt her heart begin to thud. Compared to the ocean, they were nothing. Worthless dots. Specks on a wave. Without the buoy, no one would ever be able to find them.

She did a full circle while treading water, then finally saw the buoy bouncing and hiding between the waves. She exhaled and tried to laugh it off.

"Good thing the buoy's there, since the boat's not," she told Ryan and Jake. "We might need to hang onto it for a while so we won't drift away."

Ellen checked her watch. The boat should have arrived by now. She started thinking this could be the wrong buoy, but told herself not to panic again. Of course this was the right buoy. It had to be. There probably wasn't another one around for miles. The currents couldn't have taken them that far off course.

Her arms and legs felt like rubber. Still, she forced them into doing the crawl over to the buoy. It was so much easier swimming under water than on the surface. For one thing, there were no waves to splash in her face. But it was more than that. The underwater world was more peaceful and graceful and somehow made more sense. It even made Ellen feel graceful and she never felt that way on land. She missed being in that place already, a place where a couple kicks can send you flying.

"So no boat?" Ryan asked as he reached for the buoy.

"Not yet, anyway."

Ellen kept trying to find a place on the slimy buoy to hold onto while sliding back into the water.

"What do we do if it doesn't show up?" Jake asked.

She let out a nervous laugh. "It'll show up. Don't worry."

Both Ryan and Jake looked worried anyway. Ellen turned in the direction where land should be and couldn't see anything but ocean and sky. The boat was only a few minutes late, but the panic started to creep back up again.

She kicked her legs and sensed the expanse of ocean everywhere. It radiated out from that one point for too long in too many directions. They were specks clinging to a slightly larger speck and they could easily be lost and forgotten.

CHAPTER 36

WHEN ELLEN SAW the boat speed toward them, she thought it must be a mirage. Even as it zoomed closer and closer, she kept a firm hold on the buoy just in case. The line between ocean and sky had been doing funny things, wavering with heat and wind, and she wouldn't have been surprised if the boat did turn out to be a mirage even as it motored up beside them.

She had already convinced herself that it must not be real by the time Ryan started talking to it with an indignant, "What took you so long?"

"Sorry." The driver shrugged. "We're already behind schedule."

"That's it? That's the reason we've been clinging to this buoy for the last twenty minutes?"

"Well, one scientist is a few minutes late, then another is a few minutes late, then before you know it we're all behind schedule."

"Funny how you're the one who's late but it's the fault of the scientists," Ellen said.

The driver looked at her with a blank expression, then produced a phony smile.

"Yeah, that is funny. Funny but true. Now are you ready? We wouldn't want to throw the schedule off even more."

"No, I think I'd like to hang onto this slimy buoy for a few more minutes." Ellen reached over to the boat and attempted to throw her equipment into it.

Ryan paddled over to help. Together they lifted everything into the boat without much help from the driver. She helped Ryan and Jake with their gear, then hoisted herself up with tired rubber arms and a frenzied kicking for extra lift. After scrambling in, she collapsed for a full second before bending down to pull Ryan and Jake out of the water.

Once they were all aboard, the driver punched the accelerator, almost giving them whiplash on top of everything else. Ellen's neck already felt rubberized along with her arms and legs so it didn't matter. She looked at Ryan, then at Jake. They seemed to commiserate with their tired eyes and slumping bodies.

"So we got three this time," Jake said. "That's an improvement."

"Yeah, kind of pathetic but still an improvement." Ellen looked down at the bag with their catch. The first thing she noticed was that the gray one wasn't gray at all, but a dark purplish red. The depth had obscured the color. She had never seen anything like it and wondered what species it might be. She made a mental note to check through her books and computer once they got back to the ship.

"Don't worry, I'm sure it'll keep on improving," Ryan said while slumping further into his seat.

"We should see more at night anyway," she said. "You never know, but hopefully we will."

The sun sucked all the remaining moisture away, leaving Ellen with tight, salt-drenched skin. Sampling jars clinked together with every lurch of the boat.

These jellyfish were varied at least: the strange purplish red one, a tiny comb jelly, and a light pink, almost translucent jellyfish that practically filled the entire jar. She stared at the purplish red jellyfish while the boat spastically bounced over the waves. This time she didn't have the energy to hold onto anything stable. She closed her eyes and let the motion jolt her gelatinous body in all possible directions.

Once the driver dropped them off at the research ship, Ellen brought the jellyfish samples to the lab to preserve them. She recorded descriptions of each along with the location and depth where they were found. She wanted to linger and study them some more, but needed to rest before the night dive. Maybe later this afternoon, she thought as she closed the cooler lid on her samples.

Although it was still technically morning, when Ellen opened the door and saw her bed, it felt like it had been days since she'd last been there. She peeled herself out of her wet suit and bathing suit, put on a t-shirt, then flopped down and drifted into underwater dreams filled with colors and wavy light.

She woke up starving. She looked at her dive watch, surprised that she still had it on, and saw that it was already late afternoon. Maybe there would still be some lunch scraps left. She forced herself to get up and into a hot shower.

The mess deck was mostly empty but a few researchers trickled in here and there. Everyone worked strange hours on the ship. Most were probably out on dives or taking part in experiments directly from the deck. Others needed to monitor data or equipment at all hours and took separate around-the-clock shifts.

Ellen wandered over to see what choices might be left at this late lunch hour. Everything had developed a crust around the edges from sitting under heat lamps. She chose a salad and brought it back to the clustered empty tables.

Her salad tasted a little warm but still crunchy enough. She crunched a few times before noticing Michael up in line. He walked over with his tray and sat down across from her.

"Hey, how's it going?"

"Great," Ellen said. "Just sitting here falling asleep. And you?"

"About the same. Those dives can be pretty exhausting."

"I wonder if it's because of the physical reasons or if it's more because everything's so different under water, then when we come back up everything's different again so it's a bit of a shock."

"So the thing that makes us tired is being back up here?"

"I think so. I just get used to being in such a dreamland and then when we come back up out of the water, I don't want to fully wake up."

"I guess I know what you mean," Michael said. "So when's your next dive?"

"Not until 7 tonight so I should be able to get some time in the lab first. When's yours?"

"At about 5. If we're lucky, we might get to see the shift change when some fish leave the coral to go out at night and others come back to their vacated spots to sleep."

"Do you study that kind of thing?"

"No, but it would be cool to see."

"That's true. It's as if they all have a predetermined under-standing or something."

"Apparently, they go back to the same places when it's time to sleep, and sometimes one might have to wake the other up if he doesn't vacate his spot in time. So they definitely have some kind of an understanding. It would be a chance to see the various kinds of sea life around here that use the coral for a home anyway. I suppose there could be a paper in it. But mostly, we're just go-ing to take samples of the coral."

"That's what I'm trying to do with the jellyfish. So far I've gotten four."

Michael's laugh filled the empty dining area. "You're on a roll. I'm sure you'll see more tonight though."

"I hope so. We took pictures but tonight we'll try to film some. If we can find them, that is."

"I love night diving. For fun, not so much for work."

"I should really go on more of them since you can see jellyfish more at night and everything, but I still feel strange about them."

"Why? Talk about relaxing, with everything dark and the bioluminescence everywhere, even just from moving your arms around. It's like being surrounded by stardust."

"Yeah, I guess I just feel like the night dives are much more dangerous."

"They probably are."

"Thanks, now I'll be paranoid tonight."

"Well, it sounds like you already were. So do you have your irrefutable climate change proof yet?"

Ellen rolled her eyes. "I'm working on it. Maybe I'll find some during the dive."

"I doubt it but good luck."

"Why are you so convinced it's not true?"

"I'm not convinced either way, really. I just don't think we can say definitively one way or the other yet."

"Not until the oceans start boiling?"

"Right. Well, that would certainly be proof of a warmer climate, but still not proof that humans are causing it."

"And the fact that this last decade was the warmest on record and that the average global temperature has been increasing more dramatically since the Industrial Revolution isn't proof enough?"

"The warmest on record sounds pretty scary until you realize that we hadn't been recording these things until the 1800s, which isn't that far back on a global time scale. We need long-term datasets to really look at change."

"But even if the temperatures weren't officially recorded until then, we still have a general idea of temperatures from tree rings and ice core and seafloor samples reaching back thousands of years."

"Yes, but this decade wasn't warmer than the Pliocene era."

"Not yet, but it's getting there."

Michael shook his head with a chuckle. "Why are you so convinced?"

"Look around. There are signs everywhere. But we're choosing to ignore all the signs because it's easier that way, and less troubling. Meanwhile, the Earth needs us to listen and we're not listening."

"Oh, okay," Michael said, still chuckling. "Just get me that proof and then I'll listen."

～

Later in the lab, while taking the jellyfish samples out of the cooler, Ellen's thoughts circled back to her conversation with Michael.

How could he sit back and laugh at these warning signs as if they didn't matter? It was amazing that he studied coral of all things and still didn't fully believe in climate change when coral bleaching was one of the major signs that something was wrong. If he can continue to push the thought away, then anyone who's not in the midst of studying these things would easily be able to do the same.

How ironic that we're irrevocably changing the Earth because it's easier to believe that we're not. And by the time we are able to definitively prove it, it'll be too late. The whole idea frustrated her so much that she didn't want to think about it anymore.

Ellen took out the mystifying jellyfish sample, the purplish red one. She flipped through the few books she brought on the cruise and didn't see any species it resembled. There were similarities but then there would always be something that made it different from the descriptions. A DNA test would be the only way to accurately identify it.

She took a tissue sample from the jellyfish and put it in a test tube, then added reagents to break up the cells. The cells basically had to be destroyed so that she could get the DNA out from the nucleus. The reagents would digest the cell and eventually leave the DNA to be examined.

Ellen placed the test tube in a warm water bath to help speed the reaction along, figuring she'd need to leave it there overnight to give it enough time. Then she pulled out the other jellyfish, extracted tissue samples, mixed in the reagents, and placed those test tubes into the water bath.

After doing all this, Ellen thankfully wasn't thinking about climate change anymore, only jellyfish. While examining the samples, she couldn't believe how simplistic jellyfish seemed at first glance, yet she knew they were far from it, and at the same time she felt as if there could be something more about them that she would never fully understand.

CHAPTER 37

R YAN FELT JUMPY with nervous energy. He went out on deck for some air but the heat only made him sweat more. He'd never been on a night dive. Hopefully he wouldn't screw anything up. At least Jake would be the safety diver. Then someone else would be there to make sure nothing went wrong.

The deck intensified the heat. He felt like a hamburger sizzling on a grill. His t-shirt became soaked with sweat and hung there like a wet towel. He lifted it up a little and tried to shake it dry.

Maddie trotted up beside him. She looked good in her tight white tank top. A stray breeze ruffled her gray cotton shorts, bringing them up a little higher.

"Hey there, sailor," she sang out.

"Hi." He leaned on the railing and looked out at the horizon. Maddie took that as an invitation and sprawled her arms out next to him.

"So what have you been up to lately?"

"Mostly just going out on dives," Ryan said. "We're trying to cram in as many as possible. We're supposed to go on a night dive in a few more hours."

"Lucky. I love the night dives. We'll be leaving for another dive soon but we'll be back before it gets too dark. I think we'll be doing a night dive tomorrow though. It's so interesting to see the coral when they come out at night to feed. Normally during the day they stay hidden there under that hard outer layer that they create and keep building up. But at night we get to see everything they usually keep hidden. Their true selves."

"That's pretty cool."

Maddie leaned a little closer. Ryan glanced over to see the lacey edge of her bra cupping a perfect breast. He looked back out toward the waves.

"So what do you want out of life?" Maddie suddenly asked.

"Good question. I don't know. To keep having fun, I guess. Maybe keep going on adventures like this."

The sun slipped behind a cloud and Maddie's hair took on the deeper red of a stop sign. Her eyes shimmered with green lights.

"Yeah, me too," she said. "But I do wonder if it would keep feeling like an adventure if we did this kind of thing all the time, you know? It might start to feel a little routine after a while, but I hope not. I'd love to keep doing this for my whole entire life. I want to be just like Ellen."

"Really? Why?"

"She has the perfect life, that's all. Don't you think so? Now, I know her work is really her life and all that, but I want to be like that too. I want to completely put myself into my work and make some great discovery someday. Something that will help everyone understand the world better. I never want to get married either. Anything like that would only end up getting in the way of everything."

"Do you think that's why she's not married?"

"Either that or she hasn't found the right one yet, if there even is such a thing. But I'd bet it's really just because she loves her work more than anything else. And always will. There are so few women scientists out there but plenty of female students, and do you know why? It's because they end up getting married and having children and at some point the family life completely takes over. At least Ellen didn't do that. I can't imagine her ever doing that."

"Yeah, but working all the time doesn't sound like such a great way to live to me. Wouldn't it be better to find someone to really love?"

"Oh, so you're one of those romantics, eh? I might have known."

Ryan shrugged and laughed it off. There was no way to express it in words, but he knew the only way to find true happiness was to love someone, to love fully with your whole heart. There was power in that. Not that he had ever experienced it. Still, he knew.

CHAPTER 38

━━━━━ ∿ ━━━━━

A T DUSK, ELLEN, Ryan, and Jake climbed into the inflatable boat that would take them to their night dive. The purple light brought a soft edge to the sloshing water and the droning research ship. While everyone readied their equipment, their voices stayed as soft as the light.

Ellen's gaze rested on the underwater movie camera. Now that she had a few samples tucked away in the lab, she wanted to concentrate more on filming than capturing. Then she could investigate exactly how jellyfish balance their food-energy resources.

She'd always admired their openness as they inhaled deep gulps of their surroundings. After breathing it all in, they'd basically exhale, causing water to shoot out. That action would propel them forward while catching food particles inside their bodies. In this way, they swim and eat at the same time.

She wanted to look deeper into all of it, to see what the subtle differences could be between various species, and to find out if some species are better swimmers than eaters, if some purposely swim more so they can eat more, or if they sacrifice swimming for eating or vice versa. In order to study all that, the jellyfish would be more valuable to her on film than frozen in a lab.

Ryan planned to take pictures while she filmed the jellyfish. Jake would act as safety again, this time from the boat, since they wouldn't be diving down as far.

While they gathered their gear together, Ellen watched the clouds swallow the last of the purple light. Soon they wouldn't have to venture into the water to find total darkness.

Ellen made sure she had her dive light tethered to her belt. They went over the hand signals together: moving the light in a circle meant "okay," up and down meant "yes," and moving it from side to side meant "no." If they wanted to say anything other than that, they'd have to figure out another way to communicate.

Jake checked the strobe light he'd be using to signal the divers so they'd know the boat location at all times.

"If this light would only turn on and off a little faster, we could do a disco dance out here before the dive."

"Like you remember disco," Ellen said.

"Well, no, but I read all about it in history books and saw it in action in classic movies like Saturday Night Fever. Don't tell me you remember dancing around like John Travolta."

"Not really, I wasn't old enough for that kind of thing when the movie came out. Believe it or not, I'm not as old as I might seem."

"Everyone thinks they're old until they look back and realize how young they were," Ryan said.

The last thing Ellen wanted to do was sit there and argue about how old she was. Thankfully, Jake turned the strobe light on and started singing "Stayin' Alive."

"See? I remember disco. I'd love to be able to go back in time just to attempt a few of those dance moves."

"If I could go back in time, I'd want to go to a better decade than the 70s," Ryan said. "Maybe the 1920s or the 1800s before cars. It would be fun to have to use a horse to get around."

"I think I'd want to go back and fix a few things in my own life first," Ellen said.

"Like what?" Ryan asked. "What would you want to fix?"

Ellen looked across the water at the darkening sky. "There's not enough time in the day for that one. Okay, let's make sure we've got everything all together while we still have a little light left."

Everything looked good to go. They strapped their weight belts and masks on, put their regulators in, and dove feet first into darkness.

Ellen immediately felt glad for the chance to leave that conversation and enter the silent black water. It swallowed her up and made her feel as if nothing else mattered.

She switched her dive light on and Ryan did the same. They had to stay near each other's light so they wouldn't get completely lost or tangled up in the dark. But then, light could be found everywhere. She waved her arm and watched the bioluminescence leave a trail of stardust.

She breathed deeper and sank farther into the unknown. Speckled lights darted by, as if falling stars or comets surrounded them.

Ellen readied the video camera and began taping right away. She motioned to Ryan so that he'd shine his dive light toward the bioluminescence. When he did, she saw that they were cteno-phores or comb jellies.

Ryan swam closer so that she could see the tiny rows of cilia beating along the mostly translucent oval-shaped bodies. She watched as the bristly cilia acted as paddles to push these types of jellies through the water. The light and the movement caused a diffraction pattern, resulting in flickering rainbows running down their sides.

Ellen zoomed in on a comb jelly to see the cilia up close. The entire organism was only a couple inches long but the camera magnified everything. Its bioluminescence gave off a slight blue-green glow. The comb jelly looked incredibly detailed and beau-tiful and fragile. It reminded Ellen of a soap bubble and made her think of electricity, as if she could see lightning or life flashing on inside.

She followed it as long as she could and then zoomed in on another one. It acted the same but she might find subtle dif-ferences after studying the film. She wanted to film as many as possible to determine what the differences might be, if any. There certainly seemed to be enough around. Their glow moved everywhere.

Swarms like this could be surrounding them all the time. Most blended in all too well until it became dark enough for their bioluminescence to give them away. How silly it would be if she kept searching for what constantly surrounded her. All she needed was a change in perspective in order to see what was actually there. What else might be around that they couldn't see? How many other things did they think they understood but didn't understand at all?

It amazed Ellen that ctenophores encompassed about 150 known species within the world's oceans. Some were so small that they were considered plankton while others were known to reach up to a meter in size. They didn't have stinging cells and relied on sticky secretions to catch their food.

Some species lived symbiotically with plants and animals on the seafloor while exhibiting the same color so that a pink or orange sponge or starfish would support pink or orange ctenophores. They were so varied, yet they all relied on rainbow rows of beating cilia for swimming.

Which reminded her, she really wanted to record the more common jet propulsion method on film. Technically, ctenophores weren't even true jellyfish. She stopped filming the comb jellies and searched through the darkness for larger displays of bioluminescence. Ryan saw that she had stopped filming and swung his light toward her. She gave him the thumbs-down sign to show she wanted to dive down farther. He followed her into the gloom while holding her within his light.

They didn't have to go far before Ellen saw the glow of larger jellyfish. They all looked transparent but some gave off a bluer hue than others. Ryan started taking pictures. The jellyfish sucked water in and expelled it. Ellen watched for a few minutes before remembering to use the green dye to pick up the details on film.

She reached for the squeeze bottle attached to her belt and readied the video camera while knowing she'd only have a few seconds to film everything.

Ryan steadied his spotlight on a jellyfish. Ellen began filming, then reached out with her other hand to squirt the dye. The dye was harmless but would help to show the mechanisms going on inside the transparent animal during jet propulsion.

The jellyfish sucked the dye in and Ellen watched the fluorescent green get swallowed up. She could see the dye travel through its body until it contracted and pushed the glowing green out. Hopefully this would look as good on film as it did in person.

Once the jellyfish propelled away, she found others to film. She tried to make sure to get the ones with that extra hint of blue in addition to the ones that gave off a whiter light while capturing different sizes on film.

As she watched and filmed, she felt the amazement grow within her, that amazement that came through whenever she observed life in all its forms and sizes and colors. Here is an animal hidden within the sea, pulsing with life and light. It is its own entity, yet it is part of the ocean, while all other species living within the ocean are also part of it. The ocean hummed with life. So many forms of life, so much variety, there was so much life everywhere creeping and crawling, swimming and flying. Ellen could only watch and wonder.

She checked her air and realized their time was almost up. It all went by too fast, but luckily they had captured several types on film. She motioned to Ryan that they should start heading back up. They took their time floating through the darkness.

Ellen didn't want to leave the jellyfish. While surrounding her with light, they had become like friends in some strange way. She regretted leaving their glow behind. But then once she and Ryan broke through the surface, there were stars to surround them instead, their distant lights forming obscure patterns in the sky.

They saw the light from the boat as they surfaced. Then Jake turned the dive light directly in their faces so it was all they could see. They blinked and tried to adjust their eyes as they swam toward the brightness.

Jake reached down to help them onto the boat. When they were all settled, he turned the light off so they could once again see the stars.

"How'd it go?"

"Really well," Ellen said while pulling her mask off. "We filmed all kinds of jellyfish, comb jellies, and took lots of pictures but you never really know until you look it all over."

"At least you could find them this time."

"That's true, and since we used up a lot of film, according to the law of averages we should have a few good shots. Maybe even something better than that."

"I'm glad to hear you've progressed from your one jellyfish."

"Too bad any real progress is always so slow. We should have been doing the night dives all along. The bioluminescent animals are much easier to see."

"Did you see any salps?" Jake asked.

"Now that you mention it, yes. We might have even filmed a few."

"Really?"

"Really. Have you studied the way they propel themselves through the water?"

"Are you kidding me? That's what my thesis is on."

"Well then, you might be interested in some of our film." Ellen turned to Ryan. "Think we should give him full access to it?"

"Sure." Ryan sounded like he might be in some kind of a trance.

"Are you okay?" Ellen asked.

He took a breath while looking like he wasn't sure what to say.

"I just can't believe how peaceful it was down there. It's so different at night, so much more mystical. And now here we are somehow sitting on top of it all with the stars all around us."

They looked up at the stars. There were so many more than they could ever see at home, so many that there could be more light than dark. Ellen realized ancient people would have seen stars like this. Free from the haze of modern cities, they would have felt closer to the light. No wonder the ancients thought the stars held all the answers. Maybe they did, maybe they still do, yet the modern world makes them difficult to see.

Ocean Echoes

As their boat puttered back to the research ship, they sat in silence while watching the stars above and the trail of bioluminescent light streaming through the dark mysteries in their wake below.

CHAPTER 39

I N THE LAB before sunrise, Ellen returned to the purplish red jellyfish. She searched through her books and laptop again while trying to find anything remotely like it anywhere.

It wasn't just the color that set it apart. Dark red or purple could be common colors for jellyfish, especially when found at greater depths. It was the structure of the organism that mystified her more than anything. It seemed much more sponge-like than most jellyfish, but it wasn't a sponge. It wasn't a sea squirt either. Excitement prickled at the thought that this could be a new species.

Of course, there were so many species in the world, and so many as yet undiscovered, that a new species of microbe or fungi or bacteria could be found living out in anyone's backyard. Research missions found new species all the time; especially when they ventured with submersibles or remotely operated vehicles into the deepest areas of the ocean. She told herself all this, yet she still felt the excitement creep in beneath her skin.

Ellen took the sample from the warm water bath and began a series of reactions to further isolate the DNA. She needed a pure DNA sample that could eventually be fed into a computer to determine its genetic makeup.

Unfortunately, everything had to be done in stages. She wanted an answer right away but instead had to mix and agitate different compounds and wait for reactions.

Her thoughts shifted to Michael and she consequently began to feel agitated as she mixed and stirred. Why had she agreed to prove the existence of climate change, human caused or otherwise? Obviously, she had more important things to do. Yet she still felt compelled to prove it to him, when she really had no free time at all, as if she should be researching it further right at that very moment instead of playing around in the lab.

Ellen tried to concentrate on the jellyfish sample and the chemical reactions. If this did turn out to be a new species, she would be able to name it. She tried to think of a suitable name: something that would encompass its color and structure, something that would do it justice. Nothing came to mind.

Sometimes scientists attached their own names to a newfound species. That seemed a bit narcissistic. Besides, before attaching her name to anything it would be best to learn more about it first. She wouldn't want to find out afterwards that an organism with her name turned out to be some kind of a flesh-eating monster.

This couldn't be a flesh-eating monster though. For one thing, it had no teeth. Like most jellyfish, it probably filtered nutrients out of the water while swimming, occasionally capturing and eating plankton or small ocean animals. Not too monstrous.

She put the test-tube sample down and took the frozen jel-lyfish out of the cooler to look it over some more. It didn't appear to have stinging cells but they could always be hidden within the folds. The structure seemed to be as simple as a clenched fist. Far from transparent, the dark purple color didn't give her a chance to look inside. It resembled some sponge animals but behaved like a jellyfish. The structure was gelatinous while denser than usual. It was a full-fledged mystery. Ellen felt the excitement of discovery tickle her body again.

The more she examined it, the more she thought it looked like something other than a jellyfish but she wasn't sure what that something could be. Threads of a darker red ran through the body, looking almost like arteries or capillaries, which they couldn't possibly be since jellyfish don't have circulatory systems. The darker red threads must be muscle fibers. She kept examining the jellyfish as it sat there in her rubber-gloved hand. She expected it to pulse at any second. Only then did she realize what it looked like: a human heart. She suddenly didn't want to touch it anymore and put the specimen back in the freezer.

Ellen tried to get the image out of her mind as she continued the reactions to isolate the DNA. She didn't want to handle any-thing that vaguely resembled a human heart. Could someone be playing a trick on her? Maybe someone snuck in and replaced her jellyfish with an actual heart. But where would anyone get a heart and, more importantly, why would anyone do that?

She thought of Jake. He did like to joke around. But this seemed way beyond the realm of gorilla suits or anything else he might have up his furry sleeves. Besides, he would know not to screw around with her samples. Or would he?

Ellen considered doing a dissection on the heart jellyfish, then decided against it. They hadn't seen anything like it and they might not see another one. She wanted to keep it intact, at least for now, just in case. The DNA test would tell her if it was human or not. Not that it could be a human heart, really. It just looked like one, that's all. The lab fumes must be getting to her.

She had seen the jellyfish propelling itself through the water before she put it in the sampling jar. It hadn't looked like a heart then, but it wasn't as purplish red at that depth. It had looked grayer and more gelatinous while swimming. Maybe that was the problem. It was now frozen, so it seemed solid and possibly more like an organ than in its natural, living and swimming state.

It made her think of Andrew, the bartender from Martha's Vineyard. What had he said? That the ocean had a heart? Or did he say it had a pulse? Well, same thing in a way. The thought made her regret taking the jellyfish or the heart or whatever it was out of the ocean. What if she had unknowingly taken the ocean's heart?

She remembered how mystical Andrew had been, believing in magic and spirits, embracing the unknown instead of trying to dissect and discover all the mysteries. Even though she usually thought of the more mystical side of things as silly, it still felt as if she could have learned more from him.

Andrew had mentioned she could be carrying the spirit from the outdoor church around with her. If that were true then the tourists would be disappointed. Most probably migrated there just to feel or be scared by the infamous spirit. She didn't feel any different though. That is, if the spirit was with her she didn't feel any different. Other than the fact that she seemed to be a bit irrational, thinking that she took the ocean's heart of all things and that a spirit could have inhabited her body.

She let out a nervous laugh. The sound bounced around the test tubes and back into her ears. She started to feel a little unstable and put the test tube down with a clink.

Everything had to wait for the latest set of reagents anyway. A full breakdown needed to occur. It wouldn't be ready for the DNA test until everything had been stripped down to its inner essence. Exposed and completely vulnerable. That's what she needed it to be. While waiting for the inevitable, Ellen thought it might help to get out of her lab closet.

She wandered into the main lab where the sweaty bodies were beginning to invade with their laptops and coffee. A few yawned and rubbed their eyes as the gray light of day seeped in through the portholes.

Ellen continued through the stark hallway to the galley, where Ryan, Jake, Michael, and Maddie sat at one of the tables. She grabbed some coffee and a muffin and joined them.

"There you are," Ryan said as she sat down. "We thought you might have slept in."

"Nope, I was working in the lab."

"That figures," Jake said.

Ellen gave him a half-kidding, accusatory glance. "Were you in my area of the lab recently, by any chance?"

"Me? No, I was doing the semi-normal thing and sleeping at 5 AM."

"Or maybe last night? Were you in there then?"

"No, why would I be? My area isn't anywhere near yours."

"Never mind. Just wondering if you were playing a practical joke."

"Me? Play a joke on someone? Never."

"Yeah, right. You sound real innocent."

Jake threw his hands up. "Why would you think I'd play a joke on you?"

"I don't know. I guess the gorilla suit threw me off."

"I haven't even worn that recently," Jake said. "I've been entrenched in my serious researcher mode instead."

"Okay, forget it," Ellen said.

"Why do you think someone played a joke on you?" Ryan asked.

Ellen didn't want to say. She hadn't planned for the conversation to go this way. She would sound completely insane.

"Forget it," she said. "It's not important."

But then she didn't want to forget it. She turned to Ryan.

"Remember that purplish red jellyfish we found the other day? Do you remember what it looked like?"

"It looked like a jellyfish to me."

"I've never seen anything like it," Ellen said. "Then the more I examined it, the more I started to think it didn't look like a jellyfish at all."

"What else could it be?"

"I don't know, but it looked a lot like a human heart."

"So you thought I switched your jellyfish with a heart?" Jake asked. "That would be perfect. I would have loved to do that."

"But you didn't, right?"

"No, but now I wish I had."

"Wow. Someone's been working in the lab a little too long," Michael said.

Ellen gave him a disgruntled look. "I haven't been in there enough since we started going out on the dives."

Jake started to laugh and then tried to control it, which made him laugh even more. Ryan looked like he might join in at any moment but glanced toward Ellen and managed to control himself.

"Wait a second," Jake said when he could breathe again. "Don't some jellyfish look like hearts anyway?"

Ellen thought about it. "Well, some might, a little. But not like this one. This one really looks like it."

"I've got to see this thing," Jake said.

"You don't need to see it," Ellen said. "Just picture a heart. That's what it looks like."

"Are you sure you're getting enough rest?" Ryan asked. The question only made Jake and Michael laugh harder.

"I knew I shouldn't have said anything," Ellen said while her mouth inched into a smile. "At least I'm doing a DNA test on whatever it is so we'll find out soon enough if someone snuck anything strange in there."

That only caused more laughter. In a desperate attempt to change the subject, Ellen turned to Michael and asked, "So how was your dive?"

"Not as exciting as yours, apparently. No hearts to be seen."

"But we did see some coral bleaching," Maddie chimed in.

Michael sighed. "Yes. I had been hoping we wouldn't see any at all since we're in such a remote area but there was some."

"So now you're proving climate change to yourself," Ellen said.

"No, not at all. It only proves that humans can make a slight regional impact on the environment through things like overfishing, pesticides, or cutting down trees and generating silt runoff, which can also cause coral bleaching. I'll bet when we go to the diving areas near the uninhabited islands there won't be any coral bleaching there at all."

"I'll take that bet," Ellen said.

"Yeah, me too," Jake and Ryan both said. Michael appeared to be outnumbered.

"It makes sense that some coral bleaching would appear everywhere, even in an uninhabited area, since after all it is caused by global climate change," Ellen said. "Whether or not you want to believe it, it's happening anyway."

"The climate certainly is changing," Michael said. "But it's been changing ever since the formation of the Earth. The question is: are we creating these changes on a worldwide scale?"

"I don't know what to believe anymore," Maddie said. "But I guess that's why we're doing this research. So we can figure these things out once and for all."

Ellen smiled. "Do you really think these things can be figured out once and for all?"

"We've got to at least try. That's what we're here for."

"I guess," Ellen said. "But remember, if you torture data sufficiently, it'll admit to anything."

Michael laughed. "I'll remember that when you show me your climate change proof."

CHAPTER 40

E LLEN PICKED UP a test tube, added more chemicals, then swirled it around to agitate it further. These final steps would isolate the DNA from the fragments of the exploded cells, an explosion that had occurred while the test tubes were in the warm water bath overnight.

Once she had a sample of pure DNA from each jellyfish, she brought up the software on her laptop to analyze it.

Of course, she wanted to analyze the DNA of the heart jellyfish first. She dropped the wand into the test tube and watched as the software started to do the work. It read the sample right away, but it still took too long. Ellen stared at the computer screen as it compiled the information. She couldn't bring herself to do anything else while she waited for the results.

Jake walked in just when it looked like she wasn't doing anything but sitting there.

"I'm analyzing, in case you're wondering," Ellen said. "Or the computer is and I'm watching.

Jake stared at the computer screen as it constructed a colorful DNA strand and assembled text files on the sample.

"That's really amazing software," he said.

"It's pretty new. It does everything but isolate the DNA. That we still have to do ourselves."

"At least we have some job security then," Jake said. "Can I see the heart?"

"It's not really a heart. But sure, as long as you've traveled all this way."

Ellen opened the cooler and took the dark purple jellyfish out so Jake could examine it.

"Wow, I see what you mean," Jake said as he pulled on rubber gloves. "I've never seen muscle fibers like these. They look so much like capillaries."

"I guess that's what made me start thinking it," Ellen said. "Obviously, they can't be capillaries since jellyfish don't have circulatory systems. They're just slight differentiations in color for whatever reason."

"What would cause that though?"

"Could be temperature differences or adjustments that the body might have made to swimming at different depths and pressure levels or possibly it happened because of the pulsing motion of swimming."

"So really, anything."

"I guess so. I even started to think this could be an undocumented species. I've never seen anything like it and I couldn't find a match for it in the books I brought along."

"If it did turn out to be a new species, you'd be famous," Jake said.

"Not really. New species are discovered all the time and no one cares."

"But you'd get to name it. That would be exciting."

"Yeah, I do like that part."

"*Le coeur de la mer*, except that's French, not Latin."

"Sounds good though."

"It does seem denser than the usual jellyfish, and at the same time more porous," Jake said. "Maybe something with *porifera* in there."

"Or *cor*, Latin for heart."

"Even better, how about *Corellena* for the discoverer?"

"No, that sounds too much like a disease."

"Not really."

"Well, it's too narcissistic then."

"What's the point of finding a new species if you don't name it after yourself?"

"The point is in the doing of it, not in any supposed notoriety you might get from it."

"I guess. Still, I can't wait to name some strange salp *Jakeia*."

"Talk about sounding like a disease."

"Thanks a lot."

Ellen stifled a laugh. "I just don't want to start getting my hopes up and then find out it's something we've known of all along, something that I should have remembered or known."

She glanced at the computer screen while it continued to construct the DNA strand. It wouldn't be able to tell her much until it finished compiling all the information.

"Want to see the film we took on the salps?"

"Sure," Jake said as he put the frozen sample back into the cooler. "Do you have any popcorn to go with that?"

"I guess we'll have to suffer through the movie without it."

"That's okay. Maybe we'll see a new salp species in the movie. Then I'll name it *Ellena*."

"Or *Jakasaurus*."

"That's more like it. Now I'm going to have to discover a new species just so that name can be used."

"It should be some new species of dinosaur then since that's what it sounds like, so good luck with that."

"Well, we still don't know what's hidden in the ocean depths. There could be a dinosaur or sea monster lurking down there."

Ellen rolled her eyes. "Yeah, right."

"You don't think so?"

"Sea monsters? I'm sure there are a few. It all depends on your definition of a monster. There are some pretty strange creatures down there and we're discovering more all the time. But if there is anything remotely resembling a dinosaur in the ocean, we'd know about it by now."

"Most of the ocean is still unexplored. If you were a sea monster or sea dinosaur, wouldn't you hide from us?"

"Definitely." Ellen took out another laptop and set the movie up. "Okay, ready to see some sea monsters?"

Jake rubbed his hands together in preparation for the event. "Ready."

She pressed a button and the movie blinked on, bringing them back into the dark water. Dust-like objects floated by in erratic patterns. Ellen felt more limited this way, looking only through the eye of the camera, rather than when they'd been out there surrounded by the darkness and the glow. The laptop movie made her think of looking through a window at a snowstorm in the middle of the night.

The camera tried to follow the flashlight beam but it didn't always work and so there were moments of complete darkness until the camera found the beam again. A few jellyfish propelled themselves through the dark. The camera zoomed in on those. The fluorescent dye was used and the jellyfish sucked it in, then expelled it, creating small vortex rings in its wake.

"Nice job on the dye," Jake said.

"Thanks. We used it for some salps too. How did you get interested in salps anyway?"

"I don't know. I started out studying jellyfish, but then it seemed like not that much was known about salps so I started wondering more about them."

"Not that much is known about jellyfish either."

"Yeah, but I had never even heard of salps before. I had at least heard of jellyfish. Then the way salps move started to interest me, because they're pretty much constantly swimming and eating. So it seems like they're reaching some kind of a perfect balance between getting enough energy from the food to keep on swimming, while not using up too much."

"I was wondering about that with jellyfish too."

"See? I told you they're a lot alike."

"Some are," Ellen said. "At least in the way they move through the water anyway."

"But when you really look at it, not all salps swim exactly the same. Each species swims differently. That's what I'm doing my thesis on. So far, it seems like some species are more efficient swimmers since they balance their food and energy better than others. And strangely enough, the more streamlined species aren't always the most hydrodynamically efficient."

"That doesn't make sense."

"I know. So then knowing that creates more questions. That's what I love about it."

"Sounds like you're hooked."

The movie zoomed in on the salps. Florescent dye was ejected and the salps sucked it up like the jellyfish, then expelled it to create a vortex ring. The most efficient jet-propulsion swimmers usually formed vortex rings with the water, like tiny green smoke rings.

"Maybe we should do a paper together on the jet-propulsion method of salps and jellyfish," Jake said. "I have a feeling that, even though they're swimming and eating at the same time with the same motion, more efficient swimming might not always be related to more efficient eating. Another thing that doesn't make sense, but that's why I think it's true."

"Sure, as long as you didn't replace my jellyfish with a heart."

"Unfortunately, I can't say that I did, even though I'd love to take the credit. Has the computer come up with anything yet?"

Ellen glanced at the other laptop screen. The DNA strand looked to be complete.

"We'll know in a second. I just have to scroll through this information. It better not be human."

"Don't worry, it won't be," Jake said. "Where would I get a heart around here anyway?"

"That mystified me too. But then I decided that's something I wouldn't want to know."

"Wow. That gorilla suit really threw you off, didn't it? I'm not that scary."

"Yeah, sure," Ellen said, absorbed in the text files.

"Well, what is it?"

Ellen looked up and smiled. "It's not human. In fact, this software isn't sure what it is."

"A new species then?"

"It looks that way. I'll have to send this information out to be sure, but it looks that way."

CHAPTER 41

T HAT NIGHT THE entire ocean pulsed as if it had become one living being. Ellen dove through its bloodstream, feeling the vibrations until the pulsing became her own. The ocean breathed in and out in a slow, steady rhythm. She swam as freely, as uninhibited as a dolphin. The ocean kept welcoming her in until she became part of it.

A shadow moved toward her. An enormous shadow, larger than her body, larger than a whale. As the shadow advanced, the thumping pulse grew louder. Ellen couldn't be sure if the noise was the ocean's heart or her own. The shadow overtook her while shaking spasmodically, sending chilling waves through the body of the ocean.

Ellen woke up shaking, her own heart pounding irregularly. She couldn't breathe at first and gasped at the air, wanting to breathe water instead. She longed for the rhythm of the ocean around her, to feel part of everything again.

She remembered the pulsing heart. Whatever it was, a monster, a heart, it felt real. As she tried to go back to sleep, she heard it pulsing again through the darkness, calling out to her.

When she glanced at the bathroom mirror the next morning, her reflection frightened her. She looked haunted. Dark smudges appeared under eyes that didn't look familiar. She stared closer into the mirror. Her eyes shined with an inner lunacy. She laughed, causing her reflection to look even scarier. Must be working too hard. Like usual on a cruise.

Today wouldn't be any different. The research ship would soon be docking off one of the uninhabited islands. Dives and onboard experiments were scheduled throughout the day.

She'd be going on a blue-water dive and one in shallower water closer to shore. The shallow dive was scheduled first, but it wouldn't be until 10 AM. That seemed too long to wait. She checked her laptop to see if a response had come through on the DNA information that had been sent out for further analysis. Nothing yet.

Scattered researchers sat hunched in the mess deck. A faint pink sunrise floated beyond the background windows as the ship pushed on toward its destination. No one talked at this hour, with the silence broken only by faint coughs and the clicking of laptop keys. Ellen shuffled over to the coffee station.

She brought her coffee outside while hoping the air might wake her up or at least help her feel a little more human. The image of her haunted reflection stayed with her. She hadn't fully recognized it, which made her think of the ghost from Martha's Vineyard. Andrew had claimed it would be a good thing if she carried the spirit with her. He said the spirit would help. She wasn't so sure. It might not help. It could make things worse. It could be in there tinkering around with her already fragile mind. Just for fun.

What if the ghost had decided to start showing itself? That would explain why her eyes didn't look familiar. Ellen hoped it wouldn't try to take control. She didn't want to start acting like someone else, especially if that person happened to be a ghost. It might be a psychopath. Of course, she didn't believe in ghosts. But for someone who didn't believe in ghosts, she'd been thinking a lot about them lately.

The tropical air didn't help much. Its warm dewiness brought her back into a dream-like trance somewhere between sleeping and waking. Any stray wind curled around her bare legs like a damp, twisted sheet. She leaned against the railing, felt the heaviness of the air, breathed in what felt more like water, and sipped her hot coffee.

The ship continued to sway with the motion of the waves. She could hear the waves break against the side in swishing noises, sounding almost as they would on some tropical beach paradise. She closed her eyes, hoping to be transported to that place. But when she opened them, she still leaned against a cold metal railing aboard a clanging research ship. She hadn't been whisked away. She still had to make sense of a strange jellyfish-like organism that might not be a jellyfish at all. For that matter, she still had to make sense of her life.

She stared straight down the side of the boat into the foaming water while looking for answers. Something black glistened below the surface. The darkness leapt out of the water, showing its streamlined body and white markings before diving back down. Ellen searched the water to get another glimpse, and again it leapt toward her, causing her own spirit to jump at the sight.

A Pacific white-sided dolphin dove back down and flew through the water as it sped along with the ship. It swam close to the side. Ellen thought it might be trying to communicate. She watched as it continued to jump and dive while soaring through the water. The motion looked so effortless that it shouldn't be called swimming. It seemed more likely that some unseen force propelled the dolphin.

Another appeared from the depths and kept pace with the first. Then another. Soon there were at least a dozen dolphins gliding along with the ship, their arched backs blending in with the dark blue water, becoming waves themselves.

They started chattering as they jumped; playing either with the ship or with each other, it was impossible to tell. Some seemed to look at her and smile before dipping back down. She couldn't help but smile back.

It must be a good omen. Perhaps the dolphins guided them. After all, these were the waters of mystical legends. Waters where sharks protected islanders and sea turtles could be called with song. It seemed fitting that dolphins would guide them through such a place. But how could such things be true?

Ellen had always tried to explain the unexplainable. Now, after visiting this land of magic and legends, she wasn't so sure. Maybe the opposite had been true all along and nothing could ever be fully explained. Ellen took another gulp of her coffee and wandered back into the mess deck. She saw Michael sitting there so she slumped down across from him.

"How's it going?" He glanced up, then looked a little startled. "Or is it better not to ask?"

"Who knows? I'm beginning to think that nothing can ever be fully figured out. I did a DNA test on the heart that looks like a jellyfish or the jellyfish that looks like a heart, and the program didn't know what it was."

"That's unusual. It didn't come up with anything at all?"

"It didn't even say that it was related to jellyfish. It couldn't figure out what it might be related to. I sent all the information out to see if it could be a new species or not."

"A new species? That would be exciting."

"I guess. All I really want to do is study jellyfish though. I'm not so sure I want to contend with a whole new species, as exciting as that may be."

"Maybe you should get some rest while you're waiting for the news. You look pretty tired out."

"I know. I had a crazy dream last night and now it feels like I didn't sleep at all. But I'll catch up after the cruise. I've got two dives today. How about you?"

Michael looked at his watch. "Just one for me, in about an hour. The ship should anchor in a few minutes. Then I'll be able to get out there and see if there's any coral bleaching in an uninhabited area. What was it we bet on?"

"I think we just bet. We didn't really bet on anything."

"How about if there's no coral bleaching, then I win?"

"We'll have to start keeping a score card between this and the whole climate change controversy."

"Another one I'll win," Michael said.

"Don't be so sure. I'm used to winning."

"Then this will be a first for you on both counts," Michael said as he stood up. "I'd better get ready for the dive. Get ready to be wrong."

"Make sure to take lots of pictures. And I want to hear another opinion on the whole thing, not just yours."

"What, you don't trust me?"

"Sure I trust you, but you sound like you want to win so much that you might start seeing things out there."

"Look who's calling who delusional. The person who thought a jellyfish was a heart."

Ellen laughed. "I'm pretty sure it's not a heart, even if we don't know what it is yet."

"Good luck finding that out. Now it's off to dive I go."

CHAPTER 42

E LLEN BREEZED THROUGH liquid turquoise skies with Ryan by her side. Pink and silver fish swam along with them, in front of them, and against them. At times, there seemed to be more fish than water. Then the fish would coast away to form an iridescent cloud, and there would be the turquoise sky again.

The seafloor gave off a white shine below. Red coral treetops ruffled in the water breeze. A few striped fish rested under those trees as if enjoying their shade.

Ryan swam so close that she could feel the ripples caused by his body as she searched. She felt drawn to him, but then figured it must be from sharing this underwater adventure more than anything else. At times, the beauty was overwhelming. Amazement welled up as she continued to swim through so much life.

A dark shadow appeared as a blotch on the blue-green horizon. It reminded Ellen of her dream. She didn't want to be anywhere near it and started to swim away. Then it moved closer and took the form of the heart jellyfish. She grabbed the video camera. They hadn't taken video or photos of the other one, so this was a stroke of luck.

Ellen began filming right away. She didn't notice anything different in the way it moved as compared to regular jellyfish. Maybe the film would pick up something she couldn't see. She zoomed in as far as possible and tried to swim underneath to see if anything looked out of the ordinary from that angle. Again, she didn't notice anything. It moved like a regular jellyfish, it propelled itself like a regular jellyfish, but there was something. Something was a little off. She had no idea what it was.

Ryan drew closer so he could take pictures. Ellen kept filming. Then she pulled out the sampling jar and scooped the jellyfish up into it. It would help to do a DNA test on this one to compare it with the other one. They looked the same but she couldn't be sure until the tests were done. If they weren't the same and this turned out to be a regular jellyfish, then she wouldn't be able to use the pictures and film to describe the movements of a life form that might be a new species. So she had to be sure.

She clamped the lid down on the sampling jar and held it up to take a look. The jellyfish pulsed, making it look exactly like a trapped heart. Ellen almost dropped the jar but managed to hold on and place it in her sampling bag. A queasy feeling came over her. Ryan gave her an okay sign when he saw that the sample was tucked securely away.

They swam through the liquid sky some more, but now Ellen just wanted to get back to the lab. The process should be started as soon as possible since it took so long to obtain the results. While in the collection bag, the jar occasionally bumped away at her side, a constant reminder of the work that needed to be done.

Crumbled cities of reef-building coral came into view below. They sprawled out everywhere, as organic as a human settlement. Ellen thought of them as cities or colonies because the tiny polyps continually pile on top of each other for generations. Generations upon generations. An excruciatingly slow way to grow, but then the largest living structure on Earth, the Great Barrier Reef, was built that way. She marveled that some of today's reefs began growing at least 50 million years ago, long before humans appeared. They represented so many generations, while helping future generations to grow further still.

As Ellen swam over and through these ancient pink cities, she didn't see any obvious signs of coral bleaching. Groups of fish poked at the coral. If she took more time to fully examine the reef, she felt sure there would be some signs of bleaching.

She hoped Michael wouldn't win their bet. For some reason, she didn't look forward to seeing him gloat over the fact that no coral bleaching could be found in these remote areas, even if it might be better for the world that way.

CHAPTER 43

D URING THE BLUE-WATER dive that afternoon, Ellen kept thinking about the newest sample. She had started the tests right after the morning dive and set the sample in the warm water bath. Even though it should sit in the bath for hours, she wanted to get back there, just to be near it, to somehow collect the knowledge it had yet to reveal.

Jake acted as safety for this dive. She looked up and saw him floating there, the apex holding their two points together. Their triangle moved down while attempting to perform some sort of a sweep through as much of the water as possible. She felt the futility of it. To be dangling there attached to safety lines, sweeping across and down and looking into the huge open expanse of the ocean. There seemed to be no way to adequately examine everything, to discover all its truths, to know all there was to know. Every time she thought she might be getting closer, the ocean led her off in another direction, making her realize she knew nothing at all.

Ellen swam deeper as if that would help. She didn't want to keep scratching the surface and instead plunged into the abyss.

The water shifted to a deep indigo. She knew they couldn't go much farther.

When considering the ocean as a whole, they could only swim into the smallest fraction of the surface. Even remotely operated vehicles, which could pierce the deepest ocean, did just that: they pierced an ocean of knowledge, amounting to a dot of enlightenment on the entire surface map of the Earth. A dot that could barely be seen, especially when compared to the utter vastness of the ocean. An ocean that not only made up most of the planet, but provided a home to so much life on Earth.

The darkest ocean depths stayed hidden seven miles or eleven kilometers below the surface. There was still so much to discover within those depths. She felt sure of it as she dangled there at the surface while peering into the mysteries below.

With a sudden flurry of bubbles, a dolphin dove down and looked directly at her. She could almost touch it. The dolphin held her gaze.

She started to reach out without thinking, but the dolphin had already begun its ascent back to the surface. Then another plunged down. She looked over at Ryan. He just stared. More bubbles formed around the dolphins as they continued to plunge up and down. Dolphins and humans looked at each other through all the bubbles, one life form curious about the other, trying to figure each other out.

Ellen swam up with the dolphins at first but they were too fast for her. They darted everywhere while she plodded along behind, stopping with Ryan to adjust at the correct depths. She looked around but couldn't see any jellyfish. With so much activity going on, they probably wouldn't find any at all. She watched the dolphins instead.

They started to chatter. Ellen couldn't tell if they were talking to her or to each other. At close range the clicking noises vibrated in her head.

She and Ryan kept swimming up and stopping to adjust to the pressure difference. The dolphins panicked whenever they stopped and the clicking noises grew louder. They whizzed around in frustration at the slow pace. One nudged her and tried to force her up to the surface. The dolphins screeched again, possibly telling them to hurry.

Feeling incredibly clunky and dimwitted, Ellen continued to swim up until she finally broke through the surface. The dolphins were already there, leaping into the sky.

Jake had climbed into the boat and he stooped over to help Ellen and Ryan. As soon as they were all in, the dolphins twirled and darted off through the waves, leaving the humans behind to float in their little boat.

"I wonder what they were so excited about," Ryan said as he watched them go.

"I don't know, but they must have scared away any jellyfish and probably everything else by now," Ellen said. "We might as well go back."

As she bent down to remove her scuba tank, she saw red. A red blur hovered on the ocean surface out toward the horizon. The blur appeared to be huge and spreading.

She pointed toward it. "What could that be?"

"Could be seaweed," Jake said.

"I don't think so," Ellen said. "Let's try to get a little closer."

"Okay, but if we get stuck in it, it's your fault."

He started the motor and slowly maneuvered the boat closer while keeping a good distance. Then he stopped and idled and stared while adding, "Um, I don't think we should get any closer."

It looked like blood, this dark red ooze. The redness grew steadily larger, as if it could be leaking out from the turquoise water.

As the red patch crept toward the boat, Ellen saw it was made up of hundreds of jellyfish. Each jellyfish spread out across the surface, finding and touching one another, until they formed one monstrosity. But that wasn't all. The monstrosity pulsed.

"A jellyfish swarm," Ryan said. "That's weird."

"Hey, aren't those your heart jellyfish?" Jake asked.

"I can't tell from here," Ellen said. "Let's get a little closer."

"I don't think we'll have to. They're coming toward us."

The organisms congregating together did look like the heart jellyfish, but these appeared to be lighter in color and less dense. They weren't exactly swimming by the usual jet propulsion method either. They hovered on the ocean's surface and continued to spread out. Ellen wondered if they acted differently because they were part of a group. They behaved invasively, as groups often did, whether those groups were made of humans or coyotes or jellyfish.

"Quick, get the video camera," Ellen told Ryan. "Let's try to film as much of this as we can."

"I think I'm going to back the boat up first," Jake said. "They're getting a little too close."

"Okay, but not too much."

Ryan started filming. "I can zoom in anyway, so you might as well back it up."

Ellen resorted to taking pictures. She tried to show exactly how the jellyfish were attached to each other. Each individual life form appeared to be a small part of the whole. The living being that resulted continued to grow and vibrate.

"Switch with me," Ellen said to Ryan. "I want to make sure we get a record of that pulsing."

Through the zoomed-in eye of the video camera, Ellen saw that the slight pulsing action was the result of the jellyfish sucking in ocean water. The jellyfish would take a deep gulp, then stop, then another, resulting in a spasm. It didn't look like they pushed the water back out, as jellyfish normally would. Instead, they kept swallowing.

"It looks like they're trying to suck up the ocean," Ellen said while staring through the camera lens.

Jake let out an uneasy laugh. "Oh come on. It's just a jellyfish swarm. It can't do that. Right?"

"I don't know. It could be something else. Remember, the DNA tests haven't come up with much information yet. And we can't be sure these are the same jellyfish-like organisms we did the tests on."

"Jellyfish-like organisms?" Jake asked. "They have to be jellyfish. Look at them. Even if they are some kind of a new weird species, they must still be jellyfish."

"We don't know that for sure. Not until they've been tested and examined."

Ellen watched the spasms and shaking of the overall creature. As it inhaled the water, it spread out farther as if the ocean contributed to its growth. Maybe it wasn't just inhaling water. Maybe it was inhaling life. It could be sucking up the very life and energy of the ocean.

"What the hell is that thing?" Ellen muttered. She put the camera down and turned to Jake. "We've got to get closer. I've got to take a sample."

"Take a sample of the monster jellyfish? Well, okay but if it bites I'm accelerating this boat as fast as it will go in the opposite direction."

"Don't worry, it won't bite," Ellen said. "At least I don't think so. It could sting though."

"The dolphins were the smart ones," Jake said as he steered the boat closer. "They all swam away."

"It'll be okay," Ryan added, but he didn't look so sure. He picked up the video camera and continued filming while Ellen took a sampling jar out and attached it to a long handle.

The boat idled near the swarm. The jellyfish or whatever they were continued to advance toward them. Ellen knew she'd have to scoop the sample up in one quick move. She didn't want these strange life forms to get close enough to touch the boat. They acted so invasive. They might overtake them. No one knew what they could do. It was impossible to say what kind of power they possessed.

She bent over the side, held the handle out, and scooped the sampling jar into the red gelatinous mess. Some of it oozed into the jar and she jerked the handle up so that it would stay inside.

The rest hung onto the jar for a few minutes, then detached and splashed back into the water. Strange. Even though the life forms had fused together, the resulting mass didn't act as one organism. It didn't stay together for one thing. Instead, it sacrificed a small part of itself as if giving nothing at all before plopping back down to the greater whole.

Ellen's hands shook as she screwed the cover onto the jar. She spun toward Jake and managed to say, "Go."

Jake swerved around and accelerated so fast that the front of the boat leapt out of the water. Ellen grabbed the side of the rubbery boat. She held onto the sampling jar while trying not to drop it. Ryan kept looking at her with concern. The expression on his face seemed a little too fatherly for such a young kid.

She held the jar up and stared through the motionless red blob. It looked more transparent than the other samples, which could be from sucking up so much ocean water. She kept examining it as the boat bounced over the waves.

Behind them the swarm continued to inhale and stretch out and grow.

CHAPTER 44

E LLEN BROUGHT THE new sample to the lab and started the series of reactions to isolate the DNA. She checked the other sample that had been taken during the shallow water dive that morning, but it was still too early to do anything with that one yet. She carefully placed both samples in the warm water bath.

She switched on her laptop and checked for any messages or information on the first sample. Nothing had come through yet. It remained a mystery. Perhaps it always would be.

Ryan opened the lab door. "How are you doing?"

Ellen glanced up. "Oh, great, for someone who really has no idea what's going on anymore."

"That was pretty crazy, wasn't it?"

"Yeah," Ellen said. "I've seen a lot of jellyfish swarms, but never one like that. But then, I've never seen anything like these things either."

"They do look a lot like jellyfish though."

"Right, but if the tests show they're the same as the first sample, they can't be. Otherwise the DNA test would have said they were a certain type of jellyfish or at least related to jellyfish or something on Earth. It doesn't make sense that they're not related to anything at all. Everything on Earth is related to something. Like with humans, we share most of our DNA with chimpanzees. These life forms are much more similar to jellyfish than we are to chimpanzees, but the test said they're not related to anything."

"The DNA information could be wrong. Maybe the software needs updating or something could have gone wrong while isolating the DNA."

"Maybe. But I don't think so. We even share a quarter of our genes with a grain of rice. Think of that. A cow's DNA is eighty percent similar to ours. Every living thing on Earth is related, except for these life forms."

"What do you think they could be then?"

"You'll think I'm crazy."

"No I won't. Don't you think it's a new species?"

"At first I did. But now I don't know. After seeing the way those organisms behaved today, they seemed so invasive. They kept moving toward the boat. It felt like they were going to attack us. Not only that, but did you see what they were doing? They were trying to suck up as much of the ocean as possible. They might have been sucking up the life of the ocean."

"I thought they were just moving around and pulsing."

"No, I've got it on film. They were definitely sucking the ocean up. It looked like they kept swallowing it while spreading out everywhere, like they were feeding off of it or taking samples. I'm starting to think they're not from Earth at all."

"Yeah, right."

"Remember, anything is possible," Ellen said. "We can't rule anything out at this point. I'm just saying, considering the way they behaved out there, it's a possibility."

"But aliens? Come on."

"That would explain why the DNA didn't come back as related to anything. It should have been related to something if it was from Earth."

"Then that shows there was something wrong with the test. It has to be from Earth."

"Why does it have to be?" Ellen asked. "Don't you believe that life could exist someplace else in the universe?"

"Well, yeah. There are billions of planets out there and all that. But why would an alien look so much like a jellyfish or disguise itself as a jellyfish?"

"Why not? If the objective was to sample our ocean and bring back data while remaining undetected, then why not make it look like it belongs here?"

"Usually you can convince me of anything, but I'm not sure on this one. The thought of an alien jellyfish is a little too farfetched."

"What about the way they were sucking up the ocean like that without expelling it the way regular jellyfish do? What possible reason could there be for an action like that other than to collect samples of ocean water?"

"I don't know, maybe they were just eating."

"I don't think so. Jellyfish don't eat like that."

"But you just said they're not jellyfish. You must be tired. Maybe you should get some rest."

Ellen noticed Ryan's face transform into the fatherly expression again.

"There's no time to rest. There's all this data to go through and tests to finish, plus the film and pictures to examine."

"Still, maybe you should rest."

"I'm fine. Really. Being in the lab is like playing for me. I'll finish up a few more things here and then I'll see you at dinner."

"Okay," Ryan said as he turned to leave. "But try to get some rest anyway."

Ellen couldn't help but feel annoyed. At times, she felt almost like a teacher toward Ryan. Now he seemed to be turning into her father. She didn't understand how that could have happened. It's not as if she needed parenting. If anything, he did. He was the younger one. She sighed at her laptop. Add it to the list of anomalies. Nothing made sense anymore.

CHAPTER 45

R YAN DECIDED TO find Jake to get his opinion on the whole jellyfish swarm thing. As he walked through the ship's gray corridors, he reminded himself not to say anything about the alien idea. There was such a thing as too much information. He didn't want Jake or anyone else thinking there might be something wrong with Ellen.

She looked more tired all the time. He didn't know what to do about it. She must feel tired if she looked so tired, but she kept denying it and pushing him away. He couldn't force her into slowing down and resting. Still, he wanted to take care of her, probably because she refused to take care of herself. But the more he tried to help, the more distant she became.

He found Jake in his lab staring into a tank full of salps. The salps made Ryan think of tiny light bulbs as they moved aimlessly through the water. He didn't see how they could be so fascinating.

"Hey, how are your pet salps doing?"

"Really well. I've been feeding them, the way you're supposed to with a pet. And I don't have to clean up after them or take them out for walks or anything."

"That's a bonus."

"And on top of all that, they're amazing. All they do is swim and eat and they do both constantly. They're the vacuum cleaners of the ocean."

"That's good. I'm sure the ocean needs all the vacuum cleaners it can get."

"Yeah, but it's more than that really. They live in perfect balance with their environment. Imagine a car running only on the air it moves through, while using that for enough fuel to keep moving. Salps do that every day. They get everything they need from the water they swim through and they never have to search for food. They just swim and siphon out the food while they move."

"Too bad cars can't do that."

"And not only that, they help remove carbon dioxide from the surface waters and from the atmosphere. Their waste material is full of carbon and when that carbon sinks down to the bottom of the ocean, it can be sequestered for centuries. Everyone's trying to figure out how to sequester carbon dioxide while salps have been doing it all along."

"That's great. Then all we need are more salps, right?"

"Yeah, well, there already are a lot of them out there. We just don't see them very often because they're so small and they're smart enough to stay away from the coasts. They usually come up to the surface to feed at night, then when the sun comes up they swim hundreds of meters down into the dark to hide from predators."

"That's funny that they do that. It's like they're thinking."

Jake grinned through the watery tank. "They very well could be. Who knows, maybe they think more than we do. Maybe they communicate with each other better too."

"I guess that wouldn't be too hard to do. So they could still help with the whole climate change thing?"

"We think they're already helping. I suppose we could try to get them to increase in population so they'd help some more. Salp populations can grow rapidly when conditions are right. They can reproduce by cloning themselves and by growing from fertilized eggs. But I don't know, whenever we try to do anything like that we seem to mess things up even more and upset the natural balance of things. In the Southern Ocean, when salp populations are high the krill populations are low. So it's not always good for other zooplankton to have lots of salps around. They could end up eating too much of what the others eat."

Ryan stared at the salps. They were so tiny, they didn't look like they could mess things up that much.

"What are you doing with them now?"

"I'm feeding them to measure how much phytoplankton they eat in a day, and then to see how much they grow."

"It's hard to believe they're growing at all. They look so small."

"They grow in pretty miniscule amounts. Sometimes they make me think of those sea creature pets that came with the tiny plastic aquariums. I never did too well with those. Hopefully I'll be better at keeping these alive."

Sea creatures reminded Ryan of the jellyfish. "What did you think of that swarm today anyway?"

"I don't know. I've heard jellyfish swarms can be pretty invasive, but I got this feeling like they were really coming after us."

"Yeah, that was pretty scary."

"I was just glad the boat was faster. Not that they really could have done anything to us, but they did seem like they might be kind of angry or something."

"It's not like they can have personalities though, right?"

"I wouldn't think so. But you never know. Like these salps, for instance, after a while of watching them, they start to take on different personalities."

"That's because you're trying to turn them into pets."

"Probably. But after today, there's no way I'd want a jellyfish for a pet."

CHAPTER 46

W HILE SITTING WITH everyone at dinner, Ellen sensed an un-
ease creep through her brain. She had certainly felt that
way around others for most of her life and had become used to
the feeling, but not with these people. Not yet. Until now. She
had no idea why.

She tried to shake the feeling off and glanced toward Michael.
"So did you see any signs of coral bleaching out there today?"

"I suppose I have to admit it. Yes, we did. Not much, but it
was there."

Ellen couldn't help but smile.

"Of course," he added, "it still doesn't prove that climate
change is the main cause."

"Yes it does."

"Only because you want to believe it does. Coral bleaching is
caused by any number of things or any combination of things, not
just warmer ocean waters. Besides, we already know the ocean
has been warming slightly. But that doesn't mean humans are
definitely causing it."

"That's it, I officially give up trying to convince you of anything," Ellen said. "Your mind seems made up, no matter what
kind of evidence might show up to dispute it."

"You can still convince me otherwise. You just haven't yet."

Ellen's uncontrolled laughter sounded hollow in her head. She decided to change the subject.

"Did anyone tell you what we saw today?"

"Jake mentioned it. Something about a jellyfish swarm. Interesting. They don't appear in swarms that often, do they?"

"It depends on the type of jellyfish. Moon jellies and Nomuras do, but we're not sure what we saw out there."

"Why's that?"

Ellen paused for a second. "The swarm looked like it was made up of the same type of life form as the sample I took a few days ago. The one with the DNA test that came up as inconclusive."

"The one that you thought was a heart?"

"That's the one."

Ryan's eyes lit up as if to tell her not to say any more. She ignored the look.

"Since the test couldn't give us any idea of what it was, or even what it could be related to, I'm beginning to think it's not organic."

"All life forms are organic," Michael said.

"Not organic to this planet."

Michael laughed a little too long at that one. Jake and Maddie looked at each other and joined in. Ryan kept giving her that concerned look.

"You're kidding, right?" Jake asked.

"It makes sense to me," Ellen said.

"Yeah, but you're the one who thought it was a heart a few days ago," Michael said while still chuckling. "Now you're saying it's an alien? Have you ever considered that it could just be a jellyfish?"

"Of course, but then the DNA test would have said that."

"Sounds like a bad DNA test to me," Michael said. Ryan nodded but didn't say anything.

"We'll see," Ellen said. "I've started the reactions on the other samples. We'll have to wait and find out what those tests say once they're ready."

"Including the sample taken from the swarm?" Jake asked.

"Yes, including that."

"That whole thing was pretty scary," he admitted. "After seeing that swarm, I can almost believe in the possibility of aliens."

Michael and Maddie laughed again.

"No, really," Jake said. "They were coming after us and acting like they might attack us."

"Attack of the killer jellyfish?" Maddie said while barely suppressing more laughter. "I don't think so."

"Even regular jellyfish attack at times," Ellen said. "Have you ever heard of the fried egg jellyfish? It eats other jellyfish and actually looks like a fried egg."

"Never heard of it," Michael said. "Are you sure you're not mixing fairy tales in with your science?"

Ellen ignored the question. "It's true. Look it up if you don't believe me. But the point is, we don't know everything. So then, until we know for sure about this, anything is possible."

"I do usually like to believe that anything is possible," Maddie said. "But I just don't know if anything could ever be *that* possible."

"Why not?" Ellen asked. "We're always finding out that the supposedly impossible is possible. If something isn't related to anything on Earth then it must be an alien. What else could it be? But it's not only that, it's the way the swarm acted. It hovered on the surface and kept sucking up the ocean water, maybe even the actual life or energy of the ocean. It looked like it was collecting samples."

"I thought you said it was attacking you," Maddie said.

"Well no, not attacking exactly, it was coming toward us so the swarm looked like it might attack."

Michael and Maddie laughed some more at her expense.

"I think you need some rest," Michael said while wiping his eyes.

"That's what I told her," Ryan said.

"You guys were there. You know what I'm talking about."

They looked at her and didn't say anything. Ryan glanced at Michael and then at Jake. If Ellen didn't know any better, she'd think they were conspiring against her in some way.

Maybe they were right after all. Maybe she was tired and half-crazed from exhaustion. But she still couldn't help feeling like she was onto something, like she was the only one who really knew what was going on.

CHAPTER 47

—∿—

TROPICAL BREEZES HEAVY with honeysuckle float over arid lands, swirl through palm tree leaves, and mix with ocean waves. The ocean breathes this air in and out again, changing its chemical composition as it does. The ocean is forever changed by the breeze, and the breeze is in turn transformed by the ocean's breathing.

Nearby islanders feel a difference in the air. They stare into ceremonial fires and look for answers. They call upon ancestors and spirit gods. Some let themselves be possessed with spirits to gain their knowledge. They paint their faces and bodies with the gray ash of their fires. They listen to the wind and wait for the change to come.

The redness on the ocean surface continues to grow. It grows as if it does not notice or care that the growing affects all life around it. The ocean chokes on the growth of this thing and cannot breathe as it had once been able to breathe. Ocean life swims and darts under the red cloud, feeling that something isn't quite right while looking up to see the shadow glow from above. Still, it keeps growing. It reaches for more and spreads out everywhere.

After warning the humans, dolphins abandon their feeding grounds and swim away to distant waters. Whales add news of the anomaly to their collective song for that year as they move toward Antarctica. Sharks at first think the pulsing life floating there on the surface might be good to eat, but they soon discover how wrong they were. Even they begin to stay away, leaving the waters thoroughly unprotected.

This thing keeps growing until it reaches a wall of steel. The obstacle only forces it to move down until the wall stops. The anomaly then grows underneath and up the other side of the metal wall.

∼∘

Shouts of alarm circled the deck. Ellen ran out toward the source of the noise to see people pointing over the side. She held on and looked down.

The ocean frothed with red: a living, pulsing red. They found her. Somehow they found her. She searched the ocean surface to determine how large the collective ooze might be, but couldn't see the end of it. The red gelatinous goop pulsed and sucked up the ocean as far as anyone could see.

Ryan and Michael wandered over.

"Do you believe me now?" Ellen asked.

"I don't know what to believe," Ryan said.

"Wow," Michael said as he examined the horizon. "That's one huge jellyfish swarm."

"It's a swarm of something, but it's not a jellyfish swarm," Ellen said.

"Well, it does look pretty invasive, I'll give you that. But it also looks like jellyfish to me."

"That's its disguise."

"Come on, you've heard of large jellyfish swarms like this, haven't you?"

"Yes, I've heard of them and I've even seen a few. Nomura swarms near Japan can include millions of jellyfish. The occurrences of swarms like that have been increasing because of warmer ocean waters, pollution, and overfishing. But I don't think there could be much of that going on out here near the uninhabited islands. It makes much more sense for jellyfish swarms to appear off Japan.

"Besides, in any normal swarm the jellyfish stay separate. Look at this one. They're all connected. It looks like they've fused themselves together into one living being, not millions of separate jellyfish."

"Maybe the jellyfish are different with this swarm for some reason," Michael said.

"They're not jellyfish."

"Right, it makes much more sense that they're aliens."

Ellen turned to Ryan. "Could you get the video camera?"

Ryan nodded while staring out at the swarm. He felt his way toward the door to avoid turning his back on the monster.

Michael chuckled once Ryan was gone. "Now you've got him all scared with this talk of aliens. Just don't talk to the press about any of this, whatever you do. You'll come off sounding like a lunatic."

"Is that what you think? That I'm crazy?"

Michael paused for a little too long. "No crazier than the rest of us. Maybe a little more open to all the possibilities than most."

"I know it must seem like I'm crazy. But really, I'm not."

Michael smiled at her. "That's just what a crazy person would say."

Thankfully, Ryan came back with the video camera.

"Could you start filming it?" Ellen asked. "I should really take another sample. Just zoom in as much as you can so that we can try to figure out what it's doing and how it's moving."

"Okay," Ryan said while looking through the camera lens, then grimacing. "But it looks even scarier up close. If I have nightmares, it's your fault."

Ellen ran off to find the chief scientist. He should know which researchers on board might have the kind of equipment needed to take samples from the deck. The chief scientist for this cruise, Tim McCarthy, already had some notoriety as an expert on the ocean's chemical composition even though it was constantly changing. When she found him, he was rigging a net up to the ship's huge metal crane.

"I'll need a sample of that," Ellen said when she saw what he was doing.

"No problem. Seems like there's enough to go around. What do you think of all this?"

"I don't know what to think. I've never seen anything like it."

"It doesn't seem right. We should probably change course and get out of this mess soon. I'll have to go talk with the captain."

"Good idea, but let's make sure to get some samples first."

They finished attaching the net to the crane, which could unfold from the side like praying mantis arms to lower instruments or nets into the water. Ellen watched as Tim swung the arm out and cranked the lever to bring the net down over the side. The net slowly dropped, the lever creaked, and Ellen felt the same frustration as whenever she had to wait for her laptop to make its usual updates. She worried that the swarm might disappear while the net ever so slowly crept all the way down to the water's surface.

Finally, it dipped into the red ooze. Tim reversed the cranking so that the winch would pull everything back up. The net eased out of the water but then sagged back down with the weight of its catch. Ellen could only hope it wouldn't break. The wires pulling it were steel reinforced, but the net was made of some kind of orange plastic mesh material and wouldn't be as strong as the wires. She glanced at Tim. He kept cranking the handle. She could see he was tiring from the effort.

"Need any help?"

"No, I'm fine."

She watched as the net rose up out of the waves. It bulged and overflowed with the strange red jello substance. Some of it jiggled out of the holes in the mesh and plopped back into the ocean with a splash. Ellen readied the plastic buckets that would hold the samples. She found some gloves near the buckets and put them on.

After more cranking and heaving, Tim managed to bring his catch up to deck level. Ellen looked into it from as close as she dared. It still looked like jello or that stuff called Slime that she played with as a kid. She couldn't see separate organisms inside the net. When the swarm first appeared near the dolphins, the separate life forms were visible and the overall effect looked more like a quilt. Now everything flowed together. She couldn't see any seams that might separate them.

The crane swung over the deck. Ellen helped disconnect part of the net so that the samples could flow into the buckets. Once one bucket was nearly full, Tim tilted the net back up so that the flow would stop for a few minutes while Ellen snapped a bucket lid on. They repeated the procedure until half a dozen buckets were filled.

"I'm guessing that's enough," Tim said.

"I'd say so. Just one bucket is good enough for me."

"I'll distribute them around to whoever else wants some. I guess we can dump the rest back in."

"Might as well. I don't think that many people will want samples."

Tim swung the crane around again and loosened the net. The remainder of the slop fell back into the ocean.

"It feels like I'm polluting it," he said.

"You probably are. I'm going to get this to the lab right away. I'll let you know how the tests come out, but it won't be for a few days."

"I'll be doing some tests too. I'll check in so we can compare them."

"Great, thank you," Ellen said over her shoulder as she marched off toward the door with her bucket of slop.

Back in the lab, she took several samples from the bucket and glopped them into test tubes. Now she had more than enough samples. Except for the ones from the bucket, they were all taken on different days and depths and because of that, they were all in different test stages. She labeled them carefully and mixed re-agents into some.

She was curious to know if all the tests would come out with the same inconclusive result, especially when such a differ-ence existed between the denser tissue found earlier as a solitary swimming animal and the more gelatinous substance scooped from the ocean surface. Mostly, she wanted a test to come back as conclusive of something. She wanted to figure this one mys-tery out.

Ryan opened the door to the lab. "You're not going to believe this."

"What?" Ellen couldn't bring herself to look away from the computer screen.

"The jellyfish, or whatever they are, turned back into sepa-rate organisms instead of one big thing."

"Are you sure?"

"Yeah, I even got it on film. It started forming bumps all over the place, then the bumps kind of pulled apart and now they look more like jellyfish again."

"You're kidding."

"No, I'll show you the film."

Ellen glanced at the bucket that contained the gelatinous slop. She snapped open the plastic cover and peered inside. Instead of the gooey substance that had been poured into it a few minutes earlier, several separate organisms floated there.

"They must be aliens," she said. "It's the only thing that makes any sense."

"This whole thing is really weird."

"Jellyfish don't do this kind of thing. They just don't."

After taking enough samples, Ellen made sure to tighten the lid on the bucket that contained the rest of them. She considered putting something heavy on the bucket just in case.

"Maybe they're evolving," Ryan said. "Maybe it's something they're just now learning to do."

"It seems more like a magic trick than evolution. I don't think so."

"But you did say we should be open to all the possibilities."

"That's right. As long as those possibilities make sense to me."

"Why doesn't it make sense? Maybe they've slowly learned over time that they're stronger as a group or as one huge thing than if they stay separate. Maybe the increase in jellyfish swarms has led them to this point in time where they've learned that not only can they be stronger that way, but they've figured out how to go one step further and fuse together like that."

"I don't think so. Evolution happens over many generations. Any changes really aren't that sudden. Jellyfish have survived through hundreds of millions of years. Think of that. They're among the oldest living animals on Earth. They're much older than we are. And they haven't changed much in all that time."

"So it's better to think that they're aliens, then?"

"What else could they be?"

Ryan furrowed his eyebrows in that fatherly way again. "I'm just saying there could be other reasons."

"Do you think I'm crazy now too?"

"No, you're just really dedicated to your work. I admire that in a crazy person."

"Thanks. But I'm right about this. You'll see."

"Don't get me wrong. I hope you are right. For your sake."

"It wouldn't exactly be better for the world though, having a bunch of aliens out there sucking up the life of the ocean."

"No, I guess not," Ryan said. "But if we are under an alien attack, it would be good to know."

"Right. I'd better get back to this then."

"Okay," he turned to go, then turned back. "I heard we'll be docking off another uninhabited island soon so at least we should be away from the swarm for now."

"Good. Thanks."

"What do you know?" She thought as he closed the lab door. You're not a scientist. You're just a kid. You don't understand evolution. You don't understand anything. She didn't say any of it out loud. The words pounded away in her brain as she returned to her samples.

~

Ocean Echoes

The steel wall creaked and began to hum and move. The creature sighed, for now there was more room to grow. It reached out and held onto the steel wall while detaching itself from the rest, knowing it would be carried far away. It was a sacrifice that had to be made for the betterment of the colony. Everything was for the betterment of the colony. The steel wall carried a small part to other lands as the wind carries a seed and the colony grew.

CHAPTER 48

WHILE LEAVING THE newest samples to sit in the warm water bath overnight, Ellen wished she could do the same. If she could relax, even for a minute, maybe everything would begin to make sense. But of course, there was never any time for relaxing and the only warm water baths onboard were for test tubes.

She decided to find Tim. Since he studied the composition of the ocean, he had probably been recording data on ocean temperature and salinity all along. He must have taken samples of ocean water to test the chemical makeup in different locations. That data could help bring the larger picture into focus. It would help to know if anything had changed in the water from the time period before the strange life forms appeared to when they invaded the ocean surface.

"Perfect timing," Tim said when she found him out on deck. "I just set the samples aside to react overnight."

"Me too," Ellen held onto the ship for extra support. "Do you think our test results will be the same or different?"

"They should be the same. But at any rate, it always helps to compare the tests."

Ellen nodded absently. "Did you record the ocean temperature and salinity from before the swarm appeared and after?"

"Yes. It's set up to be pretty automatic on this ship. I haven't fully looked through all the data yet, but I did notice that both temperature and salinity increased while the jellyfish were nearby."

"I had a feeling something like that might happen."

"Oh? Why's that?"

"They seemed like they were pretty determined, as if they were trying to change the ocean. So it makes sense that they did."

"But we don't know if the jellyfish changed the ocean water or if a change in the water drew the jellyfish there. It could really be either way."

"I suppose," Ellen stared at the waves. "But it did look like they were doing something to the ocean. Inhaling it or collecting it even."

The sun cast a shadow from the ship down to the water below. The shadow looked a bit menacing with its sharp rectangles and smokestacks. A green glow emanated from an island off in the distance as the departing sun angled toward it.

Tim's red baseball cap caught the sun and glowed brighter. Tiny freckles covered his face but could barely be seen. They seemed to reside beneath a layer of skin. She could be having a scientific discussion with Richie Cunningham.

"I guess it's hard to say what the jellyfish were doing," he said. "Maybe they were trying to blend in or become part of the ocean."

"Did you see how they all turned back into separate organisms?"

"I heard about it, then saw that it happened with the samples in the bucket."

"Same here. What do you think of that?"

"You're the one who studies jellyfish. What do you think?"

"I don't think they're jellyfish at all. I'm starting to think they're not even from this world."

Ellen expected Tim to laugh just as everyone else did, but instead he took a breath and said, "Well, that would explain it."

"Do you think that could be true?"

"I don't know what to believe. But I do know we can't rule anything out at this point."

"That's what I've been saying. But then everyone laughs it off and thinks I'm crazy."

"It is strange how most people believe in the idea of life on other planets, but the minute you start talking about aliens they're ready to lock you up in a padded cell."

"Maybe it's something about the word 'alien.'"

"Or it could be that people are scared by the thought and don't want to admit it so they push the whole idea away while telling themselves it couldn't be possible."

"That's a much better explanation than thinking I'm crazy," Ellen said. "I was starting to believe it myself."

"Any sane person has to be a little crazy these days. So just the fact that you think you might be crazy means you're not."

"Well, that's a relief. Thanks, I needed that."

"Any time. Let's make sure to compare those results when they're ready. We'll have to go through the ocean data more thoroughly for the time periods before and after that swarm was around."

"Sounds good," Ellen turned to go, then added, "And thank you."

"No problem."

While walking back along the deck, a wave of exhaustion hit and pulled her into a swirling vortex. She decided to go to bed without dinner. The thought brought up memories of being punished as a kid, usually for making a mess of things. Not much had changed. Then as now, she actually wanted to go to her room, partly because she didn't want to face everyone at the dinner table. At the moment, she felt much more tired than hungry and another dive was scheduled for 8 AM. So it was justified. She needed all the sleep she could get.

Once she snuggled into the scratchy blankets, she figured the exhaustion would take over right away, but it didn't. The ship clanged and creaked with sounds she didn't normally notice. She opened her eyes. Shadows danced on the walls and ceiling. But they weren't really dancing. More like slithering or leering. What could they possibly be shadows of anyway? The waves? It seemed more likely that the aliens caused them. Ellen laughed at herself. She needed some rest, that was all. She needed more rest and then everything would seem normal in the morning. Somehow.

CHAPTER 49

T IM CALLED AN early morning all-hands meeting to give everyone a chance to talk about the swarm while going over any potential dangers to divers. Ellen joined the crowd that had gathered while hoping this wouldn't make her late for her dive. She yawned. She hadn't slept at all and already felt like she might be under water.

Ryan walked up and whispered in her ear, "The dive gear's all ready to go."

"Great, hopefully we'll be able to get out of here soon."

Tim continued with his talk, "Although the ship has moved away from the swarm site, there's still a chance that divers could encounter another swarm out there. I think everyone was able to get a pretty good look at it yesterday so you know what to expect. Just be aware that it could happen again. Use extra caution while diving and make sure to monitor your dive site for any anomalies. If you do encounter another swarm, it's best to stay a safe distance away. We've got plenty of samples that we're currently analyzing so there's no need to risk your safety by trying to get any more. Just return to the ship and report back to me on the location of any swarm as soon as possible."

"Do the jellyfish in these swarms have the ability to sting?" Someone from the crowd asked.

Tim glanced at Ellen. "At this time, we don't know what type of jellyfish they are or if they are jellyfish at all, so it's best to assume that they do sting or that they can at least be dangerous in some way."

"If they're not jellyfish, what could they be?"

"We're still performing the tests, and then we'll have to see," Tim said. "You know how that goes."

The crowd mumbled. They were all used to the slow process of discovery.

"They're not jellyfish," Ellen told the crowd. "They might not even be from this planet. They're invasive and they could be following us, so don't be surprised if another swarm does show up."

Some people laughed, some looked at her with concern, others coughed and acted embarrassed. Once the trickle of laughter and coughs died down, no one made a sound.

Ellen wished she had gotten more sleep. Then maybe she'd be able to find the right words and make more sense. She shouldn't have said anything. The words were all wrong. Since there was no way of getting herself out of this hole, she dug deeper.

"Tim believes me. He said it's a possibility. I mean, look at them. Look at the film. They're sucking up the life of the ocean."

The crowd turned back toward Tim. He smiled and shrugged. With that strange expression on his face, he might as well have been making the circle motion with his finger near his ear, the one reserved for letting everyone know that a crazy person was in the room. He didn't say anything. He didn't defend her. He just stood there. So much for the flood of relief she had felt when it seemed like he believed her.

Finally, Tim took a breath and said, "Well, be safe out there today."

Most of the researchers took that as a signal to get back to work. A few glanced at Ellen, possibly trying to figure out if she could be playing a practical joke.

Ryan stood there with his hands in his pockets. She probably should have kept her mouth shut. But they should know the truth. They should be informed, warned, so they'd at least know what they were up against. Those creatures weren't jellyfish. They could be something much worse. Everyone underestimated them.

Now that silence filled the room and no one tried to argue with her, Ellen felt the need to get out of there. She backed away and practically ran down to the galley for her morning muffin and coffee.

Ryan followed and waited while she gobbled down her sorry excuse for a breakfast.

"Don't worry, there's enough time before the boat pick up. You don't have to choke on your muffin."

"I think I'm choking on more than that today."

Ryan scrutinized her, monitoring her behavior while taking internal notes. She was becoming used to that by now. At least he didn't say anything about her outburst. He probably figured it was better to pretend it never happened. Better to keep taking internal notes, as if she could be some kind of an animal at the zoo. An animal in need of some serious taming.

"We missed you at dinner last night," Ryan said.

"Thanks," Ellen took a giant mouthful of muffin. "I decided to take your advice and rest instead."

"Did it help?"

"Not really. I couldn't sleep anyway. I guess I might as well exhaust myself some more with another dive."

"We've still got a few minutes left. Want another muffin?"

"That's okay, no matter how hungry I am I don't think I could eat two muffins." She took another bite and finished it off. "All set, let's go."

Their pick-up boat puttered alongside the research ship. A few other divers piled in with their gear and tanks. The tiny inflatable felt crowded and loaded down as they took off toward the island. Ellen didn't know the other divers. They studied her strangely. Maybe they weren't really looking at her in that way, maybe paranoia took over, but it still felt like everyone stared.

As they approached the island, green mounds swayed into palm trees. The water held a clearer blue than the sky, so clear that every underwater activity could be seen from the boat. Crabs scrambled from one dark clump to another. Florescent fish flickered everywhere. The purple colors of the seafloor vegetation blurred and mixed with the turquoise sea.

"This is fine," Ellen told the driver. "You can let us out here."

They readied their scuba gear, strapped the heavy tanks on, and stepped into the blue. Ellen poked her head up and waved to show that they were clear of the boat before it sped off into the distance. This dive had been scheduled to last longer than usual.

She suspected the length of time had more to do with the boat schedule than anything else.

Ellen sank into the waves while feeling entirely unmotivated. They already had more than enough pictures, film, and samples of regular jellyfish and mysterious alien life forms. What more could they possibly want except the time to adequately go through all the data? For once, she found herself hoping they wouldn't find anything.

The water looked incredibly clear, clearer than she'd ever seen it on any dive. They might as well be suspended in midair. No wonder diving felt so much like flying. They could be diving through the sky, swimming through the air. The liquid sky shined with a silvery light.

A yellow frogfish poked his face out of a yellow coral cave, then sank back to blend in with his home. Small fish nibbled at the scales of larger fish, cleaning off parasites while finding a meal at the same time. The larger fish looked like they enjoyed being massaged by the tiny bites. They opened their mouths wider so that their teeth could be cleaned. The tiny fish flitted around and swam right into the open mouths, trusting them not to slam their jaws shut for an extra meal. A sea turtle swam by and nudged himself in for a cleaning.

More diversity can be found at a healthy reef than anywhere else on Earth and it certainly felt that way on this dive. Still, with so much life teeming and swimming and scuttling by, they didn't see any jellyfish. No dolphins either. The thought of the dolphins made Ellen smile. She hoped they would see them again soon.

Ryan looked distracted by all the ocean life, but kept swimming and investigating the coral patches. A school of parrotfish flew between them, glimmering black and silver. There were so many that they blocked her view of everything else. The fish swirled around like a mysterious dark cloud or tornado. They bumped and nibbled. Then with a final swirl, they floated away so that she could see Ryan again. Ellen signaled to him to surface.

"What do you think?" She asked when they were treading water. "I didn't see any jellyfish, did you?"

"No, even though it seems like everything else is there," Ryan said. "Maybe if we try going shallower there might be some."

"I guess we might as well try it. We've still got a lot of time. But if we don't see any, I'll be tempted to go up to that island to rest."

"Sounds good," Ryan said as he put his regulator in and ducked back down into the water.

She had been kidding about resting on the island, but maybe it wasn't such a bad idea. This dive had been scheduled for too much time and there were no jellyfish to be seen.

Besides, the island prickled her curiosity. It didn't make sense for it to be uninhabited when it looked so picturesque from a distance. Maybe something hid in its depths. For whatever reason, she wanted to find out. They swam into shallower water and she hoped they wouldn't see any jellyfish.

CHAPTER 50

E LLEN DISCONNECTED HERSELF from all the equipment that helped turn her into a fish: the regulator, weight belt, air tank, mask and flippers, and sat on the beach to acclimate to life above water again. Ryan peeled his gear off too. She figured they might as well leave it all on the beach since no one would steal it on an uninhabited island.

Her body relaxed and collapsed onto the sand. Resting there and looking up at the sky made her think of making snow angels. Too bad she didn't have the energy to attempt one. Instead, she closed her eyes and tried to soak up as much of the sun's energy as possible. Ryan sat up next to her like some kind of a guard dog. She felt his shadow fall across her body.

Now, if only he would lean over and kiss her. But of course he would never do anything like that and she shouldn't want such a thing. That would complicate everything. The last thing she needed now that the world and everything else seemed to be off its axis was another complication.

Then she felt Ryan's warm lips on hers. She must be imagining it. His lips felt soft and full and she opened herself up to them.

Nothing else mattered but the feel of his mouth. She blended in with it.

He hovered over her while still kissing, then leaned closer to kiss harder. She pulled him closer still so that she could feel his body against hers. For once, she didn't want to think or rationalize. She just wanted to feel.

They still had their scuba suits on. They must look ridiculous, like a couple of sea lions going at it, their slick skin wet and shining in the sun. She suppressed a laugh as soon as the image popped into her head. Ryan felt her stop and pulled away.

"Sorry," he said. "I don't know why I did that."

"That's okay." Her voice sounded a little shaky. She sat up and occupied herself with getting the sand out of her wet hair, then pulled everything back into place while hoping she looked a little more normal than she felt.

"I guess I thought you wanted me to do it though."

"You don't have to do everything you think I want," Ellen said while trying to brush the sand off of her back.

"Sorry."

"That's all right, it's just too complicated. Let's pretend it never happened, okay?"

"I'll try."

From the look he gave her, she didn't think he would forget but then she didn't see how she'd be able to either.

"Want to go explore the island?" She checked her watch. "The boat won't be back to pick us up for a while."

"Sure." He bounced up and brushed the sand off.

"We'll have to be careful walking around in the jungle since we don't have any shoes."

"It'll be like we're real natives then."

"Yeah, natives wearing scuba outfits."

"Pretty spooky island." Ryan looked around and then back at her like he wanted to kiss her again.

Ellen tried to ignore it. She wiped the sand from her arms and legs while fighting the urge to grab him and pull him closer.

"Okay, let's go."

They moved toward the jungle, then ventured along the perimeter. The vegetation grew in such a tangle that she couldn't see any way into it. Even though it still sounded like a fun thing to do, she didn't see how anyone could possibly run through the jungle. Not this jungle anyway. But then she'd probably taken part in enough wild activity for one day.

They searched for a path as the leaves and brush rustled around them. Ellen couldn't tell if it was the wind or if whatever might be hiding beyond the leaves caused the sound. She imagined the animals, with fangs of course, hiding in the green depths, crouching and watching, getting ready to pounce.

They curved around a bend while circling the vegetation from the beach. No path of any kind could be seen there either. Palm trees strained away, gasping for air. Their leaves gave off a ghostly tambourine rattle. Ryan was right. This island did have an eerie feel to it.

They kept trudging through the sand until they came to a slight indentation in the jungle, which funneled down to a path. Tree roots and moss made the path look dark and slimy.

"Want to try it?" Ellen asked.

"Sure, I'll be right behind you."

"Okay, but you better stay back there. Don't go running away or anything."

"I don't think there's anything in there that could make me run away from you."

"Don't be so sure," Ellen said, feeling the uneasiness again. She stepped onto the path and her bare feet slid into cold clamminess. It felt like she could be walking on someone's skin. She tried not to put too much weight down on her feet just in case.

After a few steps, the jungle closed in around them. She felt cool for the first time in weeks. Lush green life enveloped everything and brushed by her bare arms and legs. It hung overhead in twisted vines and leaves, blocking out the sky and darkening the path ahead. She walked carefully over the roots and rocks while trying not to slip and fall.

The path eventually opened to a clearing. It reminded Ellen of the island they visited when they first arrived. No ceremonial fire crackled here though. Only a few abandoned homes stood at the edge of the clearing, on the verge of being swallowed by the jungle.

Ellen turned back to Ryan. "I wonder what made them leave."

"Other than the fact that this island is incredibly spooky?"

"Yes, other than that."

"Maybe that's the reason."

Ellen laughed. "I guess it's as good as any."

"Is it time to go back yet?"

She looked at her watch. "We've still got some time. Want to look in those houses first?"

"Not really, but I guess I'll have to if you do."

She couldn't say why, but she felt pulled toward the houses. She told herself it was curiosity that tugged at her, nothing more. Still, it did feel as if something forced her forward.

Tall grass and weeds poked up between the structures. Corrugated metal walls and rooftops rusted into flimsiness. Everything smelled of rust, which also happened to smell like blood. Ellen pushed back a piece of creaky metal that might have been used as a door at one time.

While peering inside, she realized these structures weren't houses at all. Metal boxes were stacked against the walls. It looked like they'd been sitting there for at least half a century. She brushed the dust off one and opened it. Beach sand filled the space. She brought it outside to show Ryan.

"What do you make of this?" Ellen turned the opened box over and spilled the sand out. Nothing but more sand seemed to be hidden beneath the sand.

"Weird," was all Ryan had to say.

Ellen put the empty box down, turned back to the shed, and opened the creaky door to show him what hid inside.

"Do you think all these boxes are filled with sand?"

At least fifty boxes stood against the rusted wall. Ellen walked in and opened another box to make sure. More sand.

"These boxes and sheds look like they could be military." Ryan picked up the empty box and turned it around in his hands, looking for any possible clues.

Ellen walked over to one of the other sheds and saw more metal boxes stacked inside. She picked one up. It rattled and felt heavier than the others. She opened it to see bullets lined up in polished rows.

"Yep, military," she said as she showed him.

"What would anything like that be doing out here on an uninhabited island?"

"This must have been some kind of a military post, maybe during World War II."

"This place is so far from everything though. It doesn't make sense. And why would there be a bunch of sand in all those boxes?"

"No idea," Ellen said. "All I know is that lately nothing makes sense."

She put the box back in the shed and glanced at her watch. "We should get going."

Back on the jungle path, Ellen kept feeling as if they were being watched. She gazed into the green. The jungle reminded her of the ocean, flickering in the spaces between shadow and light with mystifying shades. Emerald colors exuded a liquid feel as they slid in and out of her line of vision. Her arms brushed by the colors, swimming through them as she tried to search the depths. What might be hidden there, beyond her line of vision?

A face appeared and stared back at her. Ellen screamed.

"Please, don't be afraid," the face said.

Ryan tried to force himself between the two but there wasn't much room.

"It's okay, I was just startled." She steadied herself while touching Ryan's arm.

The face moved away from the vegetation and took the form of a man. His tan skin appeared mottled on his neck and shoulder and was partially covered by a ripped t-shirt. Dappled light clung to him, making his black hair shine. His smile completely took over his face. He looked like he might hug Ellen if not for Ryan standing guard by her side.

"Do you live here?" Ellen asked.

The man erupted with a high-pitched laugh. "No, no, my island is far away from here. The ocean swallowed me up and spit me out in this land of spirits and ghosts. The ocean did not want me to fish anymore. So it rose up against me and left me here."

"Are you from Mala?"

The man nodded and gave her a curious look. "How did you know?"

"I think I met your wife. She's been looking for you. Everyone's been looking for you."

Tears welled up in his eyes. "Could you bring me back to my family?"

"Of course. We'll have to bring you to our research ship first, but I'm sure a motorboat could take you to your island from there."

"I thought I would have to build a boat if I ever wanted to see my family again and that would take a very long time. Too long, and I've already been away for too long. My name is David."

"Nice to meet you. Do you need to get anything before you leave? We have to hurry to meet our pick-up boat."

"No, I need nothing but my wife and family. I will go with you now. I only hope the ocean is not still angry with me."

Ocean Echoes

"I knew this island was spooky," Ryan mumbled behind them as they started walking. "Ghosts, that explains it."

They followed the path to the beach and hurried through the hot sand to their scuba gear. A motorboat floated offshore. They waved and yelled until it chugged toward them for the pick up.

CHAPTER 51

R YAN COULDN'T KEEP himself from smiling as they motored back to the research ship. The blue sky reflected his mood. It looked so perfect, so infinite. He drifted off into the blue while wondering why people didn't get more excited about the sky.

An ecstasy for life surged through his body at the thought. He couldn't contain everything and might overflow with it, which would be a good thing because then Ellen would have to feel it and be overloaded with it and then she would finally let herself be happy.

She worried too much. If she would only let herself feel more, without stopping to think or analyze, the happiness would overtake her too. Even if nothing ever came of that kiss, it still felt right. At least it brought them closer. Nothing else had to happen or be explained away. He didn't understand why she said it was too complicated. It wasn't complicated at all.

So there were a few roadblocks, but he didn't see them as complications. They weren't anything to worry about. Besides, whenever any obstacles come up the best thing to do is to plow right through them. Isn't that the way love is supposed to be, when you don't let anything get in the way of becoming closer to each other?

He wanted to kiss her more. When something felt that good, why would anyone want to question it or pretend it didn't happen? He wanted to reach over and kiss her again but David kept looking at them and now there were other researchers onboard. He settled for smiling at her. Maybe his feelings would radiate out enough so that she would feel them and understand. But she kept staring out at the waves.

He looked toward David and yelled over the motor, "So how long were you on that island?"

"Oh, a very long time. Days, weeks, I don't know. It felt as if time did not exist. When the ocean first spit me out, I couldn't tell what was happening. Then the island spirits helped me."

Ellen perked up at that. "How did the spirits help?"

"They talked to me, told me stories, brought me back to life. After the ocean chewed me, there was not much left. The spirits helped to heal me with their energy, though I do not yet feel whole."

"Did you say the ocean chewed you?" Ellen asked with a tinge of disbelief.

"Yes, it swallowed me, chewed, and spit me out like a broken shell. I still feel that way without my family. The ocean was not happy with me."

"You make it sound like the ocean could be alive in some way."

"It is alive. It breathes in and out, just like us. It has moods. It can be angry or calm, most times with no warning. It is filled with energy. Sometimes it can be a monster. Other times it gives us fish."

Ellen squinted out toward the horizon and smiled. "I guess that's one way to look at it."

"It is the only way," David said.

Her eyes turned toward the scar on his neck and shoulder. "Did the ocean do that?"

Sadness came over David's face. "Yes, yes the ocean was very angry with me."

"Well, I'm glad we found you out there," Ryan said.

"I am glad too." David surveyed the waves as if expecting them to jump up and bite. "I am very glad indeed."

When they pulled up to the research ship, Ryan let them know he'd put the dive gear away.

"Thanks, I should go introduce David to Tim so that we can get him back home," Ellen said before letting out a brief yawn. "All this diving can be pretty tiring."

"That and jungle exploring."

"Yes, that too."

She gave him a nervous look as if trying to figure out what he might be thinking when really he wasn't thinking anything. He waved goodbye to David, then turned his attention to the dive gear. If he couldn't kiss her again to make her feel better in that way, he'd have to try to make her happy in other ways.

CHAPTER 52

E LLEN HEARD YELLING from the deck while towel drying her
hair. She traded her towel for shorts and a tank top. Her hair
remained a wet tangled mop. She ran her fingers through it and
opened the door to chaos.

A stream of people flowed out to the deck. She figured the
ship must be sinking or on fire. Usually researchers like these
took most things in stride. Under normal conditions, they stood
back to observe and examine and didn't often run toward or away
from much. She joined the crowd and sprinted out to the deck.

Everyone hung over the railing while pointing down to the
water. Ellen looked down to see the familiar sight of the swarm.
It made her dizzy. She thought the ship had gotten away from it.
Now it seemed to be a recurring nightmare.

At least most of the ocean looked clear of it this time.
The red stain centered mainly in the water around the ship. It
didn't blanket as much of the ocean surface as before, but this
time the strange life forms crawled and slithered up the side.
Researchers pointed and panicked at the sight of the swarm
moving ever closer. Ellen watched the gelatinous mess advance
right toward her.

Ryan and Jake came over and followed her stare.

"Still think I'm crazy?" Ellen asked.

"Of course," Jake said. "But I will admit I've never seen jellyfish do anything like that. Ever."

"That's because they're not jellyfish," Ellen whispered into the wind.

"What do you think they'll do if they make it all the way up here?" Ryan asked.

"At least it's a long way up. Maybe they'll get tired partway and decide to ooze back down."

"Right. What can they really do to us anyway?" Jake asked. "I mean, at least they don't have teeth, right?"

"I didn't see any in the samples," Ellen said. "But then the samples did change into separate life forms. Who knows how much more these things can change."

The creatures weren't near the railing yet. They had advanced a couple meters above the water line but there was still a long way to go before reaching the top. Ellen visualized the swarm slipping over the railing, onto the deck of the ship, toward her, always toward her. Even if all that red looked closer to the water surface for now, the red part of the ship remained covered from bow to stern.

"That would be really weird if they had teeth," Jake said. "Do you think they might try to capture us and take us back to their planet?"

Ellen couldn't tell to what degree he was joking or making fun of her and decided the chance was pretty high on any scale.

"You never know. We think we know everything by now, and then something like this happens and we realize we know nothing at all."

"Has David been able to get back home yet?" Ryan asked.

"Tim said he'd get a crew member to bring him back in one of the smaller boats. Hopefully they got away safely before this attack."

"Do you still think they're aliens?"

"Nothing we know of on Earth looks and acts like this. Look how invasive they are. They must have followed us here. It seems like they're trying to take over or at least cause some major damage."

"So if they can't take over the world, maybe they'll take over our ship?" Jake asked. "And then gum us to death?"

"Hey, you were afraid of them when we were out on the water, remember?"

"Yes but now I'm feeling a little more superior since we're way up here and they're way down there and they hopefully can't get to us quite so easily. Even if they are trying to."

"Well, you shouldn't feel superior. We don't know what they are. They could be a higher form of intelligence for all we know."

"Yeah, right," Jake said. "I'll believe it when I see it."

"You might be seeing it soon if we don't get away from here. This ship should be moving. Why isn't it moving?"

"We're not supposed to leave this site for a couple more days," Ryan said.

"So we're just going to sit here and let them eat the ship?" Ellen could hear the panic rising in her own voice.

"Is that what they're doing?" Jake asked. "They can't eat the ship. They don't have teeth, right?"

Ryan reached his hand out to touch Ellen's arm as if to tame a wild beast.

"Maybe we should go get some lunch," he said.

"I'm not hungry. I've got a lot of work to do in the lab anyway."

Ellen thought of all the ocean life they'd seen while scuba diving: the seal family, the giant clams, dolphins, fluorescent fish, sea turtles, generations upon generations of coral. What would this thing do to them? Hopefully the research ship hadn't somehow lured the swarm here to wreak havoc on this pristine place.

The loudspeaker crackled, then whistled before Tim's voice took over with, "Okay everyone, there's no need to panic. We'll be moving away from the swarm soon, but we'll stay in the general vicinity so the planned experiments shouldn't be affected by any of this."

Ellen realized any move would be a futile one. The creatures kept finding them. She took one final glimpse over the edge. The swarm stayed where it was for now, but it still seemed to be reaching.

"Could you keep watching it and let me know if it gets any closer?" She asked Ryan.

"Sure, I'll get the camera and film some of it too."

Ellen started toward the door, then looked back to see Jake and Ryan leaning over the side, talking and laughing. She didn't have to wonder what they were laughing about. She was sure they were laughing at her. Well, lately she'd given them a lot of laughing material, especially if he'd told Jake about kissing her. How could she have let that happen? The whole thing felt like a dream: a hazy, out of focus dream that had nothing to do with reality. She had been too stressed and didn't know what was happening until it happened. Then it was almost too perfect. Maybe it had been a dream after all.

She wondered if Ryan regretted it now. He could be laughing with Jake out of embarrassment. Then to top it all off, she must look pretty scary after towel drying her hair into a mop. Those dark circles that had appeared under her eyes a while ago refused to go away. Sometimes that happened because of the change in pressure while diving. Or that spirit, the spirit from the outdoor church, could be tagging along for the ride. At times she did feel as if something or someone other than herself might be in control. If it happened to be that spirit, then that would explain something.

She wasn't acting like herself, whatever that was, whatever that was supposed to be. Like she had told Ryan and Jake, no one really knows anything. We all think we know things, we think things are certain and true, but then something always comes along to change that truth. So that, in the end, nothing is true at all.

Who knows, maybe ghosts and spirits are everywhere. We can't see or prove these things, but that doesn't mean they're not there. We may never fully understand all the mysteries. Maybe it's better that way. Because when we think we understand something like nature, we demystify it. And with that demystification, with that kind of progress if you can call it that, comes a lack of respect.

Ellen thought of the fire butterflies and the sea turtles that were called with song. Did islanders like David respect nature more because of their legends, because they believed in magic and mysteries? They chose to embrace the mysteries instead of trying to figure them out. Ellen never would have believed such things unless she had seen them happen. She still didn't fully believe them. How was it possible that sea turtles could be called with song while they were still in the same world as the one she had come from, where everything was continually mapped out, measured, and explained?

She wasn't even sure what she was thinking anymore.

She decided to hide away in the lab for a bit after retrieving her baseball cap. Back in her quarters, she attempted to brush her hair while discovering it had morphed into a mass of seaweed, then gathered it back anyway, and found her baseball cap to cover up the resulting mess. While opening the door, she ran directly into Maddie.

"Well hi there," Maddie said. "Did you see all those jellyfish out there?"

Ellen decided to let it go this time. "Yes. I was just on my way to the lab. We've got so much data now that we'll be going through it for years."

"Those ones out there sure are strange though," Maddie said. "I've never seen jellyfish creep up a ship like that. Michael and I were just saying we couldn't believe you weren't out there studying it all."

"I was out there, I just didn't see you."

"Oh, well I'm so glad you got to see it all then," Maddie said. "You kind of like him, don't you?"

"Who? Michael?"

"I think he likes you too."

Ellen wanted to run but then she'd have to somehow trample over Maddie. For some reason, Maddie kept standing there, smiling with gleaming teeth. Her red hair glowed, adding to the overall effect. Ellen blinked a couple times.

"What do you mean?"

"Oh, you know what I mean. He keeps saying how concerned he is for you and all so he must really like you. He's a great guy. He's super dedicated to his work, but then so are you. You two would be great together. Like a team of superheroes or something."

Ellen felt the heat travel from her neck to her face. "Well, I don't really have time for anything like that. And he probably doesn't either. I've got to get to the lab."

"Oh! Sorry, I didn't want to hold you up. I just wanted you to know, I mean, if you didn't already realize that is."

"Okay, thanks for the warning."

"Well, it wasn't meant as a warning, silly. He really is a great guy."

"I'll take your word for it." Ellen finally eased by the fiery barricade and was able to say those parting words over her shoulder as she hurried away.

She closed the door to the lab and exhaled her relief at the resulting solitude. The warm water bath whirred, lights blinked and buzzed, her laptop greeted her with a push of a button. All was finally as it should be.

Everyone wanted something. At times, she felt like she could be a balloon too full of hot air, continually stretching herself. Someday, perhaps someday soon, she would explode. Either that or everything would slowly leak out and fizzle away, propelling her off in an erratic direction, making her as lost as a person could possibly be. Then she would finally collapse and fall to the ground, used and spent and drained of all energy.

The memory of Ryan's kiss came burning back, making her body feel that tingling sensation again. She tried not to think about it, tried not to feel.

Frustration threatened to overwhelm her with this constant push and pull toward and away from him, as if caught up in some inexorable tidal force. Through it all, Ryan stayed there, as constant as the moon while she sent herself through these contortions that were actually caused by him. He seemed almost entertained by her low and high tides while continually shining his light toward her. She should really stop thinking about him and focus on her work, but that seemed impossible while he kept orbiting around everywhere.

She checked her messages. One of the DNA experts had finally replied. She held her breath as she read the email.

He said that, although it wasn't obvious from the test results, the DNA from the first sample did appear to be distantly related to jellyfish. He wasn't sure, but he suspected it could be a new species and would send the information out for confirmation. There would be more channels to go through in order to adhere an official "new species" label, such as a scientific peer review, but before that he wanted to check with another expert first. Ellen sighed. She was used to this laborious collective deciding and figuring out process by now, but still wished someone would stand up and say "here is a result" or "this is a truth" without having to check with every other expert first.

How could the first sample possibly be related to jellyfish when her tests proved it wasn't related to anything on Earth? The supposed expert must be wrong. Well, it was a good thing he had decided to check with someone else then. The real expert would confirm that the sample is not related to anything and that it is in fact an alien life form. That was the only possibility, the only real truth.

Ellen checked on the assorted tissue samples. There were so many now that she could barely keep track. She referred to her field journal to make sure: first the small Nomura taken on the dive outside the lagoon and the two nearly transparent jellyfish taken on the blue-water dive; then the denser purplish sample that looked so much like a heart; another heart-like life form that had been filmed first; and finally the more gelatinous samples taken when they first saw the swarm from the motorboat, then later from the deck of the research ship.

She realized they hadn't seen any real jellyfish since the swarm began appearing. The swarm could be eating the normal jellyfish or taking and replacing them in some way. Even before the swarms appeared, she remembered thinking they weren't finding enough jellyfish and that there really should be more in the area.

She jotted down a few notes then read through them, trying to make sense of it all. The only thing that did make sense, the only possible conclusion, was that these life forms were not from Earth. Everything pointed to it. Why didn't anyone else see that when it was so obvious? She scribbled in her notebook and pressed down on her pen, then turned to the samples in the warm water bath. The sample taken from the motorboat during their first swarm encounter looked about ready for the DNA test. She stuck the sampling wand in, hooked it up to her laptop, and watched as the software program constructed a DNA strand. The laptop made it look so easy. She hoped it would have more luck with the information than her brain did.

CHAPTER 53

Home rose up out of the ocean, a lush green offering of peace and promise. At times, David thought he would never see his home or family again. Now this motorboat zoomed toward home, toward everything he needed. His heart traveled faster than the boat. It leapt away, danced on the waves, and waited for him on shore.

The Man in the Rock greeted him with a satisfied smirk. He no longer screamed out at the waves. When David saw that, he thought this might not be home after all. This nice man brought him to the wrong island. But everything else looked the same: the same coral entrance and waves slurping, the same lagoon and beach he knew so well.

He wanted to jump out of the boat and swim to shore. But the ocean might still be angry with him. The waves splashed and sputtered, stammering with pent up emotion. Better to stay in the boat.

He jumped out as soon as the boat touched the sand. Only then did he notice his clothes had been shredded by the ocean's rage. His t-shirt and shorts gaped with holes like the open mouths of fish. He looked down and let out his hyena laugh, then turned back to the man in the boat.

"Thank you, my friend, for bringing me home. Would you like to meet my family? You could stay for dinner. They would like that."

"No thanks, I've got to get back to the research ship. Take care now."

With that, the man who brought him home puttered out into the waves. David knew he would remember him always and wished he could have known him better. So many opportunities for friendship are missed because of things everyone has to do or get back to.

But for now, his family was all he needed. David ran through the sand into the jungle. The path opened for him as he ran. Pointed green leaves flew up in surprise. Purple and pink flowers nodded their heavy heads, saying they always knew he'd be back. Their sweet perfume enveloped him with smells of home.

He ran to his house and threw open the door. Kalani looked up from her stew, wide eyed and startled. His children cheered and jumped on him, even his oldest. They hugged him close and hung off of him and asked a million questions at once.

"Where did you go, Papa?"

"What happened to you?"

"Why were you gone so long?"

"How did you find your way back to us?"

He had no answers. Only that love had kept him alive. And love brought him back. He felt that love grow as he hugged his children, then as he looked at Kalani. She smiled and wiped her tears away while still crying. He reached over their jumping children to hold her close.

Love welled up inside with such force that he thought he must be shining with it. He felt it everywhere, filling him, pouring out into the air. Together, they created such a powerful love. That had kept him alive. Even when everything seemed hopeless, he did not give up. He would never give up on so much love.

CHAPTER 54

ELLEN JERKED HER head off the counter. Pain crawled up her arm. She tried to discover the source of the pain but could only see that her arm was red and swelling. It burned while an invisible knife stabbed her. She leapt up from her chair. What happened? She must have dozed off but what could have happened to her arm?

She searched the lab for something to cool the pain, then noticed that the lid to the plastic bucket was ajar. The bucket that held the creatures. She peered into it. A few floated around inside, but it looked like there weren't as many in there as before. They must have gotten out. They must have stung her and then gone off somewhere to hide.

She snapped the lid back on and piled heavy books on top before running toward a sink to spray cold water on the swelling. It felt a little better with the water pouring over it but still burned. That numb feeling would never last long enough. She grabbed an ice pack from a cooler and rubbed it on her arm. Better. She found a first aid kit, wrapped an ace bandage around the ice pack, fastened it tight, then pulled her waterproof jacket on to cover everything up. She gulped down a few aspirin as if that would do anything after an alien attack. Her arm still throbbed but it wasn't on fire anymore. The pain smoldered instead.

Ellen searched the floor. She half expected to see one of those things slithering there by her feet or up a wall. But no, she couldn't find any. Maybe they were hiding. Watching her. Or else they found their way back to the ocean, which only meant they'd be wreaking havoc someplace else by now. The room started spinning, forcing her to plunk back down in her chair.

She couldn't catch her breath. If those creatures had stung her and if they were from another world, what would happen then? She thought about David's scar, and wondered if it could have been caused by the same sort of attack. David had survived at least. Survived, yes, but it might have affected him in strange ways. He said it had taken a long time to recover and the spirits helped him.

She closed her eyes. She tried to call upon the spirit from the outdoor church, her grandmother, any spirit at all, but nothing happened. Her arm only burned and throbbed more. She should have known. She was alone. She had been alone all along. There was no one there to help.

CHAPTER 55

A T DINNER, THE latest swarm was all anyone could talk about. Ellen listened to the voices as they rambled on until the sound became an insidious background moan. They all sounded so self-assured with their theories and conjectures. No one really knew what anyone was talking about, even as everyone talked on and on.

The separate voices turned into murmurs or reverberations. They swished and roared and took on the sound of the ocean. At first she thought it might be a leftover effect from all the diving. Her ears could still be plugged up. The water continued to pour in. It filled the empty spaces and became a barrier as it jostled everywhere now, making any real communication impossible.

She didn't want anyone to know about her arm. Luckily, the night brought in cooler air so keeping her jacket on might not seem too suspicious. Her arm still throbbed and now the throbbing traveled to her head as it filled with voices. There were so many voices. Michael, Maddie, Ryan, Jake. Their voices, but not just theirs. She heard David talking about the ocean and how it was alive, her grandmother's reassuring tones as she tried to get the jellyfish tentacles off, Andrew and the island chief talking of the spirits that were always there. Helping. Not helping.

Ellen felt a scream well up inside. She looked down at her plate with its lump of macaroni and cheese and almost let it come hurtling out. Then Michael asked a question. She swallowed the scream down as if it could be some kind of sustenance. It burned inside.

"Have the results come in from the samples taken during the latest swarm?"

Why were they all so interested? They probably wanted to steal her research too, just like Paul. She reminded herself not to say too much.

"No, I haven't sent those out yet," Ellen said. "I just finished isolating the DNA on those and the computer is doing the work for now."

"It'll be interesting to see the results. Have you heard back on the first sample that was sent out for more analysis?"

"I just did. He said there's a chance that it might be a new species but he needs to show the information to some other expert before confirming it."

"That's great, right?"

"Sure. He also said it's not obvious from the test results, but there's a slight possibility that it could be related to jellyfish. He wasn't sure about that part either though."

"So then it can't be an alien if it's related to jellyfish."

"That's true, but I think he's wrong."

"You think the expert is wrong in his conclusion on the very thing that he's an expert on?"

The air took on a watery haze. Ellen felt a drop of sweat trickle down her face. "He wasn't sure about any of it. If he's really such an expert, then why does he need to get confirmation?"

"That's how these things work. You know that. It's a slow process. All of our work is. Especially if this is going to be named a new species, then there are all kinds of channels to go through and paperwork to complete before it becomes official. And a scientific peer review will need to be held."

"I know, but for once I'd like to hear that something has finally been discovered or found to be true without having to go through the whole process of bringing in other experts and opinions first."

"That would be nice, but consulting others helps us to be sure of these things, especially when untraditional theories are involved."

"I don't know why I keep trying to find the truth when nothing is true."

Ryan kept looking from Ellen to Michael and back again. "But finding an unknown species is a new discovery," he said. "Even if it does need all kinds of confirmation, it's still something special."

"I guess." She didn't feel like going into all the reasons why it's not really such a great thing, starting with the fact that there are many millions or more species still unknown to humans. About eighty-six percent of the planet's species are still unknown. It wasn't as if they had found the only unknown thing.

"He's right," Michael said. "You should be celebrating."

"Except that it's not a new species," Ellen said as she stabbed her macaroni and cheese.

"What if this other expert confirms what the first one said and agrees that it's related to jellyfish? Would you still insist that it's an alien?"

"Probably," Ellen said. "It's the only thing that makes sense."

"Oh, we're making sense now, are we?" Michael asked. "Okay, let's say it is an alien. Then why would it have DNA? I would think the fact that it has DNA shows that it isn't an alien."

"Every living thing in the universe must have DNA," Ellen said. "We're all from the same universe and so we're all related even if we're not all from Earth."

Michael laughed. "Listen to yourself. Just listen to yourself. We're all related even if we're not all from Earth? There hasn't even been any living thing found outside of Earth."

"That doesn't mean it's not true. That doesn't mean it's not out there. Why would this planet be the only one with life? That doesn't make any sense. Especially when you consider that everything started from one atom, one single kernel of energy became the universe and all that there is. Every atom that's in us was once part of that single bit of energy. We're all made of the same materials, the same energy, and so is everything in the universe."

"I can't believe you're actually trying to convince us that aliens would have DNA," Jake said. "And the weirdest part is that it's working. I'm becoming convinced. But I think that's just because you're a good arguer."

"Well, I'm not convinced," Michael said. "To me, the fact that it has DNA means it must be from Earth. Let's not forget the DNA expert said it might be related to jellyfish. You're just discounting that so that you can continue on with your alien fantasy."

Ellen laughed for a little too long. Ryan gave her his usual concerned look but now Maddie joined forces with him and projected one too. She ignored them both.

"It's not a fantasy. You think I want this to be true? I know that everyone thinks I'm crazy because of it. I don't want to go around spouting insane theories. Believe me, I'd be happier if it turned out to be a new species. That would be much better all the way around. But it's not. I know it's not."

Ryan sighed. "Well, you are the jellyfish expert, so if anyone would know the difference, it would be you."

"Thanks." She crumpled in her chair, weighed down by the throbbing pain in her arm and the feeling that no one would ever truly believe her.

Michael examined his plate and took a bite of his food. He chewed slowly as if to occupy his mouth for as long as possible.

Ellen felt the need to fill the silence. "When you really think about it, how could those life forms possibly be related to jellyfish? Everyone here saw that latest swarm. Not only did they fuse together into one huge organism, but then the whole thing started oozing up the side of the ship. Nothing I've ever seen on Earth acts like that."

"You're the one who said there are attack jellyfish out there, like that supposed fried egg jellyfish," Michael said.

"That only attacks other jellyfish. And it doesn't act at all like the invasive force that spread up the side of the ship. It doesn't fuse together with others to become one gigantic life form."

"Now that you mention it, whatever happened to that ooze?" Jake asked. "Is it still out there or what?"

"Oh, it's still out there," Maddie said. "At least it was last time I looked."

"What do you think it's trying to do?" Jake asked.

Ryan and Michael both shrugged. Everyone looked over at Ellen.

"It's trying to attack the ship. It followed us here. What other reason could there be for following us? It wants to spread out as much as possible and destroy everything."

"Maybe it's just curious," Ryan said. "It could have followed us out of curiosity rather than some sort of malicious intent."

Jake nodded. "Right. Even if it is an alien, that doesn't necessarily mean it's out to destroy us. It could just be collecting data. It might be trying to determine what the ship is."

"When the swarm was in the ocean, it looked like it was sucking the ocean up," Ellen said. "Then it looked like it was collecting data. But oozing up the side of the ship looks like an attack to me."

"Oh come on," Michael said. "How can something as innocuous as a jellyfish really attack us?"

"Real jellyfish are anything but innocuous," Ellen said. "They might want you to think that, but that's how they draw you in. Jellyfish kill and injure many more people per year than sharks."

"Maybe we should go look and see if they're still out there," Jake said. "Or if they're higher up than they were. They could be waiting for darkness to set in before fully attacking."

Michael turned to Ellen. "You're scaring them. They're going to be up all night worrying about this, and then what good will they be in the morning?"

"We should go look," Ellen said. "If they're still attached to the ship tomorrow, they should be removed before heading home. We don't want to be responsible for bringing something like that closer to civilization."

"It could be just what civilization needs," Michael said.

"Funny, but I don't think so. Civilization already has enough to handle."

"They better not still be out there," Jake said. "Or I really won't get any sleep tonight. I'll keep imagining them slithering into my bed or something."

They filed out on deck and took a look over the side. The sun had set and darkness took over, blurring everything with a gray tinge so that nothing looked clear.

Maddie squinted over the side. "Looks like it's still there."

"I don't think so," Ellen said. "I think that's just rust."

Ryan left and came back with a flashlight. He slowly swept the beam down along the side.

"It's gone," he said. "Just rust and metal."

"It looks like there's more rust than I remember being there," Ellen said. "I wonder if they did that."

Michael laughed into the darkness. "You're always causing trouble, aren't you?"

~

Later that night, Ellen wandered out on deck for some air. She had changed her ice pack and her arm felt a little better. The swelling had gone down for now. It didn't look anything like the jellyfish sting she remembered from her teenage years. She tried not to think about it. Tried not to think about what that alien venom could be doing to her body or mind or both.

She took a deep breath of starlight. Even with the faint glowing lights of the ship, the stars still took over the sky. She loved being able to see the dustiness of the Milky Way, the constellations so pronounced. The stars made everything look so peaceful as they blinked their messages. But what were those messages? Would any inhabitants of those distant planets wish us harm?

Furry arms grasped her shoulders and held on tight.

"Hi Jake," she said without looking back.

"Oh come on, I can't even scare you?" A muffled voice asked.

"Guess not. I've seen too much of life to be scared off by some fur."

"I don't believe that. You just weren't looking."

"True. The stars were a little too distracting."

"Maybe I should get a vampire or alien costume. Something scarier than a gorilla."

Ellen swerved to look at him. "In this light, the gorilla is pretty scary."

"In that case, I'll have to go find someone else to scare." He held up his hands and stuck his fingers out to form claws.

"Good luck," Ellen said while drifting off toward the stars again.

She felt Jake move away, felt the absence of a person who had once been there. It caused a shiver even though no real chill could be found in the moist air.

A shrill scream pierced the night. So the gorilla had found someone to scare after all.

CHAPTER 56

E LLEN TOOK ANOTHER breath of the night air and the stars and, while hoping they'd infuse her with needed energy, headed back to the lab.

So far all her tests agreed. The DNA came from an unknown species that wasn't related to anything on Earth. Her computer generated hundreds of information files to back up its inconclusive results. After sending all of the information out for more analysis, Ellen started looking through the swarm videos.

While comparing the different appearances or invasions, she found it hard to believe that the first dark purple one they saw swimming off by itself could be the same life form as the ones congregating together in swarms. The first one was much darker and denser. Either the group became so all consuming that it altered the physical structure of the individuals or the first one really was a different life form.

Her computer only concluded that all of the samples were unknown. It didn't say they were all the same. If they were different, that would explain why the first sample had come back from analysis as possibly related to jellyfish. Maybe the swarm samples, the ones that had acted so invasive, wouldn't be related to anything. Ellen checked her email messages again. She hadn't heard back on the other samples, but then she had just sent the last ones out. The experts must be feeling bombarded by now.

Tomorrow they would begin their journey home. Ellen dreaded the arrival. Home meant a more rational place, a place where things should make sense but still didn't. While out in such a remote area surrounded by ocean and wind, it was easier to believe in all the possibilities, even if life forms from another planet happened to be one of them. There would be more pressure for things to make sense at home. And nothing ever did.

How could she explain all this? Should she, even? If the press found out, the reporters would make her look insane. They could turn her into a modern day mad scientist. That's what they would call her or worse. The more insane they made her look, the more the story would catch on and sell. She would lose her funding once and for all. She'd never have a future in science. At least she could say she had warned them once the invasions became more obvious, though that wouldn't be much of a consolation.

The jellyfish disguise could be a mechanism sent to collect data. The ones controlling those mechanisms could be more menacing than that swarm. They could be something much worse.

Ellen kept watching the video. As the swarm sucked the ocean up, it appeared to grow stronger. As it grew stronger, it spread out and covered more of the ocean surface, possibly even suffocating the ocean as it continued to feed off it. If it continued to act in this way, it would eventually kill its own sustenance. And if the ocean is a living thing, then it can be killed. Ironically, aliens might understand that more than humans. If these swarms did manage to kill the ocean, the action would indirectly kill all life on Earth. Perhaps that was the goal all along.

These life forms could be changing the ocean in order to change the planet while making it more hospitable to alien life. A higher form of intelligence would do something like that in a remote area like this, someplace where no one would notice until it was too late.

All they had to do was change the chemistry of the area; offset it a little so that the life that once flourished there wouldn't be able to do so anymore. Life on Earth would not be able to keep living if their host, their planet changed enough. If a few life forms managed to endure, they would be much different than what we see today. Possibly only bacteria, jellyfish, and aliens would be able to survive if the ocean became acidic enough.

Ellen remembered that both the ocean temperature and salinity had increased during the swarms. That must be it: they must be changing the ocean in order to change the planet.

No one would ever believe her. The only one who came close to thinking of her theories as points to consider was Tim McCarthy, even though he hadn't exactly backed her up at the meeting. Ryan only tried to placate and make her feel better. He didn't truly believe. She decided to see if she could find Tim. It might help to look at more of his ocean chemistry data.

She found him in another lab, bent over his laptop in the same way that she had just been bent over hers. Seeing him in that position made her want to stretch. She reached her arms up over her head and a yawn came bursting out. Tim jumped at the sudden noise.

"Sorry," she said. "I didn't mean to scare you. Could we look over some of the ocean data from before and during the swarms?"

"I was just looking at that." He spun his laptop toward her. "Let's see what you think."

Ellen searched through the columns of numbers. She found the latest swarm time period and compared those numbers with the ones from before the swarm. She saw the increase in temperature and salinity. But that wasn't all.

The numbers also showed a decrease in wave height, which would make sense since the swarm did seem to be blanketing the ocean in some way, an action that could suppress the waves. She wondered if the life forms could have been exerting a force on the ocean surface to flatten the waves while they continued to spread out. But there was something else. She saw an increase in carbon dioxide in both the water and the air during the swarm. That seemed strange. Normally the ocean took carbon dioxide from the air so if it increased in the water then it should decrease in the air. Unless, that is, something manipulated the natural balance of things.

"What do you think of the carbon dioxide levels?" Ellen asked.

"They go hand in hand with the pH level. The ocean water is definitely more acidic during the swarm. That could be caused by the increase in carbon dioxide. Now look at this," Tim arrowed down to a more recent time period after the swarm had disappeared.

"The levels are the same as during the swarm," Ellen said.

"That's right."

"That must mean they're changing the ocean."

"It looks that way."

"A more acidic ocean would be like poison. It would dissolve shells and kill most sea life. That could kill the ocean and all life on Earth."

"Well, the acidity of the ocean is increasing already, with or without these strange life forms," Tim said. "The increase of carbon dioxide in the air is causing it. We're causing it."

"If carbon dioxide levels keep increasing and the ocean reaches a point where it can't take any more in, we won't be able to breathe. Maybe the aliens saw what we were doing and decided to come in and accelerate the whole process."

"Why would they want to do that?"

"To kill off any life so that they can have the planet. A more acidic ocean might make Earth more like their own planet. Lucky for them, we already started the process. All they have to do now is finish the job."

Tim's eyebrows sprang up. "Sounds like you've been watching too many science fiction movies."

"I thought you were the only one who sort of believed me, even if you didn't exactly stand by me at the all-hands meeting."

"I never said that I necessarily believed you, but I do try to investigate all the options and give the benefit of the doubt to anyone. Even people with alien theories."

"Thanks a lot," Ellen said. "Did you end up doing a DNA test on your samples?"

"Yes, I'm still going through the data, but so far the tests keep saying that they're not related to anything."

"Those are the same results I'm getting. If they're not related to anything, then they must not be from Earth."

"Well, those are the preliminary results and I'm still looking through everything. There must be another reason. But I will admit your theory makes sense in a science fiction sort of way. I mean, it does explain a few things."

"Right. What else could be happening?"

"I don't know. But one thing I do know is that there's always more to know."

CHAPTER 57

THINKING SHE MIGHT have missed something, Ellen decided to look through the swarm videos again. She slowed the film down during any close-ups, reversed it, then sent it forward one frame at a time. Over and over again, she watched the organisms slowly fuse together into one living being, then separate and spread out everywhere.

"How can that be random?" Her voice echoed in the lab. No one answered.

"What's controlling them?" Again, no answer. Not that she expected one.

They must be out there even now, multiplying and choking the ocean, feeding off it and taking its life. They couldn't be that far from the ship. Ellen concentrated. She could feel them. Her breathing slowed. She felt them out there, siphoning the ocean's energy away as if it could be her own. They had to be stopped. If they were allowed to continue, all life would die.

Ellen left the lab and wandered into the storage area to grab some supplies. No one was around at the insane hour of two or three or whatever it was in the morning. She hid in the shadows just in case.

With shaky legs, she started down the metal stairs toward the lowest level of the ship. A sudden dizzy feeling made her reach out and clutch the stair rail. Steadying herself, she concentrated on each step so that she wouldn't end up in a heap at the bottom of the stairs. That's just what the creatures would want. She wouldn't give them the satisfaction.

An inflatable boat sat waiting near the closed hatch door. Its outboard motor had been stored away in anticipation of the trip home but the oars rested inside. Ellen added a flashlight, rope, sampling jars, plastic buckets, gloves, and the video camera. She pushed the heavy metal lever down and pulled at the door. It screeched at her as it opened.

After tethering the research ship to the inflatable boat, she pushed it through the hatch and into the ocean. Lights from the ship spilled out and glittered in stretches on the black water. The sparkling lights pointed toward the middle of the darkness, shiny fingers showing her the way.

Ellen pulled on the rope to draw the inflatable back against the research ship, then wrapped the rope around a clamp bolted to the floor. After tightening it, she lowered herself down feet first until she could feel the unsteady movement of the inflatable boat beneath her. While standing there and attempting to balance herself, she kept most of her weight on her hands, which were splayed out on the ship's rusty metal floor.

Rippling waves jostled the inflatable. If only she had been a surfer or a rodeo clown, then the whole thing would be much easier. She bent over and unraveled the rope with one hand, dropped it into her boat, then half sat and half fell onto the rubbery, bouncing platform.

At first and as usual, she drifted. Waves splashed against the side, spraying her arms and face. Ellen pulled on the oars to steer through it all while propelling herself farther away from the research ship and the light.

Soon darkness overtook her. She couldn't see the stars or the moon. Only a gray rectangle hovered out in the black. It was her portal, her way back, the open hatch of the research ship. She knew she shouldn't let it out of her sight even as it diminished from a hazy rectangle down to a faint dot.

Ellen clicked on her flashlight and swept the glow along the ocean surface. The water reflected oily blackness. Anything could be hidden in those depths. The surface shimmered and shined and looked sinister, holding everything back while sloshing away and laughing at her for trying to figure anything out at all. David was right. The ocean was alive. And it was impossible to understand.

"I'm trying to help you," she whispered. In response, the ocean settled down a little. It didn't splash up at her as much. If only it would completely calm down, she might be able to find the invaders.

She had to find them. She had to stop them. Dark waters hold fluid light mysteries. The words invaded her head. She had no idea where they came from, unless the words came from them. They could be putting words into her head, leading her astray, luring her farther out into the night with the promise of a mystery.

Something reared up out of the black water. Ellen swung her flashlight toward it. Nothing. Her heartbeat thudded in her ears. Soon the thumping was all she could hear. Then something else jumped off to the side. Her flashlight beam swerved to catch and hold it in its light. Again nothing.

She dipped the oars in to get away from whatever it was while balancing the flashlight on her knees to search through the black void. It was probably a whale or a shark or a fish. She had to find the invaders. She had to capture them before they did any more damage. She had to stop them. At this point, that was all that mattered.

She rowed on. Something told her to keep going, keep rowing. She took a deep breath and decided to trust the feeling as the light from the research ship disappeared in the darkness.

Sand crunched under the inflatable. Everything jolted as she hit land. Ellen swerved her head around and saw a moonlit island in her way. She dug her oar into the sand and tried to push off into the darkness again.

"Hello," the island said.

She jerked her head back to see a shadow sitting there on the beach.

"Who are you?"

"David. You rescued me, remember?"

"David? You're not abandoned on another island, are you?"

Laughter trickled through the air. "No, no, this is my home. It is very hard for me to sleep when I'm used to getting up so early to go fishing. Why are you visiting me?"

"I'm not. Well, I guess it looks like I am. I really don't know what I'm doing. I'm just looking for something."

"Ah, yes. Dark waters hold fluid light mysteries."

Ellen froze. "Where did you hear that?"

"The words came to me when I was out on my boat. Before the ocean rose up against me."

"They came to me too. Just now, tonight, when I was out on the water."

Ellen stumbled out of the boat and walked toward his voice.

"Well, that is strange indeed. These waters are strange. Very strange."

David's voice took on a hunched shape as she walked closer. When she was close enough, she could see that he sat there, crouched on a fallen palm tree.

"I feel like I'm going crazy," she admitted as she felt around for the crusty bark before sitting next to him. "Maybe the ocean is making me crazy."

"Yes, that could be. The ocean will do that. All these waves, and they never stop. Looking out at so much mystery can make anyone crazy."

Ellen sighed. "That's true."

The sound of the waves grew a little louder, a steady pulsing rhythm.

"You said the ocean gave you those scars. How did it do that?"

"The ocean was very angry with me. I did not think I would survive. A red wave like the ocean's blood rose up over me and swallowed. I don't know what happened after that. I traveled through the ocean's insides. I could not find my boat. The ocean tossed and chewed and finally spit me out on the island of spirits."

"A red wave? Are you sure it was red?"

"Very red. I had never seen the ocean look like that. It showed me its inner self."

"We've been seeing that sort of thing lately. It's an anomaly. Patches of red that look like jellyfish swarms, but that's not what they are. I thought they might have had something to do with what happened to you, but I wasn't sure."

"The ocean has always been my friend. I know it well, in a way that I know no one else, including my wife. Now I know the ocean more than ever, because it let me become part of it. This red is a sickness, and it could be why the ocean is so angry. It is sick with this rash that is spreading. We must help the ocean get rid of this sickness."

"That's what I'm trying to do." Ellen put her hands over her face and tried to rub some life back into it while forcing her eyes to open a little more.

Light filtered through the dark with the promise of dawn. In this new light, she could just make out the Man in the Rock. Morning mist crept up along his features. Ellen did a double take. The man wasn't leering. He didn't look mischievous. He had settled into himself and now looked completely at peace. It must be a trick of the light. Either that or the stress had finally made her delusional.

"Yes, he changed," David nodded. "I wondered about that too. I always thought of him as a protector warning evil away from our island. He looked so fierce, you know? I thought he would always stay that way. But everything changes. Maybe the evil is going away but I don't think so. I think he knows you will fix things and he can now be at peace. You will go back home and tell the world about this evil. Then the world will fight against it."

Ellen slumped, feeling drained of all energy. "I came out here this morning to fight against them. But then I couldn't even find them."

"This evil is too large for one person to fight. Everyone must care. You will make the world care."

"Well, I'll try. You never know what the world is going to do though."

"I think most people care already. The Earth is our only home. Everyone knows that. But they think it won't matter, that whatever they do it will not matter. They don't realize what a difference we can make, and that everything we do makes a difference."

Ellen tried to stretch her slumpiness away. The Man in the Rock became clearer with the advancing gray light. She didn't see how he could have changed so much. But then, how could sparks turn into butterflies or sea turtles be called to shore with a song?

She turned to David. "Do you believe in magic?"

"Of course, nature is magic and we're all part of that magic. You plant a seed and it grows. That seed can turn into a plant or an animal or an idea."

"I never thought of it that way but you're right, nature is a kind of magic. And the ocean and life, I guess, is magic too."

"Love is also like that. You start with something like a seed and as long as you give it all it needs, it will grow into something beautiful, something overpowering."

Ellen looked down at the sand. "Do you really think love can be like that?"

"Of course. It is that way with my wife and children and with the people in the village. If your love is strong enough, everyone will feel it. When they feel it, they pass it on, and it grows stronger still."

"I'm not sure if I've ever felt anything like that in my life."

"Maybe you have but you did not pay attention. To feel that kind of love, you must pay attention to everything. Every gust of wind, every leaf rustle, every laugh and smile to hold in your heart. When you open yourself up to the world, you will feel the love that lives there under the surface of everything."

She hadn't been paying much attention. That was true. Even as she kept trying to make a difference, to help the world somehow, she rarely stopped to notice it. But work was the important thing and if she couldn't figure this one mystery out, there might not be much of a world left to appreciate.

"When you were gone, your wife said now you know all the ocean's secrets. Is that true?"

David smiled and gazed into the distance. "No, no one will ever know all the ocean's secrets. She holds them close inside."

Ellen nodded. The ocean could be elusive. While connecting us all, it acts as a barrier. It can be felt on every shore, echoing and reverberating, giving and taking, reaching out and pulling back, incessantly mixing everything together. Ellen tried listening to the waves but still couldn't figure out exactly what they had to say. The gray early morning light continued to seep through, giving a glow to the sand. She noticed a metal bucket by David's legs.

"What's that for?"

David held it up and grinned. "Collecting shellfish. I will always be a fisherman, even if I do not have a boat."

The bucket was so dented and scratched that it could have been through a war. It turned and creaked in the wind. Ellen noticed a symbol that children began to see in the 1950s, a symbol for the modern age, the unmistakable sign for nuclear waste.

CHAPTER 58

T HE SHIP LURCHED. Ellen opened her eyes as fragments of the night came back to her. She heard David's voice whispering through the darkness, but couldn't be sure if she had actually been out there or not. It felt like a memory that she couldn't fully trust. She remembered the feel of the metal hatch door, the water spray, the scratchy tree as she sat there with David. The weightlessness of it all came back to her as she floated out to sea. She decided it must have happened even as the memory dissipated into the day.

She hadn't seen any swarms out there. She wanted to capture as many as possible, to scrape them from the surface and stop them from hurting the ocean, but then she couldn't even find them. While feeling inadequate and a little shaky, Ellen forced herself out of bed and groped around for her towel.

Her arm looked a little better. The swelling had gone down and it didn't throb as much. Now it only hurt when she touched it. She soaped her arm up in the sink while running cold water over the redness.

After stepping out to examine her arm in the light, she saw that the skin had taken on a crusty look. She figured she'd end up with a scar like David's and wrapped another bandage around it. At least she didn't need the ice pack anymore. That made it easier to hide.

Ellen pulled her baseball cap over her eyes and shuffled out to the deck. She looked over the side for any more swarms, but there were only waves. No discoloration on the ship other than rust. She tried to see through the waves directly below. No strange life forms there either. Then she stared out over the ocean surface. Still nothing. She exhaled, remembering to breathe again.

The ship plowed through an endless field of waves. They were heading to Hawaii and from there, home. In the early morning light, the ocean glowed silver. Ellen thought of all the life it sustained, from plankton and salps to dolphins and whales to humanity. She knew the ocean was worth fighting for, more so than differences in cultures or borders, since it's so integral to all life on Earth.

The ocean gave us life and continues to give us life. It produces half of the oxygen in the atmosphere while absorbing carbon dioxide. As long as it's breathing, it gives us the chance to breathe. Without a healthy ocean, humans would never be able to survive. And it might not be healthy much longer.

The sun peered over the ocean, spilling pink and orange into the sky. The celebration seeped into the waves and danced upon them. Ellen took a breath and felt the energy of the water, air, and sky seep into her. If we choose not to care, if we don't save it all while we still can, what good are we? The sun continued to rise and the colors spread into the sky.

The only way she knew how to fight was through her work. Ellen held the vision of the sunrise within her as she grabbed a cup of coffee and went back to the lab. She checked through her messages, hundreds of them, but didn't see a response from the DNA experts or anything else that looked important. She began to feel frantic with the need to communicate everything and started to write. While she was taking all her frustrations out on the keyboard, Ryan wandered in.

"Don't you want lunch?"

"Lunch? It can't be time for that already."

"What are you doing?"

"Nothing. I don't see how it could be that late."

"It is. I guess one of my duties on this cruise is to make sure you eat."

Ellen glanced up from her laptop. "What?"

"Do you want me to bring you some lunch? Bread and water? Anything?"

"No, I'll get up in a few minutes. Thanks for letting me know."

"Okay, see you there."

Ellen checked her messages again before closing her laptop. One blinked in. She opened it, held her breath, and read it. She couldn't believe it. It didn't seem possible. As she stood up from the computer, her legs shook. She almost fell back into her seat but forced herself to keep standing.

She stumbled out on deck. It could have been a trick of the light, but as the swells rose and fell, she could see the ocean breathing. She breathed along with it, steadying herself with its rhythm, then looked up to see a small city floating in the distance. The buildings towered out of the ocean with blinking lights and smokestacks spewing black air. They should still be in the marine sanctuary or near the border of it, but this floating city didn't look like something that should be anywhere near a marine sanctuary.

She joined Ryan, Michael, and Jake at the lunch table after getting her salad and lemonade.

"What's with the city out there?" She said as she sat down. "I thought Atlantis was under water, not floating on the surface."

Michael looked up. "Bottom trawlers. Major fishing fleets like that stir up so many plumes of sediment when they drag their nets across the seafloor that the effects can be seen from outer space."

"How can that be? Aren't we still in the marine sanctuary?"

"Oh, we're still in the marine sanctuary," Michael said. "But fishing is allowed here."

"What? Then how can it be called a sanctuary?"

"Good question. Fishing is actually allowed in marine sanctuaries. An area has to be declared a no-fish zone for fishing to be outlawed, and there aren't many of those."

"But if they're bottom trawling, then they're not just fishing. Those things rake huge areas of the seafloor, crush coral, and take everything away, even the next generation and the ocean life they don't want."

Michael shrugged. "They have to do it. And we do it too. Some countries don't have enough land for the kind of farming needed to feed their entire population. So they have to get a huge percentage of their food from the ocean."

"They don't have to and if they keep trying to there won't be anything left," Ellen said.

"Then we'll all be forced into changing our ways," Ryan said.

"Once the sea life is gone, then we'll be forced into changing our ways? No, I won't accept that," Ellen said. "Everything needs to change now, before it's too late."

"It might be too late already," Jake said. "I've heard predictions that the ocean will be fished out by 2050 or something like that. I wonder what will happen then."

"You're talking as if it's already predetermined and we have no control over it," Ellen said. "We can't let that happen. We just can't."

Ryan looked at her as if she might be showing her insanity again. Ellen almost started laughing at the thought, as if her insanity could be some kind of an undergarment showing through at the worst possible moments.

"But do we have control over it?" Michael asked. "Do we really?"

"Yes, of course we do," Ellen said. "We've just got to change everything, that's all."

Michael sighed. "People have been trying to do that for generations now. But once a process starts, it can't stop. That process started with the Industrial Revolution and it's been snowballing ever since. It's out of our hands."

"If we say that, then we're giving up. Any progress we've made isn't worth anything at all if we destroy ourselves in the process. The Earth is everything. It's filled with so much life and beauty and mystery. I'm not going to sit back and watch while it's being destroyed, whether it's by aliens or humans or some sickness. Even if it doesn't work, even if I can't stop the whole process, at least I'll know I tried."

"Speaking of aliens, did you get the results back on the latest samples yet?" Michael asked.

"Yes, I did, but that doesn't mean I have to tell you."

"Okay, what were they?"

"Well, inexplicably, they say all the samples are from the same species, even though the organisms from each sample looked and acted completely differently, which means they're all this supposedly new species that might be related to jellyfish."

"No evidence of aliens?" Michael asked.

"It looks that way," Ellen said. "But it's not as if we have a definitive alien, non-alien test we can utilize."

"Just when I was starting to like the idea of aliens too," Jake said. "So it's a new species then, that's it?"

"That's what the DNA experts say, but I still don't fully believe them. Tim McCarthy did some tests on the samples and his results came up the same as mine, that they're not related to anything. So the DNA experts could be wrong. They're only sifting through the information. They're not seeing what we see. Even if it ends up being true that the samples are related to jellyfish, they could still be aliens since everything in the universe is related."

"I'm beginning to think you are truly delusional," Michael said. "You'll twist and turn anything into your way of thinking, even if the truth is the opposite way of thinking."

"No one knows what the truth is. We only think we know what it is, and then someone comes along and discovers the opposite truth."

"True, I suppose, in a delusional kind of a way," Michael said. "What might be the truth as we know it in this case? Besides insisting that they're aliens, that is?"

Ryan perked up. "What if the jellyfish evolved into this new species?"

"We already talked about that," Ellen said. "Evolution takes place over many generations. Jellyfish first appeared several hundred million years ago, way before humans, and they haven't changed much since. Why would they change so dramatically now?"

"Maybe they've been changing in this area all along, but it's always been so remote that no one noticed."

"You might have something there," Michael said.

Ellen turned to him. "You really think so?"

"It's better to think that they're aliens? Evolution sounds like a much better explanation to me."

"There have been cases of jellyfish evolving slightly when they're isolated, but never enough so that they develop into a completely different species," Ellen said. "There are jellyfish that live in lakes on an island near Indonesia. Their ancestors came from the ocean during a period of rising sea levels that created salt-water lakes and then left the jellyfish stranded. Over many generations, the jellyfish survived by developing a relationship with marine algae. The algae live in the jellyfish tentacles, where they create carbohydrates that the jellyfish use for energy."

"Like with coral," Michael said. "Coral can have that kind of a relationship with algae."

"That's right. The jellyfish must have developed that relationship with the algae because there wasn't enough food left in the lakes. Jellyfish in the ocean normally feed on plankton, but over time the jellyfish in the lakes must have eaten most of that, especially since there are millions of jellyfish in these lakes and some are as large as basketballs. So they evolved by finding a new way to create energy. The jellyfish in each of the five lakes even look slightly different from each other and from the ones in the ocean. But they're all still the same species even though they evolved slightly and in different ways."

"I remember hearing about those jellyfish," Jake said. "Don't they act really weird too?"

"I guess you could say that," Ellen said. "They all swim together in a daily migration across the lake and then back again. We think they do it to keep their algae in the sun. At night, they stop moving horizontally and instead move up and down in the lake. They could do that to provide the algae with nutrients that can only be found in deeper water. So their behavior isn't that strange. There are reasons for it."

"Sounds strange to me," Jake said. "Not only are they constantly moving all together like that, but they might be doing these things for the algae living in their tentacles. It's as if they're communicating or something. Not only with each other, but with the algae."

"It does sound a little like the behavior of the alien jellyfish since they're all acting together," Ellen said. "But I bet it happens in the lakes because those jellyfish are isolated. In cases like that, it's easier to act as a community. The jellyfish have also figured out that if they do these things that are beneficial to the algae, the algae then produce more energy."

"It sounds a lot like the swarms we've been seeing," Ryan said. "One of the things about them is how much they act as a community. Like when they all fused together. Maybe they did it because they knew it would make them stronger."

"Right, but the jellyfish in the lakes only showed slight changes," Ellen said. "They didn't go so far as to change into a completely different species or fuse together into one being."

"Could there be something about this area that would have changed our jellyfish that much?" Jake asked. "Maybe the heat or the humidity or something?"

"I don't think so, but you never know," Ellen said. "I guess I'll start researching it."

CHAPTER 59

T HE LAPTOP BECKONED. Ellen felt the electric pull of the information highway, libraries linked and growing together, and all the knowledge she hadn't yet gained. She yanked her baseball cap on and went in search of it all.

Her closet lab had morphed into a disaster area: papers scattered everywhere, wires twisting and curling around everything, plastic buckets used so many times that they looked like they might have been chewed up and spit out by a sea monster. The silver laptop sat there in the middle of it all, shining with some sort of promise. Ellen opened it up and clicked it on.

She checked her messages first and found more than usual waiting for her. As she started to go through them, she realized word must have gotten out about the possible new species. The experts apparently couldn't keep their mouths shut. Researchers she didn't know were congratulating her and asking for more information at the same time. She had plenty of information, just no time to go through it all or make sense of it. At least there was nothing from the press yet. She hoped they wouldn't find out. She had no idea what to say to them.

Ellen began researching the area by doing a search on some of the nearby island names. She was old enough to have lived half her life without an internet, and even though she used it every day now, the whole thing still amazed her. All that information, ready and waiting for any inquiry, any question, any word. It was a little too easy.

The computer had developed into a better brain than hers, a brain that she carried around in her pocket and consulted because she couldn't fit all the information into her own head. There wasn't much of a need to remember anything when it could be called up in a second. But with the way her mind had been acting lately, she needed all the help she could get.

Some of the island legends came up. She noticed that most involved shape shifters, with gods turning into sharks or sea turtles to better maneuver through the ocean waters. The strange jellyfish could be thought of as shape shifters. She tried to think of all the advantages to being a shape shifter: better adaptability to the environment, disguise from any predators, possible freedom. Did they change for any of those reasons? Was that change deliberate or was it forced upon them?

Ellen found a link that promised some history of the area. She clicked on it to see a list of area leaders and the periods of war and peace that existed between them. It described how people from one island might form a coalition with those from another island in order to exert a more powerful force against an enemy island. Such things seemed inevitable.

A link further down made the words, "World War II and After" glow in bright orange. She clicked on the link. It brought her to a page with red letters. Ellen began to doubt the credibility of the information but read on.

Under the heading, "Relocation," she found a story about the evacuation of Bikini Island. A vague recollection surfaced from a history class but she couldn't remember the details. The article said Bikini and other surrounding islands became protectorates of the United States after World War II. This area included un-inhabited islands, but it was determined that Bikini would be the best one to use for atomic bomb testing because of its location and geography.

At the time, 167 people lived on Bikini. They were asked if they'd be willing to leave their homes so that atomic bombs could be tested for the good of all mankind. They were told their sacrifice would end all world wars. The people agreed and were sent 125 miles away to an uninhabited island. Evil spirits were known to inhabit this island, which was one reason no one lived there, in addition to the fact that it had inadequate food and water supplies. The U.S. government shipped the people food, but it wasn't enough and the islanders began to suffer from malnutrition.

For the nuclear testing program, hundreds of goats, pigs, and rats were brought to the area. They were placed on target ships docked in the lagoon so that the effects of the atomic bombs and radiation could be determined, not only on the warships, but on the animals.

The atomic bombs were about the size of the bomb dropped on Nagasaki. Even though the effects on life had already been seen in Nagasaki, an atomic bomb had yet to be detonated directly over water. The government wanted to know how its warships would be affected by an atomic bomb and if that effect would be different over water for any reason.

The atomic blast created a mushroom cloud that billowed out and enveloped the target ships while waves tossed them like toys in a giant's bathtub. Military personnel watched and recorded the event from nearby ships. The event took on a celebratory air. Everyone applauded their technology, their progress, their power.

A team entered the area after the explosion to record the radiation and devastation. Where ships had once been, fragments of twisted metal grasped a smoldering sky. Most of the animals had been killed. Some of the goats and pigs were treated for radiation burns.

The men who went into the area to monitor it and the ones who watched the explosion were never told that the resulting radiation could be dangerous. Thousands were exposed to heavy doses. Sailors went swimming in the ocean after the explosion and used it to make their drinking water.

Afterwards, they felt the effects. Their feet and legs or hands began to swell up to extreme proportions. Some couldn't walk because of the swelling. A sailor's leg swelled up so much that it had to be amputated. Once his leg was gone, the swelling traveled to the other leg and then that had to be amputated. Then his hand swelled up to the size of a basketball.

Ellen thought of the jellyfish swarms that swelled to extreme proportions while continually stretching out over the ocean. She wondered if the jellyfish could have been exposed to some of the radiation left over from this, but then doubted it. Bikini Island was pretty far away and this had all happened back in 1946. Still, today's jellyfish could have eventually come from the ones that were directly exposed. Could radiation cause the jellyfish to evolve in this way? Even to the point of becoming a new species with an entirely different, invasive behavioral pattern?

She remembered hearing pollution had recently caused a different type of fish to form. Researchers discovered that Atlantic tomcod living in the Hudson River went through a rapid evolutionary change while developing a genetic resistance to polychlorinated biphenyls (PCBs). For decades, electric facilities released PCBs into the Hudson River. Then researchers found that this one type of fish not only survived in that altered environment, but thrived.

The same sort of thing can happen when insects develop resistance to insecticides or when bacteria change because of certain antibiotics. When faced with something harmful in the environment, life adapts. To become less sensitive to the toxic effects of PCBs, the genetic makeup of the tomcod had to change, which then changed the characteristics of the future fish population. Ironically, a recent mandated cleanup of PCBs in the river might mean trouble for the tomcod unless they can find a way to adapt again to a cleaner environment.

Such a sudden evolutionary change made Ellen think of the newly discovered pizzly bear, a hybrid of polar bears and grizzlies apparently caused by warmer Arctic temperatures. Over and over again, life adapts. The thought gave her some hope.

Just out of curiosity, she figured it could be worthwhile to test the jellyfish samples for radiation. But the radiation might not show up in the offspring generations later, even if that is what caused their DNA to change. Or would it? More questions. She knew that radiation could change the atomic structure of animals. The more she learned, the more questions there always seemed to be.

Ellen kept reading. Another link brought her to the 1950s and another bomb. This time, the government had a hydrogen bomb to test. Government leaders weren't sure how powerful it would be, but they wanted to find out.

The bomb turned out to be one thousand times more powerful than each of the bombs dropped on Nagasaki and Hiroshima. When it exploded near Bikini Island, a fireball of intense heat four miles wide and measuring into the millions of degrees shot skyward. The blast was filled with sand, coral, plant, and sea life.

It generated winds that stripped branches from trees on nearby islands. Soon after, white, snow-like ash fell from the sky onto inhabited islands hundreds of miles away. People thought the sky and clouds had shattered. They watched as two suns rose that morning. They hadn't been told anything and didn't know what was happening.

Ellen considered whether radiation on that kind of a scale would have an effect on the surrounding sea life. Probably. It could still be having an effect. The islands they had visited on the cruise were about two hundred miles from the test site. This article said the ash fell as far as hundreds of miles away. The cloud eventually contaminated more than seven thousand square miles of the Pacific Ocean.

So much for studying a pristine area untouched by human civilization. The rain and the air must have been filled with radiation. And the air mixes with the sea. Ellen thought of David's bucket, a nuclear remnant casually tossed away for others to pick up and use. Everything is connected after all, but that's not always such a good thing, not when people did things like this.

In a way, she knew she should think of this as an opportunity to study an altered area. When scientists study oil spills, they're studying the effects of the oil. As horrible as that is, it's still an opportunity to study what happens when an area is altered in some way. Still, she couldn't think of this as an opportunity.

Ryan opened her closet lab door. "Do I seriously have to keep forcing you to eat?"

"Looks like it. Good thing you're here or I would have completely wasted away by now."

Ellen wasn't sure if she should let him or anyone else know about this new discovery. It seemed too important. But Ryan was the one who'd suggested that the jellyfish might have evolved in some way. All of them had helped her see things differently. Without them, she wouldn't have gotten this far.

She spun the laptop toward Ryan while deciding to let go of any lingering paranoia.

"Take a look at this. I was looking for information on the area, figuring I wouldn't find much, and this is what I found."

Her laptop screen showed a hydrogen bomb mushroom cloud. The image screamed in a fierce yellow and orange.

"Wow. Was that near here?"

"About two hundred miles away. But it says the contamination traveled for thousands of miles. White radioactive ash fell on the islands and the ocean. The sea life, like the jellyfish, must have been affected by it. How could it not be?"

"I wonder if the stuff we found on that island had anything to do with the radioactive tests. Those sheds and boxes looked military, remember?"

"That's right. They could have boxed up the sand to send it away for testing, then when it became obvious that the radioactivity levels were high and some effects could be seen, they abandoned the samples. That would make sense. I'm sure they just wanted to get out of there and didn't want to touch the stuff anymore. What other reason could there be for a bunch of boxed up sand lying around?"

"Do you think the radioactivity is what made the jellyfish aggressive enough to want to attack the ship?"

"Probably not, but it could have been the catalyst for their initial change. We don't know what they were trying to do to the ship. It could have been something as simple as hitching a ride like barnacles do."

"So now that they're not aliens, they're not quite so sinister?"

"Well, we don't know anything for sure yet. But if they really are altered jellyfish, then I'm guessing there isn't much of a method to their madness. They're just trying to exist and survive, like all of us."

"They're doing a good job of it," Ryan said. "It looked like they had practically taken over the ocean a few times."

"Regular jellyfish thrive in polluted waters, so it makes sense that these altered jellyfish could adapt well to radioactivity. Most of the radioactivity must be gone from the water around here by now though. Maybe this new species needs more of it and they're out searching for it. That could explain why they looked like they were trying to suck the ocean up. In a way, they could even be cleaning the ocean."

"Either that or they're aliens collecting samples."

"Right. That sounds pretty laughable now that there's another possibility. But at the time, that did seem like the only possibility."

"True, but there are always all kinds of possibilities."

Ryan searched her eyes as he moved closer. He reached out to brush the loose strands of hair from her forehead while touching her skin enough to make it tingle. Then he grazed his fingertips down along the side of her face to rest on her throat. His touch felt warm and somehow stabilizing. Ellen forced herself to turn away, disconnected from his touch, and suddenly became fascinated by the act of closing up her laptop.

CHAPTER 60

A S SOON AS she sat down to eat, Michael asked if she had come up with anything while researching. In response, Ellen laughed her most maniacal laugh yet.

"Well, there does seem to be a possible reason for a sudden change in the jellyfish. I guess that's the good news. The bad news is that it isn't good."

"Sounds scary. What is it?"

"Radioactivity."

Michael thought for a moment, going through all the labeled categories in his brain, pulling up the correct file.

"You mean Bikini Island? But that's pretty far from here and the island itself wasn't even damaged."

"It didn't seem to be badly damaged from the atomic bombs in the 1940s. Those bombs are what made the island famous. People even named the two-piece bathing suit after Bikini Island. The whole thing became a big celebration and show of technology and progress. Then there was another bomb in the 1950s. That one wasn't as famous, but it was much more powerful."

"Well now, I thought bikinis were always bikinis," Maddie said.

"No, first we bombed Bikini Island and then named a bathing suit after it to honor it," Ellen said. "Then there was a hydrogen bomb. They didn't advertise that one as much. Not only did it strip the palm trees and create a huge crater on the coral reef surrounding the island, it also caused radioactive ash to fall from the sky for hundreds of miles around."

"That's right, the hydrogen bomb was much more powerful than they thought it would be," Michael said. "They even admitted that afterwards. So you think that could have caused the jellyfish to change?"

"I think it could have been a catalyst, yes."

"I wonder. Have you tested the jellyfish for radioactivity?"

"Not yet. I'll have to do that once we get back home."

"They wouldn't still be radioactive, would they?" Ryan asked.

"It could carry through to the offspring to some degree," Ellen said. "It just might not be as obvious, but radiation can cause genetic mutations."

"Even if it didn't carry through, it could still be a reason for the initial change," Michael said. "And then that change would be included in the genetic code of any offspring after that. High doses of radioactivity can even break DNA strands, which could be why those tests kept coming up as inconclusive. I like it. I like it much more than aliens."

"I still like the alien idea," Jake said.

"It's strange, when I thought they must be aliens I went a little crazy thinking the Earth could be under attack. Now that it seems possible that humans could have caused this, it should be a relief, but in some way it's actually worse. The Earth is still under attack but we're the ones doing it. We're probably harder to fight than some outside alien population."

"Maybe not," Jake said. "Aliens can be pretty hard to fight."

"I know what you mean," Michael said. "An outside force would be easier to target and fight than a process that's gone out of control. At least in the case of an alien, you can see the enemy and hopefully destroy it."

"If we're the enemy, what then?" Ryan asked. "We can't fight ourselves. We can't undo something that's already been done, especially something that happened back in the 1940s or 50s."

"I don't know," Ellen said. "I guess we have to keep learning from our mistakes. Then hopefully we'll find better ways to live."

"Sounds like we've already made too many mistakes, too many things have gotten screwed up," Ryan said.

"Remember, we tend to think we're much more powerful than we really are," Michael said. "This reminds me of our whole climate change controversy. The Earth is huge. It may seem as if we're changing things, but nature does have a way of recovering from 'disasters,' as we've called them, like oil spills or a massive influx of pollution, even radioactivity. The Earth seems to have built-in mechanisms in order to recover or offset these things. On top of that, our environment is constantly changing regardless of what we do. So much of what we think we're changing could be due to natural cycles. Civilizations will continue to rise and fall, temperatures will rise and fall, and the Earth will endure. Even if it turns out that we are slightly changing some part of the environment, when you look at it in the context of millions of years, we're nothing. I doubt we'll have that much of an overall effect. Who's to say these changes will turn out to be negative anyway? They could have positive results too."

"I hope you're right," Ellen said. "But I don't think so."

"Well, you haven't proven it yet."

"I don't have to prove it. Take a look around. The Earth's mean surface temperature is warmer now than at any other time during the past four hundred years, and it continues to rise. Seawater is thirty percent more acidic than just four decades ago. The ocean controls the weather. As the ocean heats up, storms and hurricanes become more powerful, and glaciers melt causing sea levels to rise. Islands like the ones we visited are disappearing.

"With the rise in sea level, that extra load creates an increase in volcanic activity, earthquakes, landslides, tsunamis. We've been seeing more and more of these extreme weather events within the short time period of our own lifetimes.

"In the last two hundred years, the human population has exploded and at the same time, practically every other species has been rapidly decreasing. Ninety percent of the large ocean fish are gone, taken from the ocean in the last half century. We're currently experiencing the worst wave of species die-offs since the loss of the dinosaurs 65 million years ago. How can you sit there and say we're not changing the world while everything is changing all around us? Are the fish and the birds and the animals disappearing for no reason? Are these extinctions all part of the natural cycle of things?"

"Maybe. I'd believe that before I'd believe we're causing it all. Do you think the dinosaurs harmed the world in some way? Did they burn fossil fuels? No, they didn't, but the climate and everything else still changed."

Jake rolled his eyes at them. "You two are never going to agree on anything."

Michael ignored the remark. "Besides, the jellyfish are thriving. If radioactivity did change them, maybe that's not such a bad thing. It could be something they needed, an added ingredient, to help them survive in the future."

"Except that jellyfish thrive in polluted waters. So I don't see how it can be a good thing if they are thriving. It's a warning sign more than anything."

Michael chuckled. "Jake is right. We're never going to agree on anything."

Ellen looked at Jake and Maddie. "The students of today are the ones that are going to have to figure all this out and make it better. That is, if we ever get around to acknowledging that something's wrong."

"Speaking for the students of today, thanks a lot," Jake said.

～

Ellen sought out the haven of her lab. While talking with everyone, she felt some amount of irrationality creep through her brain again. She didn't want too much to leak out before she had a chance to stop it. Like usual, the lab provided an escape. Ever since she stopped talking about alien life forms, Ryan and Michael and everyone else hadn't seemed as worried about her state of mental health. She had fooled them all. Now hopefully they'd leave her alone.

She felt like such a fool for believing in the alien theory. Why had she been so convinced? With anything else, she had always been willing to investigate all the angles and listen to the theories, then modify and adjust her opinions before coming to a decision. But she was so sure with this one. She wanted results so badly. Something still prickled at her, as if the truth could turn in on itself again. But the feeling probably came from the fact that she didn't want to admit her tests could have been wrong or that she could have been wrong.

Now with most of the evidence pointing to the new species theory, she couldn't possibly be happy about it. Under normal conditions, she would have been thrilled to discover a new species. It was the kind of thing she'd always dreamed of while working her days and nights away: something that might make a difference, something that would make all the sacrifices worthwhile. It figured that when it finally did happen, it was for all the wrong reasons.

For one thing, this new species was created by ignorance. By the thought that whatever we do, there will be no real consequences. The whole "we can do anything" motto of the 1940s and 50s not only showed that kind of ignorance, it showed arrogance.

It was a dangerous combination and that way of thinking had continued into the present day.

As always, there was so much she didn't know. She didn't know if this new species could be dangerous. She didn't know anything about it: how quickly it might grow, if it did in fact feed on radiation, if it had been inhaling the ocean, exactly how invasive or harmful it could be. At least she had an overload of samples and more tests would be performed back home.

Ellen realized she'd never been doing this work for the notoriety or even the possibility of it. She had been working so hard all along simply because she wanted to know. She wanted to know more about jellyfish. She wanted to know more about everything. It was for the thrill of discovery, the love of it all, and it always had been. And the reason behind all of it was her absolute and total love for the world.

The research cruise would soon dock in Hawaii. There, they would spend a few days unloading their gear and samples. After packing everything up and sending it all to the institute, they would send themselves back by plane. Everything would be the same back home and yet everything would also be different.

～

Beneath the skidding waves, they clung to the metal wall. The metal hummed and propelled them through the ocean much quicker than they'd ever be able to propel themselves. They mourned leaving part of themselves back home, but they knew they were moving on to different waters, waters to feed from and stretch out in. Maybe someday they would again see the part of themselves they had left behind. They would reconnect and become stronger still. In the meantime, they let the humming metal lull and propel them forward, always forward.

CHAPTER 61

R YAN WALKED INTO the lab with a determined stride. Ellen looked down at her laptop. She'd be going through data for months, even years after the cruise. Like usual, there was no time for anything else. Yet Ryan kept acting as if he wanted more. Couldn't he see that she didn't have much to give?

He didn't say anything. Suddenly he was there, inches from her lips. He bent down and grazed her mouth with his. She felt a tingling travel from her mouth down through her body as if every cell could be waking up. He pulled her closer. Only their thin cotton shirts separated them this time. His skin felt as smooth as water. She could dive right in.

"We have to stop," she whispered while still kissing.

"Why?" He nibbled her neck and she let herself melt for a few more minutes.

"We could get in trouble. There are rules against this kind of thing on the ship. You know that."

"Well, what about after then? We'll be in Hawaii soon."

The thought of civilization slammed her back into reality. "I don't think so."

"So only on deserted islands?"

"That's right, only on deserted islands."

"And conveniently enough, we'll never be on a deserted island again." Ryan pulled away, leaving Ellen poised to kiss the air instead of his neck.

"I guess not."

"Why do you keep pushing everyone away?"

"What? I don't. If I did, none of this would have ever happened."

"Okay, except for momentary lapses of sanity, why do you push people away?"

"I've had more than a few lapses of sanity lately." Ryan turned to leave, then stopped. "You can't even give me a real answer. Why are you so hard to get to know?"

"Maybe because we're at work. Maybe work is the important thing, not getting to know each other."

"Don't you see you're using work as an excuse? You use it as some kind of a shield to make sure no one gets too close. That's not much of a life. Then it's you against the world. Wouldn't you rather share the world with other people? Embrace it, laugh at it even? Sometimes you need to stop and take the time to appreciate things like a laugh or a touch."

"Lately everyone's been laughing at me so how am I supposed to appreciate that?"

"By joining in and laughing at yourself. Then you'll realize how funny everything is and how much there is to appreciate. Everyone always takes themselves too seriously. Then they don't enjoy anything."

Ellen wished she could be more like that. It sounded so freeing, to laugh at everything, especially herself. She never wanted to take herself seriously. It just happened. She had to make a difference. She had to figure things out. The world couldn't always be laughed at, not when there were so many problems that needed to be solved.

"I'd rather look for ways to make the world better than for ways to make myself happier," Ellen said. "Because really, a better world is what will make me happy."

"Just the fact that you're part of the world already makes it better. Whether you succeed or not, whether you figure everything out or not, you still make a difference. Don't you see that?"

"No, not really. I have to try harder. I have to solve at least some of these things so that I can let people know what's happening out there."

"No one's trying to get in your way. We just want to help you."

"Or laugh at me."

Ryan grinned. "Well, that too of course."

He reached over and hugged her. She felt herself relax into his arms. This time there was no urge to kiss or touch. She felt only comfort. Only then did she realize she hadn't felt anything like that in a long time.

CHAPTER 62

A S THE SHIP docked in Hawaii, Ellen mentally prepared herself for sudden civilization. She knew multicolored flowered shirts would be blooming everywhere. Colors like that could be a shock to the system after being immersed in blue and green, rust and metal. There would be sunglasses and floppy straw hats and everything else people couldn't do without while getting away from it all.

She prepared herself for all that, but she still wasn't prepared for what happened. As she stepped off the boat while lugging her equipment, hoards of people rushed toward her. They pointed and shouted and she almost dropped the equipment. She had no idea who these people were or how they could possibly know her. A few took pictures of her stunned expression. Then she figured it out. Thanks to the DNA experts, reporters must have heard something about a possible new species and decided to descend.

Ryan tried to hold them back but it might as well have been an attempt to stop a waterfall. They flowed and dribbled out around him. She had to walk through the mass of people to find a place to put the equipment down. After placing it carefully on the dock, she turned to face them. She wiped her sweaty palms on her shirt.

They shouted their questions out:

"What happened out there?"

"Is it true that the swarms are invasive?"

"Do you think this is a worldwide or regional problem?"

Ellen put her hands up to stop the questions. She wasn't sure what to say. She opened her mouth but no words came out. She tried again and this time the words found their way.

"At this point, all we know is that it might be a new species. More tests will need to be done to confirm that and to determine any other details."

"What about the rumors that it could be an alien?"

Ellen glanced at Ryan. He shrugged slightly.

"We'll need to do more tests but at this point it just seems to be a new species."

"We heard it was invasive and growing at a pretty extensive rate out there. Are you sure it's not an alien and could this be a worldwide problem?"

Ellen sighed. Since they brought up the subject of worldwide problems, she might as well enlighten them on a few.

"Yes, it could be a worldwide problem. We have many worldwide problems. We're at the point where all that we're doing and all we've done to the Earth is coming back to haunt us in a way. We think the new species or whatever you want to call it might have been caused by radiation from a hydrogen bomb. A bomb that we exploded back in the 1950s. We're discovering our actions have consequences that can reverberate through decades or centuries.

"But beyond that, we're seeing signs that things are not right with the world. A major depletion of most species is going on while new species that thrive on pollution are coming to the forefront. We need to stop and listen to the ocean and the Earth. We need to start caring before it's too late."

"So where is this swarm now and what can we do about it?"

"It's out there and like you said, it's growing. Soon it could be everywhere. Now that we know we've created problems like this, we have an opportunity to put aside our differences and work together as a worldwide community to reverse the damage we've done. It's the challenge of our time. I only hope we're up to it."

The questions quieted after that. They didn't want to hear that they were the problem or that they had created a monster. They glanced at each other and scribbled in their notepads. Video cameras clicked off. Ellen's legs shook with nervous energy as she walked back to the ship to get more equipment to unload.

Ryan walked behind her, protecting her from any other possible onslaughts.

"Wow, that was crazy," he said when they were safely back aboard.

"Yeah, we might have to wait for them to clear away before going back down there. They shouldn't have been allowed on the dock."

"Those were some major news channels though. I'm sure they can force their way in anywhere, claiming First Amendment rights or something."

"I guess. So now they have the right to hear that everyone's screwed up the world."

"I'm sure they already knew that. That was good what you said though, that part about all this being an opportunity to work together and make the world better."

Michael walked by with a box full of equipment, set it down, and joined them.

"Just looking out over this sea of humanity," Ellen told him.

Heads and hats bobbed up and down as everyone walked away, creating ripples and waves through the crowd.

"Don't go romanticizing them," Michael said. "So they attacked, did they?"

"Yes, they had somehow heard of the possibility of aliens. I think that interested them more than the possibility of a new species or any actual scientific discoveries."

"Don't look at me. I'm the one who told you not to let the press know about aliens, remember? There are a lot of people on this ship and they all have email access."

"It doesn't matter. They'll probably make me out to be some kind of a lunatic or mad scientist but it really doesn't matter. I'm sure people already thought that about me anyway. Now it'll just be more public."

The crowd trickled off the dock and dispersed. Each person would write or broadcast a story. Ripples turn into waves. Ellen could only hope that people would listen. Maybe they would even create waves of their own.

CHAPTER 63

—◦—

THE LAB AT home looked the same. The same dust. The same echoing emptiness. The same stale smell of potential tucked away. Ellen brought in a plastic bucket full of jellyfish samples and plunked it on the floor near the counter. Far away from the sink this time.

Marcus waltzed in. He always waltzed, never walked. "Congratulations. Everyone's been talking about your strange discoveries."

Ellen smiled and wiped her hands off on her jeans. "Thanks. I wasn't so sure I'd still have a job when we came back. So we're okay with the funding for now?"

"Okay? Yes, I'd say we're okay. Program managers have been calling and asking for proposals. Imagine that. They actually want to send us more funds for once instead of cutting them to shreds."

"Before we left for the cruise, they said they wanted immediate results or they'd take our funding away."

Marcus waved his hand in the air as if everything had been easy all along. "A new species is an exciting result. Not to mention the news coverage. Jellyfish have never been so famous."

"But there's still so much we don't know about this new species."

"Exactly. We'll be going through it all for years to come. It's the best possible scenario, especially because these jellyfish are seen as threatening. For once, people want to know all about what we're doing here. That means more funding."

Ellen couldn't bring herself to feel excited about an invasive new species. Still, Marcus overflowed with excitement and she felt some of that energy trickle into her skin.

She pushed the baseball cap off her forehead and squinted at the fluorescent light. "Well, I guess we'd better get to work then."

———— 〜 ————

CHAPTER 64

B ACK ON HER falling apart houseboat, Ellen sipped her coffee and gazed out at the water's silver surface. She cradled the coffee cup between both hands, siphoning its warmth.

The November air held surprises. It could be warm and chilly all at once, depending on which river of air happened to be swirling by. The air currents were very much like the water currents, at once transporting and refreshing, forever mixing everything together.

Her seagull friend perched on the edge of the boat and watched the water while also watching her. The sun selected random objects to shine: the seagull's beak, a group of trees across the harbor fringed with yellow and red, a window from a house tucked into the trees. The water's surface sparkled with more light. Trees that were once green now glowed yellow until they took on the crystallized look of coral, an undersea world standing up to distant waves of air.

Ellen examined her arm. It didn't throb or sting anymore. When the swelling receded, it left a mottled scar. Like David's. She felt a pang, hoping he was okay, hoping he had found a way to live with the ocean that he thought of as alive. Now her arm would always remind her of David. The scar could be a tattoo with pink and brown designs. The more she looked at it, the more she knew David was right. The ocean is alive. It can become sick, just like any living being. It can give and take life. And it can be killed.

Both he and Ryan had been right about so many things. They knew that everything we do makes a difference. She couldn't keep shutting the world out. She'd have to remember to embrace the world and everyone in it more often. That would be a challenge in itself since it was so much easier to hide.

There was still so much data to go through, tests to be done, colleagues to talk with, and paperwork to be submitted on the new species. To get through it all, she needed coffee. Lots of coffee. She took another sip. Since the press conference, she had become a spokesperson for everything from climate change to jellyfish to radiation in the ocean. When dreams come true they cease to be dreams. Then all they are is reality.

An email popped in from Michael. Ellen opened it and read the words, "Where's that proof you promised me?" She laughed, figuring she'd have to add that to her ever-growing list of things to do.

She couldn't decide if the research cruise had been successful or not. If it hadn't been for the new species, she would have called it unsuccessful since they didn't find many regular jellyfish. But then the new species could have something to do with the lack of jellyfish. Either the jellyfish in the area turned into the new species or scared the others away. She doubted they would attack or eat the regular jellyfish, but then she didn't really know.

All this time, all she ever wanted was to make a difference with her research. Now she smiled at the thought. Ripples turn into waves.

The waves below sloshed a lazy rhythm. Ellen closed her eyes until the song built up inside. Then she knew what the waves had been whispering all along. It wasn't the kind of message that could be analyzed or explained. It could only be felt and all she felt was an overwhelming sense of love. The trees danced with it, the wind and the waves echoed with it. The birds sang with love and now it seemed even the ducks quacked with it. Love surged through her. It woke her up more than coffee ever would. As it built up inside, she felt the energy of so much life and love. She wondered how she could have felt so alone while love rustled all around her.

Her thoughts stretched out to the universe and how one single kernel of energy made all that there is. Every atom that's in us was once part of that energy, the same energy that made the stars and planets, the Earth and all the life it sustains. It's something we all share.

Ellen took a deep breath of ocean air. She could feel the world breathing as she breathed, with every surface wave, wind gust, and leaf rustle. She felt the tiny fish swimming beneath her and heard them jumping and plopping at the surface. She felt the pulse and hum of everything as it became her own pulse.

She felt him walk up behind her and then a hand was on her shoulder, comforting and stabilizing. Ryan leaned in and poured more coffee into her cup, filling it to the brim. She blinked her tears away and smiled a thank you.

Her seagull friend jumped up and flew. He caught an air current that brought him out over the open ocean without so much as a flap of his wings. He coasted along, past sailboats and wind surfers, then began to turn in a circle. He saw something red on the sparkling surface below, something he had never before seen. Without worrying too much about it, he flew on and dipped down to pluck a fish from the water.

The swarm stretched out and continued to grow.

Author's Note

*O*CEAN *ECHOES* TAKES place in 2010. Since then, ocean news has worsened. In real life, I see devastating ocean headlines every day.

Here are a few from 2016: "At Least 50 Whales Wash Ashore in India," "Man-Made Heat Put in Oceans Has Doubled Since 1997," "Ocean Acidification Takes Toll on Coral Reef Growth," "Fukushima Site Still Leaking After Five Years," "Scientists Say Oil Exploration Offshore Could Doom Rare Right Whales," "Coral Sanctuary Is Now a Graveyard Due to Record Warm Oceans, Scientists Find." And another one from 2015: "Ocean Life Faces Mass Extinction, Broad Study Says."

But there is also hope, and that can be seen in the headlines too: "A Robot Buoy Saves Whales from Boat Strikes," "Inside the Race to Save Cuba's Coral Reefs," "Bacteria Present a Solution for Reducing Plastic Pollution," and "Scientists Listen to Whales to Learn How to Protect Them."

Who knows what will happen in the future and what new discoveries may be made to reverse any damage. It's the challenge of our time.

A percentage from the sale of this book will go toward non-profit organizations working to protect the world's oceans for future generations.

If you'd like to see what ocean conservation groups are doing and the victories that have been made along the way, please visit these web sites:

Oceana: oceana.org
The Ocean Conservancy: www.oceanconservancy.org
Environmental Defense Fund: www.edf.org/oceans

Recommended books about the ocean:

Sea Change: A Message of the Oceans by Sylvia A. Earle

The Fragile Edge: Diving and Other Adventures in the South Pacific by Julia Whitty

The Outermost House: A Year of Life on the Great Beach of Cape Cod by Henry Beston

The Wave by Susan Casey

Acknowledgements

THERE WERE TIMES when I thought this book would never be finished or published. Thank you to everyone for cheering me on through it all.

Thank you to my parents for showing me the wonders of the world, whether those wonders were in our backyard, in our neighborhood, Up North by the Michigan lakes, or in the tidal pools and dunes of Cape Cod.

Thank you to my husband for reading through many different drafts, for welcoming the characters into our home, and for encouragement through years of revisions. To Sheila Bowen, Tom Hurst, Robin Hurst, Karen McGrath, Gail Daly, Tom Condon, Michael Condon, and Sarah Myles, thank you for taking the time to read earlier drafts of this novel and for so many helpful suggestions. Thanks Tom and Robin for the jellyfish party too. To all of those mentioned and to Leslie Sheehy and Lori Fontana, thank you for your constant encouragement through the years.

Thank you to Mario Lampic for the wonderful book cover celebrating the beauty and mystery of jellyfish and the ocean.

Thank you to Lara Trimble for suggesting that a character could be based on her brother because he's interested in science and likes to wear a gorilla suit. To fellow writing partners Amy Nyman, Dan Catalini, and Licia Sorgi, thank you for the laughs and encouragement through days and nights of writing and for reminding me that writing should be fun.

Thank you to literary agents Michelle Brower, Monika Woods, Sorche Fairbank, and Ann Collette for many helpful suggestions. To my blogging friends from all over the world, thank you for your friendship, advice, and encouragement.

To all those who asked about the book, who inspired me along the way, and encouraged me through the years, there are too many of you to name but I hope you know how much you mean to me. I've loved sharing the writing adventure with all of you.

About the Author

S HEILA HURST GREW up in Michigan and Massachusetts, contributing to a split personality involving a love of farmlands and the ocean. Early influences include Harriet the Spy and the books of Judy Blume and Laura Ingalls Wilder. Her favorite authors are John Steinbeck, Carl Sagan, and Barbara Kingsolver.

After studying journalism at the University of Massachusetts at Amherst, she worked as a reporter while writing fiction on the side. She currently edits science journal articles and is a freelance writer with articles published in *Cape Cod Life*, *Cape Cod Magazine*, *The Enterprise*, and Boston newspapers. Her short stories have been *Glimmer Train* and *Writer's Digest* finalists. *Ocean Echoes* is her first novel.

Made in the USA
Charleston, SC
21 December 2016